# A gift or a curse?

scattered around the stem. I fix it in my gaze.

*Novo*, I think. *Novo.*

It doesn't revive. It does not alter itself in any way.

But I can feel the magic in me. It's there in every breath, every angry heartbeat, its gossamer threads pulsing and tightening my chest. It's teasing, cajoling, begging to be let loose.

I try again: *Novo.*

Nothing. I slump forward, elbows on knees, chin cradled in my hands. I'm a useless witch. Tess is barely twelve, and she can alter the entire garden without a word. Could probably do it with her eyes closed. I'm sixteen and I can't manage a simple silent spell.

I don't want to be a witch. I'd stop using magic entirely if I could, but it's impossible. I tried once, two years ago.

I've never tried to suppress the magic since. I practice sparingly, grudgingly, to keep from losing control. But I follow the rules Mother laid out for us. We must use magic only in the rose garden. We must speak of it only in hushed voices and behind closed doors. We must never forget how dangerous it can be—nor how wicked.

My eyes fell on a rose, its tip

CANCELLED

# BORN WICKED

JESSICA SPOTSWOOD

PENGUIN BOOKS

PENGUIN BOOKS

Published by the Penguin Group
Penguin Books Ltd, 80 Strand, London WC2R 0RL, England
Penguin Group (USA) Inc., 375 Hudson Street, New York, New York 10014, USA
Penguin Group (Canada), 90 Eglinton Avenue East, Suite 700, Toronto, Ontario, Canada M4P 2Y3
(a division of Pearson Penguin Canada Inc.)
Penguin Ireland, 25 St Stephen's Green, Dublin 2, Ireland (a division of Penguin Books Ltd)
Penguin Group (Australia), 707 Collins Street, Melbourne, Victoria 3008, Australia
(a division of Pearson Australia Group Pty Ltd)
Penguin Books India Pvt Ltd, 11 Community Centre, Panchsheel Park, New Delhi – 110 017, India
Penguin Group (NZ), 67 Apollo Drive, Rosedale, Auckland 0632, New Zealand
(a division of Pearson New Zealand Ltd)
Penguin Books (South Africa) (Pty) Ltd, Block D, Rosebank Office Park, 181 Jan Smuts Avenue,
Parktown North, Gauteng 2193, South Africa

Penguin Books Ltd, Registered Offices: 80 Strand, London WC2R 0RL, England

penguin.com

Published in the USA by G. P. Putnam's Sons • A division of Penguin Young Readers Group 2012
Published in Great Britain by Penguin Books Ltd, 2013

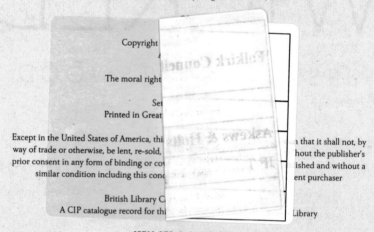

British Library C
A CIP catalogue record for thi                                  Library

ISBN: 978–0–141–34211–5

www.greenpenguin.co.uk

ALWAYS LEARNING                    PEARSON

# A gift or a curse?

My eyes fall on a rose, its tips brown and nibbled, petals scattered around the stem. I fix it in my gaze.

*Novo*, I think. *Novo*.

It doesn't revive. It does not alter itself in any way.

But I can feel the magic in me. It's there in every breath, every angry heartbeat, its gossamer threads pulsing and tightening my chest. It's teasing, cajoling, begging to be let loose.

I try again: *Novo*.

Nothing. I slump forward, elbows on knees, chin cradled in my hands. I'm a useless witch. Tess is barely twelve, and she can alter the entire garden without a word. Could probably do it with her eyes closed. I'm sixteen and I can't manage a simple silent spell.

I don't want to be a witch. I'd stop using magic entirely if I could, but it's impossible. I tried once, two years ago.

I've never tried to suppress the magic since. I practice sparingly, grudgingly, to keep from losing control. But I follow the rules Mother laid out for us. We must use magic only in the rose garden. We must speak of it only in hushed voices and behind closed doors. We must never forget how dangerous it can be—nor how wicked.

# A gift or a curse?

My eyes fall on a rose, its tips brown and nibbled, petals scattered around the stem. I fix it in my gaze.

*Novo*, I think. *Novo*.

It doesn't revive. It does not alter itself in any way.

But I can feel the magic in me. It's there in every breath, every angry heartbeat, its gossamer threads pulsing and tightening my chest. It's teasing, cajoling, begging to be let loose.

I try again: *Novo*.

Nothing. I slump forward, elbows on knees, chin cradled in my hands. I'm a useless witch. Tess is barely twelve, and she can alter the entire garden without a word. Could probably do it with her eyes closed. I'm sixteen and I can't manage a simple silent spell.

I don't want to be a witch. I'd stop using magic entirely if I could, but it's impossible. I tried once, two years ago.

I've never tried to suppress the magic since. I practice sparingly, grudgingly, to keep from losing control. But I follow the rules Mother laid out for us. We must use magic only in the rose garden. We must speak of it only in hushed voices and behind closed doors. We must never forget how dangerous it can be—nor how wicked.

Our mother was a witch, too, but she hid it better.

I miss her.

Not a single day goes by that I don't wish for her guidance. Especially about my sisters.

Tess runs ahead of me, heading for the rose garden—our sanctuary, our one safe place. Her slippers slide on the cobblestones, the hood of her gray cloak falling to reveal blond curls. I glance back at the house. It's against the Brothers' strictures for girls to go out of doors uncloaked, and running isn't considered ladylike. But we're concealed from the house by tall hedges. Tess is safe.

For now.

She waits ahead, kicking at the dead leaves beneath a maple. "I hate autumn," she complains, biting at her lip with pearly teeth. "It feels so sad."

"I like it." There's something invigorating in the crisp September air, the searing blue skies, the interplay of orange and scarlet and gold. The Brotherhood would probably ban autumn if they could. It's too beautiful. Too sensuous.

Tess points to the clematis climbing up the trellis. Their petals are brown and crumbling, their tired heads bowing toward the ground.

"See, everything's dying," she says mournfully.

I realize what she intends a scant second before she acts.

"Tess!" I shriek.

I'm too late. She squints her gray eyes, and a moment later, it's summer.

Tess is an advanced caster for twelve—much more advanced than I was at her age. The deadheads spring up, whole and white and luscious. The oaks sprout new green leaves. Magnificent peonies and lilies sway toward the sun, glorying in their resurrection.

"Teresa Elizabeth Cahill," I hiss. "You put that back."

She smiles winsomely, skipping ahead to smell the fragrant orange daylilies. "Just for a few minutes. It's prettier this way."

"Tess." My tone doesn't brook any argument.

"What good is all this, anyway, if we can't use it to make things more beautiful?"

As far as I can tell, "all this" is good for precious little. I ignore Tess's question. "Now. Before Mrs. O'Hare or John comes outside."

Tess mumbles a *reverto* spell under her breath. I assume that's for my benefit. Unlike me, she doesn't need to speak aloud to cast.

The clematises' flowers droop on their vine; the leaves crunch beneath our feet; the impatiens fall to pieces. Tess doesn't look happy about it, but at least she listens to me. That's more than I can say for Maura.

Footsteps strike the cobblestones behind us. It's a man's quick, heavy stride. I whip around to face the intruder. Tess moves closer, and I resist the urge to put my arm around her. She's small for her age, but I'd keep her this way forever if I could. An odd, pretty child is safer than an odd, pretty woman.

John O'Hare, our coachman and jack-of-all-trades, lumbers around the hedge. "Your father's wanting you, Miss Cate," he huffs, his bearded cheeks red. "In the study."

I smile politely, tucking an errant strand of hair beneath my hood. "Thank you."

I wait until he's gone. Then I turn, tugging Tess's cape up over her curls, bending to brush the dust from her ragged lace hems. My heart is pounding. If he had come two minutes earlier—if it had been Father, or the Brothers paying an unexpected call— how would we have explained this corner of the garden springing back to life?

We couldn't have. It was magic, plain and simple.

"Best to see what Father wants." I try to sound cheerful, but the unexpected summons makes me uneasy. He's only been back from New London for a few days. Does he mean to leave us again so soon? His time at home gets shorter every year.

Tess looks longingly down the cobblestone path toward the rose garden. "No practicing today, then?"

"After that display? No." I shake my head. "You know better."

"No one could see us from the house, Cate. We were behind the hedges. We'd have heard them, like we heard John coming."

I frown at her. "No magic outdoors except in the rose garden. That's what Mother taught me. She made the rules to keep us safe."

"I suppose," Tess sighs. Her thin shoulders slump, and I hate that I've taken this small happiness away from her. When I was her age, I liked to run through the gardens, and I suppose I was careless with my magic, too. But I had Mother to look out for me. Now I have to play mother for Tess and Maura, and ignore the wild girl that still bangs in my heart, begging to be let out.

I lead the way back to the house, and we troop through the kitchen door, hanging our cloaks on the wooden pegs inside. Mrs. O'Hare is bent over a bubbling pot of her dreadful fish chowder, humming a snippet of an old church song, her curly gray head bobbing in time to the music. She smiles and gestures toward a pile of carrots on the table. Tess washes up and sets right to work chopping. She loves bustling around the kitchen, dicing and mixing and measuring. It's not proper for girls of our station, but Mrs. O'Hare gave up on proper a long time ago with us.

The heavy oak door to Father's study is slightly ajar. I can glimpse Father at his desk, shoulders rounded in exhaustion, as though what he'd like the very most is a nap. But there's a stack of thick leather-bound volumes on his desk, and I have no doubt that when our business here is concluded, he'll go right back to them. And when he finishes those, there are dozens more on the shelves ready to take their place. He is a businessman, yes—but a scholar first and foremost.

I rap on the door and wait for permission to enter. "John said you wanted to speak with me?"

"Come in, Cate. Mrs. Corbett and I thought you should have a say in our new venture, since it affects you girls." Father gestures toward the corner of the room, where Mrs. Corbett sits like a fat spider on the plush red sofa, spinning her helpful little schemes.

"New venture?" I echo, striding up to his desk. Mrs. Corbett had precious little interest in us before Mother died, but she's been full of neighborly advice ever since. Her last suggestion was to send me off to a convent school run by the Sisters. I had to compel Father and modify his memory so he wouldn't make me go. He only remembers deciding it wasn't wise to send me away, not so soon after losing Mother.

Invading his mind is the wickedest thing I've ever done. But it was necessary. How could I keep my promise to look after my sisters if I was in New London? It's a two-day journey.

"I think—that is, Mrs. Corbett suggested—" Father hems and haws but eventually gets to the point. "A governess! It would be just the thing."

Oh no.

I jut my chin at him. "For what?"

Father's thin face flushes. "For your education. I'm going back to New London next week, and I'll be gone most of the autumn. That's too long for you girls to be away from your lessons."

My heart sinks. Hours snatched here and there to correct our French pronunciation and Latin translations are the only time we get with him anymore. Now we won't even have that. I learned not to count on Father years ago, but Tess hasn't. She'll be heartbroken.

I brush dust from the lamp at the corner of his desk. "Maura and I can teach Tess while you're gone. I don't mind."

Father tactfully refrains from pointing out that Tess's Latin is worlds better than my own. "If that were the only—that is to say—you're sixteen now, Cate, and—" He looks helplessly at Mrs. Corbett, who is only too pleased to jump in.

"There is more to a young lady's education than foreign languages. A governess could give you girls a bit of polish," she asserts, eyeing me up and down.

I clench my hands into fists. I know how I look: a high-necked navy frock unadorned with any frills or frippery, the scuffed boots I wear to work in the garden, hair plaited neatly down my back. It doesn't do me any favors. But it's better to be thought dowdy than to attract too much attention.

"We have our piano lessons in town every week," I remind Father.

Mrs. Corbett smirks, her eyes disappearing into the fat folds of her face. "I believe your father was thinking about more than piano lessons, dear."

I should lower my eyes like a good girl, but I don't. That sugary, overly familiar "dear" sets my teeth on edge. I square my shoulders and lift my chin and stare right into her beady little hazel eyes. "Such as?"

"May I be frank with you, Miss Cate?"

"Please." My voice is syrupy steel.

"You're of an age to be thinking about your future now, yours and Miss Maura's. Your intention ceremony is coming up soon. It won't be long before you'll have to make your choice: marry and raise a family, Lord willing, or join the Sisterhood."

I fiddle with the gold tassels on the lamp shade, a flush rising on my cheeks. "I'm well aware of my choices." As if I could forget. It feels like I spend half my days batting the fear away, refusing to let the rising panic consume me.

"Well, you may not be aware that you girls are getting a reputation. As—eccentrics. Bluestockings. Miss Maura more so than you—she's always got her nose in a book, doesn't she? Always popping in and out of that bookshop. You two don't go visiting or receive callers. It's understandable, without any mother to guide you—" Mrs. Corbett looks sadly at Father. "But regrettable. I thought it my neighborly duty to tell your father what I've been hearing."

Of course she did, the snooping, meddlesome—

*Eccentrics,* she said. Have the old cows in town been gossiping about us? What if the Brotherhood has heard? Father's a Latin scholar of some renown, and he's respected by the Brothers. Before Mother died, before he inherited his uncle's shipping business in New London, he taught at the boys' school in town. But that's not enough to place his daughters above suspicion. These days, no one is above suspicion.

I thought keeping us secluded would be safer. Perhaps I've been going about it all wrong.

My face falls, but Father takes my silence for assent. "Mrs. Corbett knows of a young lady who would do. She's fluent in French—painting, music—" His voice drones on, but I stop listening. Our governess will excel in all the pretty, useless things young ladies of our station are expected to embrace.

And she'll be living here. Right here in the house.

I grit my teeth. "Have you already retained her, then?"

"Sister Elena will be here Monday morning." Mrs. Corbett smiles.

Sister? It's worse than I thought. The Sisters are the feminine arm of the Brotherhood, only without any power: they do not preside over legal disputes, or create addendums to the morality codes, or judge the cases of girls accused of witchery. They live isolated in convents in the cities and dedicate their lives in service to the Lord, educating girls in their elite boarding schools, occasionally serving as governesses. I've never met a member of the order before, but I've seen them passing through town in their closed carriages, dressed all in black. They always look pinched and joyless. Mrs. Corbett's daughter Regina had a Sister for her governess before she married.

Is that Father's intention? Does this governess specialize in marrying off hopeless girls, like Maura and me?

I turn to Father, accusations on my lips. He wanted my input, did he? He's already made his decision! Or had it made for him by someone else.

He sees the anger on my face and droops like the poor clematis flowers in the garden.

Blast. I can't argue with him; since Mother died, there isn't enough of him left to argue with.

"If the decision's already been made, we shall make the best of it. I'm sure she'll be lovely. Thank you for thinking of us, Father." I give him my most charming smile, full of daughterly devotion. See? I can be sweet as Tess's strawberry pie when I want.

Father smiles back uncertainly. "You're welcome. I only want what's best for you girls. Would you like to tell your sisters the news, or shall I tell them at dinner?"

Oh. *That's* why he summoned me. He never intended to ask my opinion. It was only a pretense because he doesn't have the courage to tell them himself! This way, when Maura throws a tantrum and Tess sulks, he'll be able to comfort himself with *Cate agreed it was for the best.* As if I had any real say in the matter.

"No, no. I'll tell them." Better they're rude to me than to Father. "I'll be off to do that now. Good day, Mrs. Corbett."

Mrs. Corbett brushes invisible lint from her heavy wool skirt. "Good day, Miss Cate."

I curtsy and close the door behind me, cursing her black soul. She has no notion of the peril she's just put us in.

Maura's curled up on her window seat, a patchwork quilt around her shoulders, reading a Gothic novel. They're banned, of course, but she has a whole stack of them hidden under a loose floorboard in her closet. They used to be Mother's.

I sail in without knocking. She closes the book, one finger marking her place, and squints up at me with sapphire eyes.

"Heard of knocking?" she asks. "It's all the rage among polite people."

"Oh yes, I know what a stickler you are for manners," I laugh.

"What is it?" She sits up, one bare foot peeking out from beneath her navy skirts. "Tell me quickly. I've got to find out what happens to this poor girl. She's about to be ravished by a duke."

I roll my eyes. Fine reading material for a young lady. If Father caught her, even he would object. But we've more important things to worry about at the moment.

"Father's decided to hire a governess. A member of the Sisters."

Maura dog-ears her page and sets the book down.

It's not certain doom. But it will make things more difficult, particularly if the governess is the pious, talkative sort. It's hard enough keeping our secret from Father and the O'Hares and Lily, our lady's maid. Adding another person into the household—a person who will be spending all her time judging our conduct—will make things much more difficult.

"Father decided, did he? As if he'd have the gumption to come up with a plan like that." Maura taps on the window. Outside, Mrs. Corbett is climbing into her barouche, the wind flapping her cloak. She looks for all the world like a great fat crow.

I'd thought the same thing about Father, but I don't like to hear Maura say it.

"Oh, for pity's sake, don't give me that lemon face. You know it's the truth." She shoves the calico curtains aside so we can get a better look. "Do you suppose she wants to marry him?"

"*Marry* him?" Father would never remarry.

"Widowers remarry, Cate. Especially widowers with three daughters. Happens all the time in my books. She'd make a devil of a stepmother, wouldn't she?"

Maura scoots over to make room for me. We both peer out at Mrs. Corbett dubiously.

"I don't think Father seems the slightest bit interested," I announce.

"Of course he's not. Father's not interested in anything besides his books and his business. He's never even here. We'd be the ones stuck with her. Like with this governess." Maura wrinkles her nose.

I wait for the explosion forthcoming. Tess and I, we're watercolors compared with the rich oil painting that is Maura, with her flame-bright hair and a temperament to match. She's impetuous. Intractable. Easily infuriated.

"It might not be so bad. Perhaps a governess could liven things up a bit," she says finally.

I jump up, staring at her as though she's grown another head. "You want a governess? Living right here? I suggest you might practice your piano and you take my head off, but you'd welcome some stranger whose sole job is to boss us?"

"Well, I'm sick of you doing it," Maura mutters. "I'm fifteen now, Cate. I don't need you watching out for me anymore. I'm not a baby like Tess. Even *Tess* isn't a baby, not really."

I pick up the blue velvet slippers she's tossed helter-skelter by the bedside. "I know that."

"Do you? You don't act like it." Maura snarls something under her breath, and the slipper in my hand is suddenly a spider. It starts to crawl across my wrist and up my arm. I freeze, but only for a moment.

I'm not a weak, squeamish girl, afraid of things that scurry through the dark.

Maura cured me of that. My magic became evident from the age of eleven, but hers didn't manifest until she was twelve, and then it exploded overnight. She was dizzy with it. After Mother died, she was impossible. We were in mourning—we seldom went out except to services—but she wasn't cautious enough at home by half. I lived in terror that one of the servants would

11

catch her—or, Lord forbid, Father. We quarreled constantly about her carelessness. After our rows, hideous ghosts popped out of my closet; spiders crawled through my bed and wove webs in my hair. Snakes wrapped around my ankles, licking at my feet with forked tongues.

I learned to think my way out of such things quickly. And to never, ever show my fear. Mother taught us that a witch's power is all in your mind. We can't change matter, only how people see things, and—in very rare cases—how they remember them.

"*Commuto*," I say, and the spider turns back to a slipper. I toss it into a pile with the others by her wardrobe.

"Aren't you bored silly, Cate? I know I am. If I didn't have my novels, I'd throw myself right in the river." Maura's eyes snap as she stands and stretches, the fabric pulling tight through the bodice. She needs new dresses to fit her new curves. "What life do we have here, wandering around the house like ghosts? Don't you ever crave *more*?"

Do I? It's been years since I've let myself consider what I want. It hardly matters. I didn't want Mother to die; I didn't want Father to turn into a shadow of his old self; I didn't want the responsibility of policing my sisters. I certainly never wanted to be a witch in the first place.

The universe has yet to take my wishes under consideration.

Maura still thinks she can bend the world to her will. She'll learn.

A memory floats up—running through the garden, chased by a towheaded boy with mischievous green eyes. Letting him catch me and tickle me until I was breathless. The way he looked at me, his sunburned forehead nearly touching mine, his body pressing me into the grass. How he laughed and rolled away, his cheeks as red as Maura's hair, and it was suddenly evident that we were too old to play such games.

I bite my lip—an unladylike habit, I know, and one that Tess has picked up from me. "What is it you want to do? What am I stopping you from—afternoon teas at Mrs. Ishida's? Shopping with Rose Collier and Cristina Winfield?"

"No. I don't know. Perhaps!" Maura begins to pace.

Good Lord. If those sound like attractive options, she's lonelier than I ever dreamed. "No one is stopping you from making friends. You could invite the girls from town over for tea whenever you like."

"As if they would come! They barely know us and we dress like ragamuffins. Besides, you're the oldest, you'd have to host, and you'd rather be a hermit."

I sink onto Maura's bed, smoothing the yellow coverlet that Mother sewed during one of her long convalescences. Maura's right; I wouldn't enjoy making odious small talk with the simpering town girls. But I would do it. For her. To keep us safe. "Is that really what you want?"

She spins the old globe Father gave her for her last birthday. "I don't know. I want more than what we've got now, I know that. We have to start thinking of our futures, don't we? How are we supposed to find anyone to marry us if we never leave the house?"

"You make us sound like shut-ins," I argue. "We go out."

"To services and piano lessons." Maura spins the globe faster, until it becomes a blue-green blur of places we'll never see. "It's all well and good for you. You'll marry Paul and have his babies

13

and live next door forever. How you won't die of boredom, I don't know, but at least it's settled. What about me?"

I ignore the jibe. "It's hardly settled. He hasn't bothered to come home and visit me once." I arrange her pillows in a neat row, fluffing them with more force than necessary. "Maybe he's fallen in love with some city girl."

"He has not." Maura gives me a wry smile. "We'd have heard. Mrs. McLeod would have told everyone in town."

Mr. McLeod is an invalid, confined to his bed, and Paul is his mother's only child and her delight. Her cosseting drives him to distraction. It surprised me at first, him going off to university. His marks in school were never good; Father had to give him extra tutoring. Now I suspect he just wanted to escape that dreary house. Still, it's no excuse not to visit. He hasn't been home in four years. Not even for Christmas. Not even for Mother's funeral.

"Well, you'll find out next week, won't you?" Maura stands before the looking glass, running Mother's old tortoiseshell comb through her curls. "Are you nervous?"

"No," I lie. "It's just Paul. Besides, I'm mad at him."

"Well, you'll have to get over that. It's not as though you have a line of men queuing up outside to marry you." Maura appraises me, sprawled across her bed in disarray. "You ought to get the governess to order you a new dress. Something fashionable. You can't let him see you like that."

"Paul wouldn't care." Would he? The boy I grew up with wouldn't.

I ought to put my pride aside and try to please him. That's what a good, practical girl would do.

"Look at yourself." Maura tugs me up to stand next to her. My hair's falling out of its braid and there's an ink stain on my sleeve. But even at my best, I can't compare with her. Maura's always been the family beauty. My hair is straight and blond with the barest hint of red, not gorgeous bright curls like hers, and my eyes are dull gray like Father's. Worse, my pointed chin hints at stubbornness. It's an ill-kept secret, though—one you'd uncover by talking to me for five minutes.

"You look a mess," she says frankly. "But you would be lovely if you tried. You should try, Cate. Six months and you'll have to marry *someone*. You can't stay here and protect us forever."

Six months before I turn seventeen—but only three before I have to announce an engagement. The thought chips away at my composure.

Maura's right. She's saying the same thing as Mrs. Corbett—not in the same way, and not for the same reasons. But if Mother were alive, Maura and I would be attending teas, paying and receiving calls, positioning ourselves as eligible, marriageable young ladies. I've put it off, afraid of bungling it somehow, of drawing attention to us. Now I've waited too long and the delay has done just that.

We mustn't give the Brothers any reason to suspect us.

"I think we should give the governess a chance. We'll be careful," Maura promises.

"She'll be living right here. She'll never let you read those novels, or Tess continue her studies, or me spend all day in the dirt." My heart falls at the thought. Gardening is the one freedom I've allowed myself. If the governess makes me stay indoors all day painting fruit baskets, I'll go mad. "If she realizes what we are—"

Maura smirks, twisting her curls up into a chignon. "If she's troublesome, we'll alter her memory. Isn't that what evil witches do?"

I whip around to look at her. "That's not funny." My sisters don't know that I'm capable of mind-magic. It's terribly rare, and it's reckoned to be the very darkest kind of magic there is. Mother was the only one who knew, and even she was horrified.

Maura skewers her hair into place with pins. "I was only joking."

"Well, don't. It's not right to go into people's minds and muddle things! It's too invasive. It's—" I stop myself before I say *wicked*.

But Maura stares at me in the mirror, like she knows what I'm thinking. "We're witches, Cate. We were born that way. Magic isn't shameful, no matter what the Brothers would have us believe. It's a gift. I wish you would accept that."

# chapter

# 2

I know what the brothers would say: magic isn't a gift from the Lord, it's devil-sent. Women who can do magic—they're either mad or wicked. Destined for an asylum at best, or a prison ship or an early grave.

"It feels more like a curse," I sigh, straightening the hairpins on her dressing table.

"To you!" Maura slams her hand down on the dressing table, rattling the glass bottles and scattering the hairpins again. Her blue eyes burn bright in her pale face. "Because you try to pretend it doesn't exist. If it were up to you, we'd never use magic at all. We should be learning all we can, practicing as much as possible. It's our birthright."

"So you would have us practice magic in the mornings, and have the Brothers' wives and daughters over to tea in the afternoons? You don't think the two are a wee bit incompatible?"

"Why? Why can't we have both?" Maura plants her hands on her hips. "It's not the Brothers who are stopping us, Cate. It's you."

I reel back, stung, and almost knock into the globe. I steady it on the pedestal with both hands. "I'm protecting you."

"No, you're *smothering* us."

"Do you think I enjoy it?" I demand, throwing up my hands. "I'm trying to keep you safe. I'm trying to keep you from ending up like Brenna Elliott!"

Maura sinks onto her window seat, her hair as red as the maples lining the drive. "Brenna Elliott was a fool."

It isn't that simple, and Maura knows it. "Was she? Or was she just careless? They ruined her either way."

Maura raises an eyebrow, skeptical. "She was odd before."

"Odd or not, she didn't deserve what was done to her in that place," I snap.

Brenna Elliott gives me nightmares. She's a girl from town, my age. It was never unusual to find her walking down the street, deep in conversation with herself, humming beneath her breath. But she was a pretty girl and Brother Elliott's granddaughter, and everyone forgave her eccentricity—right up until she tried to warn her uncle Jack of his death, the day before it happened. After he died—right on schedule, in a carriage accident—her own father turned her in. She was accused of witchery and shipped off to Harwood. Less than a year later, she slit her wrists. When her grandfather found out, he insisted she had been simpleminded all her life—that it was illness responsible for her mad talk, not witchery. He brought her home to recover. For the first few weeks, she had to be fed like a baby and wouldn't talk to anyone. She still barely leaves the house.

I grab Maura's arm. "I'm not bossy for the joy of it. I'm trying to protect you. I won't see you shipped off to Harwood. I won't stand by and see Tess with scars on her wrists and no life in her eyes!"

"Shhh!" Maura hisses, flinging me off. "Father will hear."

I can't help it. The thought of my sisters being sent away to suffer Lord knows what because of some lack of diligence on my part—it haunts me.

I'd rather they think I'm a shrew.

"I'm going out," I announce. "You go tell Tess about the governess, if you're so pleased."

I pound down the wide wooden staircase, worry choking me. I hope Tess will be sensible of the threat this newcomer could bring. If only I could trust my sisters to be more careful, more vigilant about what could befall us—

I promised Mother I would look after them. I was the one she trusted—not Mrs. Corbett, not Mrs. O'Hare, not even Father. Their safety is my responsibility now. But they don't make it easy. They practice magic whenever my back is turned, whenever they think no one will see. They relish unconventional pursuits and unconventional books. Lately Maura's been rebelling against my rules, fighting me at every turn.

I do everything I can, but it's always too much or not enough or all wrong somehow.

The kitchen smells of cinnamon and apples. A pie sits on the wide windowsill, steam fogging the glass, leaking from the cross carved into the center of its golden crust.

I grab my cloak from the peg by the door and hurry outside. The air is sweet and acrid at the same time, a blend of smoke from the chimneys and dead leaves blanketing the ground. My favorite spot is up ahead: a bench in the rose garden beneath the statue of Athena. There, surrounded by the tall hedges, we can't be seen from the house—except from the window in the east corner of my bedroom.

I know: I've checked.

I throw myself onto the cold marble and shove off my hood. My eyes fall on a rose, its tips brown and nibbled, petals scattered around the stem. I fix it in my gaze.

*Novo*, I think. *Novo*.

It doesn't revive. It does not alter itself in any way.

But I can feel the magic in me. It's there in every breath, every angry heartbeat, its gossamer threads pulsing and tightening my chest. It's teasing, cajoling, begging to be let loose. It's always like this when a strong emotion comes over me. Particularly when I haven't let myself do magic for a few days.

I try again: *Novo*.

Nothing. I slump forward, elbows on knees, chin cradled in my hands. I'm a useless witch. Tess is barely twelve, and she can alter the entire garden without a word. Could probably do it with her eyes closed. I'm sixteen and I can't manage a simple silent spell.

I don't want to be a witch. I'd stop using magic entirely if I could, but it's impossible. I tried once, two years ago.

It was the winter after Mother died, and Mrs. Corbett and some of the Brothers' wives came to call. They kept bleating on about how sorry they were and my poor dear mother. It was infuriating. They didn't know Mother at all; she never liked any of them. They were just nosy, noisy sheep.

I thought of sheep and the magic swayed up and there it was: a great woolly creature in the corner of the sitting room, right next to Mrs. Corbett. It actually nosed her sleeve. She jumped, and I was certain she'd seen it. I was ready for the shrieks to begin—ready to be arrested and hauled off to Harwood.

Maura saved me with an *evanesco* spell. She magicked it away.

Mrs. Corbett didn't see the sheep at all. None of them saw it.

I've never tried to suppress the magic since. I practice sparingly, grudgingly, to keep from losing control. But I follow the rules Mother laid out for us. We must use magic only in the rose garden. We must speak of it only in hushed voices and behind closed doors. We must never forget how dangerous it can be— nor how wicked, in the hands of those without scruples. Mother told me these things—told me vehemently and often—sitting right here on the bench where I am now, with me listening from the grass at her feet.

I wish Mother were here. I need her. Not just to tell us how to keep the magic a secret from Father and the Brothers and the governess and all our neighbors. To teach us how to be witches and ladies and grow up without losing the best and truest parts of ourselves.

But Mother isn't here and I am. It's up to me to figure out how to remedy our reputations. I'll call on the Brothers' wives.

Buy more fashionable dresses. Smile and nod and laugh. I'll do everything in my power to make certain the new governess thinks we're ordinary, empty-headed girls who don't pose a threat to anyone.

I didn't fall to pieces when Mother died. I can't do it now.

*"Novo,"* I whisper, peeking through my hands. This time the rose morphs into a bright blossom.

The garden grows dark, the statuary looming ghostly behind me. I stand reluctantly and head for the house. It's an old salt-box farmhouse that Father's grandparents built when they settled here. Maura wishes we lived in one of the new houses in town, one with a turret and a widow's walk and scrollwork above the doors, but I like our house the way it is: sturdy and safe. If the white paint is peeling a little, if one of the dark shutters on the second floor hangs at a crooked angle, if the steeply sloped roof is missing a few shingles since the big storm back in August—well, John's been busy. The Carruthers boy quit mid-summer. Who cares if it's looking a bit ramshackle? No one comes to call on us anyway.

As soon as I turn the corner into the garden proper, I smack into someone.

I stumble back in surprise. It's seldom that I encounter any-one out here save John, our handyman. I like it that way. Tess is comfortable in her kitchen; Maura prefers the company of books over flowers; Father rarely leaves his study except for supper or sleep. The garden is *mine*.

I feel a punch of irritation at this intruder.

He reaches out to steady me, a book tumbling from his hand, and that's how I recognize him: Finn Belastra. Of course he would have his nose in a book, though how he can see to read in the dusk I don't know. He must have a cat's eyes.

"Excuse me, Miss Cahill." Finn pushes up his glasses with his index finger. He's got freckles scattered like cinnamon all over his cheeks. And his face—he's grown into it since I saw him last. He used to be a scrawny beanpole of a boy. Now he's—well. Not.

"What are you doing here?" I demand gracelessly. And dressed like that? I'm hardly one to stand on ceremony, but he's wearing a pair of ragged brown corduroy trousers, held up with a pair of suspenders, and a work shirt rolled up to the elbows.

Finn doffs his slouchy hat. Beneath it, his thick coppery hair stands up every which way. "I'm your new gardener."

He must be joking. Only, he is carrying a pail full of weeds.

"Oh," I say finally. I don't know what else is appropriate. *Welcome* would be a lie. We don't need more strangers around the place. After Mother died, I convinced Father that we could get by with only Mrs. O'Hare and John and Lily. Father agreed to leave the housekeeping decisions to me, but he's insisted on hiring a succession of gardeners. His latest scheme is to build a gazebo up by the pond, overlooking the cemetery.

Mother loved the gardens. Father's never said as much, but I think he keeps them up for her sake. He certainly never comes outside himself.

"Do you know *how* to garden?" I ask, not bothering to hide the doubt in my voice. I can't think of anyone more poorly suited to the task. The other gardeners have been brawny boys from surrounding farms, not pale, scholarly booksellers' sons.

"I'm learning," Finn says, holding out the book. It's an encyclopedia of plants.

That hardly inspires confidence. I've been pitching in, weeding plots, planting the spring bulbs. I like it. What's more, I don't need a book to tell me how. I watched Mother and John for years. I hope Finn won't go around pontificating about new irrigation methods and optimal soil conditions. He used to be the most insufferable know-it-all in Sunday school.

Finn swings the pail by its handle. His forearms are all lean, wiry muscle. "Your father heard I was looking for work and was kind enough to offer me a place here. We've been having some difficulties with the shop."

It's just like Father to be softhearted—at least where his books are concerned. I've never heard him object to the Brothers' witch hunts, but he gets quite livid about their censorship.

I shove my hands into the pockets of my cloak. "Are you—your shop isn't closing?"

"Not yet." Finn squares his shoulders—which have gotten a good deal sturdier since the last time I saw him. Or paid attention, at any rate. How long has it been since I actually looked? He's gotten awfully handsome; it can't have happened overnight.

"Good! That's good." Finn looks surprised that I care, but Mother loved the bookshop. She was a great one for reading, like Maura and Tess. Like Father.

I hesitate, feeling like I ought to say something more.

"Well, don't murder my flowers," I mutter, running a protective hand over a bush of pink tea roses.

Finn laughs. "I'll do my best. Good day, Miss Cahill."

I scowl. "Good day, Mr. Belastra."

• • •

My mood does not improve at dinner.

Mrs. O'Hare's fish chowder is as awful as I'd anticipated: salty and ill seasoned. She's an excellent housekeeper but a poor cook. I spread fresh butter on thick slabs of sourdough and ignore the bowl in front of me. Tess holds Father's bowl in her gaze, and a moment later he's declaring it a wonder.

I frown at Tess until Maura kicks me under the table.

I kick her back harder, and she jumps in her seat. The bread in my mouth turns to peppery ashes. I gag and reach for my glass of water.

"All right, Cate?" Father asks, looking up from his miraculous chowder.

"Fine," I choke. Maura gives an angelic smile. She knows I won't fight back magically, I never do, but I'm hard-pressed not to lean across the table and slap her.

"I trust you've all heard about the new governess?" Father sits at the head of the mahogany table with Tess and Maura on one side and me on the other. By rights I'm the lady of the house now and ought to sit at the foot, but I still think of it as Mother's place.

Tess and Maura nod, and Father continues. "She'll be arriving on Monday. I'll stay until Thursday to see her settled, but then I'll be traveling for several weeks. I may not be back until the Feast of All Saints."

Tess drops her spoon with a clatter. "That's more than a month! What about our Ovid?" They've been reading the *Metamorphoses* together. It's banned by the Brothers—too many strange gods and goings-on—but Father has a copy secreted away.

My heart sinks. After Mother died, after it became obvious that he would have no sons, Father started reading with Tess and teaching her the dead languages he loves. She gobbles up his lessons like a starving kitten, thrilled with any scraps of knowledge or leftover bits of affection he tosses her way.

Father gazes at an empty space on the wall. "I'm sorry to postpone our lessons."

He isn't, not truly. Maura's right; all Father cares about anymore is his books and his business. Anger rises through me. Does he even notice how Tess adores him? He isn't here to see how she mopes around the house after he leaves. It's left to me to cheer her, to entertain her with magic lessons in the garden and impromptu theatricals. It's always left to me.

"Will the governess teach us anything interesting?" Tess asks. "Or only stupid things like drawing and French?"

Father clears his throat. "Er—I imagine the latter. Your curriculum won't include anything that hasn't been approved by the Brotherhood. I know it's not what you're used to, but drawing and French—those are useful accomplishments for young ladies, Teresa."

Tess sighs and fiddles with her spoon. She's already fluent in French, Latin, and Greek. Father's been promising to teach her German next.

"Won't you be lonely?" Maura goes to the sideboard and pours Father a glass of port from the crystal decanter. "Away from home so long?"

Father coughs. Has he been coughing more lately? He says it's only the change of seasons, but his face is as tired as his eyes. "I'll be quite busy. Meetings all day."

"But wouldn't you like company? Someone to take meals with?" Maura gives him a bright, wheedling smile. She looks very much like Mother when she smiles. "You've been working too hard. I could come and look after you. I'd love to see New London."

Tess and I both swivel in our chairs. Maura has to know he'll never agree to it. He doesn't know what to do with us at home, much less in New London.

"No, no, I'm right as rain. And I wouldn't have time to look after you properly. New London is no place for a young lady without a chaperone. It's much better for you to stay here with your sisters." Father takes a spoonful of soup, oblivious to the way Maura's face falls. "Now, about this governess. Sister Elena comes very highly recommended by Mrs. Corbett. She was Regina's governess."

*And Regina married very well.* Father doesn't say it, but it hangs in the air, heavy as the evening fog. Is that what he wants for us? Regina Corbett is a simpering ninny, and her husband is religious and rich and of good standing. He's sure to be considered by the Brotherhood the next time they have an opening. There are always twelve members on the town council, ranging in age from ancient Brother Elliott, Brenna's grandfather, down to Brother Malcolm, twenty and handsome, married just last fall.

Brother Ishida, the head of the council here, reports to the National Council in New London twice a year. Generally, however, the National Council does not involve itself in small-town affairs. They are more concerned with the looming threat of another war with Indo-China, which has settled the western half of America, or Spain, which has colonized the south. It's Brother Ishida and the Chatham council that we have to be wary of. If they knew what we were, all their fatherly kindness would vanish in the blink of an eye. Young or old, they are united in their fervor to keep New England safe from witches.

I wouldn't marry a member of the Brotherhood for all the money in the Brothers' coffers.

"I remember Regina's governess," Maura says. She's tearing her bread into bits instead of eating it. "She's young. And very pretty."

I search my memory but can't come up with a face. We must have seen her at services, passed her occasionally in the street, but she was in town for only three months before Regina married.

"I met the other new member of the staff," I announce. "Finn Belastra?"

"Ah, yes." Father shakes his head. "I popped into the shop the other day and spoke with his mother. Marianne tells me the Brothers have been scaring half their customers away. Hoping to find something forbidden and shut them down, I expect. It's a shame when it's come to this, people afraid of books!"

Never mind people being afraid of *girls*. I interrupt him before he can get started. "Yes, but does Finn actually know how to garden?"

"He's a very bright young man. Would have made a fine scholar," Father says, which does not actually answer my question. He natters on about how Finn was supposed to go to university before his father died, and what a shame it is, and I'm sure Finn would be thrilled to know his mother's been blabbing his business all over town.

I make polite replies as Father segues back into the importance of learning. I think he means to encourage us about the governess, but I'm the only one listening. Maura's slipped a novel into her lap. Tess is amusing herself by making one of the candles on the wall sconce flicker. I give her a look, and she stops with a guilty smile. I shake my head and push my apple pie away, appetite lost.

After dinner, we're free to do as we please. When Father's away, occasionally we coax Mrs. O'Hare into joining us for games. Often we play at chess or draughts, though Tess is the reigning champion at both and Maura is a horrid loser. Tonight Father drifts back to his study. Maura climbs the stairs to her room with barely a word to anyone. That leaves Tess and me.

I follow my little sister into the sitting room. She settles at the piano, her fingers gliding gracefully over the keys. She's the only one of us with enough patience to develop any real skill.

I kick off my slippers and lie on my back on the tufted cream sofa. Tess's sonata washes over me. She used to play lively old folk ballads, and Maura would sing and play her mandolin. We'd push the furniture to the walls, and Mrs. O'Hare would come in and dance me around the room. The old songs were banned years ago, along with dancing and theater and anything else that smacks of the old days before the Brothers, when the witches were the ones in power. But the Brothers have become increasingly strict, and dancing isn't worth the risk.

Tess's fingers stutter and stop. "Are you still angry with me?" she asks.

"No. Yes." If I don't discipline her, who will? Father doesn't know about the magic, and he mustn't find out. Mother was convinced he wasn't strong enough to handle it. She cited his weak chest, the cough that seems to leave him a little frailer each year. But it's more than that, even if she couldn't bring herself to say it outright. Father grumbles about the Brothers' censorship and hides books in secret compartments all over the house, but that's an easy sort of rebellion. I don't think Mother believed he'd be strong enough to stand against them when it came to something that really mattered. Like us.

She loved him anyway, but I can't see how it was much of a marriage, honestly.

I sit up, hugging my knees to my chest. "You can't do magic anywhere you like, Tess. You know that. I couldn't bear it if something happened to you."

Tess looks very young in her pink pinafore, her hair in two braids that stretch to her waist. Now that she's twelve, she's been bothering me to let her put her hair up and her skirts down. I suppose the governess will advise me to allow it. I can't keep her from growing up. "I know," she says. "Me either. If something happened to you, I mean."

I glance up at the portraits above the fireplace. There's one of Father with his parents when he was a boy, a retriever puppy asleep at his feet. Next to it is a painting of the five of us—Father, Mother, Maura, Tess, and me. Tess was still a baby with pale blond hair sprouting like dandelion fuzz all over her head. Mother is looking down at her lovingly, a Madonna cradling the child in her arms. She had lost a baby between Maura and Tess—the first of five buried in the family cemetery.

"This governess—she'll be living here, taking meals with us, watching our every step. Even if you think it's to help someone— Father, or even me or Maura—"

Tess swivels to face me. "Is this about what happened at services last week?"

"No, but that's a perfect example." As we were leaving the church last Sunday, someone stepped on Maura's skirt. Her dress ripped—right across the middle of her admittedly tight bodice—exposing her corset cover for everyone to see. It would have been mortifying if Tess hadn't thought quickly and cast a *renovo* spell.

"Maura would have been humiliated," Tess argues.

"A little public humiliation wouldn't have killed her. We would have gotten her into the carriage and out of sight, and no one would have remembered it in a few days. If anyone had seen what you did—"

"They would have thought it never ripped in the first place," Tess insists. "I was very quick. They would have thought it a trick of their eyes."

"Would they?" I'm not so certain. "The Brothers have been leaping on anything that even hints of magic—and they wouldn't assume it was you—they'd think it was Maura. You meant to help, I know, but it could have ended very badly."

Tess fiddles with the lace at her wrist. "I know," she whispers.

"Brenna Elliott. Gwen Foucart. Betsy Reed. Marguerite Dolamore."

I reel off the names like the multiplication tables Father taught us. They're the four girls arrested by the Brothers in the last year. Gwen and Betsy were sentenced to labor on the prison ship off the coast of New London. The conditions there are horrid—backbreaking work and very little food. There are rats, I hear, and disease, and girls don't often survive it. But Marguerite—no one even knows what happened to her. She disappeared before her trial, taken away in the middle of the night.

"Would you have it be Maura? Or you?" I'm relentless. I have to be.

"No. No, never." Tess's rosy cheeks drain of color. "I won't do it again."

"And you'll be more careful at home, too? No more magic at the dinner table?"

"No. Only—I wish we could tell Father the truth. Perhaps he'd stay home more. Look after us better. I'll never get anywhere with my lessons this way."

I stare at the gold flowers on the carpet. There's so much hope in Tess's voice. She wants a regular father, someone she can depend upon to protect her.

But we're not regular girls. If Father knew how I'd gone into his mind, compelled him, and destroyed Lord knows what other memories in the process, would he ever forgive me?

I want to believe he would, that he'd come to understand. But he hasn't given me any reason to think he'd fight for us.

That only means I have to fight twice as hard. I rest my chin on my knees. "We don't know what he'd do, Tess. We can't chance it."

Tess's pale fingers twist in her lap. "I don't understand why she didn't trust him," she says finally. "I wish I did. I wish Mother were here."

She turns back to her piano, finding some solace in her sonata. I pick up the post from the tea table. There are a few bills for Father, a letter from his sister, and—to my surprise—a letter with no postmark, in an unfamiliar looping script, addressed to Miss Catherine Cahill. Who would write to me? I've fallen behind on correspondence with Father's side of the family, and Mother has no living relatives.

*Dear Cate:*
*You don't know me, but your mother and I were once very dear friends. Now Anna is gone, and I, who ought to be there to guide you in her absence, can be of no help besides this: look for your mother's diary. It will contain the answers you seek. The three of you are in very great danger.*

*Affectionately yours,*

*Z. R.*

The letter flutters from my fingers to the floor. Tess plays on, heedless of my terror.

I don't know Z. R., but she knows us. Does she know our secrets?

## chapter

# 3

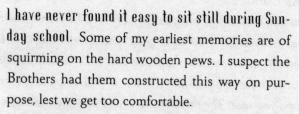

I have never found it easy to sit still during Sunday school. Some of my earliest memories are of squirming on the hard wooden pews. I suspect the Brothers had them constructed this way on purpose, lest we get too comfortable.

It's called Sunday school, but we are required to attend twice weekly: on Sunday before regular services and again on Wednesday evenings. There are two separate classes: one for children under ten, held in the classroom down the hall, to teach them basic prayers and the tenets of the Brotherhood's beliefs, and one for girls aged eleven to seventeen, to teach us about how wicked we are.

The air in here is stifling, though the wind blows cool and fresh through the trees outside. The Brothers never open a window. Lord forbid we get distracted, even by something as innocuous as the September breeze tickling over our skin.

Brother Ishida, the head of the Brotherhood's council here, teaches our class today. He is not a very tall man, only perhaps my height, but up on the dais he looms over all of us. His face is hard, and his mouth perpetually tilts down, as though he's used to frowning his way through life.

"Submission," he announces. "You must submit to our leadership. The Brotherhood would lead you down the path of righteousness and keep you innocent of the world's evils. We know you *want* to be good girls. We know it is only womanly frailty that leads you astray. We forgive you for it." His voice is full of fatherly compassion, but his eyes are contemptuous as they rove over us. "We would protect you from your own willfulness and vanity. You must submit to our rule, even as we submit to the Lord. You must put your love and faith in us, even as we put ours in him."

Maura and I exchange scornful glances. Love and faith, indeed. Back in Great-Grandmother's day, the Brotherhood burned girls like us. We are not without our faults, to be sure— but neither are they.

"We will never lead you into sin and temptation. Indeed, we will do everything we can to keep you from it. When the witches were in power, they did not encourage girls to take their rightful place in the home. They cared nothing for protecting girls' virtue. They would have women aping men—dressing immodestly, running businesses, even forgoing marriage to live in unnatural unions with other women." Brother Ishida allows himself a shudder of disgust. "Because of their wickedness, they were overthrown. It was the Lord's will that the Brotherhood take their place as the rightful rulers of New England."

I stare at the pew in front of me, at the blond curls dripping down Elinor Evans's neck. Is he right? Almost one hundred twenty years ago, in 1780, angry mobs stirred by the rhetoric of Brother William Richmond burned the temples up and down the coast—often with the witches still in them. Ultimately, the witches' magic wasn't enough to subdue their subjects—not when the witches were so vastly outnumbered. The Great Temple of the Daughters of Persephone in New London was the last to fall. Most witches were murdered; the few who were left went into hiding.

Brother Ishida's voice rises, his face going red, his black-marble eyes shining. "Our rules were made to *protect you from yourselves*. The witches were headstrong and lustful. Perversions of what women should be. Lord help us all if they ever rise again! We must never forget the evil they perpetrated—the way they corrupted our girls, and the way they used mind-magic on their opponents. These are women who left their enemies empty husks."

I can—and do—mock much of what Brother Ishida teaches, but I can't argue with this ugly bit of history. Mother confirmed the truth of it. When the early members of the Brotherhood first came to America, seeking religious freedoms, they were allowed to practice in peace. But as their numbers grew greater, they and their followers began to speak out against the witches, and they were systematically compelled to forget their objections. When the witches fell from power, the Brothers discovered asylums full of the witches' enemies, the occupants reduced to childlike states or outright catatonia.

Elinor Evans shivers and waves her hand in the air. She's a plump, placid girl of thirteen whose father is the chocolatier. "Can we go over the signs of mind-magic again, sir?"

Brother Ishida smiles. True mind-magic is rare as hen's teeth, but the Brothers like to keep us frightened of it. "Of course we can. Headache. The feeling that someone is pulling on your hair, only inside. And your memory goes all foggy." Brother Ishida's eyes sweep over the crowd of assembled girls. "But if the witch is strong enough, there will be no symptoms. You may never know that she has invaded your mind and destroyed a memory. Witches are very clever and very wicked. That is why we must hunt them down and contain them, Elinor, so they don't contaminate good girls like you."

"Thank you, sir," Elinor says, lifting her double chins with pride.

"You're welcome. We're nearly out of time. Let's go over a few of the tenets of womanhood, shall we? Miss Dolamore! What is a woman's highest purpose?"

Gabrielle Dolamore shrinks back in her seat. Her sister Marguerite is the one who was taken away last month, and the Brothers have been scrutinizing Gabby ever since. She's a tiny girl of fourteen, all birdlike arms and legs. "To bear children and be a comfort to our husbands?" she whispers.

Brother Ishida strides forward to the very edge of the dais. He's an imposing figure, cloaked in the Brothers' black robes. "Speak up, Miss Dolamore. I can't hear you."

Gabrielle says it again, louder.

"That is correct. Miss Maura Cahill! To whom do you owe obedience?"

Next to me, Maura stiffens. "The Brotherhood. My father. And someday, my husband," she replies, her voice crisp.

"That is correct. And what must you strive to be, girls? Answer all together!"

"Pure of heart, meek of spirit, chaste of virtue," we chant.

"Yes. Good job, girls. That concludes our lesson. Let us clear our minds and open our hearts to the Lord."

"We clear our minds and open our hearts to the Lord," we echo.

"You may go in peace to serve the Lord," he says.

We bow our heads. "Thanks be."

Indeed, I am thankful that it's over. I stand and arch my back as we wait for the children and adults to join us for the service proper. Some of the girls promenade down the aisle and back; others huddle together and giggle. I elbow Maura, who's staring at Brother Ishida's back as though he's a two-headed calf.

*"Perversions of what women should be,"* Maura mimics. "Because they loved other women? Or because they refused to submit to a man's authority?"

She has a point. The Brothers say that women having romantic relationships with each other is a very great sin. But in other, freer places, like Dubai, women live openly with other women—and men with men. It's not common, but it's not illegal.

"I loathe him," Maura hisses, her pretty face distorted with anger.

"Maura," I say warningly, putting a hand on her yellow sleeve.

I turn to see if anyone is within hearing distance. Thankfully there's no one's left in the pew behind us.

But Sachiko Ishida is just passing our row, arm in arm with Rose Collier. "You should see some of the new hats from Mexico City, they're so dear! All decorated with feathers and flowers," Sachi says loudly. "But Father says they're far too gaudy. Only meant to draw attention, you know. Just like rouging your face. Only ladies of loose morals do *that*."

"I hear girls in Dubai are wearing blouses separate from their skirts," Rose adds in a scandalized whisper. "And sometimes trousers, just like men!"

Sachi gasps. "How positively indecent! I'd never go that far. Father says it's only my womanly frailty that makes me wish for pretty things." She catches me looking and winks a dark eye. "I shall have to pray harder to rid myself of sin."

Is she joking? I've never seen the slightest indication that Sachi has a sense of humor. She is her father's pet, a model of good behavior, and the most popular of the town girls. Her sixteenth birthday was a few weeks ago, and he threw her a grand garden party with croquet and chocolate cake. We were not invited.

I hold back a sigh. What I wouldn't give to share in the freedoms of Arab girls. They're allowed to inherit property and go to university; they've even been given the right to vote. But we never hear about witches living there. We never hear about witches *anywhere*. It seems like most of the world's witches were drawn to New England by the promise of freedom—and within a few generations, they were all slaughtered.

Even if witches were allowed to live openly elsewhere, there's no way for us to leave New England. Girls have more freedoms in the Spanish colonies to the south, but the borders are closed. *All* the borders are closed, except for official Brotherhood business and trade. Stowaways are punished as harshly as witches themselves.

Running away is impossible. We have to stay here and solve our problems. I reach into my pocket, where my fingers brush against the crumpled note from Z. R. It's been nearly a week since I received the letter, but I'm no closer to figuring out her identity. I haven't been able to find Mother's diary, and there's no mention in her correspondence of anyone whose name starts with a Z.

Who is Z. R.? And what sort of danger is she warning me about?

Everyone from Chatham and the surrounding farms is here, stuffed into the wooden church; services are mandatory except for the very ill. Even when it became obvious that Mother was dying—and after, when the house was in deepest mourning—we weren't granted a reprieve. Brother Ishida urged us to offer up our grief to the Lord. He promised it would prove our greatest consolation. I did not find much truth in that, myself.

My eyes roam over my neighbors. The Brothers sit together in the first two pews. Their families sit behind them in places of honor. We are meant to shun worldly vices like pride and envy, but being married to one of the Brothers carries with it a certain cachet. Their wives are meek women with downcast eyes, but they dress well. Their wide bell skirts fan out around them, and their taffeta petticoats rustle when they shift. Puffed sleeves stand up on each shoulder—sentinels guarding their thoughts, lest anything shameful sneak in. And their daughters! They are pictures of garish girlishness in bright yellows and purples, pinks and emeralds, their hair in the new pompadour style instead of the simple chignons my sisters and I favor.

A half-swallowed giggle catches my attention. Brother Malcolm pauses in his sermon on charity, frowning at proof that not everyone is wholly absorbed.

It's Rory Elliott. For a moment, she smiles at all the attention and tosses her long black hair. Then she lowers her eyes demurely, her cheeks flushing as pink as her dress, and inches closer to Nils Winfield. She gets away with being scandalous because she's betrothed to Nils, and his father is Brother Winfield.

Everyone else's eyes slide away as Brother Malcolm resumes. The Lord . . . something. I keep watching Rory and see how Sachi Ishida elbows her sharply in the ribs. Rory mouths something unladylike, but folds her hands in her lap, straightens her back, and fixes her attention back on Brother Malcolm. Sachi smiles, and I wonder—not for the first time—why the town sweetheart chooses to associate with a girl like that. Rory's mother is a shut-in who never leaves their house. They say she's a drunk, and that she doesn't know who Rory's real father is. Her husband, Jack Elliott, gave Rory his name, but since he died in that carriage accident, the Elliotts won't have anything to do with Rory or her mother.

Sachi catches me staring. I raise my eyes back to the dais, where Brother Malcolm is just finishing his sermon.

"We clear our minds and open our hearts to the Lord," he intones.

"We clear our minds and open our hearts to the Lord," the congregation echoes. I mouth the words along with everyone else. Mother taught us to say the prayers before bedtime and meals when we were small, but it seemed more a matter of habit than of faith. Any real belief I had in the Lord died along with my mother.

"Go in peace. Serve the Lord," the Brothers chant.

"Thanks be."

Our neighbors file out slowly, chattering to one another, exchanging news. I want to shove them out of my way, throw elbows into their soft stomachs. I want to be home.

Instead I smooth my skirt and wait my turn to exit the pew.

Mrs. Corbett is at Father's side, nattering on about the governess. I watch them, Maura's prediction ringing in my ears. The old hag can't really be trying to entangle Father romantically, can she? He's not home often enough to be a husband to anyone. And we do not need—do not ever want—a new mother.

Father manages a smile. He used to be handsome, but perpetual mourning has taken its toll. There's a scattering of silver in his blond hair, and his face droops like a basset hound. "You must stay for dinner, then," he suggests.

Surely that's just politeness.

Mrs. Corbett simpers. At least I think that's the intended effect. Her mouth twists into a ghastly sort of smile.

Mrs. Ishida appears at the end of our pew. "Miss Cahill! I'm giving a little tea next Wednesday afternoon, and I was hoping you might like to join us. Miss Maura too, of course."

Mrs. Ishida's teas are the most coveted invitations in town.

We have never been granted a summons before. Mrs. Corbett looks up sharply, her tongue darting out between her teeth like a snake testing the air.

I clasp my hands together and stare demurely at the wooden floor. "It's so kind of you to think of us. We would be delighted."

"Lovely," Mrs. Ishida says. "We shall look forward to seeing you on Wednesday, then."

I wonder what's prompted this sudden interest in our society. I look over at Sachi, who is whispering with Rory, their dark heads bent close together. Her eyes glance off mine so quickly, they almost throw sparks. Did she set her mother on us?

"It's good for young ladies to be out in company. They won't make the right connections at home studying Cicero," Mrs. Corbett whispers. "Perhaps Sister Elena can help them organize a tea of their own. They ought to have an at-home afternoon."

Oh no. If we commence gadding about, we'll be forced to return the invitations. I am ostensibly the lady of the house, but I've never been called on to perform as such. The thought of having neighbors running roughshod through the place, poking their noses into our lives, terrifies me. I don't know how to serve tea and cakes and make polite conversation. By the time I was old enough to go visiting with her, Mother was too ill, and then we were in mourning for a year. What do polite people talk about? Not magic or books or Greek mythology. Likely not gardening.

Loath as I am to admit it, this governess might be useful after all.

• • •

43

We eventually make our way down the crowded aisle and outside. Above us, white cotton-boll clouds scud across the cerulean sky. Branches sway in the breeze, sending leaves pirouetting to the ground. On either side of the walk, white chrysanthemums bloom. The plot needs weeding.

The church and its white spire dominate the town square. The holding cell in the basement and the Brothers' council chamber serve as jail and courthouse. All of Chatham stretches out from here: the general goods store, the stationer's, the chocolatier's, Belastras' bookshop, the seamstress's, the apothecary's, the butcher's, the bakery, a few dozen homes. Most of the population of Chatham lives on farms outside town, where they grow potatoes and corn, oats and hay, apples and blueberries.

Father has escaped the dread clutches of Mrs. Corbett and is chatting with Marianne Belastra, Finn's mother. She's a thin woman with gray twining through her rust-colored hair. She has Finn's freckles—or the other way around, I suppose. Finn stands next to her, nodding enthusiastically at something Father says. His sister, Clara, tugs on the sleeve of his jacket. She's Tess's age, but tall and gangly, with enormous hands and feet that seem all out of proportion to the rest of her. Her skirt isn't quite long enough; a hint of her petticoat peeks out beneath.

"Good day, Miss Cahill," a deep voice says behind me.

I whirl around. It's been ages since I've heard that dry growl, but I'd know it anywhere.

How on earth did I miss him in church? He must have slipped in at the last minute and sat behind us.

I knew Paul would be home soon; everyone in town knows.

Mrs. McLeod's talked of nothing else for weeks. He must have come a few days early to surprise her. Still, I can't help staring. He looks so much older. A man of nineteen, not a boy of fifteen. He's taller—I barely come up to his nose now—and he's got a close-cropped mustache and beard just a shade darker than his blond hair. He looks quite the gentleman in his frock coat, lounging indolently beneath a maple tree.

"Mr. McLeod, home at last. How are you?" I curtsy, wishing I'd worn a prettier dress. Apple green looks beautiful on Maura, but it does me no favors. Why didn't I wear the mauve brocade?

"Quite well, thank you, and you?" He shifts from foot to foot. Is he as nervous as I am? His green eyes are so intent on my face, I can't help flushing under the scrutiny.

"Very well." Still angry with him.

"Mother and I are leaving. Could we escort you home?"

Oh. No gentleman's ever offered to escort me home before. I should be pleased. As Maura so helpfully pointed out, Paul is my best chance for finding a husband. If I don't get betrothed soon, Father will involve himself—or, worse, the Brothers will choose for me. They could pick anyone—a lonely old widower or a devout man poised to join the Brotherhood. I'd have no say in it.

Still, Paul didn't even bother to come home for Mother's funeral. Girls are not permitted to receive letters from men unless they are betrothed, but surely he could have written me if he'd wanted to, instead of that dry little note of condolence he sent Father. If he'd thought of me—missed me at all—he would have

45

written. We were the best of friends right up until the day he left. This man in front of me now is a stranger.

And I'm not the carefree Cate he left behind. Seeing him again—it makes me miss that girl. She didn't realize how much she had to lose. She laughed more and worried a great deal less.

"Let me tell my sisters I'm going," I decide.

Maura greets Paul with enthusiasm while Tess smiles shyly. When I say the McLeods will take me home, Maura glares at me for abandoning her and Tess to the dull politeness of our neighbors. I can't help smirking. Perhaps this will give her the chance to make those friends she's been longing for.

Paul hands me up into the McLeods' barouche, and I settle onto the leather bench next to his mother. Paul sits across from us. Mrs. McLeod nervously arranges a blanket over her lap, shivering, as the matched pair of bays starts forward. I suspect the open carriage is Paul's doing. His mother is notoriously afraid of catching a chill.

"Good morning, Mrs. McLeod," I say. "How are you?"

She gives me a sour smile as she recounts her latest aches and pains. Paul is her darling; I don't think she'd care for any girl he paid attention to, but she's always found me particularly irritating. I suspect I am too hardy for my own good.

"How was your apprenticeship?" I ask.

"Paul's become Mr. Jones's right-hand man. And he was quite the scholar at university," she gloats. "Tell her, son."

"I did well enough for all the time I spent in the library." Paul ducks his head. I'd wager that he spent precious little time in the library, compared with how much he spent wandering the city and carousing.

"He's modest," Mrs. McLeod says.

"New London is grand. Construction booming all day, every day except Sundays. New factories, new warehouses down by the port to store goods, new houses for the men making their fortunes off the factories. All the big houses have gaslights now. Some even have indoor water closets!"

"Imagine that," Mrs. McLeod breathes.

"The streets are a madhouse. Trains come and go all day long, bringing workers from the country looking for jobs. Ships come to port with goods and people from Europe or as far away as Dubai. The city is bursting at the seams. Whole families are living crowded together in three-room flats above shops and taverns. It's an amazing time to be an architect."

I can't fathom it. The only life I've known is here in Chatham. I've never been out of Maine. Never farther than the seaside. "Taverns? I don't imagine the Brothers approve of that."

Paul chuckles. "They shut them down as fast as they open. There are signs up everywhere, warning us against drink and gambling." He stretches his arms over his head, and I can't help noticing how well his suit fits. "They regulate the gentlemen's clubs with iron fists, Jones says, but he took me with him to his, and you wouldn't believe the—"

"Paul. I'm sure Miss Cahill doesn't want to hear your scandalous tales." Mrs. McLeod settles her feet on the hot-water bottle on the carriage floor. "Are you quite certain you aren't cold, dear?"

I would love to hear scandalous tales, but I can't very well say that. Instead, Paul and I both assure her that we are comfortable. I take in a deep lungful of air as we pass an orchard, the trees tangled with ripe red apples. On the other side of the lane, the trees are bare, already picked. The sweet air smells like home, like autumn. I wonder what New London smells like—smoke from all those factories? Sewage from all the people and horses?

"And now you're back for good?" I ask Paul.

"We'll see. I've missed the place." His green eyes linger on mine until I find myself flushing again.

"It hasn't been the same without Paul, has it, Mrs. McLeod?" I say lightly, deflecting the attention. She's only too glad to enumerate the many ways in which she's missed her son, how silent and dull the house has been without him, how she's been planning a dinner party to celebrate his return.

"And you'll come, of course, won't you? You and Maura and your father," Paul suggests.

"Of course." It's one invitation I can accept with ease. The McLeods are our nearest neighbors. As a child, I was in and out of their house almost as much as my own. I grin, remembering the time Paul dared me to tightrope-walk the wall around the McLeods' pigpen. I fell and sprained my ankle, then swooned from the pain and fright. Paul carried me home, terrified he'd murdered me. Once he was assured I was all right, he teased me mercilessly about being such a girl. He went about for months falling down in a mock faint.

I must have been about ten at the time. Mother was recovering from the third stillbirth—Edward Aaron. Mrs. O'Hare insisted on cleaning me up and bandaging my ankle before I was allowed into Mother's rooms. I remember her pale, drawn face and the purple shadows under her swollen eyes. She told me I had to start behaving like a lady soon, and I stuck out my tongue at her, and she laughed.

The barouche pulls up before our house, and Paul jumps out. "I'll be back directly, Mother," he says, helping me down, tucking my hand into the crook of his elbow.

He stops just outside our front door, fixing me with an earnest expression. "Cate, I was so sorry to hear about your mother. She was a great lady," he says.

"Thank you." I stare at the plot of black-eyed Susans beside the porch. "We appreciated your note of condolence."

"It wasn't enough. I wanted to come home, but it was the beginning of the term—"

Yes, the timing was inconvenient. My mother's death wasn't reason enough to miss a few classes. Never mind that Mother used to sneak him sweets that his mother forbade. When she was well enough to come outside, he used to turn cartwheels through the garden to cheer her, and when she wasn't, he'd make hideous faces at her through the window. He was my best friend, and he grew up with her, too, and he couldn't be bothered to come home for even a week.

"You couldn't have gotten back in time for the service. I know. It's quite all right." But I don't meet his eyes, and my reassurance sounds hollow. Will he notice?

"It's not. I wanted to be here for your family—for you—but—" I look up as he falters, and he leans in close. He smells spicy, like pine needles. "I couldn't come home. Financially, I mean. I was too proud to write it at the time, and my mother would murder me for telling you now. Money's been scarce."

"Oh," I say, stupidly. I've never had to worry about money, not for a minute. I've always taken it for granted that our good name is all the currency I need.

"You must have wondered why I never came home at holidays." He gives me a funny little smile, as though he hopes I did wonder.

"Your mother told everyone you were with your cousins in Providence." I'd assumed he'd made fine new friends in the city and forgotten me.

"We couldn't afford even that. I would have been sunk if Jones hadn't offered me lodging. I owe him a great debt."

Oh. I feel guilty now, for all my uncharitable thoughts. "You should have told me. You could have written."

"I wanted to." Paul smiles. "I wanted to tell you everything. But to have your father reading it all first—that made it less appealing."

"As if I couldn't get around Father," I huff, affronted.

Paul chuckles and steps closer—far closer than is appropriate. There are only inches separating us; I can feel the warmth of his body almost touching mine. "I've missed you."

I've missed him, too. But it was inevitable that our friendship would change as we got older, and perhaps the forcible separation was for the best. After Mother died, when Maura ran wild, keeping the magic a secret was hard. Keeping it from Paul would have been nearly impossible.

"Can you forgive me? I know you must have been angry."

I duck my head. "No, I—"

"I know you better than that. Come now. Mad as a hornet?"

I grin, sheepish. "A whole nest of them. It—hurt. A bit. That you weren't here."

Paul takes my hand. The smile fades from my face. "I'm sorry for it. Truly," he says.

"Paul!" Mrs. McLeod's querulous voice calls. "Let Miss Cahill go inside before she catches a chill!"

"Indeed, Miss Cahill, we know what a delicate flower you are," Paul teases.

I roll my eyes and give a very unladylike snort. "Indeed."

"So you forgive me, then?" His hand grips mine, burning warm even through the kid gloves that separate our skin.

"Of course."

Paul's eyes search mine. "May I call on you tomorrow afternoon?"

My heart beats faster. As an old friend? Or as a potential suitor?

When I asked whether he was back to stay, and he said *we'll see*—what did that mean? Does he intend to court me in earnest? The sense of panic that's been battering at me for the last few months eases just a little.

I'm suddenly very aware that he is still holding my hand.

"Yes. Only"—I wrinkle my nose—"the house may be in a bit of an uproar. Our new governess is arriving in the morning."

"Governess?" Paul's eyes go wide. "Lord help her. How many have you gone through?"

"This is the first, thank you. Father's been tutoring us, but he's going to be away most of the fall. And how do you know we haven't become exceedingly polite young ladies while you were gone?"

Paul brings my hand to his lips, turns it over, and presses a kiss to the bare bit of skin at my wrist. He's held my hand dozens of times over the years, boosted me up onto horses and into trees. This is entirely different. It leaves me gaping at him, mouth open like a ninny.

He winks at me and doffs his hat. "Because I know *you*. See you tomorrow, Cate."

## chapter

# 4

"She's here!" Tess calls. "She's here!"

She and Maura scamper out the front door before I can stop them. Father and I follow, with more decorum but just as much curiosity. Our carriage is rattling slowly up the potholed drive with the new governess inside. I'm not optimistic. After all, Mrs. Corbett recommended her, didn't she? I'd wager she's some sheltered convent girl, brought up by the Sisters to earn her livelihood teaching dull, demure young ladies to become dull, demure wives. I'm expecting a prim miss given to sprouting platitudes.

So I'm quite surprised when the carriage door is flung open and Sister Elena hops out without even waiting for John to hand her down. She swishes up to the porch, taffeta petticoats rustling, moving as though she owns the place.

Maura was right. Sister Elena is pretty—no, beautiful—with smooth brown skin and black ringlets peeking out from beneath her hood. And she's fashionable—as fashionable as the Brothers' strictures will allow. Her dress has a wide bell skirt in a soft pink that reminds me of Mother's peonies. A pleated black silk cummerbund draws attention to her small waist, and black velvet slippers adorn her feet.

"Sister Elena, welcome," Father says, stepping forward. "We're glad to have you. These are my daughters, Catherine, Maura, and Teresa."

"Cate, please," I correct.

"And Tess." Tess is half hiding behind me, her blond head resting against my shoulder.

"Certainly. If we're to dispense with the formalities, you must call me Elena. I'm so glad to meet you all." Elena smiles, her chocolate eyes tilting up at the corners. "I'm certain we'll get along famously. I've always been fast friends with my pupils."

Father looks relieved, but I bristle at her boldness. She doesn't know a thing about us, and Regina Corbett's bosom friendship hardly recommends her to *me*. Father inquires after her journey, whether the inn she stayed at last night was satisfactory, whether she might like to see her room and freshen up before they discuss our curriculum, while my temper commences a slow boil.

Elena can't be more than a few years older than me. She's a member of the Sisters, which means she spends much of her time walled up in their cloisters in New London. What can she teach us about the world or about catching a husband?

I remember Paul's words from yesterday—*Lord help her*—and grin.

"Cate?" Father says, and I startle, the mad smile slipping from my face. "Would you show Sister Elena to her room?"

"I'll do it," Maura volunteers, grabbing Elena's leather valise and leaving John to bring her trunk. "You'll be in the room directly across from mine. It's got a beautiful view of the gardens."

"Ah, yes. Mrs. Corbett mentioned you've got the magic touch with flowers, Miss Cate."

Her tongue trips over the word lightly, but I look at Elena hard. She's giving me a bland smile. Perhaps it's just a figure of speech, albeit a dangerous one.

"Thank you," I say uncertainly. "I do enjoy being outdoors."

"My late wife—" Father begins, then coughs. "She spent a great deal of time in the gardens. Cate inherited her mother's talent for growing things."

I give Father a startled look. I wasn't aware he thought I had any talent; this is the first I've heard of it. Maura leads Elena inside, pointing out the sitting room, Father's study, and the dining room before leading her upstairs. Maura bounces like a child, whereas Elena walks sedately, back straight, trailing a gloved hand along the curved wooden balustrade like a queen. I scurry after them.

"You've a lovely home," Elena says, pausing at the top of the stairs to admire the painting of Great-Grandmother. She was a petite woman with pale blond curls like Tess's. She wasn't pretty, though—she had a cadaverous face, with a complexion like old milk. But she was strong. She raised four children, buried two, and kept the farm running even after a fever took her husband.

Maura tosses her hair. "It's falling apart. It was my great-grandparents' originally—this is Great-Grandmother. Sour looking, isn't she? I'd love to move into town proper, but Father won't hear of it. It's frightfully dull out here in the country. It must seem horrid to you after all the excitement of New London."

Good Lord. "We're hardly in the country," I object. "It's only two miles to town. And Father will never move, not with the cemetery here."

Elena takes Maura's frankness in stride. "I'm very sorry about your mother. You must be tired of hearing that, I know. I lost both my parents when I was eleven. People never know what to say, do they? Mrs. Corbett told me you were in full mourning for a year. That you've put off coming out into society. Of course, with your father away so much, with no mother to introduce you, how could you? But it must be rather lonely."

"Yes," Maura says emphatically, just as I say, "We manage."

Moving away from the stairs, we pass Father's room, the closed door to Mother's bedroom and sitting room, my bedroom and Tess's, and finally come to Elena's. It's right across the hall from Maura's. "It's not very grand," Maura says apologetically, even though Mrs. O'Hare and Lily spent all day yesterday airing it out and dusting the heavy mahogany furniture until it gleamed.

Elena crosses to the window and pushes back the heavy

green draperies. Beyond the garden, the fields stretch out for acres and acres, the ripe golden wheat undulating in the breeze. "It's a lovely view. What a pretty garden."

Maura puts Elena's valise on the bed and jumps up beside it, ducking beneath the rose-colored canopy. "But we'll have to spruce up the house a bit, won't we?" she persists, eager for an ally. "If we're to have callers, I mean. Cate's got to find a husband soon."

"Maura!" I hiss, mortified. She can't wait five minutes to bring that up?

Elena smiles, even white teeth flashing against her dark skin. "When's your birthday, Cate?"

"March fourteenth," I murmur. I'm surprised Mrs. Corbett hasn't told her that, too. It seems the old bat's been quite chatty.

"She's got a suitor," Maura confides, and I fight the urge to throttle her.

"Your intention ceremony's coming up," Elena says. "Don't worry about a thing, Cate. Leave it all to me."

I stare at the dusky pink rug, resentment swelling up again. I'm hardly the type to leave the worrying to anyone else, to start with. And how can I leave my future to a complete stranger?

Maura thinks it's all very straightforward: I'll marry Paul. But he didn't say whether he was back in Chatham for good, or only for a visit. And the way he spoke of New London, with such fervor—I can tell he likes it there. What if he asks me to marry him but move away?

How did Mother expect me to keep my promise when I came of age? She knew I wouldn't be able to stay home forever.

I've got to find her diary. Soon.

• • •

An hour later, I'm kneeling on the hardwood floor of Mother's sitting room, surrounded by the contents of her writing desk. Nibs and sealing wax and parchment are scattered helter-skelter on the floor. A neat stack of correspondence, bound with a blue velvet ribbon, sits next to me. I've already read through it— twice. There are no mentions of any Zuzannahs or Zinnias anywhere. Who is this mysterious Z. R.?

I know Mother kept a diary during that last year; I interrupted her scribbling in it whenever I came into her rooms. I've never been able to find it. But I've never been as determined as I am now. I need her guidance. Not just about magic, but about my future. What did she want me to do?

I feel along the drawers, looking for a spring or a latch that might reveal a false bottom. There's nothing. I throw things back into the drawers, slide them into place, and rock back on my heels, frustrated. Elena's very presence here pinches at me like too-tight slippers. I've put off thinking about myself, concentrated instead on Tess and Maura and my promise. But I can't ignore the reality any longer. Father didn't hire Elena to teach us French and flower arrangements; he hired her to make sure that Maura and I find husbands.

The Brothers are afraid the witches will rise up again some-day, Mother said, so they loathe the idea of powerful women. We are not permitted to study and go to university as men do, or to take up professions. There are a few notable exceptions: the town midwife, Mrs. Carruthers; the dressmaker, Ella Kosmoski; and Marianne Belastra—but Mrs. Belastra took over the running of the bookshop only after her husband's death. Women are not normally granted permits to run businesses.

The Sisterhood is held up as an alternative to marriage, and an honorable one. They do the charitable work of the Brotherhood: serving as governesses and nurses, visiting the sick and dying, and feeding the poor. But no one in Chatham has actually joined them in years. The notion of spending my life studying scriptures or teaching orphan girls is odious. I'm fairly certain I'd murder my pupils. Furthermore, living in a cloister with dozens of other women sounds suffocating. Trying to keep my magic a secret would be too risky.

No. The Sisterhood is not an option.

I crawl beneath the desk, running a hand along the underside. The diary can't have disappeared into thin air. But there's nothing here. I wince as my slipper catches on a nail in the floorboard, then pull off my shoe, frowning at the run in my stockings. Mrs. O'Hare is sure to scold me again about how I go through them faster than Maura and Tess together, and—

Wait.

I inch backward. The floorboard nearest the wall tilts beneath my palm. I pull at the nail that sticks up; it comes free. I lift the board. Underneath, there's a hollow space. I thrust my arm in to the elbow, hoping I won't disturb anything crawling. My hand searches over dusty wood. It touches something small and smooth and round. I pull it out—only a gray button. It must have fallen in here by accident. I remember the dress it belonged to: high necked, with each of its gray flounces edged in black lace, and a row of these buttons up the back.

I tuck it into a drawer and keep searching.

There's nothing else.

*"Acclaro?"* I try, hopefully, and power sizzles through me. I shove my arm in again, and the illusion of emptiness is broken as my fingertips brush against a book.

The familiar blue cloth cover is grimy, but I hug it to my chest because it's a piece of her. Whatever secrets it contains, for a few minutes, she'll be with me again. Mother will be able to tell me what to do. She always knew what to do.

Thank the Lord.

"Miss Cate?"

Oh, this is just the dignified pose I'd like the governess to catch me in: on hands and knees beneath Mother's desk, one shoe off, bottom wiggling in the air. At least she didn't come in a moment ago and catch me magicking a book out of thin air. Hasn't she ever heard of knocking?

Adding injury to insult, I bump my head on the desk as I turn around.

"I knocked, but no one answered," Elena says, a smile tugging at her lips. "Mr. McLeod is here to see you."

"I was looking for an earbob," I lie. "I lost it. Somewhere."

"I see. Would you like to take a few moments to tidy up?"

Is she laughing at me? I'm offended until I look down at myself. My bodice is covered in dust from lying on the floor, my hair is falling into my face, and my hands are gray with dirt. It's hardly how I want a prospective husband to see me.

I stand, brushing the dust from my sleeves, trying to salvage some shred of dignity. "Yes, I believe I shall. Please tell Paul I'll be with him directly."

• • •

In the privacy of my room, I wipe off Mother's diary with shaking hands.

If it were any other caller, I'd feign illness and spend the afternoon reading. No one would dream I'd stay indoors for anything other than sickness. I'm desperate to know what advice she's left for me. I was so young when she died, only thirteen, and still such a child. The three years until I had to declare an intention loomed like thirty, especially without her. I wouldn't have listened to anything she said about marriage and husbands then; perhaps she was clever enough to know it, and she wrote down her words of motherly wisdom instead. My nerves jangle in anticipation like the keys on Mrs. O'Hare's belt.

But it's Paul. I can't put him off. The thought irks me. Never mind that he's kept *me* waiting for four years.

I pull on one of my nicest day dresses, a dark gray with a pale-blue sash and blue lace at the collar. I fix my hair as best I can, then head downstairs to the sitting room.

Paul is there, his long legs spread out in front of him. Elena has disappeared—presumably for her chat with Father about our curriculum. Maura and Tess crowd together on the sofa, chattering like magpies, firing rapid questions at Paul about New London. He takes up more room than I had remembered. He seems very— male, with his beard and his tall black leather riding boots and the deep timbre of his voice, dwarfing the high-backed blue brocade chair he sits in. I suppose I'm very used to living among women, with Father away so much. Not that we are very quiet women.

Paul stands when he sees me, taking both my hands in his. "Cate," he says, looking at me appreciatively.

He's seen me covered in slop from the pigpen. He's seen my hands and face smeared with strawberries. We used to roll down the grassy knoll beyond the pond until our clothes were stained green. But he's never looked at me like this. It makes me suddenly aware of every inch of myself.

"That dress is just the color of your eyes. You're lovely." He says it easily, confidently. As though he's used to telling girls they're lovely.

I flush and pull away. I'm not used to hearing it, and I can't quite reconcile this earnest, admiring man with the mischievous boy I remember. "Thank you."

"Tess tells me your father's building a gazebo down by the pond. I should like to see the progress."

"It's barely begun. They only erected the frame yesterday."

"Still. I've missed the country air. Come for a walk with me?"

Oh. He doesn't want to see the gazebo so much as he wants to go for a walk with me. *Alone.* Paul was never terribly subtle.

"Can I come?" Tess asks. I open my mouth to say yes, but Maura elbows her. Tess lets out an angry squeak, and the next moment Maura's on the floor in a heap of skirts.

"Teresa Elizabeth Cahill!" I scold. I don't know exactly what she's done, but I'm sure she used magic to do it. "We have a *guest!*" I say, pointing emphatically at Paul.

He just grins, his mouth quirking below his new mustache. New to me, anyway—who knows how long he's had it. "No, no, carry on," he says. "I'm not a true guest. I'm practically family."

Maura arches her eyebrows at me, but I scowl. "You *are* a

guest. Don't encourage them. And you two ought to be ashamed of yourselves. You're too old for this. Tess, apologize."

"She started it," Tess argues, rubbing her side.

"Because you were being a ninny," Maura says. "Paul doesn't want to go for a walk with all three of us. He came to call on Cate."

Tess gives Maura a good pinch. "I'm not a ninny! I'm cleverer than you!"

"You're hopeless, both of you. Perhaps you ought to go and ask Elena about the proper etiquette for entertaining callers." I take Paul's arm and feel his muscles twitch beneath my palm. "A walk would be delightful. Please. Before I murder them both."

I mean to sweep out dramatically, but somehow the doorsill drops away and I lift my foot into empty air. I trip forward, narrowly avoiding rapping my skull on the hall table and destroying an heirloom vase that belonged to Great-Grandmother. Instead, Paul catches me. In fact, he holds me closer than is entirely necessary. I hear a titter behind me and spin around to see Maura, her hand over her mouth, shoulders shaking. Even Tess can't suppress a smile.

Lord help me, my sisters are evil and my best friend's become a rake.

We reach the front hall just as Elena pops out of Father's study. "Miss Cate, let me fetch your cloak. Would you like Miss Maura to accompany you on your walk?"

"No, thank you." As if I haven't gone for hundreds of walks alone with Paul—in the garden, chasing each other through the cornfields, playing hide-and-seek through blueberry bushes.

Elena eyes us, and I'm suddenly conscious of the distance, or lack thereof, between our bodies. "I'm afraid I must insist that you take a chaperone. I can come with you if you'd like."

Oh, for heaven's sake. I hardly worry that Paul will ravish me in the gardens.

"Don't forget your gloves," Elena adds.

I flush, remember the warmth of Paul's mouth on the thin, delicate skin at the inside of my wrist. Perhaps she's right. We're not children anymore. The way Paul looks at me—it's like he remembers that kiss, too, and might enjoy taking other liberties if I were to allow it. No man's ever looked at me like that before. It's a heady feeling.

Still, I don't care to have Elena telling me what to do, much less following us and eavesdropping on our conversation. I feel nervous enough as it is.

"Where's Lily? Lily!" I call.

Our maid appears from the kitchen, wiping wet hands on her apron. "Miss Cate? I was just helping Mrs. O'Hare with the dinner pre—"

"Never mind that. Grab your cloak. Mr. McLeod and I need a chaperone for our walk."

Lily has great meek brown eyes, like a cow's. "Yes, miss."

Once I'm properly cloaked, Paul and I stroll through the gardens, Lily following at a discreet distance. Geese fly overhead in inky formations, honking against the eggshell sky.

"I'm sorry about all that mayhem. My sisters—"

"Are adorable girls, as ever," Paul finishes. "No need to apologize."

"They're ill-mannered beasts!" After witnessing their behavior today in front of both Elena and Paul, I'm starting to believe we may actually require a governess.

"They're high-spirited," Paul says. "It must be grand, having sisters. You're lucky. Being an only child is lonely."

I don't remember a time before Maura was toddling after me, pulling at my hair, stuffing my toys in her mouth. "Is it?"

"At times. Take Father's debts. If I'd had a brother to share the burden, to confide in—it would have been a relief."

"You can confide in me," I suggest. "We were like brother and sister, growing up, weren't we?"

Paul's mouth twists into a frown. "Is that how you think of me? As a brother?"

I don't know what to say. I was still a child when he went away. I've thought about us marrying, but as a solution to the problem of my future, not as a romantic daydream. I have fond memories of the boy who chased me through the gardens, but the man who's standing in front of me now with the beard and mustache is a stranger. We can't simply pick up where we left off.

"I can assure you, Cate, I don't think of you as a sister." Paul stops walking. Runs a hand over his beard. Shuffles his feet. There's a faint flush on his cheeks when he finally looks at me. "You've always known your own mind, and I won't rush you. We have plenty of time to get reacquainted before December."

December? That's when I have to announce my betrothal. Is he implying—?

I stand there staring until Lily dawdles up to us, and then I give her such a glare that she scurries back, mumbling apologies.

"I'm sorry. That was forward of me, wasn't it?" Paul gives me a rueful smile. "This isn't—it's not going according to plan. You said that bit about us being like siblings, and I couldn't bear thinking—"

"You had a plan?" I give him an impish smile, brushing my hand against the tops of the Autumn Joy sedum. They've got rusty red heads like broccoli that stand out well against the backdrop of goldenrod.

"Fool that I am, yes. I planned out what I was going to say on the train."

"On the train?" I gape at him. "Before you even saw me again? What if I was perfectly hideous? What if I'd got spots and a double chin?"

"You'd still be my Cate. And besides, you're lovely. You look quite like your mother, you know."

It's the nicest compliment anyone could pay me. I suspect he knows it. My resemblance to Mother isn't obvious, as it is with Maura; my hair has only the slightest hint of red and my eyes are Father's. But sometimes I catch a hint of her sharp nose or the determined set of her shoulders in the looking glass.

"Thank you. That means a great deal. But what if—what if I'd turned into some mealymouthed miss with nothing to say but 'Yes, sir' and 'How clever you are, sir,' the kind who laughs at all your jokes?" Paul laughs at this, so long and so loudly that Lily looks over at us with alarm. I elbow him. "Hush!"

"Well, my jokes are good, but not as good as that. You could never be that kind of girl." Paul tucks my arm into his and continues on through the gardens. For once, I'm immune to the heady scent of the roses, of the plot of blue monkshood overrun with weeds.

All I can think is that this is it: the moment that decides my future. It's happening sooner than I expected. I'm not ready. I don't know what Mother would want me to do.

"Don't look so terrified. I don't expect an answer now. I haven't even asked the question yet." Paul smiles.

"You're mad." But I'm relieved.

"And you're even more fun than I'd remembered." Am I? I don't feel like much fun. Perhaps he's attributed the change to my growing up, becoming a young lady. Perhaps this is how all girls feel, stifled and muted. "A life with you will never be dull, will it, and that's just what I want. Think about it, Cate. That's all I ask. Can you do that?"

"I suppose. Only—you didn't say how long you were staying in Chatham. Will you be going back to New London soon?"

Paul comes to a halt right in front of our little fountain—a statue of Cupid, with water coming out of his bow. "I've only just gotten back. Are you trying to get rid of me? Is there someone else—another suitor?"

"No," I blurt before I think. Aren't girls meant to be coy and mysterious? Perhaps I ought to let him think that I have half a dozen men at my beck and call. But he'd find out soon enough that it wasn't true.

"Ah." Paul leans down, his warm breath tickling my neck, his voice a husky whisper. "Would you miss me if I went away again? Is that it?"

I step away, well aware of Lily's eyes on us. "I asked if you were back for good, and you said we'd see. What does that mean?" My words come out sharper than I intend.

"It means I came back to see you. There are a lot of girls in New London, Cate, and I may have gone a little wild at first.

May have called on a few of them, even fancied myself in love. But none of them were you. So after my apprenticeship ended, I decided to come home. What happens next—I suppose that depends on you. I know you were angry with me. Did you miss me at all? Even a little?"

I can't help laughing at his mock pout. "Of course I missed you. But I—" My eyes fall to my feet, embarrassed. "Where do you mean to live? Here, or New London?"

"Ah. I see." Paul shifts back into seriousness. "I'm afraid there's not much business for an architect here in Chatham. Jones has offered me a position as his assistant. I've saved up a bit, and— if I were to marry, I could take a house in a decent part of town. I couldn't imagine my Cate happy in a cramped little flat with no garden."

*My Cate.* It's both sweet and surprisingly possessive. How long has he been saving up to rent a house for us? How long has he entertained the notion of asking me to marry him? It feels like the time I fell off the pigpen fence, all the air knocked out of me. Paul sees my face. "I think you'd like the city, once you got used to it," he says hopefully.

I look at the spiky yellow dahlias clustered around the base of the fountain. I've never wanted to live in the city. But if it were just me, perhaps I could get used to it. "My sisters. I couldn't leave them."

Paul cocks his head at me, clearly puzzled. "They could come visit us. They would always be welcome."

He doesn't understand. How could he? "Things are different now. Without Mother."

I bolt, walking as fast as my skirts and stays will allow. If I can't marry Paul, what will I do? Fear grips me. Perhaps Mother always expected me to marry and move away. Maybe my promise was meant to last only while Maura and Tess were young. Maura's always insisting that they don't need me the way they used to.

I wish I could believe that. Z. R.'s warning comes back to me. *The three of you are in very great danger.* But why? Does someone else know about our witchery?

Paul hurries after me. "I know this must seem very sudden, after I've been away so long. Just think about it. Please."

I nod, blinking back tears. This is ridiculous. Now he's going to think I *am* a delicate flower.

We wind through the garden toward the sound of hammering. Lily trails behind us, picking a bouquet for the kitchen table. On the hillside, Finn Belastra is kneeling in the skeleton of the gazebo, pounding the floorboards into place. He looks odd in his shirtsleeves, a hammer in his hand instead of a book.

"Is that Finn Belastra?" Paul asks. "The bookseller's son?"

"Indeed. He's our new gardener." I raise my voice. "Mr. Belastra, the gazebo is coming along nicely!"

"Happy to have me away from your flowers, are you?" There's a gap between his two front teeth. It makes his smile a bit rakish and all the more charming. He reaches for a sheaf of papers, waving them at me. "It's all a matter of following directions!"

"Belastra!" Paul calls out, and Finn's smile vanishes. "Good to see you. Taking up horticulture, I hear? Or are you planning to give me a run for my money?"

"Mr. McLeod is an architect now," I explain, then wince at the note of pride in my voice. I'm acting like a betrothed already, as though his accomplishments somehow reflect well on me.

Finn scrambles to his feet to shake Paul's hand. "Welcome back, McLeod. I trust you enjoyed your studies?"

Paul shrugs. "Well enough. I didn't spend as much time in the libraries as my mother or my professors would have liked, but I scraped by. Not like you. Cate, did I ever tell you how Belastra could identify any point on the globe? Always showed the rest of us up. The Brothers used to try to best him, but they never managed it either. And it wasn't just geography. The man's brilliant."

"You give me too much credit," Finn objects.

Paul shakes his head. "You were best in our class in every subject. We were all in envy."

"Funny way you had of showing it," Finn mutters, turning back to his plans. It hits me suddenly that, all of Paul's joviality aside, they do not much care for each other.

Paul chuckles. "Poor Belastra got the stuffing knocked out of him on a regular basis. Schoolboys are cruel creatures. The Brothers rarely intervened, but your father! Lord, I've never seen him so angry. He was teaching Latin once and caught us kicking Belastra's books around the school yard. The lecture he gave would have squeezed guilt from a stone."

"Father can be quite eloquent when he wants." On the subject of books, particularly. I wonder if he would have been half so passionate if he'd caught the boys kicking Finn.

Paul pushes against the frame of the gazebo, as if testing its soundness. "I'm surprised you're not off at university yourself, Belastra. It would suit you. Me, I spent most of my time rambling around the city."

Finn's smile goes tight behind his papers. "Some would say that's missing the point of university."

I wince, remembering Father's talk about what a fine scholar Finn would have made.

"Well, in any case, I'm glad to be back." Paul gives me an unmistakably warm glance. "Let's go down to the pond, Cate, shall we?"

The trees around the pond bow their golden heads, making bright offerings to the sky. Paul picks up a pebble and skips it across the mirrored surface. I count aloud as I used to when we were children: two, four, six, eight hops before it sinks.

I try to focus on the beauty all around us. On the geese, squawking their way south. On Paul's reminiscing. But my eyes are drawn to the family cemetery on the other side of the pond. In the back, their flat headstones weather worn and crumbling, are the graves of Great-Grandfather and the two little girls who succumbed to the fever. Great-Grandmother is buried next to her husband. Father's uncle, from whom he inherited the shipping business, another aunt and uncle, and a baby cousin who died in infancy all rest nearby. Then there's the tomb where Father's parents were buried: Grandfather before I was born, and Grandmother when I was so young, she's only a hazy memory of the soft yarn I wound for her and the smell of the oranges she loved. Beside their tomb is the one where Mother rests. *Beloved wife and devoted mother.* There's a quote, too. Poetry.

Next to Mother's tomb are five little headstones all in a row. Three brothers who died before they took a single breath. One who lived for two glorious months, months when Mother sang around the house. Then there's the last little grave: Danielle. The one the midwife urged Mother against for the sake of her own health. The one who killed her in the end.

She was only another girl anyway.

I can't help wondering why we weren't enough—why Mother was so determined to give Father a son. A son could have guaranteed that the house and the business would stay in the family instead of passing to our cousin Alec. A brother could have provided a handsome dowry to ensure that we married well. But none of that is a substitute for a mother's guidance.

"Cate? Are you all right?" Paul's peering down at me.

I force a smile. "Oh, I was daydreaming, wasn't I?"

He grins, obviously jumping to the conclusion that it's his proposal I've been thinking about.

"That's all right. I ought to be going. You know how Mother hates to let me out of her sight," he jokes, checking his pocket watch. It was his father's; he got it right before he left. I remember how proud he was, showing it off to everyone. Mother told him every gentleman should have one. "That would be a benefit to moving to New London, you know. If we stayed here, Mother would insist we live with them. She means well, but she'd drive you mad with all her fussing. And she keeps the house hot as Hades."

I laugh, but only because it's expected. I wouldn't relish being Agnes McLeod's daughter-in-law, with her constantly peering over my shoulder, communicating disapproval in her language of sighs. But I'd do it. If Paul weren't so determined to move to New London, I could marry him and live right next door.

Now it seems impossible. Unless Mother's diary releases me

from my promise, I'll have to say no, and Paul won't understand why. It will ruin everything, and I'll have to find someone else to marry me, and quickly, too, before the Brothers feel the need to involve themselves.

Unless—no. I shake the thought off as quickly as it comes. I won't compel him. Bad enough that I'd have to keep secrets from him. I won't have a marriage based on treachery.

I frown at my reflection in the pond, wishing with every fiber of my being that I weren't a witch.

## chapter

# 5

I'm about to scurry upstairs when Elena pops out of the sitting room like a frighteningly cheery jack-in-the-box. Has she been lurking there, waiting for me to come in? I hope she doesn't expect me to confide in her about Paul's visit.

"May I have a word, Miss Cate?"

"I—yes, of course."

She leads me back to the sitting room and gestures at the sofa. As though it's her house, not mine. She sits in the high-backed blue brocade chair Paul recently vacated, but where he slouched, legs long, she perches delicately, her back ramrod straight, her petal-pink skirts pooling around her feet.

"You don't seem like the type for prevarication,

so I'll be blunt," she says, folding her hands neatly in her lap. "You're the eldest. Your sisters look up to you."

I open my mouth to protest, but she waves away my words. "They do, whether they want to admit it or not. If my time here is to be a success, we'll have to get along. I don't imagine you wanted some stranger coming and traipsing around your home. But it's obvious that your father is worried about you girls growing up without a woman's influence, and I suppose a governess is better than a stepmama, is it not?"

Lord, but people are taking me by surprise today.

"I don't intend to boss or mother you. I'm barely eighteen," she confides. "It would be nonsense to pretend that I'm so very much wiser. But if we can come to a mutual understanding, I think my time here can be beneficial for both of us."

I lean forward, curious. "How so?"

"It seems you've been isolated since your mother's death. Maura feels the lack of companionship. I can be a friend to her. Let's be honest, shall we? My job here is less about teaching you French—I understand Tess is already quite fluent—and more about teaching you how to make conversation with dull people you don't care for. Whatever your reasons for keeping apart"— she fixes me with a look that's more than a little unnerving— "you're clearly beginning to attract attention. Mrs. Corbett says you've developed a reputation as bluestockings.

"The Brotherhood is quite firm about women's roles. We are to be seen and not heard. Men want wives who are meek and agreeable, not clever and opinionated. You must learn to be more pleasing, Cate. For your own safety. I can help you do that."

I narrow my eyes. "Become a pretty little doll, you mean?"

"Become a woman who knows when to keep her mouth shut." Elena's voice is like a whip, and I flinch as though she's struck me. "Has it occurred to you that not all women who refuse to flout convention are mindless? Perhaps it means that they're clever enough to remain inconspicuous."

Is she implying that our reputation is my fault? That I've mishandled things because I'm not *clever* enough? I've kept my sisters out of Harwood, away from the Brotherhood and their snooping informants. Whatever the old cows in town might say about us, I consider that a success.

"Is that what you did with Regina Corbett? Taught her to be less threatening?" I smirk.

Elena doesn't rise to the bait. "Regina has no brains to speak of. Her mother paid me handsomely to ensure that she married suitably. She had no other options. You and your sisters are a different case. You could do very well for yourselves."

"What does that mean? To do well?" I'm curious. Her frank assessment of Regina—it almost makes me like her.

"You could marry, too, if that's what you want." *Like Regina,* her tone seems to say dismissively. *Like every other empty-headed nitwit.* "It seems you have a suitor. Or. There's the Sisterhood. The three of you are scholarly, are you not?"

"Tess and Maura are." My face burns, remembering Father's impatience with me. I struggled to keep all the old gods and goddesses and their exploits straight, I faltered over which declension to use, I butchered my pronunciations. I can add and subtract and multiply numbers in my head faster than he can, but what good is that besides keeping the household ledgers? Women aren't allowed to have their own money.

"Well." Elena's mouth purses, and I find myself unhappy to have disappointed her. "The Sisters would allow you to continue your education. Their libraries in New London are marvelous. The gardens, too. And they appreciate learned women."

"We are not a very pious family," I point out.

She shrugs one enormous puffed sleeve. "There are ways around that. They took me in when I was orphaned. Gave me a home and an education. If you're interested, I'm certain I could get them to grant you an interview. Or Maura. Even Tess—girls start at the convent school at ten."

The way Elena describes the Sisterhood, it doesn't sound so impossible. The three of us could stay together, at least, and look out for one another. But wouldn't we have to take orders swearing to uphold the Brotherhood's teachings? Study scriptures and pray all day, surrounded by dozens of other religious girls— girls who would surely condemn us if they learned what we are?

"You've been here only a few hours. I think deciding the course of our future is a bit premature."

"I disagree. It's vital for girls your age to consider your options. Lord knows there aren't many." Elena rolls her eyes, her exasperation obvious. It makes me wonder how she fits in with the Sisters. Aren't they meant to be models of womanhood? She hardly seems the meek and subservient sort. "You could be happy in New London; I feel certain of it."

"You barely know me," I point out, bristling. "How do you know what I'd like?"

"Well, you don't seem very happy here," she says bluntly, and I wince. It's not Chatham that's the problem; I love my garden and our house and the rolling farmland that surrounds it. It's the Brothers and the looming deadline for my intention that plague me. "Just think about it, Cate. Don't jump to conclusions before you gather all the facts. It is possible for other people to have clever ideas, you know."

I open my mouth to argue—to rail at her for her impertinence—but Elena just smiles and sweeps out of the room.

I don't know much about the Sisters. Mother studied at their convent school when she was a girl, but she seldom spoke of it. She met Father when she was sixteen and left the school a month later to marry him. It happened so fast; I used to think it was all very romantic. Now, knowing how little she trusted him with the things that really mattered, I wonder whether she had other reasons for wanting to leave the Sisterhood.

I'm just outside my room, eager to get back to Mother's diary, when Maura charges up the stairs behind me, grabs my wrist, and drags me into her room. "What?" I ask, annoyed.

"What do you think?" she whisper-shrieks, closing the door.

I bounce onto her bed, rumpling the coverlet. Lily must have been in already; Maura never makes her bed. "Of what?"

She curls up in her window seat. "Of Elena, goose."

"Oh." I can tell by the excitement in her voice that she likes her. "Too soon to say. I wouldn't go telling her any of our secrets yet."

"So I shouldn't have let her read my diary then?" Maura asks, wide eyed with alarm.

I shoot to my feet, not realizing the joke until she giggles. "You don't really keep a diary, do you?" I sigh.

"Not really," she clarifies. "Lord, you're jumpy as a cat. Sit down."

I sit, grabbing one of her pillows, turning it over in my hands. *Family* is embroidered in wobbly pink letters across the front, surrounded with hearts and flowers. I have a matching one in blue. "I don't like having a stranger around."

"Yes, you've made that abundantly clear. She seems nice, though, doesn't she? Not at all what I expected. I remembered she was pretty, but her dresses! I helped her unpack her things and they're all like that. All fancy brocades and those taffeta petticoats and silks. She even has"—Maura lowers her voice, flushing—"silk underthings. And she has the dearest kid gloves for church, and the prettiest green velvet slippers with little embroidered pink roses! I told her we don't have anything new, and she said she'd talk to Father about it, that perhaps we could get something made up quick in time for Mrs. Ishida's tea, if he's willing to pay a bit extra."

"We don't need all that," I argue.

"We do, too. Just because you're content to tramp around the gardens like some—wait. How did your visit with Paul go? He was flirting with you, wasn't he? Where did he learn that, I wonder?"

I think of what Paul said about going wild in New London. I don't like the idea of him flirting with other girls, escorting them home from services. Not one bit. But he came back for me, didn't he? I think of his voice in my ear, his breath tickling my neck, and hug Maura's pillow to my chest. I wonder what it would be like to have a proper kiss. Or improper, depending.

I giggle. "It was good to see Paul. I missed him."

"He makes you smile," Maura observes. "You ought to flirt back. Did he give you any hints? You know—about marrying you?"

"He said we'd have plenty of time to get reacquainted before December."

"Cate!" Maura shrieks, leaping on me, knocking me over sideways, puppylike in her excitement. "Why didn't you come tell me straightaway?"

"Because he didn't ask me officially, not yet. He hasn't even spoken to Father. And because I can't—I don't know if I can say yes."

My sister stares at me, her face two inches from mine, sapphire eyes wide with puzzlement. There's a tiny scar on her chin from when she had the chickenpox. "Why not?"

"Because he's going back to New London. The man he was apprenticing under offered him a position in his firm."

Maura sits up, brushing her hair out of her face. "Lucky thing. I'd give my right arm to live in New London. You didn't—oh, Cate, you didn't refuse him, did you, just because of that? I know you wouldn't relish the idea of living in a little flat somewhere with no trees and no garden. But there are parks in the city, aren't there? And eventually he'll make enough money to buy you a proper house and—"

"He said we could rent a house. It's not that." I stare at the coverlet, at Mother's neat, even stitches. "I can't just leave you and Tess."

Maura kicks me. "Yes, you could. We'd come visit you, silly."

"But it's so far. It's not just in town, or the next town over; it's two whole days away. I'd never forgive myself if something happened."

There's a silence, and then Maura shoves me with both hands. I roll off the bed and stumble awkwardly to my feet. "Don't you dare!" she hisses. "Don't you dare use us as an excuse not to marry him, Cate. We can take care of ourselves."

I wrap my arms around myself, miserable. Can they really? I wish I knew.

"Perhaps we needed you a bit—right after Mother died—"

A bit? I stiffen, thinking of the nights the three of us slept in one bed, curled together like kittens. When Maura grew pale and thin and hardly left her room, I coaxed Mrs. O'Hare to make all her favorites. After she cleaned her plate, as a reward, I'd take her out to practice magic in the gardens. When Tess had scarlet fever, I refused to leave her side. I read to her during her convalescence until my own throat was raw. I tried to make up for Mother's absence. I never quite managed, I know—no one could—but I tried so very hard.

"I don't care what you promised Mother," Maura continues, frowning at me fiercely. "You are not responsible for us, do you understand me? If you want to marry Paul, you had better say yes when he asks you. There's no guarantee he'll ask twice."

Dinner is a strange affair. Mrs. Corbett is here, prattling on about Regina's advantageous marriage. She's in absolute raptures over how lovely Regina's estate is and to what great effect Regina's decorated the rooms. She eyes our own dining room with clear distaste. The heavy red damask paper on the walls hasn't been replaced since Father was a boy, and the flowered carpets are starting to show signs of wear. The mahogany table and chairs have curved backs decorated with scrollwork and dragons, in the old Oriental style instead of the new Arabian fashion. All the houses in town have gaslights now, but we still rely on candles. Father insists on it.

I hear the hum and buzz of conversation but barely take in the words; I find myself watching Elena instead. I wish I could read people the way Tess can. She's the observant one, brilliant at seeing motives and desires written out on people's faces, in the pauses between their words. All I notice about Elena is her impeccable table manners and her sycophantic flattery of Mrs. Corbett.

The soup is salty but serviceable; the boiled codfish is decent if dull. But when Lily brings out the main course, I wince at the platter of gray, overcooked roast. I can't bring myself to complain to Mrs. O'Hare, but it's rather mortifying to serve our guests meat that's tough as shoe leather.

Except when I bite into it—it's not. I ladle a bit of the thin, watery onion gravy: it's seasoned to perfection. After I capture a forkful of mashed potatoes, only to have them melt buttery in my mouth, I'm afraid to try anything else. The limp string beans, the historically dreadful stewed squash—I'm certain it's all delicious.

I stare at Grandmother's pale blue china in horror. Tess

promised me! Improving dinner for Father's pleasure is one thing—still dangerous, but it's unlikely that he would notice the discrepancy. But to risk it in front of guests—

I glare at her, but she shakes her head, eyes wide. We both swivel to Maura. She's listening to whatever Mrs. Corbett and Elena are saying, purposely not meeting our eyes.

I concentrate on my dinner, pushing against the glamour until it gives way. The next bite requires a goodly amount of chewing, so I let the glamour slip back over me.

No one in her right mind would *choose* to taste this food.

I glance around the table again. Father is scooping up his potatoes; Mrs. Corbett is dabbing her greasy lips with her napkin. Even Elena is taking delicate bites of the squash. It was a ridiculous gamble, but it doesn't seem any harm was done. This time.

As soon as we've eaten Tess's fruit compote and apple tart, I make my excuses, pleading a headache. Maura, who knows my constitution is quite strong, offers to keep me company. I refuse. I need to read Mother's diary in private. My heart hums, hopeful, in my chest. Whoever my mysterious correspondent is, she wouldn't have told me to look for the diary unless it contained something that would help. There have been times I have resented Mother for leaving me with so much responsibility and so little guidance. But she must have always intended me to find it. I feel silly for not looking sooner. Perhaps I could have saved myself a great deal of worry.

Mrs. O'Hare has started a fire in my room to ward off the

chill. I kick off my slippers and grab the quilt from the foot of my bed. Mother sewed it especially for me, embroidering it with the blue daylilies that were my favorite flower when I was little.

I fling myself onto the faded violet settee with Mother's diary in hand. I took a few things from her sitting room when she died—this settee, the rose-patterned rug next to my bed, her little watercolor painting of the garden. If I bury my face in the arm of the settee and breathe in deep, sometimes I think I can still catch the scent of the rose water she always wore.

The September wind whistles at the windowpanes and the candle dances on my table, throwing eerie shadows against the walls. If I believed in ghosts, tonight would be a perfect night for an apparition.

If Mother's spirit could give me answers, I'd welcome it and gladly.

*You must watch over your sisters for me. Keep them safe. There's so much I wanted to tell you. And now I haven't time,* Mother lamented the last time I saw her. She was pale as a ghost and fought for each breath. Her sapphire eyes, so much like Maura's, had dimmed, as though part of her had already gone ahead into the next world.

I promised, of course. What else could I do? But it was a heavy promise for a girl of thirteen.

I flip open the diary, eager for advice. It begins in my twelfth year. Her first real mention of me comes after my magic has already manifested:

*I worry for Cate. It is not an easy burden to be a woman, much less one with powers such as ours, and she is a bold, outspoken child. The combination will be dangerous if she does not learn to hide her true self. When she is a little older, I will teach her all I know, lest she suffer the same fate as her godmother. I must go into town at the earliest opportunity, before my condition begins to show, and see Marianne. Perhaps she will have some news of Zara.*

I break away from the page for a moment. I can feel my pulse twitching in my fingertips as the questions tumble through me. Zara? Was Z. R. my godmother? Was she a witch, too? What happened to her? I don't remember her; I don't remember Mother even mentioning her. Later, in another entry:

*I have been to visit Marianne. Together, we read the registry of trials. Neither my knowledge of magical history nor all of Marianne's scholarship can make sense of the Brothers' sentencing. Some girls are condemned for witchery and sentenced to a lifetime at Harwood on precious little evidence, whereas others are acquitted and simply disappear. I fear they have been murdered; we find no trace of them after they leave Chatham, and we hear of similar disappearances throughout the country. I can find no rhyme or reason to it. I do not think I will ever see Zara again. And what of her research into the prophecy? It is vital to our future and the future of every witch still in New England.*

I skim over Mother's joyous accounts of her pregnancy, her fervent, futile hopes that this child would be born healthy and male. Three weeks later:

*Today was my last visit to town; perhaps I should not be jostling about the roads even now, but I would not trust John or even Brendan—[Father!]—to deliver Zara's book back to Marianne. I worry for my daughters. What concessions will they make to keep themselves safe? What if Emily Carruthers is right and I do not survive this confinement— who will teach them? Cate is already capable of mind-magic, a gift so rare and frightening, I would not have anyone but Zara or myself instruct her in it. I have tried to make her aware of how very, very wrong it can be to invade others' minds. It puts her at such great risk—from the Brothers and from those who would seek to use her as a weapon.*

I bite my lip. So my godmother was a witch, then—and capable of mind-magic. I remember how horrified Mother was when she discovered what I could do. She made me swear on the family Bible—then on my sisters' lives—that I would never use it except to protect them, and that I would never tell *anyone* I could do it. Mother claimed it made women go just as power mad and wrongheaded as the Brothers; *that*, she said, was why the witches fell.

Then, two months later:

*Maura has come into her power overnight. She is not as careful as Cate. I have warned her that she must not be seen, even by her father or Mrs. O'Hare. I have tried to impress upon her that she can trust only Cate. I hope she will heed me, but I am too tired to be stern with her. I have not the vigor of earlier confinements. Emily is worried about my successful delivery, but I worry only for my girls. What if Tess is cursed with this magic, too? I cannot stop thinking of that damned prophecy. Emily says I am thrice blessed with daughters. How little she knows of blessings and curses. I wish Zara were here.*

By the time I come to the end, the candle has burned down. The fire is only ashes in the grate; I'm shivering, huddled beneath the quilt. I've been so absorbed, I barely registered the sounds of Mrs. Corbett's carriage rumbling away or of Tess calling my name outside my door. I ignored her and she went away eventually.

Mother's handwriting goes fainter as her confinement progresses, as though she hasn't the strength to push the pen into the page. She begins to write every day—rambling entries full of worry and doubt. She worries whenever Maura and I have one of our rows; she frets over whether Tess, only nine at the time, might prove a witch as well. But there's nothing here for me. No message to guide me, no helpful words on what she would have me do when I came of age.

Eventually I come to the last page, dated the day before she died. After the last little grave was dug on the hillside. Her handwriting changes here: it's all dark slashes. There are places where it's torn clean through, as though she used all her energy to convey one last vehement message.

To my relief, it is addressed to me.

*My dearest, brave Cate:*

*I am so sorry. I did not want to burden you too young, but it seems that instead I waited too long. I have not taught you enough about your magic—what you are capable of, and what you must guard against.*

*Before the Great Temple of New London fell, the oracle made one last prophecy. She foresaw that before the dawn of the twentieth century, a trio of sisters will come of age, all witches. One of the sisters, who will be gifted with mind-magic, will be the most powerful witch born in centuries—powerful enough to change the course of history— to bring about a resurgence of the witches' power or a second Terror.*

*Cate, I am so worried for you. It is very rare to have three witches in one generation. If Tess manifests as well, it seems terribly likely that you are the ones they have prophesied. You will—*

No. Please, Lord, no.

I slide off the settee onto the floor. I just lie there for a moment, in a heap of petticoats, my mind reeling. This is mad. It's impossible.

Only—there are three of us, all witches. I can do mind-magic. Tess will come of age just before the turn of the century. We fit the bill exactly.

The Lord does not hear the pleas of wicked girls.

I do not feel brave. I feel small and frightened and furious. I have enough on my plate without worrying about some damned prophecy made a hundred years ago. I came to this diary looking for help, for guidance, and instead Mother's heaped more responsibility onto my head.

But there was more. Perhaps some of it's actually useful. Something to tell me what I ought to do, besides cowering here in the corner.

I pick up the diary again.

*You will be hunted by those who would use you for their own ends. You must be very, very careful. You cannot trust anyone with your secrets.*

*There is more, and it is worse. I have been frightened to write it all here, lest it fall into the wrong hands. You must seek answers. Those who love knowledge for its own sake will help. Until you know the whole truth of the prophecy, you must not share it with anyone. I am so sorry I am not there to protect you, but I trust you to take care of Maura and Tess for me.*

*Love always,*
*Mother*

I hurl the diary across the room. It hits the wall with a satisfying crack.

It's rare that I've let myself feel angry with Mother. She's dead; she can't defend herself. But now I'm shaking with it. How could she? How could she die and leave me here to deal with all of this alone?

My magic rises, baited by my fury. I haven't lost control in years, not since the episode with Mrs. Corbett and the sheep, but now I'm tempted to let go.

I could smash everything in this room and take pleasure in the breaking.

But I don't.

I'd only have to fix it before Father or Mrs. O'Hare saw.

I close my eyes. I take deep breaths, the way Mother taught me.

When I feel convinced of my own calm, I pick up the diary. I go back and reread the last page. It's mad. Perhaps Mother was delirious when she wrote it. Even if she's correct—even if there is such a prophecy—there must be other sisters who are witches. Other girls who can do mind-magic besides me. I'm not *that* powerful.

An uncomfortable voice niggles at me. *How do you know? You don't know what other witches are capable of,* it points out logically. *You don't even* know *any other witches.* I've always known more must exist besides Mother and my sisters and me, but I've never met one. At least, I've never met one who's admitted what she was. I went to Sunday school with Brenna Elliott, and Marguerite and Gwen and Betsy. But I never saw any signs of magic in them, and most of the Brothers' claims seem rather dubious—

Fear prickles my arms with gooseflesh. What if it's true? What if it *is* me?

If I'm fated to bring about the resurgence of the witches' power—if the Brothers found out, they would kill me. Immediately and without trial. They would believe they were doing it for the good of New England. Perhaps they'd make an example of all three of us—burn us at the stake, or hang us in the town square, the way they did in Great-Grandmother's day. They stopped because normal people began to object to the brutality of it. But they'd bring those methods back to show their strength, to frighten witches and normal girls alike into submission. I have no doubt they're capable of it.

How can I have that on my head?

I curl into myself, wishing there were someone else who could take this burden for me.

Mother must have written more. She couldn't leave me like this, without telling me what to *do*! I find the magic coiled inside my chest, waiting. *"Acclaro,"* I whisper. I turn the pages frantically, hoping that more words will appear in the black end-papers.

Nothing happens. I say it again, louder, and push down the tide of rising panic. I scrutinize each page, waiting for a message to leap out at me. But there's nothing added to the blank pages at the beginning or end—no secret words crisscrossing the other entries, nothing circled or underlined in code. Nothing at all.

I feel for a trace of her magic, but I don't sense anything. Did her strength fail before she had time to write more?

I try again and again. I try different spells; I try until I'm exhausted and my power feels faint and far off. Tears begin to blur her words. I swipe irritably at my eyes and toss the diary onto the bed, striding to the window, the quilt falling to the floor behind me.

The gibbous moon peeks in through the daylily-dotted curtains. I look down at the statue of Athena in the garden, stark in the moonlight. Goddess of wisdom and war.

Mother didn't trust Father to fight for us. Truth be told, she didn't do a very good job of it herself. She left me with a diary full of cryptic warnings and a responsibility that should have been hers.

I will keep my sisters safe. Whatever happened to Mother's friend Zara, whatever happened to Brenna Elliott, I will not let it happen to Maura and Tess. Not while I have breath left in my body.

chapter

# 6

I'm standing on the raised dais in the back room of Mrs. Kosmoski's dress shop, wearing only my chemise and corset, with all of them examining me like livestock on the block.

"Too thin," Mrs. Kosmoski says, clucking disapprovingly.

"That can be fixed," Elena insists. "We'll give the illusion of curves. Padding in the bust and a bustle in back?"

Mrs. Kosmoski nods. "It'll mean more work. I'll need to have both my seamstresses up all night."

"Whatever you need," Elena promises. "As long as they're ready by next Wednesday. We can have the girls come in the morning for last-minute alterations. This tea is their equivalent of a coming-out party. They can't go looking like this."

Mrs. Kosmoski eyes Maura's high-necked green sprigged muslin. "Indeed," she agrees, her voice dry. She's been arguing with my orders for years now, suggesting brighter colors, busier patterns, more current fashions. I've resolutely ignored her advice—until now, when I have no choice.

Elena's gotten Father to loosen his purse strings; the three of us are to have new wardrobes. She declared all our old things frightfully outdated and frumpy. Tess is pleased at the thought of graduating to longer, grown-up dresses; I'm the only one who isn't elated.

I'm too preoccupied with wondering if I might be the most powerful witch in centuries.

Elena circles around me. "What a waist, though. Twenty inches, Cate?"

I nod and she lets out a low, unladylike whistle. "Most girls would murder for that."

Across the room, Maura glowers. Much to her chagrin, she's never been able to cinch her corset tighter than twenty-four.

"At least I don't need a padded arse!" she mutters, glaring at me.

Tess hides her giggles behind her hand.

Mrs. Kosmoski's lips tighten. For someone who works with ladies' fashions and forms all day, she's something of a prude.

"Maura!" Elena touches one of the perfect black ringlets that frame her perfect, heart-shaped face. "Please. We do not use such unladylike words."

Mrs. Kosmoski takes my measurements. She's a tall woman with a head of thick, dark hair perched on a swanlike neck. Her pearl earbobs swing back and forth as she and Elena talk.

I let her poke and prod me as I watch my sisters whispering

on the pink love seat. Tess is paging through a book of patterns, the dimple in her left cheek coming out as she mocks the outlandish fashions from Mexico City.

The dress shop is meant to be a feminine oasis, and perhaps that should make me feel safe here, but everything from the rosebud paper on the walls to the pink velvet love seats sets my teeth on edge. Bouquets of roses litter every available surface, perfuming the air with their sweet scent. It feels gaudy and oppressive to me, but Maura adores it. She's like a child at the chocolatier's, giddy with all the choices before her.

Elena encourages it. And Mrs. Kosmoski is taking Elena's every suggestion as gospel truth, hungry to hear what the ladies are wearing on the streets of New London. Aren't Sisters meant to forgo sins like vanity and pride? Surely Elena's love of fashion falls into one of those categories. Today she's wearing a gorgeous peach silk that Maura keeps reaching out to stroke. It practically glows against her dark skin.

"I'm finished, Miss Cahill," Mrs. Kosmoski says. Her breath smells like peppermints.

"Excuse me, ma'am." Gabrielle Dolamore, one of Mrs. Kosmoski's seamstresses, pokes her dark head into the room. Oh good, another person to see me in my underclothes. "Miss Collier is here for her alterations."

I pull on my chemise cover and petticoats and my plain brown dress. It used to be a rich chocolate, but now it's faded from repeated washings and looks more mud colored. Maura does up the buttons in back, her fingers nimble and familiar against my skin. "Stop being such a grump," she admonishes. "This is meant to be fun."

"I've got a headache." It's been present for two days straight, since I read Mother's diary. I reach up and massage my right temple. I've got to share this secret with someone, and soon, before it drives me mad. Mother confided in Marianne Belastra. Dare I do the same? *Those who love knowledge for its own sake*— that describes the bookseller more than anyone else.

"Just think of Paul's face when he sees you in these dresses. He'll be mad with lust," Maura teases, eyes dancing.

"Hush!" But now I can't avoid thinking of it. Paul must be used to city girls and city fashions. It strikes me, all of a sudden, that I *do* want him to think I'm pretty. I want him struck dumb with it.

I lean down and button my boots, wretched all over again. Perhaps I *should* marry him and move away—the farther the better. If this prophecy is true, I'm putting my sisters at risk every moment of every day.

"Hello," Rose Collier says, passing us on her way to the inner sanctum.

Tess practically skips to the counter to examine the bright spools of ribbon.

"Oh," Maura breathes, running her hand over a bolt of luxurious sapphire silk.

I slouch on a settee in the corner. It's impossible to care about new dresses with so much to fret about. But that's my conundrum, isn't it? I've still got to find a husband, still got to look pretty and proper, no matter what terrible thoughts lurk inside my head. I cringe as Rose's giggles swoop through the air and attack my eardrums.

"This violet would be divine on you, Cate," Elena says, handing me a color sample. "It would make your eyes look lavender."

I examine the swatch and shudder. "But it's so—bright!"

"Exactly," Elena agrees. "You're a pretty girl. Why hide away in those dark dresses? What do you think, pink for the sash? All your dresses should have sashes to show off your waist."

She's determined to involve me in this. "*Not* pink." Pink is for empty-headed girls like Sachi Ishida. Like—I wince as her laugh pierces my skull again—Rose Collier.

"Blue then. Peacock blue," Elena presses, undeterred.

The bells above the shop door chime, and we all look up. It's Brothers Ishida and Winfield, flanked by two enormous guards. My heart drops like a stone.

At the counter, my sisters inch toward one another. Behind them, Gabrielle Dolamore drops a skein of pink ribbon. It unspools slowly across the floor, coming to rest right at the Brothers' feet.

"Good morning." Elena curtsies, her face smooth and unconcerned. I suppose that's the security of being a Sister; she knows they'll never come for *her*. "Mrs. Kosmoski is in the back with a customer. Shall I fetch her for you?"

"No." Brother Ishida's pause seems to stretch out for eternity, a leaden weight in my lungs. "Gabrielle Dolamore, you are under arrest for crimes of witchery."

*Thank the Lord.* It's my first, uncharitable thought, even as Gabrielle lets out a strangled scream. The Brothers' guards approach her from either side, and she shrinks back against the rack of ribbons. It's no use. They turn her roughly and grab her wrists, binding them with coarse rope—as though that would keep her if she had magic to stop them! But it makes her seem very small, helpless against the two hulking men dressed all in black. One of them has a hooked nose and a jagged scar over his chin, and he smiles as though arresting wicked girls is a good day's work.

"Don't. Please don't. I haven't done anything!" Gabrielle gasps.

"We'll determine that," Brother Ishida snaps, folding his arms over his chest.

"Wh-what have I been accused of?" Gabrielle asks. "By who?"

"Whom," Brother Winfield corrects odiously—as though grammar matters at a time like this. It feels as though they've sucked all the oxygen from the room. From the whole town. My breath comes in shallow gasps.

"There's been a mistake. I haven't done anything!" Gabrielle cries.

Maura and Tess shrink together, grabbing each other's hands. Mrs. Kosmoski stands slumped in the doorway to the inner room, her perfect posture abandoned. She presses both fists against her mouth as if the barrier is all that keeps her from protesting. But she doesn't make a move to help Gabrielle. I wonder if she's suspected this would happen ever since Marguerite was arrested.

"Please, let me go home to my family tonight. I'll come tomorrow for the trial. I haven't got anything to hide. I'm innocent," Gabrielle insists, her brown eyes shining with tears. She looks around the room, searching our faces for reassurance, but we have none to give. Her innocence is irrelevant—only the Brothers' perception of it matters.

"We do not trust the word of witches," Brother Ishida growls. "Liars and deceivers, all of you."

"I'm not a witch!" Gabrielle is hysterical now, tears weaving wet trails down her cheeks. She struggles against the guards, her boots scuffing the wooden floor as they drag her forward. One man holds the door open while the other pulls Gabrielle through it. She trips over the flowered rug and the guard kicks it aside.

Gabrielle casts one last desperate, pleading glance at us over her shoulder. No one moves. Then she's gone. The Brothers sweep out after her like ghosts, and the door bangs shut behind them. We're left in a great gaping silence.

"I apologize for the interruption, ladies," Mrs. Kosmoski says finally. She crosses the room and straightens the rug, but her brisk movements don't hide the tears in her eyes. "I daresay I could use a good bracing cup of tea. Angeline, could you fetch the ladies some tea?"

I barely hear her; it sounds as though she's speaking from very far away. My hands are clenched together in my lap, my breath coming fast.

If the Brothers are this cruel to an innocent girl, what would they do to us?

Visions of my sisters sinking, struggling, arms and legs shackled, or screaming as their hair catches fire—

"Cate." Elena puts a concerned hand on my shoulder. "Are you faint? You look a little pale."

I *feel* pale. Pale and cowardly and powerless. We all just stood here. We let them take Gabrielle and we didn't lift a finger to help her!

What could we have done? Nothing, I know—not without

looking as though we were sympathizing with a witch. But it still rankles. She's just a frightened little girl, only fourteen years old—

If it were us, no one would come forward to help either.

Fury slides through me, more bracing than smelling salts. I will *not* let the Brothers make me into some scared, swooning creature.

"I did feel a little faint for a minute. All the excitement. I'm fine now," I lie. I summon up a smile, sitting up straight and running a hand over my chignon.

Mrs. Kosmoski sits in the chair beside us while her daughter scurries up to their flat to put on some tea. For once, the seamstress looks at me kindly. "I don't blame you, dear. No matter how often you see it, it never gets any easier."

"Has she worked for you very long?" Elena asks, pausing over a watered blue silk.

"Almost a year. She and my Angeline are the same age. Gabby's always been a good girl. A hard worker. Not that I'm defending her, mind—" Mrs. Kosmoski flushes, as though she's suddenly remembered that pretty, fashionable Elena is still *Sister* Elena. "It's the Brotherhood's job to determine the righteous from the wicked. But their poor mother, losing two girls. Marguerite was arrested last month. It was a very strange case—no trial, and the family hasn't gotten any answers about where they took her."

"Are there other children?" Elena asks.

"Another girl," Mrs. Kosmoski says, tracing the pineapples and berries carved on the arm of her chair. "Julia's only eleven."

Three sisters. Is it a coincidence, or something more sinister?

I think back over all the recent arrests. Last spring, there was a trio of sisters arrested in Vermont. Will little Julia Dolamore be dragged away next?

Tess picks up the spool of ribbon that Gabrielle dropped and begins to slowly, methodically rewind it. "Thank you, dear, you don't have to do that," Mrs. Kosmoski insists.

"I don't mind," Tess says. She organizes things when she's upset. Maura's moved back to the counter, ostensibly looking through the dress patterns, but I can tell by the rapid way she flips the pages that she's not any calmer than Tess.

"Well, I daresay the Brothers know best, but it is distressing." Mrs. Kosmoski stands up and brushes her hands together, as though wiping away the whole unpleasant scene. "Did you decide on fabrics?"

And that's it. Mrs. Kosmoski, Elena, and Maura go back to debating the merits of heart-shaped necklines versus square, buckled belts versus silk cummerbunds. I can't believe they can carry on as though the question of pink taffeta or blue brocade actually matters.

Gabrielle is innocent. I am not. I have been wicked and deceitful; I have used mind-magic against my own father. The Brothers' words drum through my head. I am a witch. It should have been me, not her.

But I thank the Lord it wasn't. What kind of girl does that make me?

A half hour later, our business mercifully concluded, we step into the cool September sunshine. Across the street, the chocolatier's door stands open, and the wonderful, bittersweet smell of dark chocolate wafts toward us. Now we're off to the stationer's to choose calling cards.

Tess and I lag behind. "Are you all right?" she asks, gray eyes searching mine.

I nod. It's hard to hide anything from my little sister; she's entirely too perceptive. She and Maura would be furious with me for keeping secrets from them, no matter what Mother's instructions were. At least now I can blame my distress on the ugly scene we've just witnessed. "As well as I can be after that display. You?"

Tess bites her lip. "Poor Gabby. I just wish we could have done something to—" She stops midstride, her hand flying to her mouth. "Goodness, what's wrong with her?"

Brenna Elliott stands outside her grandfather's gate. She turns in and then, apparently thinking better of it, retreats back to the safety of the street. She repeats the motion again and again, as if unable to make up her broken mind, muttering to herself all the while.

Her hood has fallen off, and her long chestnut-colored hair is a mass of knots. Maura and Elena give her a wide berth as they pass. Tess lets out a disgruntled little huff under her breath.

"Miss Elliott?" she asks, approaching Brenna gingerly. "Are you unwell?"

"Tess," I hiss warningly. We shouldn't be seen talking to a madwoman.

Tess is too kind to care. It's one of the many ways in which she's a better person than I am.

Brenna turns her wasted face to us. Her blue eyes are haunted as a graveyard. The sleeves of her dress hug her wrists, hiding her scars, but they show in the hunch of her shoulders and the pallor of her face. "My grandfather is dying," she says. Her voice is threadbare, as though it doesn't get much use.

"I didn't know he was ill. I'm so sorry," Tess says, looking up at Brother Elliott's house. There's no sign of Dr. Allen's carriage out front, no activity to suggest the bustle of a sickroom or relatives coming to pay their final respects.

"He's quite well today. He'll die next week," Brenna continues. Tess and I glance at each other, shocked. I thought Harwood had cured her—or at least taught her not to go around prognosticating on the street. She clutches suddenly at her hair, yanking on it in anguish. "Oh, this is bad. Very bad. Not good at all."

"Is there anything we can do? Can we fetch someone to help you?" Tess asks.

"I think she needs more help than we can give her," I whisper. Brenna has always seemed to live inside her own head, in a world of her own imagination. But this—this is downright spooky.

"You." Brenna grabs my arm. She was always tall and willowy and pretty—so pretty that people forgave some of her eccentricities. Now she looks emaciated, as though a single strong gust could knock her down. "Did you get the note? I was very careful with it. Clever, she is."

My heart leaps into my mouth. I fight the urge to yank away, but I don't want to make matters worse. "I don't know what you're talking about."

Brenna's blue eyes aren't dead now; they're frantic. "Good girl. No questions. Mustn't ask questions! They'll come for you."

Her hands are ungloved; her nails dig into my arm. "It's all right," I soothe her, as I would Tess after a nightmare. "It'll be all right."

"Your godmother, she asked too many. The crows came for her." I freeze. The note. Did Brenna deliver the note from Zara? "That's what they do with bad girls. Lock them up and throw away the key."

"Harwood, you mean?" Is that what happened to Zara? Did Brenna see her there?

Brenna nods, tapping her temple. "Lucky one. Not mad. Not yet."

Does she mean herself or Zara? I look around, spooked, as though my godmother might be lurking behind the bushes.

"Everything all right?" Maura calls. She and Elena have stopped a few yards ahead.

"Yes!" I call back, trying to escape Brenna's grip. "We're coming!"

"Don't go! You mustn't let them take you." Brenna looks down at Tess, then back at me. Her eyes are sad blue pools. "Powerful. So powerful. You could fix it all. But you must be careful."

"Yes. We'll be very careful," I promise, but something inside me wilts. First the prophecy, now Brenna. What if she's not mad—what if she can genuinely sense the future? I don't want to be powerful. I want to be normal.

"You should be careful, too," Tess suggests, looking worried. If anyone else hears Brenna talk like this, they'll have her shipped right back to Harwood.

"It's too late for me." Brenna falls against the gate, her ratted hair covering her face. "Go away now. I'm very tired, and I need to visit my grandfather."

Tess slips her hand into mine, and we turn and walk down the street, where Maura and Elena are waiting for us outside the stationer's.

"What on earth was all that about?" Maura asks.

I shrug, ignoring Tess's eyes. "Lord knows. She's mad, isn't she?"

At home, I change my nice buttoned boots for old mud-splattered ones and head outside. The sun's disappeared behind the clouds. Not quite raining, but threatening it. I hope it holds off a little longer. I need cheering, and I'm happiest when my hands are busy in the earth.

I stride into the rose garden—only it's already occupied. Finn Belastra sits on the bench—*my* bench—beneath the statue of Athena, a book open on his lap, munching on an apple.

"What are you doing here?" I demand crossly. He might be nice to look at, but I need a few hours alone with the roses and my thoughts.

He jumps up. "I was just"—he chews furiously—"eating my lunch. Obviously. Am I in your way? I can go somewhere else."

"Yes." It sounds horrid, even to me. I sigh. "No. I was going to do a bit of weeding. I'll come back later."

"Oh." Finn looks at the snarl of red and pink tea roses. "You don't have to do that. I've been working on the gazebo, but I can find time to—"

"No, I like it," I interrupt. "I want to do it myself."

Finn grins, gap toothed and boyish. "Ah, then you must be my elf."

"Pardon me?" I tuck a strand of hair beneath my hood.

"I noticed someone's been weeding and planting the spring

bulbs. I fancied you had a garden elf. I imagined him short. And green. You're prettier." He flushes behind his freckles.

"Why, thank you," I laugh. I hardly imagined Finn Belastra the fanciful sort. He always seems so serious.

"I should have suspected," Finn says. "Your father mentioned one of you was good with flowers."

"He did?" That's twice now. Perhaps Father pays more attention than I give him credit for. I'm not certain whether I ought to be pleased or alarmed. Frankly, we've come to count on his obliviousness. "Well, that would be me, then. Gardening helps clear my head."

"Well, no need to come back later. I don't mind if you want to puzzle something out. I'll finish my book."

The gold lettering of the book in his hand catches my attention. "Wait. *Tales of the Pirate LeFevre*?"

"Even a scholar needs leisurely lunchtime reading, Miss Cahill. Are you familiar with the dreadful adventures of Marius the pirate? They're quite entertaining."

"I prefer the stories of his sister Arabella," I blurt before I can stop myself. I can't believe Finn Belastra reads pirate stories. I assumed he would be struggling through some incomprehensible German philosophy.

Finn lowers his voice to a confidential whisper. "Arabella was my first literary infatuation. I had a mad crush on her."

I squeal. "I used to want to be just like her! Remember when she saved Marius during the shipwreck? And when she was captured, she chose to walk the plank rather than sacrifice her virtue to that awful captain. And the time she dressed in Marius's clothes and fought the duel with—" I catch myself gesturing wildly with a pretend rapier.

"With Perry, the soldier who accused the pirates of not having a code of honor?" Finn finishes. "That was a good one."

"She obviously made quite an impression on me. She was a model of—of courage and resourcefulness," I say quietly, folding my hands behind my back.

Finn peers down at me, curious. "I didn't think you were much of a reader."

My face falls. "Did Father tell you that?"

"No. I presumed—you pick up books for your father, but I've noticed you rarely get anything for yourself."

He's right. I can't remember the last time I voluntarily picked up a book besides an almanac, to see when to plant the bulbs or herbs. But I used to read—not ever as much as Tess or Maura, but more than I do now. I spent loads of summer afternoons in the gnarled arms of our apple tree, immersed in *Tales of the Pirate LeFevre*.

Maura's always loved the fairy tales and romances that Mother favored, but I liked the adventure stories from Father's library best. I used to beg him to read them to me—the more bloodthirsty the better. Tales of evil kings and rascals and pirates and shipwrecks. Once I persuaded Paul to help me build a raft, and we paddled it across the pond. It started to take on water out in the middle, and we had to swim to shore. I came home looking half drowned and gave Mrs. O'Hare quite a shock.

I shrug, smoothing my skirt. "Young ladies aren't meant to read pirate stories."

Finn laughs and tosses his apple in the air. "I thought your father believed in educating his girls."

"Father believes in reading for edification, not enjoyment."

"Well, then, he and I will have to agree to disagree on that. What's the point of a book you don't enjoy?" Finn holds out his dog-eared copy. "You can have mine if you want. We have half a dozen in the shop."

I'm half tempted. It would be nice to climb a tree again and let my mind wander to foreign ports and deserted islands along with Arabella. *She* never had to worry about finding a man to marry. They all threw themselves at her—except when she was dressed as a boy, of course. And once even then.

Unfortunately, I live in New England, not aboard the *Calypso*. And I do have to worry about marriage. And the Brotherhood and now this damned prophecy.

"No, thank you." I walk past Finn and kneel before the tangle of roses. "I still have my copy. I just don't have time to read anymore."

"That's the saddest thing I've heard all day," Finn says, swiping his hands through his messy hair. "Reading is the perfect escape from whatever ails you."

But I can't escape.

"You seem—upset," he continues carefully. "I'm sorry for bothering you."

"I'm not *bothered*," I snap, deftly separating one branch from another. I'm angry. Why aren't girls ever allowed to just be angry?

Finn kneels next to me. He reaches out a hand to help and promptly stabs himself on a thorn. "Ouch." A drop of blood wells up on his finger, and he sticks it in his mouth. He has a nice mouth—red as a cherry—his lower lip a bit fuller than the top.

I rummage in the pocket of my cloak and pull out an old handkerchief. "Here," I offer, practically throwing it at his head.

"Thank you." Finn catches it and wraps it around his forefinger. He reaches into the bushes again.

"Let me," I insist. "You don't know what you're doing." I remember when Mother planted these. I won't have Finn ruining them, pulling out flowers instead of weeds.

There's a pause, and I fully expect him to scramble away, tired of being snapped at by this mad, pirate-loving harridan of a girl.

"Show me what to do, then," he suggests, his face earnest. "I'm the gardener. I ought to know how."

I sigh. I want to resent him for being here, in my place; for being a boy, with all the freedoms I lack; for being the sort of clever son Father wishes he had. But he's making it difficult. He's not at all the conceited prig I thought he was.

And he's let me take all my anger out on him without a single word of complaint. As though he knows it's what I need. I'm a little afraid of what I might do—what I might say—if he doesn't go away now.

"Not today," I say. "Please. I just want to be alone."

Finn stands up and gathers his book and his lunch pail. "Of course. Some other time, perhaps. Have a good afternoon, Miss Cahill."

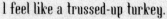

I feel like a trussed-up turkey.

Maura and I went back to Mrs. Kosmoski's this morning for last-minute alterations. Angeline, red eyed and bereft at the loss of Gabrielle—who was sent away without trial, like her sister before her— tucked and pinched while her mother stuck us with pins. Now our new dresses fit beautifully. We are perfectly fashionable—and I feel perfectly ridiculous, a silly wedding cake of a girl in my violent violet dress with the enormous puffed sleeves. The tiered skirts—four yards of brocade—flare into a bell; the rear is padded and ruffled like the underside of an umbrella. Elena's laced my corset so tight, I can barely breathe, much less protest.

My hand, encased in an elbow-length gray kid glove, rests daintily on John's outstretched arm. He smiles as he hands me down—or perhaps he's laughing at me behind his whiskers. I'm none too steady in my new heeled boots, picked up yesterday from the cobbler's.

Maura sails ahead of me, hips swaying in her voluminous cornflower-blue dress. She's all graceful curves and poise. She looks beautiful: chin held high and confident, cheeks flushed with excitement. Her dress has black lace trim and a matching black buckled belt, unlike my peacock-blue monstrosity of a cummerbund.

The Ishidas' maid directs us into the sitting room. A dozen ladies are sipping tea from china cups painted with pink cherry blossoms—a nod to the Ishidas' Japanese heritage. When the Daughters of Persephone established the colonies, they abolished slavery and promised religious freedom. Witches from all over the world flocked to New England. Two centuries later, there are faces of every color on the street, and a dozen families of Japanese origin in town. There was some ugliness during the war with Indo-China, but that was twenty years ago: now the Ishidas are one of the most respected families in Chatham. Still, Mrs. Ishida is always careful to stress that their ancestry can be traced back to *Japan*, lest the neighbors confuse one Oriental face with another.

"Miss Cahill, Miss Maura, good afternoon! Don't you both look lovely?" Mrs. Ishida coos.

I force a smile and make an appropriately insipid response. The room is already full of the Brothers' wives and daughters. Mrs. Ishida directs us through the pocket doors to the dining room, where Sachi and Rory are pouring tea and chocolate at a long table laden with dahlias.

"Miss Cahill, Miss Maura, we're so glad you could come," Sachi says. Her delicate doll's face is dominated by striking, almond-shaped eyes set off by thick black lashes. "Miss Cahill, that's such a lovely shade of purple! Why, your eyes look almost violet in this light!"

"Thank you," I murmur. "It was very kind of your mother to invite us."

Rory tosses Sachi an arch look across the table, and Sachi laughs. "Oh, that was my doing; Mama would never think of it. I just saw you at church the other day and thought, why, it's silly we don't know each other better. We're all of the same age, and you don't live so very far away, and my father thinks very highly of yours. We ought to be friends. Are those new dresses you're wearing?"

"Our governess convinced Papa we needed a new wardrobe," Maura says. I raise my eyebrows. We haven't called him Papa since we were very young.

"Lucky ducks." Sachi pouts. "My papa says I have far too many dresses as it is and lectures me about greed when I ask for more."

"Your dress is magnificent," Maura gushes. It's garish, actually—an orange taffeta with tiny pink polka dots, and Sachi's got a ridiculous pink feather tucked in her hair. But she's so beautiful that she manages to make it look tasteful rather than ostentatious.

"Milk or sugar?" Rory asks. She has the same dark, lustrous hair as Sachi, but otherwise they couldn't be more different. Where Sachi is tiny and petite, Rory is tall, with an ample hourglass figure that she takes pains to show off. Today she's dressed in a red satin frock with a heart-shaped neckline that's far too low cut for a day dress.

"No, thank you, I take my tea plain."

Sachi hands Maura a cup of hot chocolate. "You've got a new governess, haven't you? Is she very dreadful? Mine's always yammering on about French. As though I'll ever go to France! I'll be lucky to get a wedding trip to the seashore."

"Should we be expecting news of your betrothal?" Maura asks, choosing a gingersnap from the plate on the table.

"Oh, not for a few months yet, I expect," Sachi says airily. "I'm going to marry my cousin Renjiro, you know. Father's been planning it since I was a little girl. His family lives in Guilford. We're going to visit in November, on the way to Papa's National Council meeting in New London. I imagine Renjiro will propose then."

Maura gives me a sly look. "If my sister plays her cards right, she'll be living in New London soon."

I shoot her a murderous glare, but it's too late. "Is that so?" Rory drawls.

"Have you had a proposal? I saw Mr. McLeod escorted you home from services on Sunday," Sachi says.

"We were only getting reacquainted. We were fast friends as children." I turn away, trying to discourage the conversation, inhaling the spicy scent of the pink dahlias. They're just the color of the polka dots on Sachi's dress. I wonder if she did that on purpose.

"Well, you're not children anymore. Mr. McLeod's gotten awfully handsome. Yum," Rory says, popping a whole gingersnap into her mouth. She's got an overbite that gives her the slightest rabbity look.

Sachi laughs and swats at her. "You needn't be coy, Miss Cahill, you can tell us. We're really not the blabbermouths everyone thinks."

"Cate's being modest. He came back from New London especially to court her," Maura brags. "He's mad about her. I expect he'll propose any day now."

Sachi looks at me, her dark eyes impenetrable. "Will you say yes?"

I'm saved by the arrival of Cristina Winfield. She saunters in, kissing Rory on the cheek in greeting, and then they're busy inquiring about *her* newly announced betrothal.

"Did Matthew kiss you when you said yes?" Rory asks.

Maura and I drift out of the way, choosing little cakes to accompany our tea.

"Don't think you'll get off so easily, Miss Cahill; we're not finished with you yet!" Sachi warns me.

I wander into the sitting room. Why did Sachi invite us, and why is she suddenly so curious about my prospects? We've barely spoken a dozen words to each other our whole lives. She and Rory are inseparable, the kind of close that doesn't allow room for anyone else, and she has all the other girls in town vying to be her friend—proper town girls who don't need a governess to tell them how to dress and how to behave.

Maura takes a chair next to Rose and is drawn into an animated discussion about Mrs. Kosmoski's newest shipment of silks. I'm left to perch on the green-and-gold-striped sofa between Mrs. Ishida and Mrs. Malcolm. The latter has dark circles under her eyes, but she's full of cheery talk about her new son.

Mrs. Ralston, another of the young wives, boasts about her latest goddaughter.

The word strikes a chord with me. I had a godmother once, and I'm in a room with the biggest gossips in town.

I put a hand to my temple, a brave smile on my lips. I'm the picture of one of the swooning, consumptive heroines in Maura's novels.

"I wish *I* had a godmother," I sigh. The sadness in my voice isn't entirely feigned. "It would be such a help, now that Maura and I are older. With Mother gone . . ."

Mrs. Ishida's feathery eyebrows fly up to perch on her hairline. "But you do. Or—well. You did."

"I did? I don't remember her." I scan the room, puzzled, as if expecting her to pop out from behind the gold damask curtains.

Mrs. Winfield's ash-blond hair is pulled back so tightly, it gives her a pinched look—unless that's just the natural shape of her face. "I believe she moved away," she says. "When you were still very young."

"Oh. That's a pity, that she didn't take the responsibility more seriously. I know that to *some* people, it means a great deal." If I know these women at all, they won't be able to resist. The Brothers' wives each have half a dozen namesakes scattered throughout Chatham. Parents hope that it will provide some measure of safety for their baby daughters, when they grow up to be suspect young women. It doesn't actually work that way, but it remains a point of pride for the Brothers' wives. They all flock to visit newborns, vying to be the first to call at a house with a new baby.

Mrs. Ishida takes the bait. "Your dear mother, Lord rest her soul, was just lovely. So sweet, and so devoted to family matters. I can't see how she was friends with that woman."

"And to entrust her with the spiritual guidance of her first-born! I wonder that she didn't choose someone else. Someone more respected in the community," Mrs. Winfield huffs, pursing her lips. Someone like her, she means. "Zara Roth was a scandalous creature. You're better off not knowing her. I fear what kind of influence she would have been on you poor, impressionable, motherless girls!"

"Miss Roth did seem harmless at first," Mrs. Ishida allows. "A bit—intellectual. A governess, you know, from the Sisters."

My godmother was a Sister *and* a witch? I clasp my hands together docilely, but inside I'm wishing I could grab these women by the shoulders and shake them until the whole story spills out.

"She was a bluestocking," Mrs. Winfield adds. She pronounces the word as if it's something shameful—almost the way people say *witch*. She lowers her voice, and Mrs. Malcolm and Mrs. Ralston lean in closer to hear. "I loathe being the bearer of bad news, but I daresay you're old enough to know the truth. Miss Roth—your godmother—was tried and convicted of witchery."

They watch me with eager eyes, thrilled that the conversation has taken such a shocking turn. My hand flies to my mouth. "Oh, how dreadful! I can't believe Mother was taken in by that sort of woman!"

Mrs. Ishida pats my arm comfortingly. "I'm afraid so, my dear. When they raided Miss Roth's room, they found a number of heretical books hidden away beneath her floorboards and in cupboards and things. All about"—she mouths the word as though it's a curse—"*magic.*"

I wish *I* had those books. Mother taught Maura and me very basic spells: namely, how to create and reverse glamours. I know witches are capable of other magic. Mother always said she'd teach us more. Later. But now it is later, and she isn't here.

"What happened to Miss Roth?" I ask, trying to sit still. My starched taffeta underskirts announce every shift of my body against the sofa.

"She was sent to Harwood." Mrs. Winfield wags her head, the jeweled comb in her hair catching the light from the chandelier. "I'm sure your dear mother would never have associated with her if she'd known. They were old school chums. Studied together in the Sisters' convent. I'm sure she thought Miss Roth was a good, upstanding, religious woman. She was a Sister, after all! It was quite shocking. They cast her out after her arrest, of course."

"Of course. Is she still there in the asylum?" I ask, shuddering.

"I imagine so. She could hardly be allowed out in polite society," Mrs. Winfield says, waving her green silk fan to disperse the heat of the crowded room.

"You must let us know if you need anything, Cate. I may call you Cate, may I not? You poor girls. It's not an easy thing, coming of age without a mother's guidance," Mrs. Ishida sighs sympathetically, dabbing at her eyes with a lace handkerchief. "My mama died giving birth to my youngest brother, and my father never remarried. I understand full well how difficult it can be."

Somehow I doubt that. She didn't have to worry about getting arrested for being a witch, did she? But Mrs. Ishida carries on, reminiscing about her own dear departed mama, and the conversation drifts away from Zara Roth. The message is clear: women who are too opinionated or too educated, too odd or too curious, are punished. They deserve whatever fate they get. Women like Zara.

Women like us.

We stay the requisite half hour. The rest of the conversation is dull as dishwater: Cristina's engagement to Matthew Collier, Mrs. Winfield's suspicion that her maid stole her jade earrings, everyone's advice to Mrs. Malcolm for her son's teething. When we rise to leave, Mrs. Ishida thanks us for coming and declares us welcome every other Wednesday. "Your mother would be so proud of what lovely girls you've turned out to be," she declares, touching her pressed-flower cheek to mine.

I smile even as my rebellious heart trips over her presumption.

Across the room, her daughter smirks at me unnervingly.

Mrs. Ralston and Mrs. Malcolm make us promise to call on them during their at-home afternoons. After the briefest hesitation, Cristina and Rose follow their lead, asking when our afternoon is, and Maura glibly declares that we'll host two Tuesdays hence.

In the carriage, my sister grins at me. "Everything went well, didn't it?"

"I suppose." Aside from learning that my godmother was a member of the Sisterhood, a witch—and a convict to boot.

"Oh, hush. I think we were a smashing success!"

"Lovely," I mock. "Everything was just *lovely*!"

Maura laughs—not the polite titter she uses in company, but her sweet, full-out laughter, like a stream bubbling over rocks. It's my favorite sound in the world.

"I was tempted to start counting how many times Mrs. Ishida said it," she admits, kicking off her pointy new shoes and massaging her pinched toes. "What a limited vocabulary that woman has."

"I doubt she's allowed to read anything but scriptures, if that. The last thing Brother Ishida wants is a wife who can challenge him."

"I imagine he just practices sermons over supper anyway." Maura mimics his oily voice. *What good is teaching a woman to read? Really, girls, you should try not to think at all if you can help it. It might hurt your pretty little heads. Lord forbid, it might make you question us. You mustn't ever question your betters, and remember: even the stupidest of men know better than you!*

I laugh. "Poor Sachi. I can't imagine growing up in that house, with a father like him."

"Me either. Father's not much use, but at least he's not a tyrant."

There's a little catch in her voice, and I sober. "I'm sorry he won't take you with him."

"It's all right. Someday I'll get away." Maura stretches her legs out so her stockinged feet rest in my lap. "I'll marry an old man who's rich as Midas and loves to travel, and I'll make him take me everywhere. Perhaps he'll be an emissary from the Brothers to one of the European courts."

"You wouldn't marry someone who worked for the Brothers."

"I might, if he'd take me to Dubai. Maybe I could do away with him and stay there forever. A widow in Dubai—imagine! I'd get to wear trousers and read whatever I please!" Maura laughs at the shock on my face. "I don't think I'll marry for love. I'll have to be pragmatic."

"You?" I scoff. She's always been the romantic one, the impulsive one, prone to tantrums and tears. "You've got a year and a half. That's plenty of time to find a man to suit even your high expectations."

"I don't think so." She wiggles her toes at me. "What about you? Do you love Paul?"

I glare at her. "Why on earth did you tell Sachi and Rory that he means to propose? I told you I don't know if I can accept."

"And I told *you* that's nonsense," Maura returns, pulling the pins from her hair. "Besides, I couldn't think of anything else to say. You weren't much help at making conversation."

"Now they'll be gossiping about us all over town." The carriage pauses as John exchanges pleasantries with Mrs. Corbett's coachman, just coming out of her lane. Besides the McLeods, she's our nearest neighbor. She rents a small, square house with gray shingles, barely visible through the orchards surrounding it. I can't help thinking she ought to live in some Gothic mansion, replete with cobwebs and headless statues. It would suit her better than an innocent-looking little cottage.

"At least it's the normal sort of gossip. Isn't that what we want?" Maura asks.

I fall quiet. She's right. Marrying Paul, going to tea with the Brothers' wives, gossiping with Sachi Ishida about my betrothal—those are all things a normal girl would do. But what will *I* do?

"You will marry Paul, won't you?" Maura asks, her forehead wrinkled with concern. The carriage jolts forward, the horses' hooves clopping against the hard-packed dirt road. Clouds of dust rise up, and I sneeze, leaning away from the window.

"I don't know, Maura. He hasn't asked me yet."

Maura sits up and puts her feet back on the wooden floorboards. "He will. And you mustn't let some misguided notion of duty toward Tess and me stop you from saying yes. It would be a wasted sacrifice. If you don't choose for yourself, the Brothers will choose for you. What good would it do any of us to have you miserable? Your husband could still take you away anywhere he wanted. You'll be happier with Paul."

I bite my lip. How can I explain my doubts without telling her about Mother's diary or the prophecy?

"You really think I'd be happy with Paul?" I ask.

She smiles, pleased that I'm asking for her advice. "I do. He wouldn't suit me, but possibly he's perfect for you."

Lord, but she's full of backhanded compliments today. "You don't think he's handsome?"

Maura twirls one red curl around her finger. "I suppose. Rory thought so. What do *you* think? You're the one who'd have to share his bed."

"Maura!" I bury my face in my hands, mortified.

"Well, you would. Come, Cate, we're sisters. Do you find him handsome?"

I nod, remembering his lips against my wrist. "Yes."

"It would be a good match. None of the McLeods have ever

been in any trouble, and he's got excellent prospects. He could probably have any girl in town. Did you see the way Rose was looking at him last week at church? But he doesn't even glance at other girls. It's obvious he worships you."

"He does?" I ask, and Maura nods vehemently.

If my sisters and I were ordinary girls, would I want a life in New London with Paul? He told me more about the city last time he called: the restaurants with spicy, exotic Mexican dishes; the long rambles he takes along the piers to watch the ships coming in; the zoo full of animals from all over the world. It sounds grand. Every day there would be an adventure. And he wants to show me all of it.

If I were a brave girl—an adventurous girl, like Arabella— that's what I'd want, too. It's what Maura wants. Her eyes lit up like candles when he spoke of it.

Sometimes I wonder if he chose the wrong sister.

Maura stretches back against the leather bench like a cat. "I see the way he looks at you when you're not paying attention. All moony. His eyes have this sort of *gleam* in them."

"A *gleam*?" I tease. "Oh, heavens!"

"You shouldn't laugh, Cate. He'd make you a good husband, I expect. Only—" Maura hesitates. "*Are* you in love with him, do you think?"

"I don't know," I say truthfully. "I care about him."

"But does your heart pound when he's near?" Maura's blue eyes go dreamy. "In my novels, the heroine's heart always pounds. Do you feel like swooning when he touches your hand? Or when he says your name? Do you feel as though you'll die if you're apart from him for a single day?"

The pragmatic one, is she? I burst into laughter. "No, I can't say I do."

She frowns. "Then it must not be love. Not yet, anyway."

Elena leaps on us the second we get inside, eager to hear how it went. The three of us gather in the sitting room: Elena perfectly poised in the blue chair, Maura bouncing on her end of the sofa as she brags about how popular we were. I collapse onto the other end of sofa, exhausted, but my conscience batters at me until I thank Elena and assure her that we were a credit to her teaching. Maura regales her with the details: how gaudy and grand the Ishidas' house is, with its silks and chandeliers in every room; how bold and fashionable Sachi's dress was; how Cristina said she'll declare her intention to marry Matthew Collier on Sunday at church.

"Soon it'll be your turn, Cate," Elena says. "Mr. McLeod stopped by this afternoon while you were out. He was very sorry to miss you."

Maura laughs. "I told you! He's pining over you!"

"Are you pining, too?" Elena's eyes feel like searchlights.

I bury my face against the curved back of the sofa and groan. "That's none of your business."

"Cate!" Maura chastises. "Don't be rude."

I want to point out that it's Elena's prying that makes me speak rudely, but she's hardly the first to ask. Sachi and Rory felt it perfectly within their rights to question me about Paul; Mrs. Winfield and Mrs. Ishida made insinuations; Maura interrogated me on the way home. I won't have any peace until I announce my decision. It's down to ten weeks now.

"It *is* my business, actually. Your father hired me to see to it that you girls make suitable arrangements." *Arrangements*, she says—not *marriages*. But it's mortifying to have it laid out so plainly. Father didn't trust me to find my own husband, so he brought a governess aboard to help. "Marriage shouldn't be entered into lightly, Cate. If you're unsure—we can talk about it. You do have other alternatives. The Sisterhood—"

"I don't want to join the Sisterhood," I snap.

Elena leans forward, tapping her nails against the wooden arm of the chair. "Do you want to marry Mr. McLeod?"

"I don't know," I say miserably. I raise my eyes. "I don't know what to do."

"What else is there?" Maura demands. "You only have—"

"I know!" I shout. "Ten weeks! *Do you honestly think I could forget?*"

"Cate—" Maura looks shocked. It's a rare thing, my raising my voice with them.

"Leave me alone, please," I beg, scrambling out of the room. "I just want to be alone."

"Cate!" Maura calls after me, but Elena tells her to let me go.

I burst outside without grabbing my cloak. I'm almost running—I don't know where—there's nowhere to go. I stumble in my stupid heeled shoes and wish I could kick them off and run barefoot like I used to. I'm tired of stays and petticoats and heels, of hairpins that bite into my scalp and tight braids that make my head ache. I'm exhausted with trying to be everything—an unassailably polite young lady, a stand-in mother, a clever daughter, an agreeable would-be wife and—

I don't want to be any of those things! I just want to be me. Cate. Why isn't that ever enough?

I come to the little meadow by our barn. I wish I could just hide away somewhere no one can find me.

Inspiration strikes. It's not proper, but—bother proper.

I bend down, unbuckle my shoes, and kick them off. They land in the shade of the wide, gnarled old apple tree. It's been years, and I'm not entirely confident I can still manage this. I launch myself at the tree anyway, grasping the branch next to my head, clambering onto the thick, knotted lower limb. I'm not terribly graceful about it. My stockings tear straightaway, and I almost fall back down because of the weight of my skirts. For a minute I hug the tree, teetering unsteadily, but then I find my balance and turn around and climb higher. I sit astride the third limb on the right, five feet off the ground, legs and skirts dangling. My childhood self would laugh to see me settle for this when I used to climb twice as high.

I pull the pins out of my hair and toss them to the ground one by one. I tilt my head back and look up, up, up through the arching, apple-laden branches at the sky. It's very blue today—there's probably a word for this precise blue. Tess would know. I ought to spend less time trying to get a husband and more time studying the sky, learning the names for all the different blues. I laugh, a little giddy.

"Miss Cahill?"

I lean forward, steadying myself with both hands on the limb in front of me, peering down through green leaves, right into Finn Belastra's astonished face.

A lady wouldn't be caught dead in this position. But a gentleman—wouldn't a true gentleman ignore me and walk away, to spare me the embarrassment?

I give him a weak wave.

Finn chuckles. "Are you a tree sprite now?"

"I'm pretending to be twelve again." I scrape frantically at my hair, wishing I hadn't thrown all the pins away. I must look a fright. He's always handsome, even covered in sawdust from the gazebo, with that ludicrous hair and his glasses all crooked.

He sets down the ladder he's carrying. "Twelve wasn't my best. Thought I knew everything. Got my arse kicked on a regular basis."

"Twelve was heavenly!" I protest. "No responsibility. I could do anything I liked."

"Such as?" Finn asks, leaning against the knobby trunk.

"Running through the fields. Climbing trees. Reading about pirates. Splashing around in the pond, pretending to be a mermaid!" I laugh, remembering.

"You'd make a very fetching mermaid." His eyes are admiring. "Will you toss me an apple?"

I pluck an apple and throw it to him. He ducks.

"You were meant to catch it," I point out, swinging one leg over the branch, scrambling to find my footing on the lower limb.

"You surprised me with your excellent aim. It's—"

I glower at him. "If you say 'good for a girl,' I'll never forgive you."

"I wouldn't dream of it. You terrify me," he laughs.

"Don't tease," I protest, hugging the tree trunk again. "I'm mortified enough as it is."

"Why? Do you need help? Do you want me to catch you?"

"Certainly not," I say, chin in the air. I just don't want him seeing up my skirts. Or to see me falling on my face, if it comes to that. "Avert your eyes, please."

"Don't hurt yourself." Finn sounds worried.

"I won't. This is hardly my first time climbing a tree. Now turn around."

Finn obediently turns his back, hands shoved in his pockets. I hang on to the branch and let myself drop. The shock of landing sends pain shooting up both my legs. "Ouch," I breathe.

Finn whirls around. "Are you all right?"

"I'm fine. Just—I'm so sorry." I finger-comb leaves from my hair. My new dress is half ruined, a bit of lace has come loose from the hem, and my stockings are entirely shredded.

Finn leans over and plucks a leaf from my hair. "Why are you apologizing?"

I bury my face in my hands. An hour. I wanted one hour to be invisible, and I couldn't even get that. "I—well. I'm a bit old to be climbing trees, aren't I?"

"Are you? It's your tree, isn't it; I don't see any reason you shouldn't climb it if you like." Finn sets up the ladder beneath the tree.

"I hardly think the Brothers would approve. I look like a vagrant."

"You look beautiful," he disagrees. This time his blush spreads all the way to the tips of his ears. "The Brotherhood would suck all the color and joy out of the world if we'd let them."

I'm silent, fascinated. He rakes a hand through his tousled

copper hair. "I—now it's my turn to apologize. I shouldn't have said that."

The grass is cool against the soles of my feet. "But you did. Is that what you really think?" I ask, voice low.

Finn turns back to me, his brown eyes serious behind his glasses. "I don't think the Lord wants us to be miserable, Miss Cahill. It's not a prerequisite for our salvation. That's what I think."

chapter

8

I'm not nervous. Not until I push open the heavy door to Belastras' bookshop the next morning. Then I'm struck with the sudden, ridiculous urge to pick up my skirts and run. I glance back at the carriage, but having seen me safely inside—or close enough—John's already driving away toward the general store. It would hardly be appropriate for me to run down the street after him.

I'm meant to be having a lesson in watercolors at home, but I informed Elena I wasn't inspired by the basket of fruit and asked to paint the garden instead. When she agreed—landscapes are apparently all the fashion now—I sneaked over to the barn and asked John if I could ride along into town. There was one name, besides Zara's, that came up again and again in Mother's diary. One person she trusted with her secrets. Marianne Belastra.

"Could you shut the door, please?"

That's Finn's voice. Drat. I assumed he would be working on the gazebo.

I step all the way in.

Belastras' is a fire warden's nightmare. Labyrinthine bookshelves stretch from floor to ceiling. The shelves always seem to be full, no matter how many books are banned or censored by the Brothers. The place smells like Father's study: sweet pipe smoke mingled with woodsy parchment. Dust motes sail in on sunbeams at the front, but the back of the shop hovers in shadow.

I have never felt comfortable here. I can't understand the way Maura and Father can linger for hours, stroking spines with loving fingers, paging reverently through old texts, mouths and eyes moving in silent worship.

I don't understand their church any more than I understand the Brothers'.

Finn Belastra strolls out from behind a row of bookshelves. He's wearing a proper jacket today instead of shirtsleeves. "Can I help you find—oh, good day, Miss Cahill."

I shrink back toward the door, feeling shy after our arboreal encounter yesterday. "Good day, Mr. Belastra. Is your mother here?"

Finn shakes his head. "She's feeling poorly. Headache. I'm looking after the shop for her. Is there something I can help you with?" He sorts through a stack of books on the counter. "We don't have a package for your father. Did he have something shipped?"

It's been difficult to slip away from my sisters and Elena's interminable etiquette lessons to see Marianne. It never occurred to me that when I finally got up the nerve and the opportunity to ask, she wouldn't be here to answer my questions.

"I'm not here for Father." I fidget, trying to tamp down my irritation. It's not Finn's fault that his mother's ill, or that today is unlike any other day I've set foot here.

"Oh." Finn gives me that winsome grin of his. "Have you come looking for Arabella?"

"No. I'd hoped—is there any chance your mother could come down and see me, just for a moment? It's important."

Finn pushes his spectacles up his nose. "I know you lack confidence in my skill as a gardener, but I can assure you I'm a very good bookseller. What is it you're looking for?"

I can't ask him for books on magic. But if I turn around and leave, my trip will be a waste. Who knows when I'll get another chance to come into town without my sisters?

"I've heard you keep a register of trials." The words are out of my mouth before I can think of the consequences. What if Finn doesn't know his mother keeps it?

He squints at me. "Where did you hear that?" There's a touch of iron in his voice. "And even if we had such a thing—what would a girl like you want with it?"

"A girl like me? What sort of girl would that be, exactly?" I ask, hurt. "A girl who doesn't go around with her nose stuck in a book all day? I'm not allowed to have an interest in—in local history?"

"That's not what I meant," Finn says hurriedly. "It's not something we go lending out on a whim, is all. Why do you want to see it?"

"I had a godmother," I say slowly. "She and my mother were school friends. But she was arrested for witchery. I wanted to read about her."

Finn comes closer. "And I can trust you with it?"

I throw my hands up into the air, frustrated. "Yes! I trust you not to go murdering my flowers, don't I? We all take our chances."

Finn tilts his head and studies me for a long minute. Evidently, I pass muster. "All right. Wait here." He opens the door beside the stairs and disappears inside the closet. A moment later, he emerges with a ledger, the sort used to keep records in a shop. "Follow me."

I follow him down the twisting rows of books, nerves swarming like butterflies. He stops before a desk in the very back. "Do you know what year she was arrested?"

"No. Well—less than sixteen years ago, but more than ten. If she was my godmother, she would have been present at my christening, but I don't remember her at all."

"The entries are chronological, of course," Finn says. He leans against a bookshelf while I situate myself in the desk chair.

"Of course," I mock. I look up to find him staring at me. "What?"

"Your hair." My hood's fallen off, revealing the braids wound around the crown of my head. Maura did them for me this morning, practicing one of the styles in Elena's fashion magazines. "It's pretty. That style suits you."

"Thank you." My eyes fall to the ledger, my cheeks burning. "Are you going to hover? I promise I won't run off with this."

"No, I'll leave you to it." But he hesitates. "Mother would prefer the Brotherhood not know about this record. If the bell above the door rings, you might put it in the drawer and occupy yourself with something else. For your own safety, as well as ours."

"I—yes. Of course. Thank you."

I wait until his footsteps have receded to the counter. I can hear every step of his shoes against the creaking wooden floor. It's so quiet in here, I can barely think—not like the quiet of outdoors, where there are always insects buzzing, birds singing and scolding, and wind rustling through the trees. This is an eerie, dead silence.

When I flip open the book, the cover falls back against the desk with a sharp crack. I page back sixteen years to 1880 and scan the list of names in the left-hand column.

*Margot Levieux, aged 16, and Cora Schadl, aged 15,* the first entry reads. *12 January 1880. Crime: caught kissing in the Schadls' blueberry fields. Accused of deviance and lust. Sentence: Harwood Asylum for both.*

Sent to Harwood for the rest of their lives for kissing another girl? That seems unduly severe.

This register is fascinating! I've never seen the Brotherhood's accusations and judgments laid out plainly before. Normally they're shrouded in mystery and spoken of only in whispers, like bogeymen under the bed.

Halfway through 1886, I find the name I'm looking for.

*Sister Zara Roth, aged 27. 26 July 1886. Crime: witchery (known). Accused of possessing forbidden books on the subject of magic and spying on the trials of the Brotherhood. Accusers: Brothers Ishida and Winfield. Sentence: Harwood Asylum.*

It's no more than what I discovered at the Ishidas' tea. My godmother managed to smuggle a letter out of an asylum for the criminally insane. Only—how did she know that we're not safe? Unless—did Brenna predict something?

I continue my reading. Mrs. Belastra writes about the sentencing of girls here in Chatham and also notes what she hears of trials in nearby towns. The vast majority of girls are transported to the coast and put to hard labor. A few, like Brenna, are sentenced to Harwood. A few more are dismissed with only warnings, and Mrs. Belastra notes that all of them subsequently moved away or disappeared.

What happened to those women? Living in Chatham after a trial would be difficult, knowing the Brothers' vigilant eyes—and spies—are everywhere. Did the women flee to a bigger city, where it might be easier to slip into the crowd unnoticed? Or did something more sinister befall them?

Mother noted in her diary that there was no discernible pattern to the sentencing, and as far as I can tell, that still holds true. Women who steal bread from shops or take a lover are sentenced to backbreaking years at sea, whereas some women accused of witchery are found innocent and dismissed outright. How is that possible, with all the Brothers' paranoia about magic? Unless—unless they aren't as oblivious as I thought, and they know how rare true witchery is. That's almost worse. It would mean the increase in arrests isn't due to any wrongdoing at all; it's only meant to keep us frightened.

I turn back to the register. The accused are anywhere from little girls of twelve like Tess to housewives of forty like Mrs. Clay, one of the most notorious cases of the last ten years. Mrs. Clay confessed she had lain with a man not her husband. The town's gossips never revealed his identity, but it is written here in Marianne Belastra's neat penmanship: *Mrs. Clay charged that if she were deemed guilty, so was Brother Ishida, for he was the man with whom she had committed the crime of adultery.*

Brother Ishida? I think of his cold eyes and his thin lips, and my skin crawls. It is always women who are punished.

I swallow my revulsion. There's one more thing I need to see. I flip to last October and scan the row of names. *Brenna Elliott, aged 16. Crime: witchery. Accuser: her father. Sentence: Harwood Asylum. Released summer 1896 at her grandfather's insistence. Obvious attempts at suicide.*

Ten months in that place and Brenna would rather have died. My godmother's been there for almost ten *years*.

I march to the front of the shop, where Finn is reading a book, his chin cupped in his hand, eyes moving rapidly across the page.

"Thank you, Mr. Belastra. That was very helpful."

"Did you find what you were looking for?" Finn's brown eyes search mine.

I did, but I'm no closer to learning anything new about the

prophecy—or knowing what I'm going to do at my intention ceremony. "Yes. It turns out she was scandalous. Sentenced to Harwood."

"I'm sorry to hear it." Finn stands behind the counter. "Is there anything else I can help you with?"

"No. In fact, I'll thank you to forget I was ever here." I pull up my hood and head for the door. Outside the wide picture window, Chatham looks still and sleepy in the midafternoon sun. It's enough to trick one into forgetting, sometimes.

"Wait! Miss Cahill, you haven't been accused, have you? Or one of your sisters?"

I whip around. Finn's shoulders are tense beneath his jacket, his jaw set. "No! Of course not. Why would you suggest that?"

He frowns. "You asked to see the register."

"I told you, I was curious about my godmother! And besides, if we *were* accused, I hardly think I'd be sitting here reading a book! What use would that be?"

"What would you do? If you were accused?" Finn's eyes are intent. Curious.

I suck in a deep breath. No one's ever asked me that before, but it's a question that haunts me. If someone unsympathetic caught us doing magic, I would be forced to erase his memory. I'm not without qualms about it. But I'd do it.

I can't very well tell Finn Belastra *that*.

"I don't know," I say. That's true as well. If we didn't know about the informant until it was too late—if the Brothers and their guards came to our home and made an accusation the way they did with Gabrielle—I don't know what I'd do. I don't think my magic would be strong enough to modify half a dozen memories.

I've spent hours strategizing, but I don't have a solution. There aren't any solutions.

That's the point, I suppose. We are at the Brothers' mercy.

"I would run," Finn says, trailing his hand over the smooth oak of the counter.

My head snaps up. I don't know what I expected him to say, but that wasn't it.

"You're a man. They'll never accuse you of anything."

There's a grim look in his eyes. I didn't imagine the book-seller's awkward, clever son could look so foreboding. Like a force to be reckoned with. "I meant if Clara were accused. Or Mother. I would take them and run. We'd try to lose ourselves in the city."

My hood falls down again. I ignore it, transfixed. I've never heard a man talk like this before. It's treasonous. It's—fascinating. "How would you escape the guards?"

Finn lowers his voice. "Kill them, if we had to."

As if it's as easy as that! Just a dash of murder!

"How?" I can't keep the skepticism out of my voice. I can hardly imagine Finn Belastra prevailing in fisticuffs with the Brothers' burly guards.

He bends and draws a pistol out of his boot. I drift closer. I should be horrified—a good girl would be—but I'm captivated. John has a hunting rifle, but he uses it for rabbits and deer for our dinner; it's not meant for shooting *people*. Even the Brothers' guards don't carry guns—at least not openly. Murder is a sin.

But then so is witchery.

Finn balances the pistol in his hand. He seems easy with it. "I'm an excellent shot. Father took me out every Sunday after services."

My eyes meet his. I have the sudden, unprecedented urge to confess. To tell him I'd do murder for my sisters, too, if it came to that. I'd do anything.

So would he. I can see it on his face, clear as day.

"Why would they be after you?" I ask. Is Marianne a witch, too? Is that why my mother confided in her?

"Mother's too independent for their liking. They suspect she flouts their rules and sells banned books. They're right," he says, his mouth quirking into a smile. "And they're none too happy with me, either. They offered me a spot on the council. Said they'd give me a place teaching in the school if I closed down the shop. I think I wounded their pride when I refused them."

Foolish. No wonder they're so intent on ruining his business. His family would be safer if he'd said yes. "Why did you say no?" I whisper.

He bends over the counter, lowering his voice to match mine. Our faces are only inches apart. He smells of tea and ink. "This place was my father's livelihood. His dream. I won't give in to their fearmongering."

"It's brave of you. To say no to them."

His cherry lips twist. "Brave, or foolish? Brother Elliott passed away last night. I imagine they'll be after me to take his place. If I refuse them again, they may retaliate."

I freeze. Brenna's prediction came true, then.

"Why are you telling me this?" My voice comes out strangled.

He has to know I could report him: for the register, for the pistol, for threatening the Brothers.

Finn bends and slides the pistol back into his boot. "Perhaps I wanted to prove that you could trust me, too."

I do. I want to. It stuns me, how much I want to. I've known Paul since I was a baby, and I've never come so close to telling him my secrets. "Why?"

He straightens. "Even Arabella needed help occasionally."

Poor misguided, chivalrous man. If I were mad enough to confide in him, to tell him what I am, he'd have nothing at all to do with me. Not if he wants to protect his family.

"You—you've already been very helpful," I stammer, raising my hood back over my hair. "Thank you, Mr. Belastra."

He studies me for a moment, trying to read me like one of his books. Blessedly, he doesn't ask questions that I can't—won't— answer.

"You're welcome, Cate."

chapter

9

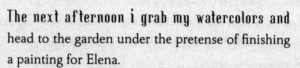

The next afternoon i grab my watercolors and head to the garden under the pretense of finishing a painting for Elena.

A goldfinch squawks nearby, lifting off with an angry flutter of wings. It swoops in a circle before settling in a nearby oak.

I feel rather like squawking myself.

Instead I walk toward the hammering on the hillside. Finn is perched on the top rung of a ladder, nailing a roof beam into place. "Mr. Belastra!" I call.

Finn turns, startled. His movement sways the ladder, which slumps sideways, taking him with it. I cry out a warning, but it's too late—Finn windmills his arms, snatching at empty air. He lands awkwardly, one ankle crumpled beneath him.

I run toward him, throwing my watercolors and sketch pad to the ground, cursing this damned corset.

"Are you all right?" I crouch beside him.

He's sitting up, but his face is ashen beneath his freckles. He turns his head and curses like a sailor.

I gasp in mock outrage. "Mr. Belastra, I wasn't aware you knew such words!"

He tries to grin, but it comes out a grimace. "Large vocabulary."

"Shall I fetch John? Do you need help?"

"I can manage," he huffs. From my vantage point I can see the back of his neck flush pink beneath his collar. He's got freckles there, too.

I wonder how many freckles he's got. Are they all over, or just where the sun's touched?

"—your arm?"

I'm too mortified to meet his eyes. "What?" Good Lord, why am I thinking of Finn Belastra without his clothes on? My mind's gone all muddled from the excitement of his accident.

"Your arm? Could you help me up?" he asks.

"Oh. Yes!" He grasps my shoulder and heaves himself upright, letting out another string of curses. I stand, too, and grab the overcoat he's left folded on the floor of the gazebo.

We begin the slow walk back through the gardens, Finn leaning against me, his arm slung around my shoulders. I can't help assessing him from the corner of my eye. Now that I know how fiercely he'd protect his mother and Clara, I—

I can't help but think of him differently. If he was handsome before, now he's doubly so. Still, I can't go falling in love with the gardener. That's like something out of one of Maura's novels. And with the Brothers watching the shop so closely, any alliance with the Belastras would only put us under more scrutiny.

Finn catches me staring. "Don't worry, I won't faint," he jokes.

"I hope not. I don't think I can carry you."

We limp along to the kitchen door. Finn props himself against the brick wall while I call for Mrs. O'Hare. She stops dinner preparations—possibly for the best—and bustles over. The kitchen smells like freshly baked bread.

"Finn fell off the ladder," I announce. We deposit him in her old brown-flowered armchair by the fire.

Mrs. O'Hare clucks her tongue. "Oh, dear. Should I send for Dr. Allen?"

Finn shakes his head. "No, thank you. Just let me get my boot off and assess the damage."

"Of course. I'll get you some tea," she says, ruffling his thick hair like a child. Mrs. O'Hare knows no strangers.

Finn pulls off his work boot and wriggles his gray-stockinged toes. When he attempts to roll his ankle, he lets out a pained hiss through his teeth.

Mrs. O'Hare hurries over, clucking. "Poor boy. Is it broken?"

"Just a bad sprain, I think."

Mrs. O'Hare snatches up her sewing basket from the corner. Some of our chemises and stockings are piled there, waiting to be mended. I blush, hoping Finn won't notice them. "Let me see. I've dressed more than one sprained ankle in my time. Cate here can attest to that," Mrs. O'Hare says.

"No, no, I can do it," Finn objects.

"Nonsense! Just give me one minute." Mrs. O'Hare lifts the lid to stir something bubbling over in the pot. It lets out a tempting aroma of onions and butternut squash. Perhaps tonight's dinner won't be a travesty after all.

"Could you do it?" Finn asks, his voice low.

"Me?" I'm hardly a nurse. "You'd be better off with her."

He looks at Mrs. O'Hare, busy over the pot of soup, then lifts his pant leg slightly—just enough to reveal the pistol strapped to his shin. "Please, Cate."

Oh. I nod and kneel beside him. "Yes, of course."

Mrs. O'Hare chuckles when she sees me fumbling with her roll of bandages. "You, playing nursemaid? What's gotten into you?"

I blink up at her innocently. "I ought to learn how, shouldn't I? In case anyone ever takes pity and marries me?"

"Lord help the man," she laughs. "All right, but don't tie it too tight or you'll cut off his circulation."

I give Finn a wicked smile. "Don't you think a peg leg would be charming? Like a pirate? The first mate on the *Calypso* had one, didn't he?"

"It would add a certain rakish factor. Have you got a spare eye patch?"

"Be serious, you two. Gangrene is no laughing matter," Mrs. O'Hare scolds.

I look up at Finn, and his brown eyes collide with mine. My hand freezes an inch from his leg. I stare at him, stomach fluttering with nerves. I don't know why I feel so shy all of a sudden. It's not as though I've never seen a boy's bare leg before. When

Paul and I were children, he'd roll his pants up to his knees and I'd hitch up my skirts and we'd wade in the pond, trying to catch minnows in our hands.

But that was Paul, and we were only children. Somehow this feels a different thing entirely.

"Get on with it," Mrs. O'Hare prompts, and I do, wrapping the bandage snugly over Finn's instep and up his calf—which is sinewy with muscle, covered in fine coppery hair and more freckles. I'm fascinated by the pattern they form over his skin. Do they go all the way up his leg?

I flush scarlet at the thought.

"Now, you have some tea and leave that leg propped up for a bit, and then we'll have John drive you back to town. Good work, Cate," Mrs. O'Hare says.

I hang up my cloak in confusion. If I were to take notice of a man, it should be Paul. *But does your heart pound when he's near?*

My heart's a hummingbird now, fluttering madly in my chest.

I drag a chair across the room to sit beside Finn. He's staring at me, his eyes big and owlish behind his spectacles. "You needn't stay here with me, you know."

"Haven't anything else better to do." I shrug. Then I'm struck by the fear that perhaps he'd like me to leave. "Unless—do you want me to go?"

He chuckles—a nice, low hum of a laugh. I've never noticed that before. "No."

"What, haven't you got a book in your coat pocket?"

"I do, actually. But I only bring it out in dull company."

Does he mean he enjoys my company? I smooth my green

144

skirt, glad for once that I'm wearing something pretty, without mud on the knees and ragged hems.

We're still sitting there, smiling foolishly at one another, when the kitchen door bangs open and Paul strides in, stamping his feet.

"There's my girl! I've been combing the gardens for you. Maura said you were working on your watercolors." He grabs up my hand and kisses it. I give him a warning look—he ought to know better than to take such liberties, especially in company. "Belastra, what have you done to yourself?"

Finn sips his tea. "Fell off a ladder," he says coolly.

Paul's lips twitch, and I feel a surge of protectiveness. "It was my fault," I blurt.

"How's that?" Paul cocks his head at me, confused.

I shift in my wooden chair. "I startled him."

"No hard feelings. You did a grand job bandaging me up," Finn says.

"Cate?" Paul laughs until he sees Finn's smile, and then his jaw sets. "I ought to fall off more ladders myself, if it means having such a pretty nurse."

"Stop," I protest.

"Seriously, Cate, I could help John finish the gazebo. I wouldn't mind an excuse to come by. I might even be able to make a few improvements to the design while I'm at it," Paul muses, grinning.

"That's not necessary. I'll be right as rain in a few days," Finn says.

"What?" I exclaim. "No. No more ladders for you. I won't have you breaking your head next time."

Paul chuckles. "Bossy as ever, aren't you?"

Lord, I've just ordered Finn about the way I would my sisters. I grimace. "I'm sorry. I didn't mean to be so forward, I—"

"I don't mind it," Finn interrupts. His hand, on the arm of his chair, is very close to mine, on the arm of my chair. If I stretched out my fingertips, we'd be touching. It is suddenly, unaccountably difficult to resist. My entire body is tilted toward him. Is it very obvious, how enticing I find him? I fold my hands together in my lap.

Paul is watching us, a strange look on his face. "I don't suppose you do. I like a woman with spirit myself."

"With spirit?" I glare. "You make me sound like a horse." Like something to be tamed and broken.

"Hardly." He grins, grabs a wooden trowel from the hook on the wall, and takes up a fencing position. *"En garde."*

I look to Finn, mortified. Paul and I used to spar in the garden with sticks—and through the kitchen with cutlery—but that was when I was twelve. I shake my head. "Paul, no."

Paul flourishes his would-be rapier at me. "Come now, I might actually stand a chance at besting you this time. I've been practicing at Jones's club."

Finn chuckles. "My money's on Cate."

"A gentleman's wager?" Paul suggests, dropping a coin from his pocket on the table.

Neither of them have the money to waste on something so silly. "No, no betting. There's only pride at stake," I announce, seizing a long-handled spoon from the table and advancing on Paul threateningly.

"Cate!" Mrs. O'Hare wails. "I was using that. Put it down, you'll get soup every—"

"Excellent!" I land a hit on Paul's shoulder. The spoon leaves a squash-colored smudge on his gray overcoat.

"I'll get you for that!" Paul waves the trowel at me. "This is a new jacket!"

We duck and dodge around the kitchen table, the icebox, and the stove. Mrs. O'Hare's alternately chortling and urging me to behave like a proper young lady. I'm laughing, my hair tumbling out of its pins and down my back.

"Get him, Cate!" Finn yells.

I look at him over my shoulder, and he smiles. I catch my breath.

Paul sneaks up behind me, trapping me against his broad chest. He spins me around and taps the crown of my head with the wooden trowel. "Got you," he says softly.

It's under the guise of play, but it feels more than that. Staking his claim.

"Miss Cate?" The hall door flies open. One look at Lily's face and I know something is wrong.

I disentangle myself from Paul. "What is it?"

"The Brothers are here."

I freeze, but only for a second.

Maura or Tess? What could they have done when I wasn't watching?

Why wasn't I watching them better?

"Thank you, Lily," I say, and my voice doesn't shake at all. I want very badly to look at Finn, but I don't. If I do, I might beg him to let me borrow that pistol.

"Cate, your hair!" Mrs. O'Hare rushes over to fix it. When she's finished, I smooth the wet grass from my hem and straighten my shoulders. I take some strength from the brave smile Mrs. O'Hare puts on, and then I follow Lily out.

Brother Ishida and Brother Ralston wait for me in the sitting room. Brother Ralston is a whiskered man with a big belly and a forehead so furrowed it looks like a spring field. He teaches literature and composition at the boys' school; he's a friend of Father's.

"Good day, Miss Cate," he says.

"Good day, sir." I kneel before them.

Brother Ishida puts his plump, soft hand on my head. "Lord bless you and keep you this and all the days of your life."

"Thanks be." I stand but bite my tongue. I don't dare ask why they are here. It would be impertinent.

They make me wait a long minute.

"Have you had any correspondence with Zara Roth?" Brother Ishida asks.

I raise my head, relief flooding through me. "No, sir," I lie. "I wasn't even aware I had a godmother until Mrs. Ishida told me about her. Isn't she in Harwood Asylum? I didn't think the patients there were permitted to write letters."

"That is true, but there have been unscrupulous nurses willing to post a letter in the past. You haven't had any contact with her whatsoever?"

I make my gray eyes go wide with puzzlement. "No, sir. Never."

"If you hear from her—if she attempts to contact you in any way—you must let us know immediately," Brother Ralston urges.

I clasp my hands before me and lower my eyes to their boots. "Of course, sir. I'd tell you straightaway."

"She was a wicked woman, Miss Cahill. A witch masquerading as a devout member of our Sisterhood. She was treasonous to our government and to our Lord. I do not know why your mother, Lord rest her soul, would have appointed such a person to be your godmother." Brother Ishida's dark eyes focus on me, as though I am somehow tainted by association.

I glance up at the family portrait—Mother, serene and beautiful—and shake my head sadly. "I don't know either, sir. Mother never mentioned her."

"We hope it was only a matter of womanly frailty on her part," Brother Ralston said. "You must be wary of the devil's tempting whispers masquerading as the voice of friends, Miss Cate. Trusting the wrong sort of people can lead down dark paths."

"We hope you will not follow in your godmother's footsteps," Brother Ishida says. "We noted that you visited Belastras' bookshop yesterday."

I start. They were following me? Why would they follow me? But Brother Ralston makes a calming gesture, as though I'm some skittish filly. "We have been watching the comings and goings of the bookshop for some time. It does not behoove a young lady of your station to linger in such a place, Miss Cate. The company a girl keeps is vital to her reputation."

"I was only there on an errand for Father," I lie.

"You didn't leave with any parcels," Brother Ishida says.

"I thought your father was in New London," Brother Ralston adds.

Lord, they *are* monitoring things. I think quickly. "I was delivering a message. Finn Belastra is our new gardener. Only I got to talking and . . ." I hope they won't ask why John couldn't deliver the message. Or whether Finn and I were alone together in the shop.

Brother Ralston smiles fondly, only too willing to believe in my womanly frailty. If it weren't to my advantage, I'd slap the smile from his face. "Ah, that makes more sense. Your father's said you aren't the clever sort."

I grit my teeth. "I confess I don't see the appeal in so much book learning." I give them a look of doe-eyed distress, fluttering my spindly blond lashes. Sachi Ishida herself would be proud.

"There's no harm in that. Too much knowledge turns a woman's head," Brother Ralston says.

"You won't ever miss your godmother, Miss Cahill," Brother Ishida says. "You have all the guidance you need. It is our duty to care for our sons and daughters, and we are happy to do it."

I mask my fury with a smile. "Yes, sir. I'm very grateful for that."

"When do you turn seventeen, Miss Cahill?"

Oh no. "March fourteenth, sir."

Brother Ralston peers down at me, his jolly blue eyes uncomfortable. "You are aware of the importance of your next birthday, correct?" I nod, hoping that will be all, but he continues. "Three months before your birthday, you must announce either your betrothal or your intention to join the Sisterhood. In mid-December, there will be a ceremony at church in which you will pledge yourself in service to your husband or to the Lord. We take the declaration of intent very seriously."

"One month before your ceremony, if you have not identified

a prospective suitor or received an offer from the Sisters, the Brotherhood will take an interest in the matter. We will make a match for you," Brother Ishida adds. "We consider it an honor and a privilege to help our daughters find their place in our community."

Brother Ralston looks at me anxiously. "That's mid-November."

A chill runs up my spine. Today is the first of October. That's only six weeks. I've got to make a decision even sooner than I thought.

"We've already received a few inquiries for your hand," Brother Ishida says. "Your devotion to your sisters since your mother's passing has not gone unnoticed. We know of several widowers who have small children requiring a mother's care. Brother Anders and Brother Sobolev would both make fine husbands for you."

I can't marry either of those old men! I won't. Brother Sobolev is a dour man with seven children ranging in age from eleven to two. At least in heaven his wife has some peace. And Brother Anders is older than Father—he's forty if he's a day, he's got five-year-old twin boys, and he's bald.

"Yes, sir. Thank you," I murmur.

"Very well, then. We're finished here," Brother Ishida says. "We clear our minds and open our hearts to the Lord."

"We clear our minds and open our hearts to the Lord," Brother Ralston and I echo.

"You may go in peace to serve the Lord."

"Thanks be." And indeed I am thankful. Once they're out of my sight, I'm so thankful, I could spit.

How dare they! How dare they come here to my home and tell me to keep my mouth shut and my head empty and find a husband before they have to do it for me!

I listen as the Brothers' carriage rattles down the drive, and then I stalk back toward the kitchen. The magic ripples through me like rough waves on the pond during a storm. I take a deep breath, pressing my palm against the chilled windowpane in the dining room.

A flash of red catches my eye. Maura is walking in the garden with Elena, arm in arm beneath the oaks. A hint of Maura's bright hair shows beneath her hood. I can never get her to leave her blasted novels and come outside with me. But for this stranger with her pretty dresses and pretty ways, Maura's all too willing. She listens to Elena, adores her, but I'm the one who spends all my time worrying over how to keep her safe.

Only—which decision would keep her safer? Should I marry Paul and move away, never see my sisters but once or twice a year, and leave them to Elena's guidance? Or stay here in Chatham and let the Brothers marry me off like some prize filly, keeping a watchful eye out, ready to wield my mind-magic if my sisters come under suspicion?

Neither option feels tenable.

There's a cracking like ice on the pond in March. The glass windowpane breaks into tiny fissures beneath my palm.

I take a deep breath. If I'd lost control in the kitchen, in front of Finn and Paul and Mrs. O'Hare—

I don't like to think of it. I must be more careful.

*"Renovo,"* I whisper. The glass repairs itself.

In the kitchen, I'm greeted with a flurry of questions. Paul's soup-splashed frock coat is thrown over the back of a chair, and he's pacing in his fawn-colored waistcoat and shirtsleeves. "What did they want?" he demands.

Mrs. O'Hare lifts her eyes from the table, where she's kneading dough again, even though there's a fresh loaf on the windowsill. "Is everything all right, Cate?"

But it's Finn I look to, still in his chair by the fire. He doesn't seem frantic like the others, though his thick hair is a bit more disheveled than before, as though he's been running his hands through it again. His expression is cool. Calculating. Like he's been doing mathematics problems in his head—or thinking how to get me out of trouble, should I need it.

"It was nothing. I'm fine," I insist.

Paul moves closer, hovering. "Cate, the Brothers don't just stop by for—"

I round on him, temper exploding. "I *said* it was nothing!"

He holds up both palms. "Yes, yes, all right." I can tell he doesn't believe me, but what should I say? That they want to marry me off to ensure I won't be troublesome like my godmother and could he help me with that, please? It's humiliating.

"John should have the carriage ready," Finn says. He winces as he stands. Mrs. O'Hare's lent him her wooden walking stick. "Thank you again."

I try to smile, but it falls short. "I'll see you out."

Finn clears his throat. "It's fine. I'll manage." He limps to the door.

"Sit and have some tea with me. You look exhausted," Paul urges, pulling out a chair.

"In a minute. Let me see Finn out first." I storm past Finn and outside before either of them can argue it further. I'll have to accede to a husband's orders soon enough; I won't do it now.

I get several yards down the garden path before Finn catches up. "I could have managed on my own, you know. I don't want to cause trouble with your fiancé." He leans heavily on the walking stick, his face aimed at the ground.

"He's not my fiancé," I snap, plucking a black-eyed Susan. What sort of insinuations was Paul making while I was gone?

Six weeks. That's so little time. Six weeks ago, I didn't have a godmother or a governess; I didn't know anything about this prophecy; I barely knew Finn to say hello to.

"Oh? He—well. I apologize. Obviously I jumped to the wrong conclusion." Finn smiles.

"Obviously." I yank petals from the flower in my hand—he loves me, he loves me not—and brush off a twinge of guilt. There are no promises between Paul and me. I said I'd think about his intentions, and I am thinking. "The Brothers—they asked me why I was at your shop. They knew I was there, and for how long, and that I left without a package. They're watching the store. I didn't want to tell you in front of Paul and Mrs. O'Hare."

Finn presses his lips together. "That's nothing new. I'm sorry if it got you into any trouble, but—"

"Not at all, they think I'm practically illiterate!"

"What?" Finn leans against the stone wall bordering the edge of the garden.

"Apparently everyone knows I'm not the clever sort," I hiss, tossing the ruined flower to the ground. Finn stares. Then— brave man—he reaches out and takes my hand in his.

It's enough to still the anger in me.

"Don't let them make you feel small. It's their specialty, but anyone with half a brain can see how clever you are." He gives me a sideways glance. "And brave. You barely hesitated when you heard they were here."

"You think I'm clever?" Him? The brilliant scholar?

"I do." His fingers curl around my palm, his touch comforting and disturbing all at once. My heart flips over in my chest. "What else did the Brothers ask you about?"

There's the noise of carriage wheels rattling over a pothole. John's driving out of the barn. I drop Finn's hand and move a respectable distance away. "Is your mother feeling better?"

Finn looks puzzled. "Yes. She's back to minding the shop today."

"I might stop in tomorrow. I have a question for her." It's reckless, I know, with the Brothers watching. But how else am I to find out about this blasted prophecy? I'll have to dream up another errand for Father. "Will you be there, do you think?" I try to ask carelessly, as though it doesn't matter, but I find I rather want to see him again.

Finn smiles. "In the morning. See you tomorrow, then."

"See you," I echo.

I lean against the wall, destroying another black-eyed Susan, watching him hobble down the path and feeling like tomorrow is a very long time to go without seeing him.

No good can come of this.

Back in the kitchen, Paul's sitting in Finn's chair. Mrs. O'Hare has made herself scarce. He jumps up when I come in.

"I'm tired," I say shortly. "It's been a very taxing morning."

"Is that so?" Paul works his jaw in that way he has. Another thing that hasn't changed—I can still tell when I've annoyed him. "Well, I'm not going anywhere until you tell me why the Brothers were here, so you may as well have out with it."

I pick up the loaf of bread on the windowsill and carry it to the table. "It's nothing."

Paul leans across the table, bracing himself on his tanned, thickly muscled forearms. "It's not nothing to me. Not if it involves you. And you didn't seem to mind telling Belastra. I wasn't aware the two of you had become such close friends."

Finn was right. Paul is jealous.

"We're not. I don't even know him. Barely." Paul and I glare at each other for a moment. I've lost my temper with him more times than I can count, but I shouldn't take advantage of his good nature. He's only worried about me.

Truth be told, I'm worried about me, too.

"It had to do with the bookshop," I explain, silver knife flashing as I slice the bread ferociously. "The Brothers suspect that Mrs. Belastra's selling banned books. I was there yesterday, delivering a message for Father. They saw me come and go and questioned me about whether I'd noticed anything untoward."

"That's it?" Relief washes over Paul's face.

"Mostly. They wanted to remind me about my intention ceremony, too," I sigh.

Paul looks stricken all over again. "You wanted to tell Belastra about that?"

"No, I wanted to warn him about the Brothers watching the shop."

"Oh." He grabs his jacket from the chair. "There's nothing between you two, then?"

"What would be? He's our gardener." I try to sound properly incredulous, but I can't help remembering the flushed, freckled skin on the back of Finn's neck. The warmth of his fingers cupping my palm.

"I don't know. I've been away." Paul swings his jacket over his broad shoulders. "How am I to know who's been calling on you?"

"Finn Belastra has not been calling on me, I can assure you."

He steps around the table, planting one arm on the wall behind me, trapping me between the icebox, the table, and his body. "Good. I don't think Belastra's the sort of man to suit you."

Presumptuous creature. "Oh? And what sort of man would that be?"

Paul tilts my chin up with one finger. His eyes are dancing, confidence restored. His finger traces the edge of my jaw in a way that leaves my mouth dry and my pulse hammering.

"Me."

chapter

# 10

The next morning I stride down Church Street looking very proper in my new, fur-trimmed gray cloak. When I pass Mrs. Winfield outside the chocolatier, she stops to compliment it and ask after Father. She exclaims how dreadfully we must miss him, and I agree without explaining that living with Father these days is rather like living with a very dull, studious ghost.

It wasn't always this way. He used to bring us chocolates and pick wildflowers for Mother on his way home from teaching at the boys' school. When she was well and the weather was nice, we went for long Saturday drives. Mrs. O'Hare would pack us lunches of bread and sharp cheese and fresh strawberries, and after we ate, Father would read us stories about Odysseus and Hercules and the heroes of old. He did the same in the winter, when the wind sobbed in the chimneys and the fire roared comfortably in the sitting room. Sometimes he even did the different characters' voices.

I thought he would get past his grief eventually. It seems not.

As Mrs. Winfield talks, I scan the cobbled sidewalks around us. I have the itchy sensation of being watched. Is the old biddy in brown an informant for the Brothers? Or perhaps it's Alex Ralston, tying his horse to the hitching post outside the general store. Normally I would discount the feeling as paranoia, but ever since I discovered the prophecy, I feel as though we must be particularly careful, as though putting a single foot wrong could cost us dearly.

Eventually, Mrs. Winfield grows weary of her gossip and disappears into the chocolate shop. I linger in front of the stationer's, staring at their display of calling cards. After a few moments, I continue on, and meander up the steps of Belastras' bookshop. Clara is tending the window boxes, pinching withered blooms.

As I enter, Mrs. Belastra glances up at the bell. She's standing in the middle of the store, shelving a box of books. "Miss Cahill," she says. "Finn told me to expect you."

"Yes, I—I was hoping you could help me. With some research."

Her brown eyes are very like Finn's—kind, but calculating. Under her gaze, I shift from foot to foot, suddenly ashamed of all the times I've been brusque with her. I've never bothered to make more than polite conversation when I pick up books for Father or accompany Maura. Not because the Belastras aren't of our social class—though they are not—but because I don't like being here. I've practically pulled Maura's arms off to get her out faster. And now I come calling to beg for Mrs. Belastra's help with secrets that could get us both arrested?

She would have every right to refuse me.

"I don't know what Finn told you," I say, squaring my shoulders. "But I've just discovered my mother's diary, and she wrote about some curious things—things that I found rather alarming. I would appreciate any help you can give me."

I'm at her mercy. I don't know what else to do. If Marianne decides not to help me, I'm sunk.

"I'll do what I can." Marianne doesn't quite smile, but her shoulders relax. "I was very fond of your mother."

"I didn't know you were friends. Not until I came across her diary. She mentioned you in it. She said—that is—" I crane my neck, looking toward the back of the shop.

Mrs. Belastra catches my meaning. "We're alone. Finn's upstairs. I thought you might prefer to keep this conversation between us."

"I would, thank you."

I hover just inside the door. The sunlight from the wide picture window catches at the small ruby on her ring finger. Her hair is pulled back in a tight chignon—like the rest of her appearance, more serviceable than fashionable. There are crows' feet at the corners of her brown eyes, and permanent lines of worry etched on her forehead, but there are laugh lines around her mouth, too. She was a beauty once, I can tell. She has Finn's square jaw and full, red lips and his handsome snub nose.

When did I come to think Finn's nose handsome?

"My friendship with your mother came about because of our

mutual love of books," Marianne explains, waving a slim volume of poetry at me. "We were both very fond of the Romantic poets. And after Zara came to town—"

"You knew Zara, too?"

A smile tugs at her lips. "As well as anyone could. She was a private sort of person. Very brave—foolhardy, some would say, about her own safety. Her research was her guiding passion. Finn said you came to read the registry and find out what happened to her."

I stare down at the gleaming wooden floorboards. The shop smells of wax and lemons, as though Marianne's been doing her fall cleaning.

If Zara was so important to Mother, why didn't she ever mention her? Was she afraid to frighten us with stories of girls being locked up in Harwood? "I didn't even know I had a godmother until I read the diary. I don't remember her at all."

"You would have been only six when she was sent away. That last year, she traveled a great deal—and when she was in town, the Brothers were watching. It was only a matter of time for her. She and your mother met here sometimes, but Zara was afraid of casting suspicion on Anna."

*Anna.* It's been so long since I've heard my mother's given name. I force back a desperate swell of missing her.

"Why did you stay friends with her? If it was dangerous?"

Marianne smiles as though it's a reasonable question and not an impertinent one. "Some things are worth the danger, aren't they? I don't believe anyone should be allowed to dictate what I read or who my friends are. It gives me pleasure to know that I can thwart the Brotherhood in some small way. And I thought Zara's work was important. She studied the oracles of Persephone, and that last year she was researching a prophecy, which, if it comes to fruition, could very well influence the course of history."

I bite my lip. "Mother wrote about the prophecy, but not much. Do you—do you know more about it?" I ask, praying that Mother's faith in Marianne was not misplaced.

Marianne gives a brisk nod. "A bit. I have something that might help. Why don't you go sit at the desk in back, and I'll fetch some books."

I wind my way back to the desk where I read the register of trials. Marianne's spectacles lie on the desk, along with a cold cup of tea and a note jotted in her neat penmanship.

Is Marianne a witch herself, or just a scholar and purveyor of books? Does Finn know how deeply his mother is involved in the study of magic? Women have been murdered for less.

Marianne joins me, carrying two packages wrapped in cheese-cloth. She unwraps them to reveal two handwritten manuscripts. According to the ornate blue script, the first is called *The Tragic Fall of the Daughters of Persephone*. The second is badly water damaged, the bottom right corners stained, the ink illegible in places. It is titled simply *The Oracles of Persephone*. In small letters beneath the title it says *Z. Roth*.

My fingers dart out, running over the words. When the Daughters of Persephone made the laws, education was available for everyone. Girls like Tess were allowed to study mathematics and philosophy right alongside boys, and some of them became scholars of great renown. Now girls aren't permitted in the village schools; the desire to learn anything beyond needle-work from one's governess is suspect. The writings of women have been banned and burned, witches or no.

"Zara wrote this?" I feel a dash of pride at having such a progressive godmother.

Marianne slips on her spectacles. She looks even more like Finn now. "She did. Her research on that last prophecy is what had Anna so worried."

I stare at her expectantly, but she flips open *The Oracles of Persephone* and turns it toward me. "You ought to read it for yourself. Words mean more that way."

I lean over and read the section she's indicated.

*By the time of this writing, the author suspects there are only a few hundred witches alive in New England. All of the priestesses in temples across the country have been dead since the summer of 1780. Women suspected of witchery were burned and beheaded in mass numbers into the early nineteenth century.*

*The Great Temple of Persephone was burned to the ground at sunrise on 10 January 1780. The doors to the temple were locked and barred from the outside to prevent escape. Several priestesses jumped from the roof rather than be consumed by fire.*

*The Book of Prophecy was burned to ashes—and with it, records of hundreds of years' worth of the oracles' work. But it was rumored that one final prophecy was made— a prophecy that gave hope to the doomed priestesses. It foresaw that before the turn of the twentieth century, three sisters—all witches—will come of age. One of them, gifted with mind-magic, will be the most powerful witch in centuries, capable of bringing about a new golden age of magic— or a second Terror. This family will be both blessed and cursed, for one sister will*

The words end abruptly. The bottom right corner of the page is smudged, completely illegible.

"One sister will what?" I demand, my eyes flying up to Marianne's.

"I'm afraid I don't know. Zara hid the manuscript on the porch roof of the Coste boardinghouse before she was arrested. Fortunately, the Brothers did not find it. Unfortunately, parts of it were destroyed before I was able to retrieve it."

"But I need to know. Mother was worried—was afraid that *we* were the sisters of the prophecy," I whisper.

"I know," Marianne says. Her face furrows. "I think Anna knew the rest of the prophecy, but she didn't share it with me. Neither did Zara. I was their friend, yes, but I was not privy to all their secrets."

I dig my nails into my palms. "It can't be right."

"The oracles were never false. You can read more about the other prophecies in—"

"I don't care about the other prophecies!" I stand so quickly, the chair tumbles over. "This—it can't be about us. There must be other sisters who can—who are—" Even now, I can't bring myself to confess, to say the words out loud.

"Can one of you do mind-magic?" Marianne asks.

I stare at the woven red rug beneath the desk. She takes my silence for the admission of guilt that it is. "Good Lord," she breathes.

"But does that mean that we're the sisters? Absolutely? Perhaps there are others who can—"

Marianne puts a hand on my shoulder. "I don't think so. Even without taking that into account, having three witches in one generation—I've never heard of it before. Even in the old days." Before the Terror, she means. "And now—you read it yourself. All the priestesses were murdered, and there were witch hunts well through the beginning of this century. Some witches chose not to marry and have children. For those who did—it is very rare that more than one daughter manifests powers. Three witches in one generation is a precious thing."

"Precious?" I choke. "It's not precious, it's horrible!"

"I know you didn't ask for this kind of responsibility. But you could have the opportunity to change history. To give women back their power. Did Anna tell you anything else?"

"Anything that would tell me what to do, you mean? How to keep Tess and Maura safe? Anything *useful*?" I slump against a row of bookshelves. "No. My intention ceremony is so soon, and I don't know what to do. I'll have to marry, I suppose."

Marianne takes a deep breath. "You should know all of your options. Sit down, Cate. I have something to tell you."

I sit, fingers tapping a nervous rhythm against the desk.

"I notice you didn't mention the Sisterhood."

I shake my head. "Wouldn't we only be in more danger there?"

"Less than you might think. The Sisters—Cate, they're witches."

My jaw drops. "All of them?"

Marianne nods. "Since the Sisterhood first began. They're the Daughters of Persephone re-formed. It's a very important secret, very closely guarded."

"But then—there must be more witches than Zara thought, aren't there?" I ask, hopeful. If there are more, perhaps we're not the three sisters after all.

"No. There are a few dozen Sisters, and perhaps fifty pupils at any given time. Some of the girls receive their training in magic and then go back out into the world. Some stay and become full members of the order."

"Wait." I gasp as another realization nearly bowls me over. "So our governess—Elena Robichaud—she's a witch?"

"She must be." Marianne leans over the desk, as though she's worried I might faint from the shock of it. "I imagine she's been sent to see if the three of you could be the sisters from the prophecy."

I think of Elena, giggling with Maura in the sitting room. Walking arm in arm through the garden. "She's a spy, then."

Marianne puts her hand on my shoulder again, her long fingers kneading as if to reassure me. "Yes. But the Sisterhood will do everything they can to teach and guide you. They'll want to keep you safe from the Brothers at any cost."

I bite my lip. "But how did they know we might be witches in the first place? We've been so careful."

"When Anna was in the convent school, they made her use

her mind-magic against their enemies. I imagine any daughter of hers would have been of interest to them. And the fact that there are three of you . . ." Marianne takes off her spectacles, her brown eyes peering down into mine. "I've wanted to reach out to you girls for some time—it was a matter of finding the right opportunity. The Brothers think me eccentric, and I was afraid taking an interest might not reflect well on you. But I want you to know I'll do everything I can to help. You mustn't ever hesitate to ask."

Tears spring to my eyes. She knew about Mother's mind-magic—and now she knows about mine—and she would be our friend anyway. "Thank you. That—it means a great deal," I say softly.

A door opens above us and footsteps come limping down the stairs. It's Finn, disheveled in boots and shirtsleeves, his hair sticking up impossibly. "Cate? I thought I heard you."

"Finn." His mother gives him a quelling look. "We're just in the middle of—"

Finn sobers. "What's the matter?"

I struggle to compose myself. "Nothing's the matter. Everything's grand."

"Could you give us just a moment, please?" Marianne asks, and Finn obediently heads off to the front of the shop. She picks up Zara's book and holds it out to me. "I know this must be overwhelming, Cate. If you girls are the subject of the prophecy, it's a very great responsibility. And a great hazard. Perhaps putting it into the context of the oracles' other prophecies would help. Anna truly believed—"

The bell above the door stops her.

"Mama!" Clara rushes in. "Brother Ishida and Brother Winfield are coming!"

I bolt to my feet. Marianne's already rewrapping the histories and dumping them into my arms.

"What do I do with these?" I ask, panicked.

"Into the closet," Finn orders from behind me.

"What?"

"Cate, I haven't time to argue with you. Get in the damned closet!"

I didn't know Finn had a voice like that. He gives me a not-entirely-gentle push toward the front of the shop, and I stumble forward. He throws open the door beside the one that leads up to their flat—the closet he retrieved the register from yesterday. There's a towering bookshelf inside with a few leather-bound ledgers. Are we meant to hide in here? It doesn't seem very hidden.

But Finn shoves the big bookshelf aside like it weighs nothing. Behind it, there's a narrow door set a foot up the wall. He bends and steps through and beckons to me. I peer doubtfully into the tiny room beyond. It looks like a root cellar. There's barely space for Finn to stand upright. Stacks of books line the earthen walls, and frankly, it looks like an ideal home for spiders.

"Hurry," Finn says. He holds out a hand to help me over the sill, but I climb in on my own. Mrs. Belastra hands him a candle and Clara throws my cloak at me and shuts the door. I hear the scratching of wood against the wall as they shove the bookshelf back into place. I put the books down, carefully, on top of one towering pile.

Just as the closet door slams, I hear the jangle of bells above the Church Street entrance. The heavy tread of men's boots. Brother Ishida's unmistakable voice, greeting Mrs. Belastra.

I've hardly gotten my bearings when Finn blows out the candle, plunging us into darkness. In my haste to get away from the damp wall, my foot nudges something on the floor. Another stack of books. I teeter, windmilling my arms. If I knock them over, we'll all be caught.

Finn catches me and pulls me back. Right up against him.

Brother Ishida is asking Mrs. Belastra for a list of her recent customers. I freeze, my mind sifting through all of our purchases. Only linguistic textbooks and scholarly tomes. They'll assume I've been here on Father's behalf.

"No customers at present, Mrs. Belastra?"

"Not at present. Business has been a bit slow for some reason or other," she says, and I can hear her cheeky grin.

"Didn't Miss Cahill come in earlier? We didn't notice her leaving."

"She went out the back. Wanted to get a look at my roses."

Finn grabs my hand.

Normally I'd yank away from him. I'm not easily frightened; he should know that by now.

Except I am quite frightened, actually. So I twine my fingers with his and squeeze back. His hand is warmer than mine. There are calluses at the base of his fingertips. Are they from the hammer and trowels he's been wielding in our gardens?

My heart stops as the outer closet door opens and those heavy footsteps move in our direction. I hold my breath, lungs strangling in my chest. Finn goes still as a stone beside me. The only sound is the rapid, uneven beating of my own heart.

But the footsteps move away, and the door bangs behind them.

It's only when I taste salt that I realize tears are running in a silent river down my face, dripping off my chin and onto the cold stone floor.

Finn is still clasping my hand. Now he reaches out and wipes a tear away with the soft pad of his thumb.

How did he know I was crying? He can't see in the dark, and I never cry.

His thumb slips down over my cheek and rests softly, sweetly, on the curve of my bottom lip.

"It's all right," he says. He's so close that his warm breath tickles my neck.

I turn and nestle my hot face into the soft cotton of his shirt. He smells of rainy spring days and old books. His hands move to my back and hover there, tentative, as if he expects me to push him away.

I have never been this close to a man before. Something stirs deep, pulsing through my body, and it's quite like the tug of magic, but it's not the magic; this is something entirely different, just between Finn and me and this moment.

His hands are firmer now. One settles at the small of my back, its weight burning through my dress and corset and even my chemise. My skin shivers under his touch. I should back away.

I should but I won't.

I want his hands on me.

If I could see his face, would I have such bold thoughts?

My hands slide up his chest. My mouth reaches for his.

Our noses bump in the dark, but Finn tilts his head sideways until his lips touch mine. They brush back and forth, testing. Tasting. He waits, but I only press closer, and he reads that for the invitation it is. His kisses grow bolder. My toes curl in my slippers; my fingers clench the fabric of his shirt; fireworks explode in my belly.

His mouth explores the sharp line of my jaw, then moves to the hollow of my throat.

"Finn," I sigh. Never in my life has my voice sounded like that.

I knot my fingers in his hair and pull his mouth back to mine.

His hands move over me, light as feathers, stroking my back, my hip. Tangling in the sash around my waist, anchoring me tighter against him. My body burns wherever he touches.

I've never devoted much thought to kissing. Never had cause to. But this—oh, this is lovely. Mad and hungry and lovely. I could stay like this for hours.

And then the outer closet door bangs open, and Clara's voice calls out, "They've gone!" and we spring apart, both of us breathing as though we've run a footrace.

Something soft crunches beneath my slippers and I look down.

There are feathers. Feathers everywhere—scattered over all the books, tangled in Finn's hair, caught in my skirts, blanketing the floor in white.

Oh no.

There were no feathers here before.

Finn is bending down, picking up a white plume the size of his palm. That means he can see them, too.

I didn't mean to, but I thought of feathers and here they are.

I squeeze my eyes shut. Why now? I've never made anything appear out of thin air before except that sheep.

*Evanesco.* Please, Lord, *evanesco.*

They do not disappear.

Of course they don't. I have clearly used up my store of good luck for today.

"What the devil?" Finn mutters, and even though I can't see his face in the darkness, I know that the space between his eyebrows is tucked into an upside-down V. "Cate, do you see—?"

*"Evanesco,"* I blurt, and now they're gone.

Finn stares at his empty hand.

What have I done?

I think I can trust Finn, I do, but with this? This is everything. If it were only my secret—

But it isn't. It's my sisters', too.

*You will be hunted by those who would use you for their own ends. You must be very, very careful. You cannot trust anyone.*

I stare at him, glad now that he can't see my face. *"Dedisco!"* I say, careful to enunciate each syllable, my focus sharp as a surgeon's scalpel. I only want him to forget the magic and the feathers. No more and no less.

But my magic isn't necessarily so precise.

"Finn? Cate?" Marianne Belastra throws open the secret door. "Is something the matter?"

Finn stands blinking in the sudden light. "No," he says.

"Nothing," I say.

"You'd best get home, Cate," Mrs. Belastra says. "Let me give you a book on gardening in case the Brothers think to look for it. You can see that manuscript another time."

"Yes," I agree numbly. I can't stop looking at Finn, searching his face for any hint of what he remembers. He's not looking at me. That's good; he's not horrified I'm a witch. But what *does* he remember?

Did I erase our kiss along with the feathers?

"Thank you, Mrs. Belastra." It's hard to talk around the lump in my throat. "I'm sorry if I've caused any trouble for you."

I'm heading toward the front door when she stops me, her hand catching my elbow, and points toward the back. "That way, Cate. They'll be watching the front."

I nod and stumble through the maze of books. Of course. What am I thinking?

Finn. I'm only thinking of Finn.

I can't even look at him, much less say good-bye.

## chapter

# 11

Sunday is Lily's day off, so I ask Tess to fasten my corset, then dress myself. I'm wearing one of my new frocks to church: a royal blue with cream-colored lace at the wrists and throat. The wide gored skirt is free of any frills or frippery, and the plain cream-colored sash ties in a neat bow at the back. I smile at my reflection in the glass. I feel almost pretty. Will Finn think I'm pretty?

Maura's giggle floats down the hall. She and Elena must be primping together. They seem more like friends of late than teacher and pupil, and their closeness unnerves me.

I need to talk to Elena. To confront her with what I know.

Their footsteps approach, and I think quickly.

Asking to speak with Elena alone will only ensure Maura's interest in the conversation. I need a pretext. I pull the pins from my chignon and shake my hair out.

Maura pokes her head in the door. "Almost ready? John's brought the carriage around front."

"Almost. Elena, would you mind helping with my hair?" I smile bashfully. "I'm useless with these pompadours."

Elena looks surprised. "Of course. We'll be down in just a moment," she tells Maura, who troops downstairs with Tess. "You know, I brought a stack of ladies' magazines from New London with step-by-step instructions. You can borrow them if you like."

"That would be lovely, thank you." I sit at my wooden dressing table before the looking glass. Elena stands behind me, brushing my hair, teasing it up at the crown. I meet her dark eyes in the mirror. Her black curls are swept up, just a few perfect ringlets left to frame her face. My hair won't curl without irons and hours of effort.

"Is there something you wanted to discuss?" she asks carefully.

I might as well say it straight out. "I know you're a witch."

She doesn't even hesitate; her hands stay busy in my hair. "When did you figure it out?"

"That doesn't matter. You haven't been honest with us. You being here—it's no coincidence. You've been sent to spy on us."

"Not *spy*. I've been sent to protect you. It had already been confirmed that at least one of you was a witch, but the Sisters were eager to—"

I twist around to face her. "Confirmed? By whom?" I've

175

always known the Brothers have spies in Chatham. Do the Sisters? Are there other witches in town besides Maura and Tess and me?"

Elena sits on the settee, arranging her inky blue skirts elegantly around her feet. "I'm not at liberty to say. I can assure you it's not someone who means you ill. I was sent to discern which of you could do magic—and to my astonishment, I discovered all three of you can. That's very rare. Exceedingly so."

My first instinct is to deny it, but Elena raises a hand, forestalling my argument.

"Maura told me. Don't be angry with her, please. I know you've worked very hard to keep it secret, and you've done a good job of it."

Not good enough, apparently. My temper simmers. "So now you've gone and told the whole Sisterhood?"

"Not yet. I'm also meant to find out what kinds of magic you can do. Mind-magic, for example." Elena cocks her head at me. "Maura says she's never tried it. Have you?"

"No. Good Lord. It's bad enough being a witch, isn't it? That's the last thing I'd want." I turn back to the mirror, bolstered by the half-truth.

"You don't like being a witch?" Elena's smooth brown forehead wrinkles, as though I've divulged something deplorable. "Why?"

"Why would I?" I make a face and slip on Mother's sapphire earbobs.

"Maura said you've taken the Brothers' sermons to heart. That you think magic is wicked."

Maura talks too much. "She thinks magic is a toy. Do you

know how many times Father or the servants have almost seen something she couldn't explain? It's a wonder we haven't been discovered."

"It's to your credit, I'm sure." Elena twists the silver ring on her finger, the symbol of her marriage to the Lord. "The Sisterhood could help you, Cate. I know how much your sisters mean to you. We could help you keep them safe. You *must* let us help you. The three of you may be in more danger than you can imagine."

"Because of the prophecy?" As soon as the words are out of my mouth, I want to bite my tongue.

"How do you know about that?" A slight arching of her brows—that's the only sign of her surprise. She'd make a marvelous card player.

"Mother told me. She was worried because—well. There are three of us." I fiddle with the white lace cloth that drapes the dressing table.

"You ought to know, Cate, that the Brothers are aware of the prophecy. They found a record of it in the home of a witch they arrested." Elena frowns. "Haven't you noticed they've been cracking down on girls the last few years? Trios of sisters, in particular. How long will it be before they turn their attention to you?"

The Dolamores. And those girls in Vermont. I wonder how many other trios of sisters are left in Chatham. In New England. It's not uncommon to find families of six or seven children, particularly on the farms outside town—but how many have three girls?

"Cate!" Maura hollers from downstairs. "Hurry, or we'll be late!"

"Just a moment!" I call.

"I'm sorry," Elena says, "that I haven't been more forthright with you. You must understand—the true nature of the Sisterhood and the prophecy are vital secrets. We do not share them lightly."

I bite my lip. "Does Maura know?"

There it is again—that tiny lift of her brows. She stands. "You haven't told her?"

"Not yet. I'd like to tell her and Tess myself."

"Of course." Elena leans down and adjusts one of the pins in my hair. I fight the urge to flinch away from her. "Please, think about it. The convent in New London is beautiful, and it's very secure. Even if you're not the three sisters, we would welcome you there. If you *are*—there isn't any other place in the world where you'd be as safe."

I stand, eager to put distance between us. My trust isn't as easily won as Maura's. "Why do you think it's us?"

She smiles. "Let's just say I have a very strong hunch one of you can do mind-magic. Your mother could, couldn't she? Even within the Sisterhood, that's a rare and fearful thing. You may not be capable of it—or you may—but those who are learn quickly. I'd like to try to teach you. All three of you."

"No." I back toward the door. "I don't want you teaching my sisters that!"

Elena's a few inches shorter than me, but the look she gives me makes me feel like a stubborn child. "Cate. Mind-magic has unfortunate side effects if it's used too often, that's true. But wielded responsibly, it's not inherently worse than any other kind of magic. That's just the Brothers' paranoia. It can help protect a witch from those who would do her harm. Your sisters have a right to know what they're capable of. It could save them someday."

*"Catherine Anna Cahill!"* Maura screeches. "We're going to be late!"

Elena laughs. "Think about what I've said, Cate. I know you're used to doing things on your own, but you don't have to anymore. We're here to help."

Brother Sutton is leading Sunday school today. He's tall, with skin the color of walnuts, and close-cropped fuzzy hair. He's got a rich, melodious voice, and he smiles and gestures as he talks, like an actor in the now-defunct theater. If he weren't preaching about the evils of mind-magic, I'd almost like listening to him. It makes me uneasy that it's come up two weeks in a row. This time, Hana Ito asked him why a girl would ever do something so wicked.

"Perhaps this sort of magic doesn't seem so wrong at first. Say you were roughhousing with your brother and knocked over your grandmother's china vase. It wasn't very ladylike, but these things happen." Brother Sutton smiles, indulging our girlish faults. His brown eyes are warm. "Say your grandmother has passed on and the vase is a treasured reminder of her. You're afraid your mother will be heartbroken. Afraid of being punished. So you lie and say it was your brother who knocked it over. Instead of lying—which is wicked in itself, girls, you should never lie to your parents—a witch might choose to do mind-magic. Erase her mother's memory of that vase altogether. It would save her from punishment and save her mother from grief. Perhaps she even convinces herself it's the noble thing to do."

I stare at the pew in front of me, at the mass of blond curls bobbing as Elinor Evans nods, and I feel sick with guilt. Mother taught me how to do mind-magic in the months before she died, letting me practice on her. I still remember the look on her face when she realized I could do it—a mix of pride and fear.

The Brothers act as though mind-magic is common as dirt, as though there are witches practicing it all around us and we must be ever vigilant. But if I'm to believe Elena, it's a rare gift. If there are only a few hundred witches left in total, how many of us are capable of it? Thirty? Ten? Fewer? There was Mother. Zara. Elena. And me.

"You might think that erasing one little memory isn't so bad. But it is," Brother Sutton insists. "What if your grandmother gave that vase to your mother as a present on her wedding day? What if she bequeathed it on her deathbed, along with her last words of motherly love and advice? What if those memories are gone now, too? Mind-magic is never noble, girls. It is always a selfish, wicked thing to do."

Twice now, I've modified people's memories. Both times I've convinced myself it was justified. But in protecting us, I've hurt them. What if the thought of sending me away to school was linked to Father's memories of me as a baby, of my first words or steps, of some precious moment over my cradle with Mother?

And Finn. There's no way to know what memories I erased along with the feathers. It could be one of his shooting sessions with his dead father, or his favorite book, or some other memory he cherished. But I can't help praying: please, *please* let him remember kissing me.

I am wicked in many ways.

"Cate?" Maura elbows me. The sermon is over and girls are stretching, standing, moving to their customary pews to await their families. "Elena and I are going to take a turn around the room to stretch our legs. Would you like to join us?"

"No, thank you." I stand to let them leave, then sit back down, determinedly facing front. I want to squirm in my seat and look for Finn, but I won't. I've got more sense than that—and more important things to fret about.

Sachi and Rory pause their promenade at the end of my row. "Good morning, Miss Cahill!" Sachi chirps.

"Do you mind if we sit with you for services?" Rory asks. I can hardly say no. She doesn't wait for an answer anyway, pressing in beside me, her yellow taffeta skirt taking up an enormous amount of room. Sachi squeezes in after her. It's a good thing Father's not here—he'd never fit. But why do they want to sit with us? They usually sit with Mrs. Ishida and the Winfields in one of the front pews. Tess stares at me, flabbergasted, but scoots over to make extra room.

"Are you engaged after church?" Rory asks. Her cheeks are suspiciously rosy despite the Brothers' stance against women making up their faces. "Would you like to join us for tea at my house?"

I shake my head, staggered by the sudden attention. We've known each other since we were children—why are they so interested in me now? Is it really just because I've got new dresses and a man's attention?

"Please say yes," Sachi says, fluttering her thick, dark lashes at me. "There's something we'd like to talk to you about."

That sounds dire—and quite mysterious. I don't dare say no. "I—yes. All right."

"Excellent. Don't bring your sister. Just the three of us. It'll be very intimate."

When Maura and Elena come back, they're astonished to see Sachi and Rory, but well mannered enough not to comment on it. I barely hear the sermon, too busy wondering and worrying about Sachi's invitation. Then it's time for Cristina to get up on the dais and declare her intention to marry Matthew. Intention ceremonies can be odious, particularly when it's a match forced by the Brothers or a girl's parents. Today isn't like that. Cristina's beautiful, her pale hair done up in elaborate curls, her cornflower-blue eyes shining as she looks down at Matthew, sitting in the second pew behind his father. Cristina promises to serve him faithfully for the rest of her life, and his answering grin lights up the plain wooden church. The congregation fairly roars its support.

Will that be me, in a few weeks, announcing my engagement to Paul?

My resolve wavers, thinking of Elena's promises. The Sisterhood could take all three of us. They'd make sure we were safe. But what would they expect of us in return?

Afterward, I whisper to Maura that I'm going to Rory's for

tea and will see them at home. Then I'm surrounded as a flock of town girls rushes to pay court to Sachi and Rory—and now to me.

Rose Collier, thrilled with her brother's betrothal to her best friend, chatters on about how excited she and Cristina are to attend our tea on Tuesday. Rose links her arm through mine as though we're bosom friends, and I have to force myself not to jerk away. Two weeks ago I overheard her and Cristina laughing at me outside the dry-goods store. They were poking fun at my old blue-checked frock and the unfashionable way I braided my hair. Rose said I'd never catch a husband looking like such a sourpuss, and Cristina imagined I thought I was too good for the boys in town anyway.

Now they adore me, just because Sachi's marked me as her new favorite. Because I've let Elena do my hair and dress me like a doll. Because I smile even when I think they're cabbageheads.

By the time Paul rescues me from the crowd, my face hurts from smiling. He tucks my hand into the crook of his elbow and leads me out onto the lawn. Eyes follow us, and our neighbors' whispers fill my ears.

"What a throng. May I escort you home, milady?" he asks.

"Thank you, but I'm having tea with Sachi and Rory." They've left already, Rory winking at me and Sachi promising they'd have the maid hunt up some scones.

"I thought Mrs. Ishida's grand teas were on Wednesdays."

"No, this is just tea at Ror—how on earth do you remember that?" I laugh, pulling my skirts in close to keep from trampling the flowers lining the sidewalk.

"You weren't home on Wednesday afternoon when I called. Lily told me where you were, and I have an excellent memory when it pertains to my favorite girl." Paul smiles.

He's shaved off his beard and mustache, and his cheeks and the tip of his nose are red, as though he's been spending time outdoors.

"You're staring," he notes, voice low.

His face looks familiar now—like the boy I used to play with. "You're sunburned."

"I've been fixing up the barn," he says, "and building a shed behind the house. My shoulders are red as a lobster. Wearing this suit hurts like the dickens."

I look at his broad shoulders admiringly. His lips twitch as though he's guessed what I'm thinking. "I've shaved as well," he points out.

"I noticed. I like you clean shaven," I say, then realize how proprietary it sounds.

"I understand mustaches tickle." He grins, and when I catch his meaning, I stare at the chrysanthemums in confusion. What would it be like, kissing Paul? Different from kissing Finn? I imagine Paul has more experience with girls, but I can't imagine anything nicer than the kiss in the closet. I go hot and prickly all over, remembering Finn's mouth on mine, his hands on my waist.

"Cate," Paul says, his voice low. "You're blushing."

His green eyes are fastened on me, intense with—lust? Love?

"I—I have to go," I murmur. What's wrong with me, thinking about kissing two different men in the space of two days?

"Can I walk you to the Elliotts'?" he asks.

"No, thank you. It's not far." I gather my blue skirts and make my way through the crowd quickly. Just as I'm about to turn onto Oxford Street, the hair on the nape of my neck prickles. I hesitate, scanning the lawn behind me.

Finn's eyes meet mine, just for a minute. He's standing beneath a red maple, talking with Matthew Collier. His hair is sticking up impossibly.

He doesn't smile or acknowledge me in any way.

My heart sinks. Did I erase our kiss?

Or does he remember, and regret it now that he's seen me flirting with Paul?

Four blocks away, on a little side street filled with ramshackle row houses, Sachi Ishida is standing in the Elliotts' front yard. She's twirling a red rose between her thumb and forefinger. Rory is sitting on top of the wrought-iron gate, swinging back and forth and giggling.

"Cate Cahill!" Sachi pronounces. "Just who we've been waiting for."

"We were afraid you'd back out." Rory hops down off the gate. "We hear you're a troublemaker."

I freeze on the empty sidewalk. I've done magic and told lies. I've read forbidden books; I've kissed a man and liked it. But Sachi Ishida can't know any of that, can she?

The shrewd look in her eyes alarms me more than all the Brothers put together. It was easy enough to trick her father, but Sachi looks at me as though she's ferreted out the inner workings of my mind and uncovered all the secrets of my imperfect heart.

Rory opens the gate for me. I hesitate and she laughs—all sharp notes and broken edges. I can't help noticing that her eyes are like her cousin Brenna's. They're not quite so empty—but they're not altogether *right*, either.

I step into the yard, overgrown with weeds and dandelions.

"We need to talk, Miss Cahill," Sachi says. "Oh, ouch!" She makes a little face, throwing the rose to the ground. A bead of blood wells up on her index finger.

Rory leans away, scrunching up her nose. "Ugh!"

"Don't be such a baby," Sachi snaps. I expect her to pull out a handkerchief, but instead she closes her fist and squeezes it. A moment later, she holds her finger up for inspection.

No blood. No puncture. Not even a mark to suggest it was ever there.

Sachi Ishida just did magic.

Right here in the yard. Right in front of Rory and me.

Did she *heal* herself? I've never even heard of that sort of magic.

Sachi smiles. She's pretty as a picture in her pink dress, every flounce edged in lace. "As I said, Miss Cahill, I think it's time for us to have a talk. I suspect we have more in common than either of us thought."

I go very still. "I'm sure I don't know what you mean."

Sachi Ishida, a witch? With her father the head of the council? It's not possible.

But there's no other explanation for what I just saw.

"Rory's mother is indisposed. We'll be left alone here," Sachi explains, walking up to the front porch. I can't help but follow.

Up close, the Elliott place is even more ramshackle than it

looks from the street. The blue trim around the windows is cracked and peeling. There's a broken board on the front porch, and others feel ready to give way beneath my feet. I feel a pang of sympathy for Rory.

And yet the most popular girl in town strolls in without knocking and hangs up her cloak as though she's perfectly at home. The Elliotts' sitting room isn't grand and fashionable like Mrs. Ishida's. It's clean but shabby; the rugs are worn clean through in places, and the striped wallpaper is faded and out of fashion. Still, it seems cozier.

Sachi sits in a bulky chair of brown leather. I take the seat opposite her. She rings for the maid, then sends her off for tea and scones while Rory flits around the room, tidying things up, moving like a bright, restless yellow butterfly.

My mind is still reeling. Sachi's always seemed so proper, and Brother Ishida is the very definition of strict. It's hard to imagine magic taking place right under his nose.

"We've been watching you," Sachi says finally.

I leap up, expecting men in dark cloaks to explode into the room.

"Rory and me," she clarifies. "Lord, but you're jumpy. Sit down."

The cracked leather armchair behind me shoots forward, knocking into the back of my knees.

She moved the chair. It was a foot behind me. She *moved* it.

I do not sit. I stride forward until I'm looming over her. "How did you do that?"

She doesn't look intimidated. "How do you think? Magic."

Mother never taught me how to move objects. How to heal

myself from a cut or scrape. Or, for that matter, how to magic things out of thin air, the way I did by accident with the sheep and the feathers.

I'm starting to think there were quite a lot of things Mother didn't teach me.

And now I'm here in this room with another witch, a witch who happens to be the daughter of the most important man in town, and I'm at a distinct disadvantage.

"Cate. Don't waste my time." Sachi tosses her dark, shining hair. "I'm not an informant for my father, if that's what frightens you."

I flush. "I'm hardly frightened. What do you imagine you could tell him?"

"Come now. It's to our mutual advantage to be honest with each other. I am a witch. I strongly suspect that you are one as well."

I steeple my fingers together, trying to look careless. "What on earth gave you that idea?"

"Rory stepped on your sister Maura's skirt a few weeks ago at church. I was right next to her and heard it rip, and I saw the tear across the bodice, and then a moment later it was gone. As if by *magic*. And the way she whipped around and looked at you—" Sachi laughs. Maura did look at me—probably because she was afraid I'd murder Tess for doing magic in church. "She knows what you are, doesn't she? Besides, your godmother was a witch; I heard Mama tell you. It wasn't much to put two and two together. Who'd give a baby a witch for a godmother unless the baby was likely to be a witch, too?" Sachi smiles triumphantly while Rory looks back and forth between us as though we're playing at lawn tennis.

I lift my chin. "What if you're wrong?"

"It would be my word against yours, and my father's head of the council." Sachi smirks. "But if I were wrong, you'd have swooned or called me names or run out the door twice over, wouldn't you? Any good girl would."

She's right.

Sachi Ishida isn't a cabbagehead at all. She's much cannier than I've ever given her credit for.

I'm impressed.

The maid brings a pot of tea on a silver tray with a plate of blueberry scones. "Thank you, Elizabeth. I'll pour," Sachi says.

I wait until the maid leaves before speaking, and even then I keep my voice to a whisper. "Fine. What if you're right? What if I am—what you say?"

Sachi hands me a cup of tea—plain, the way I like it. The cup has a little web of cracks around the handle. "Then we can pool our knowledge. I hear you've been visiting the bookshop. Everyone says they've got books on magic—on the history of witchery, too. My father hasn't been able to find them, but he's certain they exist. I want to know what's in them. Mrs. Belastra would never give them to me, but she might let you see them."

I take a sip of tea, eyeing Sachi over the rim of the cup. "You haven't told anyone about this suspicion of yours, have you?"

"No. I wouldn't do that. Honestly, I wouldn't," Sachi swears.

"So you're not blackmailing me?"

Sachi sets her teacup down with a clatter. "No! I can be

useful, too, you know. Father trusts me. He thinks Rory and I are just silly little girls. I can see why you've stayed home so much, if you're afraid of being discovered. But it must be awfully dull. I can make you the second-most popular girl in town. Or third, after Rory." She rolls her eyes as if to show just how little she thinks of the town girls and their limited possibilities. "If you're my new best friend, Father won't suspect you."

I look at Rory, who's nibbling on a scone. She's pulled the pins from her black hair so it falls in soft waves over her shoulders. Why are we having this conversation here, in front of her?

"No," Sachi snaps, smacking a small bottle out of Rory's hand. It rolls across the rosewood tea table. "Do you want to be like *her*, drunk by midafternoon?"

Rory sinks onto the sofa. "No," she says pitifully. "But I didn't want any of this, did I?"

The penny drops. "You're not a witch, too?"

"Why not?" Rory grits her jaw, her overbite pronounced, and stares at the bottle. *"Evanesco,"* she says, and it disappears.

"Good work," Sachi praises.

This is without a doubt the most bizarre afternoon of my life.

It seems my sisters and I aren't the only witches in town after all.

"The drink—it dulls the magic," Rory explains. "I don't feel it *at* me all the time."

"You don't feel much of anything, and that's a problem," Sachi says. "You've got to keep your wits about you. Brother Winfield is itching for a reason to make Nils stop seeing you."

Rory slumps across the sofa, kicking her voluminous yellow

skirts out of the way. Crumbs drop carelessly to the threadbare carpet. "What do I care if he does?"

"We need Nils. He helps you keep up appearances," Sachi says patiently, as though she's said it a hundred times before. It's the same tone I use with Tess and Maura.

I think of how Rory's always smiling up at Nils, always touching him. "It's all just for show? You're not really in love with him?"

Rory barks her broken laugh. "Lord, no. He's dumb as bricks. Handsome, though, isn't he?"

I frown, and Sachi looks at me hard. "Oh, and I suppose you've never used anyone or lied to keep your secret safe?"

But I have. And I will again.

"Fine," I say. "You're right. I'm a witch."

It's a dangerous thing, saying those words out loud. It feels momentous.

Sachi smiles. "Prove it."

It's a challenge, and I've never been one to back down from a challenge. Not when Paul dared me to climb an apple tree or walk the pigpen fence, and not now.

I peer at the picturesque forest scene carved into the tea table, at the spot where Rory's bottle disappeared. I can feel the glamour hovering over it, the magic practically shimmering in the air. My sisters and I are fairly well matched, which makes breaking their glamours difficult. Apparently it's easier if the witch isn't as strong as you—and Rory's not. I push against her magic until her glamour cracks and I can see the bottle again. The golden-brown liquor winks in the sunlight. *Commuto,* I think. But it's still only a bottle. I take a deep breath. My magic feels tenuous at best, whisper-thin and shaky.

"Forget everything else and concentrate," Sachi

says. I glance at her, expecting scorn, but she's smiling as though she's eager to see me succeed. Mother never looked at me like that when we practiced. Anything to do with magic left her pinched and anxious.

Sachi's right. Finn—the prophecy—Elena—the knowledge that my sisters and I aren't the only witches in town—it's all swirling around in my head, splintering my focus. I'm lucky I didn't make the sitting room an aviary. I draw in another breath, filling my mind with a single intention, repeating the words over and over again.

*"Commuto,"* I say clearly.

Now there's a sparrow perched on the table where the bottle was. Brown feathers, white chest. Rory shrieks, leaping out of her seat.

"I knew it." Sachi throws her hands up, triumphant. "Nice work, Cate."

"It isn't nice, it's horrid. Birds carry disease!" Rory protests.

"Real birds do." Sachi pushes aside the heavy velvet drapes and unlatches the window behind her. She shoves it open, and cool air rushes into the room.

*"Avolo,"* she says, and the sparrow flies out with a flapping of wings.

"Show-off," Rory complains, shivering. "Now where's my brandy gone?"

Sachi looks at me, black eyes dancing. "Check the bushes?"

"How long have you been practicing?" Rory asks. She kicks off her slippers and stretches out on the red-flowered sofa as though we're old, familiar friends who no longer need to stand on ceremony.

"Since I was eleven." They both look impressed, so I don't volunteer that I've hardly practiced since Mother died—that the spells I mastered at thirteen are the only ones I can manage at sixteen.

"I didn't start until I was thirteen," Sachi says. "Father preached against women's inherent promiscuousness all through dinner and I went upstairs so angry, my magic exploded. I smashed all three of my looking glasses and the music box Renjiro sent me from New London. It took me a week to figure out how to fix them, and I had to find excuses to keep the maids out of my room the whole time. Couldn't have Papa thinking his little girl had a temper."

The first time I did magic, I was eleven, Maura barely ten, and Tess seven. It was a drowsy summer day and Paul was away. I was bored with being cooped up in the house, so I wheedled my sisters into coming outside and playing with me. The smell of roses and freshly cut grass surrounded us as we drew on the flagstones with chalk.

Maura and I got into a row about whether I'd smudged her drawing on purpose. She shoved me and I tripped into Tess, who fell and tore her stockings and scraped her knee. Maura said it was all my fault and that she was going to tell Mother. Tess just sat there, lip wobbling, knee bleeding. I was so angry, I wanted to shake Maura—I wanted her to be the one crying, her dress torn and smudged with chalk and blood.

I felt my anger simmer faster and faster until it boiled over. Something inside me swayed up and out my fingertips. Her green dress ripped. White chalk Xs slashed across the skirt. Blood splattered. At first I thought I was only imagining it, but then Tess's eyes went wide as saucers and Maura started screaming her head off, and I knew they could see it, too. I tried to bribe them with promises of stories and sweets. I wasn't much for listening to the Brothers' sermons, but I knew about witches: how their magic sprang from Persephone's marriage to the devil, how they were born wrong and wicked.

"Was your mother a witch?" Rory stretches her arms over her head, her fingertips dangling toward the floor.

I pluck at my blue skirt with nervous fingers. "She was."

"And your sisters?" Sachi asks.

"No," I say quickly. The Brothers can't hurt Mother now, but my sisters are another matter. "They've been very accepting, but it's just me."

"You're lucky we found you, then." Sachi gives me her sly smile. "Mine comes from Father's side. He doesn't like anyone to know, but his great-grandmother was a witch."

"I don't know where mine comes from," Rory says. "Certainly not my mother."

"You aren't anything like her," Sachi says, patting Rory's dark head. "You're so much stronger."

Rory knocks her hand away, and Sachi sighs. I get the impression this is a frequent argument between them.

"What can you do besides illusions, Cate?" Sachi asks.

"That's all, as far as I know. Mother only taught me a few spells before she died." I reach for a blueberry scone. No matter how nice Sachi is, I'll never tell her about the mind-magic.

"Animating objects is harder. It takes more energy than illusions." Sachi's teacup hovers off the table a few inches, then floats back down to its blue saucer, clicking gently into place.

"It's not as easy as she makes it look. Things—well, they don't always move where I want them," Rory adds.

Sachi gives Rory a sideways look. "If you didn't drink, your focus would—"

*"Agito,"* Rory interrupts, and a thick leather-bound Bible flies right off the bookshelf, zooming across the room toward Sachi's head.

*"Desino,"* Sachi fires back, and the book falls harmlessly to the floor. "Very good, Rory."

"Stop lecturing me then and let Cate try it."

"Me? Here?" I glance nervously toward the hall. Birds and feathers aside, I've never performed magic in front of someone besides Mother or Maura and Tess. I can't help feeling shy, as though Rory's asked me to undress.

"It's safe. Elizabeth's gone out to the market, and Rory's mother won't come down until supper," Sachi says, her eyes flicking up to the ceiling.

But it's a new kind of spell. Who knows what could go wrong?

"No one will care if you break something here," Rory says from her prone position on the sofa. "Mother never notices if the dishes go missing."

"All you have to do is pick an object and focus on where you want it to go. Pinpoint the location *exactly*. If you get distracted, it may end up somewhere else," Sachi instructs. *"Agito* is the best spell, although sometimes I use *avolo* to make things go faster. If you set something in motion, *desino* will make it stop."

I'm slow at languages, but even I recognize that much Latin. I set my teacup down. *"Agito?"*

It doesn't move. I try again, more forcefully, imagining it three inches to the right. *"Agito!"*

Still nothing. Frustration chokes me.

I look up at Sachi, cheeks flushed. "I can't do it."

Sachi just laughs. "You can't expect to master a spell in two minutes. Watch us for a bit."

Rory sits up, and they call out spells, sending things flying around the room: books, pillows, Rory's slippers, the sugar bowl. Rory pulls the pins from Sachi's hair, and the next minute the sofa floats a few inches off the floor—with Rory still on it, squealing. They're playful with magic in a way I've never been. They make it look *fun*.

It makes me wish things were different. That *I* was different.

Mother was very clear; magic was not a thing to play with. Inheriting it wasn't a gift or a mark of pride. It was a burden, and a heavy one, and we had to learn to wield it well enough to make sure we were safe.

What would it have been like to learn magic without all her warnings, without the fear and anxiety that pervaded all of our practices? Would the Brothers' lectures still make me feel sick with guilt?

"Keep trying," Sachi says, and I do. Once the teacup rattles promisingly, and they both stop their own efforts to watch. I try again. This time, it scoots forward three whole inches.

Rory puts her fingers in her mouth and gives a piercing whistle. "Brilliant! It took me weeks to learn that."

"Me, too. You're amazing," Sachi proclaims. "You must have a natural gift for this sort of magic."

197

I look at her suspiciously, but she's not mocking. She actually thinks I'm good. Lord, but I have misjudged these girls.

Half an hour later, I climb into our carriage. Sachi and Rory stand at the gate, waving and calling that they'll be at our tea on Tuesday. The carriage jolts over the cobblestones, but I'm so exhausted, I could nap. I feel as though I've been clobbered over the head with a shovel; there's a dull ache in my temples and my legs feel leaden. Is this why Mother didn't tell us it was possible to animate objects? Was she waiting for us to be older and stronger?

She knew she was dying, though. If she was worried for us, she should have taught us everything we were capable of. Why didn't she want us to be as powerful as possible?

*Because she thought it was wrong,* a small voice inside me suggests, and I go still with the certainty of it. She wanted us to be normal girls, safe and ordinary.

But we're not. And seeing Sachi and Rory—seeing how free and fearless they are—it makes me wonder. Perhaps Maura's right. I've been trying to follow Mother's example because I had no other. I thought keeping us safe meant hiding our magic away, resenting it for the danger it put us in. Perhaps it doesn't *have* to be that way. Lord knows, now more than ever, we need every possible means of protecting ourselves.

John drops me off in front of the house and helps me down. I don't go inside; instead I walk toward the garden. I owe my sisters an apology. I should have been helping them learn instead of preventing them. It's important to keep up a veneer of respectability, yes. To dress well and fit in with our neighbors.

Elena can help with that—and Sachi, too. But beneath that—as long as we're careful—we could be learning new spells.

We're not alone in it anymore. We have Sachi now, and Rory. Elena, backed by the entire Sisterhood. The thought brings me a surprising amount of comfort.

I work out my thoughts as I walk. The apology's muddled—I hate admitting when I've been wrong—but the plan of action, moving forward, is good. Perhaps if I let Elena teach us animation and healing spells, she'll tell the Sisters that we've been cooperating, and they'll be satisfied with our progress. It's not a permanent solution—but it may buy us a bit of time, enough for me to learn more about the last part of the prophecy. For me to figure out whether the Sisterhood can be trusted.

My face falls. Only—I haven't much time to spare. The early October sun is warm, the sky a bright robin's-egg blue full of puffy white clouds, but autumn is here and November is coming. If I don't make up my mind soon, the Brothers will force my hand.

I'm so absorbed in my thoughts that I don't notice the butterflies until they're flying past my head.

Blue butterflies with gold wings. Pink butterflies with orange spots. Butterflies with tiger stripes and topaz eyes.

I've never seen anything like them.

I stop, amazed. They're flying in a steady stream out of the rose garden.

I hear a bubbly laugh and hasten forward. It's Maura. I'd know that spun-sugar laugh anywhere. But if the butterflies are moving—when did she learn to do animation spells?

I slip around the tall hedges into the garden, hoping to surprise her.

I'm the one who's surprised.

Elena Robichaud sits on the bench, a thin cigarette between her lips. She's blowing smoke rings. As each ring rises, she transforms it into a butterfly that flutters after the others.

And Maura—Maura's sprawled on the grass in one of her old dresses, her red hair shining in the sun, watching Elena with adoration.

Elena glances up. "Hello, Cate." She gives one more puff on her cigarette. The smoke ring becomes a butterfly with velvety, ruby-tipped wings. Then she takes the cigarette from her lips, tosses it to the ground, and crushes it beneath one boot. "Maura and I were just going over animation spells. Would you like to try one?"

Anger rolls over me. All her pretty words of friendship aside, I don't like this woman. I don't trust her with Maura. When we were very little, Maura used to look at *me* with that sort of hero worship—like she would follow me anywhere, embark on any mad scheme I suggested.

There's a book at Elena's feet, brown with white lettering. I focus on it. I shut out everything else, and I do not let the possibility of failure enter my mind.

"*Agito.*" At the Elliotts', I gave the teacup a gentle tap with my mind. There's nothing gentle in the way I heave this book now.

It whizzes through the air and flies across the garden, landing exactly where I wanted it: at the foot of the statue of Athena.

"Cate!" Maura gasps. "Where did you learn that?"

I stride into the center of the garden. "Elena, I'd like to talk to my sister. Alone."

"We're having a lesson," Maura says haughtily, resting on her elbows. "You're interrupting."

"A good thing, too!" I wave a hand back toward the house, half hidden behind the tall shrubbery. "I hardly think this is what Father hired her to teach us!"

"I wasn't aware you knew how to do animation spells," Elena says.

"Neither was I," Maura grumbles, standing and brushing bits of grass from her pale yellow skirt.

"Oh, for heaven's sake, I just learned it today." But I feel a twinge of guilt for the other secrets I'm keeping from my sister. There are so many: my mind-magic, the prophecy, the letter from Zara, kissing Finn. If I was angry to find her practicing magic with Elena without my permission—well, multiply that by ten, and I imagine it's still not as furious as she'd be with me.

"Liar, you did not!" Maura gasps, planting her hands on her hips. "I've been trying all afternoon and I can't move anything yet."

I sigh, leaning down to yank out a fast-growing weed. "Yes, well, occasionally I do manage to pound something into this thick skull of mine."

"That is quite fast, though," Elena says slowly, and my stomach plummets. Why did I have to go and boast?

"Whatever you want to talk about, you can tell Elena. She wants to help us," Maura insists. She reaches down, plucks a pink rose, and tucks it behind one ear.

I take a deep breath. "So she says."

Elena stands, scowling. "If you'd stop being so childish and admit that—" She gathers herself, running a hand over her hair. "No. You're right. The two of you ought to talk. I'll be in my room."

Maura and I watch her go, swishing elegantly out of the garden, her dark skirts hissing against the cobblestones. Somehow, I feel as though I'm the one who's come off badly in this.

"What's wrong with you?" Maura demands.

"She's a stranger! And you *told her* about us!" Maura doesn't answer. I stride forward until we're nose to nose, my heeled shoes clapping against the cobblestones like a horse's hooves. "Didn't you?"

Maura crosses her arms. "Oh, what if I did? Do you think I need to ask your leave?"

"Yes, actually! You *should* ask my leave, and Tess's, too. It's not only your secret, Maura."

"What do you think she'll do, expose us to the Brothers? She's a witch herself. She wants to teach us things. She knows heaps of spells we don't. We can trust her, Cate."

"Can we? She hasn't been entirely honest with you." I bite my lip, ignoring the fact that I haven't either. I sit on the bench, the marble still warm from Elena's body. "With any of us, I mean. It's no coincidence that she ended up here, in a house with three witches. The Sisterhood—they're all witches."

"All of them?" Maura gasps. I nod, but her reaction isn't what I expected. "That's—Cate, that's dozens of witches in the convent in New London alone! Elena's been hinting about my joining the Sisterhood, and I didn't understand why, but—oh! That makes sense now, doesn't it?"

Maura's eyes are sparkling with excitement, her cheeks flushed. She catches at my sleeve. "We could join them! They could teach us all about magic, and we'd be in New London, and we wouldn't have to marry any wretched old men!" She twirls around, her pale skirts flaring out around her. "It's absolutely perfect!"

Oh no. "Maura," I say gently. "It's not that simple."

"Why not? It's not as though you're in love with Paul. You said yourself you don't really want to marry him. We could all stay together, and we'd be safe from the Brothers."

She looks so happy. So pretty, spinning around in the sunshine.

And she's right. Now that I know what the Sisterhood is, it's a viable possibility. It's certainly better than marrying an old man and playing nursemaid to half a dozen brats. But something about Elena's promises feels disingenuous. It's got to be difficult, keeping the Sisters' true nature a secret. Would they ask me to use my mind-magic on their enemies, like in the old days? Is that why Mother married Father and fled to the country?

*You will be hunted by those who would use you for their own ends. You cannot trust anyone.*

Was Mother being over-cautious, or was her warning justified? What does she know about the Sisterhood that I don't?

Maura reads the doubt on my face. "Or you could marry Paul after all. If Tess and I joined the Sisters, we'd all be in New London together! You have *choices*!" she chirps.

Do I? Then why don't I feel happy about any of them?

She spins around again, then falls over into the grass, dizzy and delighted with the prospect of escape. Our little corner of the world is enough for me, but it isn't enough for her. Maybe it's all the grand romances she's read; maybe it's the stories Mother used to tell over her cradle. She wants more than this. She said it last week, quite plainly, but I don't think I realized how much she wants it until this very moment.

Elena saw it straightaway. She's a canny girl, Elena. She says she's here to protect us, but meanwhile she's been trying to recruit Maura. Does she think Maura's the prophesied one? Or does she just suspect that once she has Maura, Tess and I will fall in line? She has to know how much I love my sisters, how inextricably my promise to Mother has become woven into my life. I'd give up my own happiness if it would ensure their safety. If the Sisterhood is what they want, if it would ensure the Brotherhood couldn't touch them—I don't see how I could object.

"Elena's wonderful," Maura continues, scrambling back to her feet. Her hair is disheveled; the pink rose has fallen to the ground. "She's clever and kind and she's been nothing but generous. You ought to be nicer to her."

"She may be all those things, but she hasn't been exactly forthcoming. She was sent here to spy on us and see if we were witches. I think it's reasonable that I was suspicious."

"Well, now that you know why, you ought to apologize for being so rude." Maura sits next to me and gives me a hug, looping her arm around my waist. "I know you're not used to me being close with anyone else, but her friendship is important to me. I wasn't angry when you were invited to tea with Sachi and Rory and I wasn't. You can't be peering over my shoulder trying to protect me all the time."

I watch a lone purple butterfly flapping its way back through the garden. It lights on the yellow goldenrod, wings twitching. "I'll always want to protect you. No matter what."

Maura shakes her head. "Well, stop it. Think about your own future for once. The Sisterhood might be the perfect solution for all of us."

The door to Elena's bedroom is open. She's a dark silhouette against the bright window, a picture framed by green curtains.

"I was expecting you," she says, turning. Her petal-pink lips are pursed, thoughtful. "I told you before, Cate, we needn't be adversaries. But I'll tolerate only so much rudeness. I think you owe me an apology."

I close the door and lean against it. "You should have talked to me before you started teaching Maura magic."

"You're not her mother," Elena says bluntly. She sees the stricken look on my face and holds up a hand. "I don't say that to hurt you, Cate. But she doesn't need your permission, and neither do I."

It does hurt me, whether she means to or not. I stalk into the middle of the room, practically vibrating with anger. "I could dismiss you, you know."

"The Sisters would only send another girl in my place, and she might not be as patient as I've been." Elena shakes her head, silver earbobs swinging. "I don't want to fight about this. But I have a job to do here, and I will do it, regardless of your co-operation. Do we understand each other?"

A trickle of fear slides down my spine. "Perfectly."

"Good. Now. Maura's a bright, curious girl. It isn't fair to hold her back."

I loom over Elena, glad for once of my height. "Don't you tell me about my sister. I know her better than you do."

"Do you?" Elena cocks her head doubtfully. "Because I must admit, I don't think keeping things from her is very kind. The prophecy affects her future, too. She'll be furious when she finds out—and rightly so. What if she's the most powerful? She ought to know, so she can protect herself."

I frown. Loath as I am to admit it, what she's saying makes sense. Maura and Tess do deserve to know. The secrets have been weighing on my conscience for days. "I told her about the Sisterhood, just now."

"Only in an attempt to warn her away from trusting me, I'm sure," Elena says.

Am I that transparent? "Well, I'm not convinced we *can* trust you. If we wanted to join the Sisterhood—what would that entail?"

Elena settles into one of the high-backed green chairs beside the hearth and indicates that I should take the other. I perch uneasily, poised for flight. "There are a few dozen other students, all witches, ranging in age from ten to twenty. You'd be instructed in the various kinds of magic, as well as the history of the Daughters of Persephone. If you are the three sisters, it is the very safest place for you. You'd be well cared for, given anything you need."

I hesitate. "And if we don't want to go?"

"Why wouldn't you?" Elena throws her hands up in the air. Her silver ring catches the sunlight. "You can't tell me you want to stay in this poky little place forever. Your neighbors are fools. Your father's never home. What's left for you here?"

I stare past her, out the window at the newly shorn fields. It's not my neighbors or Father who makes this place feel like a home. It's the graves on the hillside. The rose garden. Tess, playing the piano after dinner. Maura, acting out scenes from her novels. Paul. Finn.

There's me. If I decided not to go, would Maura and Tess leave me behind?

"It might not seem very grand to you, but it's still our home."

"Maura hates it here, and Tess feels stifled. They'd have access to a marvelous education—magical and otherwise—with the Sisters. I think they could be convinced quite easily. So this must be about you. Is it because of Mr. McLeod?" Elena clasps her hands together in her lap. "Maura says he intends to go back to New London. You could still see him from time to time. If you aren't the most powerful, after you finish your schooling, we would consider allowing you to leave the order and marry. We have a network of former pupils who remain our eyes and ears all over New England."

Who spy for them, she means. I keep my face purposefully blank, focusing on the wallpaper over her shoulder. It's a pale green with leafy pink tulips. "What if I am the most powerful?"

"Then we'd need you to remain with the Sisters. You haven't made Mr. McLeod any promises, have you?" Elena leans forward, gripping the curved arm of her chair, then relaxes. "It doesn't matter. Engagements can be broken before you declare your intent. The Brothers wouldn't get involved if you discovered a religious calling."

I grit my teeth together. "I'm not engaged. Not yet."

"Really? What's prevented you? His interest seems clear enough," Elena muses, and I wish I could snatch my words back and stuff them back down my throat. "Perhaps it's time you do a little thinking, Cate. You're so preoccupied with your sisters—have you ever taken the time to search your own heart?"

What does my heart want? I stare down at the dusky pink rug.

I picture myself kneeling in a garden of my own. It's not a grand, winding labyrinth of hedges and flowers and statuary. There's no gazebo, no pond. There's a red maple or two, and some rosebushes with red and white buds. I'm planting bulbs and roots that will grow into tulips and peonies. My hands are deep in the cool, moist soil. Sitting on a bench nearby is a man, reading aloud from a book, the way Father used to in the evenings.

The man is not Paul McLeod.

He's got brown eyes and spectacles and messy hair that refuses to lie flat. He's got a map of freckles over arms that are surprisingly strong. He's got a smile that makes my heart pound when he stops and looks over at me midsentence.

"If you're capable of mind-magic—" Elena's breath catches. "You could help other girls like you, Cate. There are other young witches out there, alone and frightened. And girls who aren't witches, too, for that matter—who are just odd and unlucky. They're all at the mercy of the Brothers." She slaps her hand against the curved wooden arm of her chair. "It's not fair that girls have to grow up in fear, forced into making decisions about their future before they're ready. If you're the most powerful, you could help us change that. You could help the women of New England regain their independence. That's a marvelous thing, Cate. You can't ignore that."

Elena's dark eyes are flashing, her serene face animated with the promise of this new future: a future where witches and women reclaim their power. I fall silent. She's right. But this new responsibility is much bigger than anything Mother asked of me. The Sisters' expectations, this prophecy, the notion of being responsible for the welfare of dozens of girls—it's all very daunting.

Elena watches me. "Do you swear to me you've never tried mind-magic?"

"Yes." Perhaps I can use Maura's talkativeness to my advantage. Elena already thinks I'm conflicted about my magic—and that's not entirely untrue. "I've always been frightened of it. The Brothers say such awful things."

"It can be dangerous, in the wrong hands," she admits. "If you can't do it, there's no harm done. You can join the Sisterhood or not, as you wish. But if you can—better for everyone that we know it now. We'll make sure you're safe, and you won't make any promises you can't keep. Perhaps we ought to have a lesson tomorrow. All three of you can try. Then we'll know the truth, won't we?"

No! I'm not ready. I need more time to weigh Elena's words and Mother's warnings.

"Tomorrow?" I jump to my feet. "No. That's too soon! Tess is only twelve, for heaven's sake; you can't have her trying magic that powerful yet. What if it went all wrong?"

Elena tilts her head. She's lovely in that high-backed chair, regal as a queen. "Her magic seems quite stable to me. I've been here two weeks, and I haven't seen her lose control once."

Tess rarely does—even last year, when she was first learning. That's not the point. I set my jaw. "I don't want you teaching her mind-magic. Or Maura either. If I find out you are, I'll have you dismissed."

"I don't think Maura would like that." Elena smiles. "She's grown rather attached to me."

I head for the door. "I'll do what's best for us whether Maura likes it or not."

Elena leans back in her chair. "Even if she hates you for it?"

My smile feels like it could crack in half. "It wouldn't be the first time."

"This might be different. If you send me away, she'll only come to resent you more and more. I hardly think that's what you want. Especially if you are the three sisters."

I pause, my hand on the doorknob. "What's that got to do with anything?"

"The last part of the prophecy. You don't want to take any chances, do you? Tempting fate and all." Elena shivers, and her eyes—I know that look. It's the way people looked at us at Mother's funeral. Pitying. "I don't blame you for being upset about this, Cate. It's quite distressing. I promise you, we will do everything we can to keep you safe. *All* of you."

She knows about the last part of the prophecy.

I can't bring myself to admit that I don't.

Even if I don't understand it, her pity could be useful. I turn to her, letting my eyes fill with tears. It's not difficult. "We just need more time. Please. Give me a few more days to tell Maura and Tess, and let them get used to the idea. It's all very sudden."

Elena frowns. "All right. I suppose a few days won't hurt. But I expect you to keep your word, Cate. There will be consequences if you don't."

# chapter

# 13

I find tess in her bedroom, nestled in her canopy bed, reading a book twice as thick as my arm. When I slam the door behind me, she sits up, throwing the blankets off. Her curls are mussed into a frizzy halo around her head.

"What's wrong?" she asks.

"Nothing," I snap. "Everything's just grand. Would you like to learn a new spell?"

"From whom?"

"From me, silly."

Tess stares at me, gray eyes searching as though she's trying to puzzle out the joke. "You hate us using magic."

I sit next to her, ducking beneath the gauzy green canopy. "I don't hate it. I've been worried it would hurt us. But I've been thinking, and I wonder if we ought to practice more and learn some new spells. We'll still need to be careful, but—"

I'm cut off by a mouthful of hair. Tess flings herself at me, squealing, puppylike in her excitement. "Will you teach me now? Where's Maura?"

I take a deep breath. Tess's room smells delicious, like cinnamon and nutmeg. I glance over at her bureau and, sure enough, there's a plate with freshly baked pumpkin bread. Her own handiwork, no doubt. "Elena is going to teach her, I think."

"Elena? Our governess Elena?" Tess gapes at me. "How— why—how?"

By the time I'm finished explaining about Elena and the Sisterhood, Tess's eyes are round as saucers. "You know, she hinted at it the other day, during our French lesson—but I thought perhaps I was imagining it. I didn't say anything about the magic, I swear."

"I'm not angry—not with you, at any rate. I'm not certain we can trust her."

"You don't trust anybody," Tess points out, the dimple in her cheek showing.

"What do you think? Do you like her?"

Tess taps a finger against her mouth, thoughtful. "I don't *dis*-like her," she says finally. "But I'm not certain she has our best interests at heart, if she's been sent here to find out if we're witches and report back to someone."

I throw up both hands, thrilled to have my suspicions seconded. "Try telling Maura that!"

Tess gives me a look, and for a moment it's as though our roles have been reversed and she's the older, wiser one. "Cate," she sighs, as though I'm frightfully dim-witted. "We can't tell Maura that. She'll think we're jealous."

"Yes!" I groan, falling backward onto the bed. "She thinks I'm upset because they've become so close."

Tess rolls her eyes. "Well, it is annoying. Maura's so besotted with her—she hangs on Elena's every word like she's the most brilliant girl in the world."

I laugh and muss Tess's hair. "We all know that's you."

"I'm serious. Maura's started adopting the way Elena talks, and all her little mannerisms. She's desperate to impress her. But I suppose it makes sense. I'm Father's favorite. You were Mother's." Tess says it matter-of-factly. "She wants someone all her own."

I've never once thought of it like that. "How did you get to be so clever?"

Tess giggles, falling back next to me. "It's not clever. It's just paying attention to people."

Whatever it is, I wish I had her talent for it.

"Time for lessons," I declare, sitting up.

"Wait." Tess sits up, too, her hair tickling my arm. "Where did you learn new spells? Mrs. O'Hare said you went to the bookshop—did you find something about magic there?"

The story of the prophecy can wait. "No. I learned them from Sachi Ishida."

"Sachi Ishida is a witch?" Tess whisper-shouts.

I laugh and tell her how Sachi and Rory ambushed me over tea. Then I gather my energy. I think of Elena's ultimatums, letting my anger feed the magic but keeping it at an even, steady boil.

214

*"Agito,"* I say, and Tess's ragged old teddy bear, Cyclops, soars into the air.

*"Desino."* It thumps back on top of her pillows like a kite without wind.

Tess stares at me wide eyed.

I'm surprised, too. I didn't think I'd get it on the first try.

"You just learned that today?" she asks.

"I did." I hold my breath, expecting her to say it's impossible. To call me a liar.

"That's marvelous!" She bounces on the bed. "May I try?"

"Absolutely. Just—"

"Be careful," we say in unison, and I laugh. Am I that predictable?

Tess focuses on Cyclops's placid, one-eyed face. He lost one of his black button eyes years ago, but she wouldn't let Mrs. O'Hare replace it. She said it made him more interesting, and changed his name from Barnabus.

Tess takes a breath and lets it out slowly. *"Agito,"* she says, but nothing happens. She tries again, scrunching up her face. Her expression is just like Father's when he's translating a difficult passage.

"It's more difficult than illusions," I explain. "You have to sort of—harness your energy. I felt like I could nap for days on the way home."

Tess pouts. "You made it look so simple."

"It's not. It took me an hour to move a teacup. Rory said it took her weeks."

"Then I'll have to keep practicing, won't I?" From this angle, her jaw is shaped like mine. Pointy and stubborn.

"Let's practice together. You can help me with my silent spells, and I'll help you with animation. Give us a few weeks, and we'll be the cleverest witches in New England!"

Tess grins at me. "You don't ever do things halfway, do you?"

I suppose I do not.


The following afternoon, after our lessons proper, Tess and I closet ourselves in Father's study to practice again. I suppose I'm feeling rather bold, breaking the no-magic-in-the-house rule Mother set, but now that Father's gone and half the inhabitants of the house are witches, it doesn't seem quite so dangerous.

Tess sits dwarfed in Father's leather desk chair and I lie on the curved red-velvet sofa. We take turns trying to float different objects from Father's desk: paperweights and pens, stamps and sealing wax. We both show marked improvement. I manage half a dozen silent spells under Tess's tutelage, and she hovers Father's copy of *The Metamorphoses* a good six inches off the floor.

Tess is pleased with our progress, but the rapidity of it worries me. We've both picked up animation much faster than Sachi and Rory said they did. Even casting silently doesn't seem so difficult for me anymore. I always thought myself a poor witch, but now I wonder whether my lack of progress was due to lack of interest rather than lack of skill.

Perhaps it's the difference in our ages, but there's no jealousy, no sense of competition between us. It helps that although Tess is the far better scholar—better at piano and chess, too—we seem evenly matched in our magic. It's actually *fun*. I only feel guilty that it took me this long—this threat of losing her to Elena—to make me appreciate Tess more. To start seeing her as a friend, not just a baby sister.

A rap on the door interrupts us. "Miss Cate, Mr. McLeod is here to see you."

"I'll be right there, Lily."

Tess dances over to the settee, poking me with the fountain pen she's just floated up to the ceiling. "Are you going to marry Paul? Lily and Mrs. O'Hare were gossiping about it in the kitchen when they thought I wasn't listening."

I swat at her. "I don't know. What did they say?"

Tess chews on the end of the pen. "They think you'll have to. But they don't know about the Sisters, of course. What they really are."

"Do you think—" I push my doubts aside for the moment. If it's what Tess wants, what Maura wants, I'll have to give in. "Do you *want* to go to New London and study with the Sisterhood? You can't formally join them until you're old enough to declare an intention, but Elena says they accept girls as young as ten in their school. She said their libraries are amazing, and they'd let you read whatever you like."

"Elena told me about the libraries. They do sound tempting," Tess admits. I give her a tight smile. Elena did, did she? But Tess shakes her head, braids flying. "Still, I think I'd rather stay home and study with Father, and bake with Mrs. O'Hare, and take walks in the garden. Elena tries to make New London sound fun, but it just seems—noisy. And crowded."

"Well, you have years to decide yet," I assure her, though I don't know if it's true. If we are the three sisters, will the Sisterhood let her stay home until she's seventeen? "It's only Maura and me Father's worried about. Well—mostly me."

"Just wait until it's Maura's turn," Tess says. "You know how she changes her mind. Even if she goes to the Sisterhood early, she's likely to get to New London and decide she wants to marry a sailor instead. With you, at least we all know that once you make up your mind, you won't change it."

"I want to stay in Chatham, especially if that's where you'll be," I admit. "It's just a matter of figuring out how. I could try to persuade Paul to stay here with me, but—"

Tess throws her arms around my waist. "Do you think he would? I don't want you to go. It'd be so lonely without you, Cate."

I hug her tight. "I don't want to go, either."

"But you might have to." She pulls away, her little face woebegone. "If you're his wife, you'll have to go and live with him wherever he wants."

Tess is right. I could be packed up and moved to the other side of the world if my husband wanted it. I'd have no more say than the footstool.

"Do you really think Paul would drag me off kicking and screaming? That's what he'd have to do, to take me away from you."

Tess smiles, her dimple flashing. "You promise?"

"I promise." But my conscience gives a great loud pang. I don't know if I can keep that promise. Even if I can wrangle Paul into staying in Chatham, if the Sisters discover that I can do mind-magic, I don't think they'll allow me to marry. Elena talked

218

of women gaining their independence—but what about *my* independence?

My temper rises. It's one thing for me to decide, voluntarily, to forgo marriage and join the Sisters and work toward their cause. I haven't ruled it out. But I don't care for being forced into anything. No matter how safe and beautiful it is, a cage is still a cage.

Paul's waiting in the sitting room, but he hasn't removed his gray overcoat. He stands up and hands me a bouquet of white roses. I bury my face in them, inhaling deeply. "They're lovely, thank you."

He smiles. His sunburn has faded, and his green eyes are bright against his tanned skin. "They're not your favorites, I know, but Mother's garden is anemic compared with yours."

Clever boy. Flowers and compliments on my garden are the surest way to my heart, and he knows it. "Have you been waiting long? I was studying with Tess."

"It's all right. Maura stopped by and kept me company for a few minutes." Paul leans against the piano. "Your sisters are getting to be proper young ladies, aren't they? I can remember when Tess was crawling over the floors and we had to keep her from putting dirt in her mouth."

"She did have a talent for chewing on everything in her path. I think she ate half a worm once." I laugh, remembering how revolted Mrs. O'Hare was to find the other half still squirming in Tess's hand.

Paul nods sagely. "Possibly it was for scientific purposes."

"Possibly. She was very inquisitive, even as a baby."

"There was that entire year when all she said was 'Why?' And you made up those ridiculous reasons for things." Paul tilts his head to one side in that funny way Tess has, and pitches his voice high. He's always been brilliant at impersonations. "'Why do horses have four legs? Why isn't snow blue? Why? Why?'"

I laugh, trailing a hand over the closed lid of the piano. "Well, how am I supposed to know why bumblebees can fly and Tess can't? Aside from the wings, I mean."

Paul brushes a stray hair away from my face. "You're beautiful when you laugh."

The smile slips from my face. How did we go from reminiscing to flirtation? "Do I usually look haggard?"

"You're always beautiful to me," he says tenderly, stroking my cheek. "But you worry too much. I'd take away some of your troubles if I could."

I wish it were that easy. I pull away, smiling stiffly. "I manage."

"I know you do. I'm not criticizing you, Cate. I'd like to help. Whatever it is. You can count on me," he says, uncharacteristically earnest. Then he grins. "Shall we go for a walk?"

I glance out the window, uneasy. It rained this morning, but now there's a fresh wind whipping at the trees, sending the gray clouds skimming across the sky. I've been cooped up inside all day; I do want to go out. But what if we run into Finn?

"Let me guess, it's too cold," Paul suggests. "You're afraid to catch a chill."

I smack his arm lightly. "I am not!"

"You've been spending too much time with Miss Ishida. You'll become a delicate flower yet," he teases.

If only he knew. Rory turned one of the buttons on Sachi's

bodice into a centipede, and she hardly blinked. Sachi Ishida's a good deal hardier than anyone suspects.

"Nonsense," I laugh. "Of course I'll go."

I bundle up in my cloak and call for Lily. Once we're out in the gardens, my nerves stretch out like a thin ribbon. The wind whips my skirts around my ankles and tugs threateningly at my hood. I find myself listening for the sound of hammering at the gazebo. I don't hear it; I wonder if perhaps Finn isn't here at all. Perhaps he was needed at home today. My heart sinks at the thought. The truth is, I've come to crave the sight of him.

I turn my face up to the sky, reveling in the breeze that buffets my cheeks. At least I'm not cowering in the house.

"Let's go in here and get out of the wind," Paul suggests, tugging me into Mother's rose garden. "Lily, could we have a moment?"

They don't give me a chance to object. Lily scurries away, smiling fit to burst, and then it hits me: they've arranged this.

He's arranged this.

For all my brave talk of asking him to stay in Chatham, I don't feel ready.

"Cate," he says, like he relishes the taste of my name on his tongue. He stands tall, his shoulders broad, his stance wide. "I know this is your favorite place. That's why I wanted to say this here."

I open my mouth, but he puts up a hand to forestall me, chuckling. "Just listen for a minute. I love you, Cate. I've always loved you. Ever since you took that dare and walked that pigpen fence." He laughs a little. "The sky is just the color of your eyes today, do you know that?"

"Paul, I—" *Stop*, I want to say. *Don't do this. Please.*

He plows ahead, heedless. "I know this is unconventional. I haven't had a chance to speak to your father yet. But I thought it might suit you, asking you first. I can't imagine he'd object if you were happy. I think I *can* make you happy, Cate. And I would be truly honored—that is to say, you'd make me very happy if—will you be my wife?"

My eyes fall to the ground in confusion. Paul would be a good husband to me. He would be a partner, not a master. He makes me laugh. He's handsome. And I do love him.

I should say yes. I should say yes and then I should ask whether he would consider living in Chatham, at least for the first few years of our marriage. Just until Tess marries. After that, she'd be safer. But I can't ask Paul to give up his job and rearrange his life for an engagement that I might well be forced to break. It's not fair to him.

Or to me. I think back to my conversation in the carriage with Maura. I don't feel butterflies when Paul says my name, when he touches my hand. I don't miss him on the days he doesn't come to call. Whatever being in love is—I don't think I feel that way toward him.

I can't bring myself to say yes. Not yet. Perhaps in a few weeks, I'll be able to find a way around Elena and the Sisters. Perhaps when I've forgotten the way Finn's kisses made me feel—how tempted I was to tell *him* about the magic—I'll be able to say yes in good conscience.

"Paul, I—" How can I put him off in a way that won't hurt him?

But the moment I look up, he knows. He sets his jaw in that

way he has and shoves his hands into his pockets. "I've rushed things. I was afraid I was too late, but you need more time."

I feel a great glad swell of relief. "Yes," I say, finally meeting his eyes.

"You're not saying no, though?" His eyes are worried, vulnerable.

"No," I assure him. "I'm not saying no."

"Good." He waggles his eyebrows at me. "Am I allowed to try to convince you?"

How? Will he suggest setting up an architecture practice in Chatham? My head spins, pragmatism warring against Maura's ridiculous notions of romance.

"Certainly." I smile, tilting my head at him in that coquettish way Sachi has. "What did you have in mind?"

One of his arms snakes out and pulls me close, wrapping me right up against him. His mouth slants down, moving urgently against mine. My body responds; I feel warm and wanted. My arms lock around his neck; my mouth moves tentatively against his. When he takes my lower lip into his mouth, heat simmers through me. I press closer. Kissing is nice.

But even as the thought skims across my mind, I'm pushing against his chest. Remembering a kiss that felt more than nice—it felt *right*.

Paul steps away. He's smiling. "Was that all right?" he asks. "You don't feel the need to slap me for being too forward, do you?"

"No," I say, my eyes falling to his boots. "I think I can forgive you."

"Good. So. You're not certain if you want to marry me," he says. "But you like kissing me well enough?"

"Do we have to talk about this right now?" I beg, mortified. How is a lady meant to respond to a question like that? He is handsome, and he knows it. In another life—a life where I wasn't a witch, perhaps, and had no need of Belastras' bookshop and the secrets hidden there—it might have been my first kiss. It might have been enough.

"I'll take that as a yes," he says, cocky as ever. "Is it moving to the city that worries you? I know you'd miss your flowers, but there are grand parks. We could go for walks every evening when I got home from work. I could take you down to the shipyards, too, to watch the ships coming in. I'd love to show you New London, Cate. It's magnificent."

His voice is quick and passionate. He adores it there, that's clear. He won't change his mind. And I won't ask him to.

"My sisters," I say, fumbling for excuses. "Things have changed since Mother died. I feel responsible for them. Moving so far away—it's not just a few hours. If something happened and I wasn't here—"

Paul looks puzzled. "But Maura told me she's planning to join the Sisterhood. If she does, she'll be right there in New London."

She did, did she? "There's Tess. She's still so little—and Father's never home anymore. How could I leave her here with just a governess and a housekeeper to look after her?"

"She could visit as often as you like." Paul reaches out and takes my gloved hand in his. "Cate, I love that you're so devoted to your sisters, but is there something else that's giving you pause? Tell me the truth."

I stare at the rose petals the wind has scattered along the cobblestones. "No," I lie. "Nothing else."

Paul searches my face for the truth. "Are you certain? It's not—it's not because of Belastra, is it?"

"What?" I gasp, tugging my hand away from his. "No!"

"I know you, Cate. You can deny it all you want, but the way you look at him—"

"How?" Have I been telegraphing my feelings all over town? Does *everyone* know?

"Like you're fascinated."

"I don't know what you mean!"

"Cate. Show me the respect of not lying to my face, at least."

I whirl around, turning my back to him. I didn't know it was possible to feel this entirely mortified. I'm half tempted to try and vanish myself.

Paul lays a hand on my shoulder. "It's all right. I understand. I don't like it, but I understand."

I peer up at him quizzically.

"I had a bit of a failed romance in the city," he confesses.

"You fell in love with someone?" I'm not certain of my feelings for him, but I have to admit I don't relish the idea of him courting anyone else.

He turns me to face him. "I thought so, at the time. Her name was Penelope. She was very proper and very pretty. I met her at a colleague's dinner party. After dinner, she played the piano and sang for us. She had the voice of an angel."

I picture this Penelope with hair like ripe wheat and giant, innocent blue eyes. The sort of girl who's never had to worry about anything more pressing than hair ribbons or a torn hem. I hate her.

I shove a strand of hair back under my hood—perhaps a little more forcefully than necessary. "What happened?"

"I called on her a few times, squired her home from services once or twice, and was nearly ready to propose. Then she announced her intention to marry someone else. I was devastated. Drank myself into a stupor. Truly, though, it was the best thing that could have happened to me."

"What? Why?" I want to poke her imaginary eyes out for hurting him.

"We were too different," Paul says. "When she wasn't singing, she was quiet as a mouse. Never a word to say for herself. Her blushes were captivating in theory, but once the newness wore off, she would have driven me insane with boredom."

I bite my lip. "How do you know it's not the same with me?"

"Because we're alike, you and I. We want adventures, not quiet nights at home by the fire. I think I could make you happy if you'd let me." Paul's voice goes gravelly, and he takes both my hands in his. "Just promise me you won't go off and marry someone else. Can you do that? For your old friend, at least?"

I squeeze his hands, grateful for his understanding. "Yes, of course. I promise."

"Good." Paul pulls me into his arms again, but this time he just holds me. I tuck my head under his chin. He smells like pine trees and horses and leather. It's very comforting; I let myself sink into his embrace.

Then there's a clatter of metal behind us. We spring apart.

Finn. He's got a pail of weeds in one hand; he's picking up

his shovel with the other. When our eyes meet, he stumbles away, fast despite his twisted ankle.

My heart stops for a moment, then gallops on ahead.

I want to chase right after him. I don't care how big a fool I'd look.

But I can't. I'd be no better than that Penelope. Paul's just proposed; I can't go chasing after another man, one who may not even want me.

Paul wants me; he's been clear as crystal about it. He loves me, and he's my best friend. I push aside what I want.

Paul and I watch Finn's retreating figure until he disappears behind the hedges. Then I turn to Paul, smiling up at him through the horror in my heart. "Will you walk me back inside, please?"

Paul and i walk back to the house in silence. At the kitchen door, he stops, leaning against the white clapboard wall. He's the picture of a handsome city gentleman in his gray frock coat, his blond hair trimmed neatly. He studies the white clematis crawling up the lattice, and then he turns to me, frowning.

"I think I've made my feelings clear. I don't know what more I can do."

I reach out, put a tentative hand on his arm. "Nothing," I murmur. "You've been—you're amazing. I just need time to think."

Paul twines my fingers with his. "I'll give you time, but the Brothers won't."

I hunch into myself, watching him stride away toward the barn. In fact, I'm still standing there when he emerges on his big bay stallion and canters across the fields to his house. He waves a hand, and I wave back.

I should go inside and tell my sisters about his proposal. Let them hug and congratulate me, let Mrs. O'Hare squeal and Tess bake me an apple pie for after dinner. Pretend for one day that I'm a normal girl, marrying a good man. Tess would be sad, but she'd forgive me. I daresay Maura would be thrilled to have me settled and out of her way.

But what would Elena do? Would she insist on testing me for mind-magic immediately? If she did, she'd find out straightaway that I could do it, and then what? I suspect she'd ship me right off to the Sisters.

I press my hands to my face, willing back tears. That's not what I want. I don't want to go to the Sisters. I don't want to marry Paul. I want—

Finn. I want Finn.

I hesitate, but only for a minute. Then I'm scrambling through the gardens after him, praying he's still here. It's hard to see around the hedges; I'm not sure which direction he's gone. I follow my instincts through the winding paths until I come out into the open.

He hasn't left. He's up at the gazebo. In the last few days, he's erected the railing. His hands are braced against it, and he stares off across the fields toward town. He's wearing workman's clothes—brown corduroy trousers, boots, suspenders, and a chocolate-colored shirt that matches his eyes.

My slippers sink into the wet grass. My hems grow damp and heavy; the mud sucks at my skirts. I feel like the earth itself is pulling at me, slowing me down.

I hurry into the gazebo, leaving muddy tracks across the wooden floor. It smells of sawdust and wet earth and worms. There's a stitch in my side that aches something fierce; I'm panting with the exertion of my chase. The wind rips my hood off and sends my hair cascading down over my shoulders.

"Finn," I say, shoving my hair behind my ears.

He turns. I wish I were like Tess, I wish I knew how to study people, but I can't read the expression on his face.

"I wanted to explain what—what you saw—" I stammer.

He picks up a broom and begins to sweep up piles of sawdust. "You don't owe me any explanations, Miss Cahill."

Oh. I shrink back from the ice in his voice. I don't know what I expected, precisely, but I expected him to *care*. He just saw me in another man's arms—and not just any other man, but one I'm fairly certain he dislikes. I kissed someone else! He didn't see that, but if I saw him with another woman—the thought of it makes me feel hot and sick. He can't think I go letting men make love to me on a whim.

I shouldn't be kissing anyone else. I feel it with an aching certainty, like a bruised bone. Something passed between us in that dark room, something a little bit sacred. I blush at the memory of his lips on mine. Of his hands on my waist like feathers. That had to mean something, whether he remembers it or not.

"I wanted to set things right," I say, flushing.

"If you'd like me to offer my resignation, I will. I won't hold any hard feelings." He doesn't even look at me, just keeps sweeping, the broom scratching furiously against the floor.

I hadn't thought about his job. Is he afraid it wouldn't be appropriate to continue working here, after what happened between us? That Father would dismiss him if he found out?

Does that mean he remembers?

"But you need this job," I point out. Business at the bookshop has slowed to a trickle.

Finn throws the broom to the floor, scattering one of his neat piles. I cough as a cloud of sawdust fills the air. "I don't need your charity. If having me on the premises bothers your fiancé—" Finn takes a deep breath. "I owe you an apology, Miss Cahill."

There are only a few feet separating us, but it feels wide and uncrossable as an ocean. "I have the utmost respect and admiration for you," Finn continues. "I never meant to imply otherwise. You were obviously in distress, and I certainly didn't mean to take advantage. It was a—a momentary lapse of judgment. I don't know what came over me, but I can assure you it won't happen again."

I stare at him, my eyes getting wider and wider as the truth sinks in. He remembers kissing me. He is *apologizing* for kissing me.

"It won't?" I choke, feeling oddly crushed.

"No." Finn swipes a hand through his hair, leaving several strands sticking straight up. "My behavior was unforgivably forward. I assure you that I take all the blame upon myself. I don't hold you in any less regard. I got carried away and—I should not have— Knowing that you were practically betrothed to another man, it was conduct most unbecoming on my part."

I step toward him, chin leading the charge. "You got *carried away*? By a momentary lapse of judgment?" I mimic his starched voice. *"You kissed me!"*

Finn runs a hand over the stubble on his chin. "I—yes. There was no disrespect intended. I hope you don't feel as though your reputation has been compromised in any way."

"My reputation?" I fly at him, shoving his chest with both hands. He stumbles back against the railing. "I'm not some fainting flower! I was there, too. I kissed you right back! If there's blame to be taken, half of it's mine!"

He grabs my wrists. "Cate," he says, and I'm pleased that he's dropped the Miss Cahill nonsense. "I apologize if I've offended you, but I don't quite understand which part of my behavior is the issue."

I remember the hunger in his hands moving over me, the press of his body against mine. "Apologizing for kissing me! Saying it was a lapse of judgment! You certainly seemed as though you liked it!"

His grip slackens. "You want me to tell you—that—I liked it?"

"Well, it would certainly be better than apologizing for it," I snap. "How do you suppose that makes me feel?"

He squints at me. "I haven't the foggiest idea."

My head droops, anger fading. I try to back away, but he has a surprisingly strong grip. "It's mortifying, is what it is. I came chasing after you like a madwoman to tell you that what you saw between Paul and me isn't what you thought—that I didn't say yes—and here you go acting as though kissing me was some horrid—"

Finn claps a hand over my mouth. "McLeod proposed to you, and you refused him?"

I nod, feeling suddenly, excruciatingly nervous. "I told him I need time. To think."

Finn steps away and swears in a very creative fashion. I stand there, twisting my hands together, gnawing on my bottom lip.

"Cate. I'm sorry." Finn's voice dips low, velvety. "Kissing you—I liked it."

I freeze. "You did?"

The space between us feels charged. Finn smiles a slow, deliberate smile, and I wonder how I could ever have been blind to how very handsome he is. "Very much."

"But you said it was a lapse of judgment." I need to know.

"I misunderstood your feelings. You did run out of the shop like the hounds of hell were chasing you," he points out.

Because I wasn't certain if he remembered. My happiness wavers. If he knew, what would he think of me?

"Your mother was there. And the Brothers were watching," I say.

His chocolate eyes are fixed on mine. "You've been avoiding me ever since. You've hardly come outside."

"You didn't call on me." Hurt slices through me. "You were right here and you didn't come to the house. You didn't even say hello at church."

Finn shakes his head. "It seems we've been at cross-purposes. I saw you and McLeod together at services and I thought—I've been dunderheaded about it. Will you let me take responsibility for that?"

233

My lips twitch. "You may have full credit for dunder-headedness."

"Thank you. So. Just to be quite clear—you don't feel compromised?"

The Brothers teach us that lust and wickedness go hand in hand. A lack of modesty is a horrid thing in a woman. Women are meant to be chaste, just as we are meant to be subservient.

We are not supposed to enjoy kisses.

But I don't feel it was wrong. On the contrary, letting Finn kiss me—kissing him back—it feels as though it was utterly *right*.

"No," I say slowly, raising my eyes to his. "I don't feel compromised at all."

Finn only looks at me, but it's such a look. It tickles over my skin like a touch.

"McLeod. You didn't tell him no."

"I didn't tell him yes, either," I point out.

He reaches out to trace the curve of my cheek. Can he feel my pulse pounding? His eyes never leave mine. He's barely touching me, but my breath catches, and my tongue darts out to wet my lips.

It's all I can do not to grab him by the collar and pull his mouth to mine.

He laughs, a little hoarse. "Do you want me to compromise you further?"

"I do." Is that too honest? "I don't see the point of pretending that I don't like"—I hesitate, my face burning—"being kissed. By you. I do like it."

He grins, but takes a small step backward. "That's quite

convenient, as I'd like to kiss you again. Not now. Not here, where anyone could see us. But soon. At great length."

I look around, half surprised to find us still in the gazebo, in the middle of my father's land. I've forgotten myself entirely. "I suppose we are being rather scandalous."

He arches an eyebrow. "I'd say so—the lady of the house flirting with the gardener. I imagine your father would have some choice words for me."

My lips curve into a slow smile. "Don't worry about that. I can handle Father."

"I'm sure you can. You're ferocious." Finn chuckles, but then his face falls into serious lines. "I can't—my family—I'm responsible for Mother and Clara now. The bookshop is barely afloat. No one wants to come inside with the Brothers watching us day and night. I don't think they'll give up until they find an excuse to close us down. I'm not able to make you any promises, Cate."

I lift my chin. "I didn't ask for any, did I?"

"No. But you'll need them, and soon. If not from me, from— someone else." Finn's eyes fall to his scuffed brown boots. "I can barely support the three of us, much less—hell, I'll put it plainly. I can't afford a wife. I would understand if you accepted McLeod. I'd hate it—but we can still pretend this conversation never happened. I wouldn't think less of you."

"I would," I snap. "I'd think a good deal less of me, marrying a man for his money when it's someone else I want."

I want Finn. Staggeringly. More than I've ever wanted anything for myself in my life.

But it's impossible. What am I going to *do*? Now that I understand how I feel, how can I reconcile myself to anything else?

"I can't ask you to wait for me. I don't know when—if—my circumstances will improve. Even if they did—life with me would be very different from what you're used to. Mother and Clara make their own dresses. They don't have maids; they cook our suppers and keep house themselves." Finn's face is serious, his brow furrowed. "You'd be a shopkeeper's wife, not a gentleman's daughter. Mother and Clara aren't invited to take tea with Mrs. Ishida."

As if I care what Mrs. Ishida thinks! If that were the only thing standing between us—but it's not. Allying myself with the Belastras would draw the Brothers' keen eyes on our entire family. And if they realized what we could do—what *I* could do—

The prophecy said that if I fell into the wrong hands, it would create a second Terror. How many innocent girls would be murdered? I don't know if the Sisterhood itself would be safe from a second onslaught. Would any witches survive it? Would witches become extinct?

I slump back against the railing. No matter how much I want Finn, it's impossible.

My silence doesn't go unnoticed. "I'm sorry." Finn's handsome face twists in anguish. "I'd give you more if I could. I'd give you the moon."

"It's all right," I say softly, blinking back tears. Time to change the subject to something less perilous. "Speaking of tea—Maura and I are hosting our first tea tomorrow afternoon. Your mother and Clara ought to come, if they're not otherwise engaged."

Finn hesitates, his brown eyes intent on mine. "Mother and Clara aren't usually invited out."

I lean back against the gazebo. "Neither were we, until recently."

"That's different. You must know that." I'm silent, staring out over the pond and the cemetery on the other side. Finn sighs. "I'm not too proud to say it. Your father's a businessman, yes, but a gentleman and a scholar first. Mother's a bookseller and a bluestocking. The Brothers' wives don't consider her their equal because she's a shopkeeper. The shopkeepers' wives believe she thinks she's too good for them."

"I'm the hostess now. Your mother and Clara are perfectly welcome here."

"I'll extend the invitation, then. It's very sweet of you to offer." Finn reaches over and twines his fingers through mine. He brings my hand to his lips and breathes warm air onto my palm. "I meant everything I said. I want you, Cate. But I can't give you what you need."

"What if I need *you*?" I whisper. I feel us tilting toward each other like trees in a strong breeze. I've been craving the sight of him for days, but now it's not enough. I'm not sure who moves first. The inches between us are erased until I'm in his arms and my mouth finds his.

His lips are soft and fierce all at once. They taste like tea and rain. His hands go inside my cloak; one curls around my waist, the other around the nape of my neck, anchoring my mouth to his. My hands rove over his chest, feeling the muscles bunch beneath my fingertips. His lips trace a path along my jaw, stopping just below my ear. When he catches the lobe in his teeth, I gasp. My hand clenches on his collar, and he claims my lips in another searing kiss.

When I finally draw back, gasping for breath, my lips feel swollen, my chin raw from the sandpaper stubble of his. We're still wrapped up together, his arms around my waist beneath my cloak. "I ought to be more of a gentleman, but I'm afraid I lose my head around you," he says, his cherry lips inches from mine.

"I don't mind," I assure him, my arms still looped around his neck.

"I got that impression, yes." He grins. "But you should go in now, truly. If you stay here, I'll have to kiss you senseless and someone will see us eventually. Don't look at me like that. I don't want to let you go."

"I don't want to go." But he's right. I press a quick kiss to his lips, surprising us both with my boldness. Then, laughing, I back out of the gazebo.

I hurry back through the gardens, full up with joy. The wind is fall-brisk; the sky overhead is a soggy gray. Chilly raindrops scatter across my face. It doesn't feel right. There should be robins building nests, not geese scurrying south. The spiky dahlias should be just poking their green noses through the soil. Normally I love the bittersweet brilliance of fall, but today—for the first time in ages, there's no room in me for mourning.

I want springtime and sunshine.

"Poor lovelies." I catch myself cooing foolishly at the flowers. Has love turned me into a dreamy, muddleheaded girl already?

Panic blares through me, and I stop abruptly, clutching at the half wall. I love him, but I can't have him. It's irresponsible to pretend I can. It will only end in heartbreak for the both of us.

My mood swings dangerously, and I can feel the magic rush

up. I try to tamp it down, but it's no use. I squeeze my eyes shut, helpless as it spills up, out of my throat, out of my fingertips.

The garden explodes, defiant, into spring. The grass goes emerald around me. The hedges shrink. The flowers draw back into the soil, except for the long-dead tulips, which rise again.

The warm sun beats down on my horrified face.

*"Reverto!"*

It doesn't work. I can't feel any power at all.

It's gone, used up. I'm empty.

This hasn't happened in years.

I run down the path, desperate to know the extent of the damage. This isn't like what Tess did, magicking one little corner of the garden. It's everything. Over by the barn, the apple tree is heavy with pink blossoms. The stubble of cut wheat on the hillside waves tall and golden. I pray it hasn't stretched all the way back to the gazebo and the fields beyond.

I explode into the kitchen, slamming the heavy door open.

Tess is here, peering into the oven. "Cate? What is it?"

"I need you," I pant.

She doesn't ask questions. We run into the garden, Tess blinking at the sudden sunshine.

"It was just raining a minute—oh." She looks around at the greenery, then closes her eyes. A moment later, they snap back open, surprised. *"You* did this? By yourself? It's strong. I can't push past it."

I'm too upset to take offense. "Fix it!" I wail.

She pauses a moment, focusing. *"Reverto!"*

It doesn't work. Tess sucks in a breath, displeased. I panic.

What if John sees? What if *Finn* sees? I can't erase his memory again. I won't.

"Tess, we have to do something. There are *tulips*!"

"We'll fix it. We'll do it together," she says. We link hands. I feel a flicker of power as we say the Latin together. The sky goes gray just as the kitchen door flies open.

Maura runs out, Elena right behind her. "Tess, what did you do?" Maura demands.

Tess throws her hands up. "It wasn't me, it was Cate!"

Maura shivers in the cold October wind, wrapping her arms around herself. "It was strong. I tried to fix it from the window and I couldn't."

"Neither could I," Tess observes.

Elena stands back, eyes narrowed, her silk skirts billowing. "Nor could I."

Fear crawls over me. I know what she's thinking. "It was only because I was upset. I didn't mean to cast at all. I was just thinking of spring and—" I fumble for the words, tugging my hood back up over my hair. "It spilled out."

Elena nods. "What were you doing just before this?"

"Nothing," I lie. "Walking in the garden."

Her dark eyes rake over me. I wonder if I look disheveled. "You weren't with Paul?"

Do I look like I've been kissed? Can she tell, somehow? I shrink into my cloak, forcing myself not to touch my lips. "No."

"I don't care about your romance, I care about the magic. Tell me the truth—were you with him just now?" Elena presses.

"No! Why would it affect my magic if I was?"

"Paul left ages ago," Tess says, brushing raindrops from her cheeks. "I saw him out the kitchen window."

"How interesting. I don't know what could have caused it, then." Elena's lips are pressed together, a thin pink slash across her face. Somehow she knows I'm not being entirely honest. But I'll never confide in her about Finn. She may have insinuated herself into our household, but she's not my friend.

I've got to find time to see Marianne—alone, and soon. I need her advice. She's the only one I trust to help me.

I only hope she won't hate me for entangling her son in this mess.

"What do you think?" Maura asks, twirling in front of me in the front hall. She's wearing another new gown. This one is jade green with pink piping, and she's borrowed those green velvet slippers of Elena's that she's been coveting since Elena first arrived.

"Pretty. Where did you get the earbobs?" I ask, arranging an armful of red roses into Great-Grandmother's cut-crystal vase.

"Borrowed them from Elena. Aren't they divine? She's so generous," Maura gushes, fiddling with a jade teardrop.

"I know you admire Elena, but don't you think you're taking it a bit too far?" Maura's hair is teased up into a pretty pompadour with a few little tendrils escaping in front of her ears—just the way Elena wears hers.

Maura's smile slides right off her face. "You can't just say I look pretty and leave it at that, can you? You've got to find something to criticize. I think you're jealous."

Oh, Lord. "Jealous of what?" I ask, stepping back to admire my handiwork.

Maura puts both hands on her hips. "I'm prettier than you."

I look at myself in the warped glass over the hall table: gray eyes, pointed chin, strawberry-blond hair swept up into the braided crown I've come to like. I'm not a beauty; I'm rather ordinary. But Finn likes me. The memory brings a soft smile to my lips, a flush to my cheeks.

"You're much prettier," I admit. "I've never denied that."

"I'm a better witch, too. What happened yesterday in the garden—that was just a fluke," Maura continues.

"Possibly." I poke another rose into the vase. "I don't know what caused it."

"If it'd been me who made the garden explode, you'd never let me forget it. You'd go on about it for weeks. But because it was you, it's forgiven. It was just an accident." Maura's voice is all bitterness. What a time to have this conversation. Mrs. O'Hare and Lily are in the kitchen cutting the crusts off cucumber-and-watercress sandwiches and setting out Tess's cakes. Our guests will be here in a quarter of an hour.

"It *was* just an accident," I point out. "I know full well how dangerous it was. I would never have done that on purpose!"

"Elena thinks it's very odd that your magic was so strong," Maura says, eyeing me suspiciously.

"Well, Elena's a meddling little—"

"I won't hear you say anything bad about her, Cate. She's my friend. And she's an excellent teacher. I've already learned how to do healing spells. It's a nice change, having someone who actually encourages me. She likes me."

I roll my eyes. "I like you. You're my sister, Maura, I love you."

"It's not the same! You don't treat me like a person. You're always so dismissive. Even now, you're barely paying attention to me." I stop fussing with the flowers and look at her. "When you do pay attention, it's only to scold. You never want me to practice magic, even though you know I love it. You don't even want me to join the Sisterhood. You'd rather have me marry some awful old man I didn't love than be happy!"

I pull her down the hall, away from the kitchen and anyone who might overhear us. "That's not true. Of course I want you to be happy."

"Prove it then." Maura's blue eyes are calculating. "I don't need your permission, but I'd like your blessing. Give me your blessing to join the Sisters."

Did Elena put her up to this? I can't give her my blessing. Not without knowing the full meaning of the prophecy. If the Sisterhood were our best option—if it were that simple—Mother would have told me so plainly. "Is that really what you want?"

Maura nods furiously. "It is. I'm not a child, Cate, I know my own mind. I want to study magic in New London."

"But what about marriage? And children? Would you give all that up?"

She looks down and fiddles with the gold bracelet on her wrist. "I don't want to get married."

"It might be different, if it was a man you loved," I point out, thinking of Finn. Not that that's new—I've been thinking of him all day in scattered quiet moments: while Elena corrected my French, while I took out stitches in my embroidered pillowcases, while Mrs. O'Hare scolded me for my half-eaten breakfast. Somehow, in just a few weeks, he's become the stuff of my daydreams.

"That's not what I want," Maura says flatly, running a hand along the curved wooden balustrade at the foot of the stairs.

"I didn't think it was what I wanted, either. I've changed my mind."

Maura frowns. "So you are going to marry Paul, then. Did you even consider joining the Sisters? You're determined to keep the three of us together, but only if it's the way *you* want! You'd have me give up my dreams, without you sacrificing a thing!"

"I didn't say I was—" I protest, but she's already stomping upstairs, presumably to Elena's room. I sit on the bottom stair and bury my head in my hands.

There's a swish of skirts behind me. "Excuse me," Elena says, squeezing past. "Did you and Maura have a row? She's in her room slamming things about."

I raise my head. Elena's rearranging my roses.

"Why can't you just leave things alone?" I snarl, stalking toward the kitchen. "We don't need you. We were fine before you came!"

Mrs. Corbett is the first guest to arrive. Lily takes her cloak while I draw her into the sitting room. She settles her wide bulk on the cream-tufted sofa, and I fetch her a cup of tea and a few of Tess's lemon poppy-seed cakes.

"How is our dear Elena working out?" Mrs. Corbett asks. "I do hope you're making her feel at home."

"Oh, she's made herself indispensable. We couldn't have managed any of this without her." It's true. Elena chose the gowns we're wearing, decided on the menu, drilled us on proper etiquette, and instructed us at which houses to leave calling cards with our names and new at-home afternoon. I ought to be grateful. Instead, it only makes me resent her more.

"I knew she would be the perfect fit. Not as sophisticated as her previous pupils, I told her, but you needed her more. I can tell a difference in you girls already. You looked so smart at services—and just look how well turned out you are today," Mrs. Corbett says, glancing up as the Winfields arrive. She acts as though we went around in trousers before Elena! "It's marvelous, the changes she's wrought in you. Give her a few more weeks and you'll be almost unrecognizable."

"Er—thank you." The smile pasted on my face never wobbles. Where's Maura? She's the one who thinks Elena hung the moon in the sky; she ought to be the one stuck singing her praises. But no, she and Tess are pouring tea and lemonade for the other guests, leaving me trapped on the sofa with this old battle-ax.

"I'm glad to hear things are going smoothly. I would so hate to have to trouble your father with any unfavorable reports," Mrs. Corbett hums.

Her threats set my teeth on edge. She *would* write him and tattle; it's just like her.

"Tess has been writing Father. I daresay he'll be pleased with our progress. You were right, Mrs. Corbett. It's high time Maura and I were out. Past time, truly. I don't know what I was fretting over. Everyone's been so kind. Particularly Mrs. Ishida. Maura and I were delighted to be invited to tea." It's prideful, but I can't help myself. I've heard Mrs. Corbett is never invited to the Brothers' wives' functions.

"Ye—es." Mrs. Corbett blinks slowly, like a lizard in the sun. "I noticed that you and Miss Ishida have become particular friends."

"Sachi's marvelous. I take her as a model of what a proper young lady ought to be." I shoot a desperate glance toward the door, wishing Sachi would come and rescue me.

"Your father couldn't ask you to keep better company. Miss Ishida is above reproach," Mrs. Corbett agrees. But her eyes rove over me like tiny, suspicious brown spiders, as though she's just praying to find something wrong.

Have I overdone it? Perhaps I ought to be less cloyingly agreeable.

Mrs. Corbett glances up at the family portraits above the fireplace. "Have you made any decisions about your intention? I saw you speaking with Paul McLeod at church. The McLeods are a good family. Respected."

Paul. I've hardly thought of him all day. "I haven't made any decisions yet," I murmur.

"Cate!" Sachi swoops in. She's wearing a diamond comb in her hair and a bright turquoise dress. "Good afternoon, Mrs. Corbett. You're looking well. Excuse us, won't you?"

She whirls me out into the hall and collapses into giggles. "The look on your face! Like someone was plucking out your eyelashes!"

I scowl, leaning against the banister of the staircase. "She's an interfering old toad."

Sachi casts a look over her shoulder. "Never liked her much myself. Wearing all that black like a big carrion bird. It's carrying mourning a bit far, don't you think? Her husband died four years ago. And always going on about Regina this, Regina that. Regina Corbett's nothing but a—"

"Cabbagehead," I pronounce gleefully.

"Indeed," Sachi agrees. We pause to greet Mrs. Ralston and Mrs. Malcolm as Maura ushers them into the dining room. "So. Have you found any books for us yet?"

"I haven't been able to get away, but I asked Mrs. Belastra to bring one with her."

Sachi arches her eyebrows. "You invited her here? Today?"

"I did. Why?" I tamp down the rush of defensiveness.

"She's a shopkeeper, Cate."

"That's snobbery."

"No, it's fact," Sachi says, leaning down to smell the roses. "The other ladies will cut her. Everyone will whisper behind her back, and she'll be miserable. Did you invite Angeline Kosmoski and her mother? Or Elinor Evans?"

The dressmaker's daughter and the chocolatier's. "No."

"No, of course you wouldn't, and Marianne Belastra is less respectable than any of them. You know the Brothers have it in for her. My father loathes the idea of all that information just sitting there in her shop, available to anyone."

"People would still buy books without Belastras'. They'd order them from New London."

"People with money, perhaps. And then they'd have to come through the post. Father has a source at the post office. Old man Carruthers reports on forbidden materials."

"He goes through people's mail?" My eyes widen, momentarily diverted. "Imagine all the gossip he must have!"

Sachi glances into the sitting room, where her mother is holding court, her green silk fan waving briskly. "My point is, you're taking a risk. It's one thing to drop by the bookshop. People will assume you're running errands for your father. If you associate with Mrs. Belastra socially, people will talk."

I don't like it, but I'm practical enough to recognize the truth when I hear it. It's just what Finn was warning me about. A love match might be romantic in Maura's novels, but not here. Not involving a family with two strikes against them—their poverty and their willingness to go against the Brothers.

If I married Finn, it would put my sisters in danger.

But am I strong enough to give him up?

All day I've been turning the problem over in my head like a mathematics equation. I wish it were possible, but I don't see how I could marry him, no matter how much I want it. Want *him*. A nervous blush sweeps over me. I've never thought of what goes on between man and wife before, but now—I can't help but wonder what it would be like to share Finn's bed.

Sachi elbows me. "That's a secretive look. Do tell."

I hesitate, caught. I do need advice. Both times my magic's run amok lately, it's been because of Finn. Because of kissing Finn, to be more precise. Is that a normal thing for magic to do? The only person who would know is another witch, and I certainly can't ask Elena. But I can't ask Sachi either—not here, not with half the town coming and going.

I pitch my voice low. "I can't tell you here."

Sachi leans in. She smells of powder and lemon verbena.

I shrink back against the wooden banister of the staircase, blushing hotter. "My magic has been—unwieldy. In certain—situations. Certain company."

Sachi smooths her black hair. "What kind of company?"

"Men. Well. One man," I amend.

"Intriguing. I'll bring Rory, that's her specialty," Sachi giggles.

"Do you have to? I'd rather keep this private." I look nervously at the cluster of ladies in the sitting room, sipping tea, nibbling on Tess's lemon poppy-seed cakes. Rory stands out in her orange dress, prowling like a restless tiger from group to group.

"I daresay you would. But I'm hardly an expert. Do you want help or not? If it's got to do with a man, Rory will know."

"I do want help. But Rory—well, she is a bit—flighty. Can I trust her?"

Sachi purses her lips. "You trust me, don't you?" I nod. "Then I give you my word on Rory. Can you meet us Friday night? Late?"

I'm no coward, but I don't relish the thought of traipsing into town alone in the dark. "I thought—can't we meet at Rory's tomorrow?"

Sachi tosses a demure smile at Mrs. Collier and Rose as they come through the door. "Mrs. Elliott fired Elizabeth. The new girl's a busybody. We'll get rid of her, but it might be a few days until we have the house to ourselves again. If you want to wait—"

"No." I can't afford another mishap. And I can't bear the thought of avoiding Finn. "Sooner is better."

"We could meet somewhere on your property. If you're not afraid to go out after dark, that is." Sachi smirks.

I can't trust the rose garden anymore, not with Elena creeping around like a ghoul. There's one place that might work. It's not a place I relish going, not even in broad daylight, but what choice do I have?

"On the other side of the pond, there's a graveyard. I'll meet you there Friday night. If you come across the fields, no one can see you from the house."

Sachi's lips twitch. "Witching hour in a cemetery. It's the perfect place for our little coven's first meeting."

Half an hour later, I'm in the process of being bored to death by Rose Collier. She's inclined to proclaim everything "darling" in the same way Mrs. Ishida employs "lovely"—my gown, Tess's pumpkin bread, the paper on the sitting room walls. We soon resort to making observations about the weather. It's a fine day, perfect Indian summer, unusual for October in New England; I've never seen such a blue sky; and oh yes, I'm quite glad we thought to serve lemonade as well as tea.

I'm watching a lone housefly buzz against the window when Rose lets out a little hum of disapproval. "Shouldn't she go to the kitchen with her delivery?"

Marianne Belastra hovers in the doorway, looking as uncomfortable as Sachi predicted. She wears a high-necked, rust-colored gown with an out-of-fashion bustle and straight sleeves. The color and style flatter neither her complexion nor her figure.

"Look, she's brought her odd little duckling with her. That child's shooting up like a weed, Mama says. You'd think she'd be ashamed to traipse around in public with her ankles showing. What kind of mama would allow it? But Mrs. Belastra doesn't care for anything except her books, I suppose."

Rose's voice is full of feigned pity. She clearly expects me to respond in kind. But my heart clenches at the sight of Clara, trailing awkwardly after her mother, dressed in a brown pinafore that's too childish and too short.

I peer into the dining room at Tess. She's expertly pouring tea, engaging the matrons in effortless conversation, acting as though their gossip is as fascinating to her as Ovid. She's a pretty girl with none of Clara's awkward growing pains, but just a few weeks ago she would have been strange and unfashionable, too. Elena's lessons have given Tess poise; her orders at the dress shop have turned us all from odd ducks into swans. Whatever her faults, Elena has taught us to blend in.

No one rises to greet the Belastras. Teacups pause midair as rattlesnake whispers slither through the room. Clara stares at her feet, her face going a blotchy red beneath her freckles, her dark eyes hooded with misery. It's plain she'd rather be somewhere else. Anywhere.

And here I thought I was doing them a kindness.

"Mrs. Belastra, thank you so much for coming." My voice rings out clear as the brass church bells. "We're delighted to have you both. Would you like some tea? Clara, let me present my sister Tess; she's just your age."

The running patter feels stilted on my tongue, but I think I carry it off passably. This is Finn's sister. I can't let her stand here, defenseless, while these stupid women snub her and call her names.

I usher the Belastras into the dining room as though they are our special guests, pouring tea for them, urging them to try

Tess's desserts. I want to pull Marianne aside and ask her for advice, but I can't be seen whispering with her here. And with magic off-limits, I have no idea what to say to Finn's mother. I feel irrationally terrified that she can read my thoughts and know I've been thinking of her son in wanton, lustful ways.

Fortunately, Tess is much less awkward. She sizes the situation up in an instant.

"Do you bake, Miss Belastra? I made the poppy-seed cakes myself."

Clever Tess. I cast an admiring glance at her. She knows the Belastras can't afford a housekeeper, and with Mrs. Belastra in the shop all day, it's likely Clara does most of their cooking. Acknowledging that she spends time in the kitchen too puts them on more equal footing. Clara confesses to a mishap with a crust, and soon they're giggling and chattering like magpies.

I wish I had some of Tess's skill. I ask Marianne how business is going, and she tells me about a shipment of Brotherhood-sanctioned morality tales for children that have come in. When I ask what she's reading herself—a question Tess always adores—she enthuses about a French poet she's just discovered.

I fiddle with the pink and red roses on the table and glance back into the sitting room. Around the piano, Maura is chatting gaily with Cristina Winfield and a few other girls from town, and Sachi and Rory are whispering together on the settee. All normal enough. But several of the Brothers' wives and Mrs. Corbett are clustered around the sofa, and I wonder what they're discussing. Have we made some misstep? Is everything up to standard?

"This is a coming-out of sorts for you, isn't it?" Marianne asks, startling me from my reverie. "You ought to get back to your true guests."

I look up in surprise, ashamed to have been caught wool-gathering. "You and Clara are as much our guests as anyone."

"It was sweet of you to invite us, Cate, but you're a sensible girl. Associating with my family has no advantages for you. You must realize that."

I do, but somehow all my good sense flies out the window when I think of her son.

Has Finn told her about us? I wince at the thought. She and my mother were friends, but that doesn't mean she'd want her son to marry a witch.

Her no-nonsense tone is just like his. *I'm not too proud to say it.* The difference in our stations does matter. Not to me, perhaps, but in the eyes of everyone else. We Cahill girls may have our secrets, but money helps us hide them. We don't have to live right in town; we don't depend on our neighbors' custom for our livelihood. Father may not approve of the Brothers' censorship, but he keeps on their good side, and they don't come searching the house for banned books. It's not perfect, but it's easier for us than it is for Clara Belastra.

"I'll be fine," Marianne assures me, misunderstanding my silence. "I've long since made peace with my place in this town. Go. Enjoy your tea."

Shame rises in my stomach, but I go.

chapter

# 16

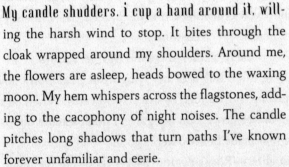

My candle shudders. i cup a hand around it, willing the harsh wind to stop. It bites through the cloak wrapped around my shoulders. Around me, the flowers are asleep, heads bowed to the waxing moon. My hem whispers across the flagstones, adding to the cacophony of night noises. The candle pitches long shadows that turn paths I've known forever unfamiliar and eerie.

Something brushes my hair. I jump back, hand flying to my face. It's only a crumpled leaf twirling to the ground. I laugh, small and shaky, and taste smoke in the back of my throat. The fires are banked for the night, but gray plumes drift like ghosts above the chimneys. Wind knifes in at my wrists and ankles. I pull my cloak tighter and walk faster.

The gazebo looms monstrously at the top of the hill. This is the most dangerous part, when I'll be visible from the servants' quarters. I pray that Mrs. O'Hare and John have no cause to be up and looking out windows.

I take a deep breath and dash forward. It's only a few yards before the candle snuffs out. Lord, but it's dark.

Up ahead, I hear the lapping of pond water against the bank and smell dank, earthy mud. It's soothing, a familiar sound amid the strange hooting of night birds. I listen harder and make out feminine voices drifting across the water. In the cemetery, shades dance among the headstones.

They're there, gathered behind Mother's tomb.

I hate the thought of her lying inside, her body slowly decomposing, surrounded by insects and earth. When he's home, Father leaves flowers on her grave. I don't see the point. Everything that made her Mother is gone.

Laughter—Rory's distinct bark—echoes in the night.

"Hello?" My voice comes out hoarse.

Sachi steps out from behind the tomb. "Cate?" Her lantern throws strange shadows, turning her pretty features monstrous.

"Spooky, isn't it? Would you like some sherry?" Rory asks, holding out a bottle.

A tall, thin figure peers around the tomb, her hood obscuring her face. There's only one other person they might bring on such a mad, macabre adventure.

"Brenna?"

Brenna twirls around the graveyard like a child, sidestepping the little tombs next to Mother's. She's singing to herself:

*"Days we spend planting flowers,*

*Nights spent warm in our beds,*
*Lives of sunshine and showers,*
*We're all food for worms in the end."*

Appropriate for the setting, I suppose, but hardly comforting.

"Rory wanted to bring her." Sachi does not sound pleased. "And she knows about us."

I whirl on her, angry. "You told her?"

"*I* didn't tell her anything." Sachi's voice is tight.

"Nor did I! She just knows things," Rory explains, tugging Brenna back to us. "That's why they took her away."

"She's mad," Sachi argues, crossing her arms over her chest. "They took her away because she told your stepfather he was going to die."

"But I *do* know things." Brenna's voice is mournful. "If only I could remember them."

"What don't you remember?" I ask. It's a foolish question— how can she know?—but Brenna takes it seriously.

"Holes in my head," she explains, tapping her temple. "The crows put them there."

"Crows?" I ask. Sachi shrugs.

Brenna shudders back against the marble tomb. She squeezes her eyes shut, like a child trying to shut out a nightmare, and wraps her arms around herself. "They came to my trial," she whispers. "The Brothers left me alone with them. I was so frightened. I thought they would peck out my eyes, but they only took my memories."

"When she came home from Harwood, she didn't remember any of us at first. She'd only talk to Jake," Rory says. Jacob is Brenna's brother, a gentle tower of a boy.

"M-mustn't ask questions," Brenna stutters. "You'll be punished!"

Another shiver presses along my spine, but this one has nothing to do with the cold and everything to do with Brenna's creepy chatter.

"That's enough. Keep her quiet," Sachi orders. "We didn't come all the way out here to listen to her nonsense. Cate has something to tell us."

"Hush," Rory says, putting an arm around Brenna. Brenna is several inches taller, but she bends like a reed, all the energy draining out of her. "Sit."

They all crouch on the cold marble dais around Mother's tomb. Brenna stares into the darkness, her eyes unfocused. Sachi draws her knees into her chest and buries her face in her cloak. Only Rory seems unaffected by the cold, bouncing in her seat like a child.

Now that the moment's here, I feel awkward.

What happened in the secret room—and then again at the gazebo—it's private. What should I say? That now I've seen how brave and loyal and handsome Finn is, I can't un-see it? That his kisses make me reckless? That I can't bear the idea of giving him up, even if marrying Paul would protect our reputations? I need to know how to keep control of the magic, even when I don't feel entirely in control of my own heart.

I only wanted to ask Sachi, not an audience of three. But I need answers.

I kneel on the cold grass, the dew soaking through my cloak. "Twice now, I've cast without intending to. On Monday it was powerful—much more so than usual. I couldn't reverse the spell by myself."

"What were you doing right before?" Sachi asks. One long black braid falls over her shoulder. "When I first started manifesting, strong emotions made my magic go awry. There were some very close calls around my father."

"Ah. Well. I—actually, I was—" How does a lady admit to lustfulness?

Brenna laughs softly, and I want to crawl behind the tombstone with mortification.

"Stop it," Sachi says, swatting her on the shoulder.

"Don't touch me," Brenna hisses, leaping up. She scales the tomb behind us, perching at the top like an eerie gargoyle.

"Oh, good Lord," Sachi says. "Brenna, come down from there. It's disrespectful."

"I can hear very well now," Brenna calls. "Go on! Tell us more about the kissing!"

"How—?" I turn to Rory, amazed.

"I told you, she knows things. Besides, you said it had to do with a man." Rory gives me her rabbity smile. "He looks as though he'd be quite good at it."

"He does?" Of course I find Finn handsome—devastatingly, distractingly so. But somehow I didn't imagine that he'd be the sort Rory would—

"Oh yes. I've never kissed anyone with a mustache," Rory admits, her face perplexed. "I don't suppose I'll ever have the chance now. Does it tickle?"

A mustache? But Finn doesn't have a mustache.

It wallops me over the head. Paul did. She thinks I'm talking about Paul. They've seen him flirt with me and ferry me home from services. They've heard the gossip. He's hardly been subtle.

It's easy enough to let them think it. I'm not ashamed of Finn. I don't care whether Sachi approves of the Belastras or not. But I don't see any point in correcting their assumption.

"Rory! Don't jump to conclusions," Sachi scolds. "Not everyone is as shameless as you."

Above us, Brenna sings tunelessly, kicking her legs.

"No, it's true. That's what prompted it. Both times," I admit.

"More than once, was it?" Rory crows.

My face flushes, but I plow on. "Both times, I felt—well, I felt—"

"Lustful," Rory says. "Wanton. Shameless!"

I flush hotter. "My feelings were—quite intense. I imagine that's why the magic went wrong. But I can't risk that happening again. How do you control it?"

Rory takes another long sip of sherry. "I don't," she says.

I throw my dignity to the wind. "Tell me, Rory, please."

Rory scowls, her dark eyes defiant. "I don't know how to control it and I don't particularly care to learn."

"What do you mean? Doesn't Nils notice? He could tell his father and have you arrested!"

"Nils is generally more focused on other things." Rory smirks. "Sometimes I cast without meaning to, like you said. But more often my magic goes dormant, and I can't cast for hours after we lie together."

I didn't expect that Rory's courtship with Nils was entirely chaste—after all, that's why I sought out her advice—but I'm still shocked that they lie together. I've heard of girls who've gotten with child and been forced to stand before the Brothers in their shame. I pluck a blade of grass and twirl it through my fingers. What would it be like to lie with a man? I think of the freckles spread over the muscles of Finn's forearms, over his calves, on the back of his neck, and wonder what it would be like to see more of him. All of him.

"Love-drunk," Sachi says scornfully, eyeing the bottle in Rory's hand. "Except, of course, you don't actually love Nils."

Rory glares and tilts the bottle to her mouth. She holds it there, her throat working until it's empty, then tosses it aside. It knocks against one of the small gravestones next to Mother's. "Do you hear the frogs, Brenna? I'm going to go look for them."

Brenna leaps down to follow her cousin. As she passes us, she gives Sachi a fearsome look. "You'll be the one to ruin Rory."

Sachi jumps to her feet, furious. "What do you know? You're mad as a March hare!"

"I know too much," Brenna says, her throaty voice sad. "They'll kill me for it."

The hair rises on the back of my neck. Sachi and I exchange wide-eyed glances. I summon up my courage. "Wait," I say, and Brenna stops trudging toward the gate. "Did you see my godmother? Zara. Was she in Harwood with you?"

Brenna nods, her hands tugging at her hair in distress.

"Can you truly see the future?" I ask. "Do you know what I should do?"

"Yes—and no. I'm broken." Brenna heaves a great, mournful sigh. But she paces back to me, standing very close—so close I can smell the sherry on her breath. My palms tingle. Am I really asking advice from a mad, drunk oracle? She peers down at me with her strange eyes. "You're lucky. He loves you. But the crows—oh, the crows don't care for love. No. It's always duty with them, isn't it?"

"That doesn't make any sense," Sachi mutters.

Brenna reaches out and grabs the front of my cloak in both hands. Her voice is urgent. "You can stop it. But not without a sacrifice."

I trip away from her, sprawling on one of the baby headstones.

Brenna runs off, and Sachi pulls me back to my feet. "There are not many things in life that frighten me, but she's one of them. I wish Rory would stay away from her."

I lean down and pick up the discarded bottle. I don't believe that Mother's spirit lingers here, but leaving trash is disrespectful to the dead.

"Will Rory be all right?" I ask, concerned. Between the liquor and Nils and her magic, she's taking far too many chances.

"At the pond or in general?" Sachi sighs. "She'd never do anything to hurt any of us, if that's what worries you. Only herself."

"Why?" I sit next to Sachi on the tomb. The marble is cold under my thighs.

"She hates the magic. Nothing I say seems to make any difference. She's so blasted careless," Sachi swears. "It's almost as though she wants to get arrested. Father looks the other way where she's concerned, but for how long? Even his nepotism can stretch only so far."

I wish I were more like Tess. I don't know the right thing to do, to say. I never imagined I'd be sitting in a graveyard at midnight, listening to Sachi Ishida pour her heart out. I know that mix of love and worry well. It's just how I sound when—

My eyes pop. *Nepotism.* Vocabulary has never been my strong suit, but if it means what I believe it means—

"Oh. She's your sister? Your father—"

Sachi curls into herself, a small dark figure against the white marble tomb. "You mustn't tell."

I think of Mrs. Clay, the woman from the registry who accused Brother Ishida of adultery. "Of course not."

Sachi grips my knee. "No one can know. No one. Rory doesn't know it herself."

I look at her solemnly. "No one. I swear it."

"I've never told anyone else. I've wanted to—I almost did tell her once. After they took Brenna away. The notion of her being sent to Harwood—I couldn't bear it."

That, I understand. "What made you decide against it?"

"I was afraid she'd do something rash. She drinks too much. Usually she just gets sleepy, you know, and a bit silly. But I was afraid she might confront Father."

"How long have you known?" I trace the letters carved on Mother's tomb: *beloved wife and devoted mother.*

"Since we were ten." Sachi passes her hand over her face. Six years. Lord, how exhausting it must have been, keeping a secret like this for so long. "Her mother came to the door and insisted on seeing Father. She was drunk, but not so drunk she didn't make sense. She wanted money, and she laid out very plainly why he ought to give it to her."

"Why didn't he arrest her?"

Sachi squints, trying to make out Rory and Brenna crouched

on the bank of the pond. "Because of Rory, I suppose. Father's a hypocrite and a coward, but he wouldn't want his bastard raised in an orphanage. And there was a scandal before. Another woman. He had her tried and sent away. I don't think he could risk it again. It wouldn't serve his standing in the community," she mocks.

I reach out and squeeze Sachi's gloved hand.

"I've always wanted a sister," she says. "I didn't know she'd be so broken."

There have certainly been days when I've wished Maura were easier to manage. But then she wouldn't be Maura, would she? Who else would act out the plots of romance novels I'll never read? Who else would sing bawdy songs, push the furniture to the walls, and dance across the sitting room with me?

I look over at the five small headstones, my gaze lingering on the last one. Danielle. She would be three now: a toddler running pell-mell through the house. What would it have been like if she'd survived? If Father had had a baby to care for, would he have stayed home more, or would he have remarried and foisted us off onto someone else?

"We don't get to choose who we love. Or stop loving them when they're difficult."

"No." Sachi sighs, swiveling toward me. "I knew you would understand."

She stares at me expectantly. A cloud passes over the moon, shrouding us in darkness, and I watch the warm orange flicker of the lantern. I don't know what she wants me to say. Just because she confided in me, am I obliged to return the favor? I don't know how female friendships work. The trading of confidences— is that expected?

"It's not Paul I've been kissing," I say finally. "It should be. He asked me to marry him. It's Finn Belastra."

Sachi laughs. "The bookseller? Isn't he a bit—"

"If you say he's beneath me, I'll slap you."

"I was going to say serious. He looks quite serious!" she protests. "I can't believe you've been keeping this all to yourself. What are you going to do?"

I lean back against the tombstone, groaning. "I don't know. It's down to nine weeks now. Five before your father would give me to Brother Anders."

Sachi shudders. "That's revolting."

"I know. But I can't marry Paul when I'm in love with someone else."

Sachi grabs me by the shoulder. "Yes, you can. To save yourself, you can. Do you think I love Renjiro?" She laughs, and it's Rory's laugh, bitter and humorless. "I do not. He's an idiot. But we do what we have to do, and it could be worse."

We could be in Harwood. We sit together in glum silence. "I suppose so."

"You have a lot of secrets, Cate Cahill. That wasn't what I expected you to tell me," Sachi says.

I bite my lip. "What do you mean?"

"Your sisters. One of them is a witch," Sachi prompts me.

"No." I pull my cape more tightly around me. "What makes you think that?"

"You said your magic went awry and you couldn't reverse it yourself. You didn't come to Rory or me. You'd only go to another witch. Who else is there?"

My mind whirrs frantically, trying to come up with a pat

explanation. No matter how friendly and open Sachi's been, she's still Brother Ishida's daughter. It's one thing to tell her my own secrets. That can't hurt anyone but me.

There's a great splash, a mad cackle, and then Rory's plaintive voice. "Sachi!"

I jump to my feet, relieved at the interruption. "The pond is freezing. She'll catch her death."

Sachi pulls her cloak tighter around her shoulders. "You don't have to tell me now. But I want you to know you can trust me, Cate. If you ever need me, I'll help. So long as it doesn't put Rory in danger."

"Thank you. I'll keep that in mind," I say.

But I hope I won't need her help.

That night, I dream I'm at one of Mrs. Ishida's teas. In the dream, I'm wearing Marianne Belastra's awful rust-colored dress. It's starched and it itches. Whenever I move, the skirts rustle, loud as a fire crackling, and everyone looks at me. Sachi and Rory bend their dark heads together and whisper behind their hands, and I just know it's me they're whispering about.

What have I done wrong? I feel suffocated—by their stares, by the high ruffled collar of this dress. My hands fumble at the buttons but I'm too rough; one button falls off in my hand. It's gray; it doesn't even match. Is that why they're laughing at me?

That button—it's familiar somehow.

I fight my way back to consciousness, gasping for breath. The gray button. It was beneath the floorboards with Mother's diary.

I leap out of bed. The light coming through the windows is weak and watery; the gray sky is streaked with palest pink. It's been only a handful of hours since I went to sleep. I inch the door open and pad barefoot down the hall in my chemise. Around me, the house is silent.

The button is still where I left it, in the right-hand drawer of Mother's writing desk. Small, plain, unprepossessing.

I weigh it in the palm of my hand. Now that I know what I'm looking for, I can feel the magic in it, pulsing strong and steady as a heartbeat. Does that mean my magic is stronger now than Mother's?

*"Acclaro."*

The button reveals itself as a note, folded twice over and sealed with wax.

Mother used her best blue stationery. The handwriting isn't the dark, frantic scrawl at the end of her diary. This was written before—deliberately. Thoughtfully.

Why didn't she give it to me sooner?

My hands shake as I begin to read.

*Dearest Cate—*

*If you have found this, I am gone. Have you read my diary? If not, you will find it nearby. That is the place to start.*

*I do not know how to tell you this . . . I am not as brave as you, my dear girl, but you must know it. You must know it and do everything in your power to guard against it.*

*If Tess is a witch, then the three of you may well be the three sisters of the oracle's last prophecy. The prophecy foretells that one of the sisters will be the most powerful witch born in centuries—powerful enough to bring about the resurgence of the Daughters of Persephone or, if she falls to the Brotherhood, bring about a second Terror. But only two of the sisters will survive to see the twentieth century— because one sister will kill another.*

*My heart breaks to think it—I cannot imagine such a thing. All sisters have their petty arguments and jealousies, but I have seen how you and your sisters love one another. Yet your godmother spent years researching the oracles, and she found no fallacies. The prophecies of Persephone's oracles always come to pass.*

*You must find a way to prevent this, Cate.*

I stop reading, though there is more.

I go back and reread my mother's words, sure I've misunderstood.

No, it says it quite plainly: *one sister will kill another.*

It can't be me and Maura and Tess, then. I might want to slap them sometimes, Maura especially, but I would never harm them. Never.

I keep reading.

*If Tess has manifested, I imagine the Sisters are watching the three of you closely. Mind-magic is a rare gift. If they discover that you possess it, they will want you to join their fight against the Brotherhood. They can offer you many things—protection and education among them. But they don't think of individuals, only the legacy of magic.*

*I do not regret many things in my life, Cate, but I used mind-magic at the Sisters' behest when I was at their school, and I do not believe it was warranted or right. I used it again to escape that life, and I have never forgiven myself. It is wrong to go into the minds of others without their consent. I have tried to instill in you the belief that it must be used only under direst circumstances. The Sisters would have us wield it freely to regain the witches' power. Their goals are worthy, but their methods can be suspect.*

*I would not have you forced into a war you did not choose, but with your gifts, I fear it is inevitable.*

*Be careful, Cate. Choose wisely. Protect your sisters.*

*Love always,*

*Mother*

By the time I finish, I'm hunched over on the floor, my knees tucked to my chest. Bile rises in my throat, and I force it back down. It leaves my mouth dry and sour.

Now I remember Elena's warning that making Maura angry was tempting fate. She promised to do everything she could to keep all three of us safe—but the way she said it, with doubt in her voice—and the way she looked at me when she said it, her brown eyes filled with pity—

Brenna's haunting voice: *You can stop it. But not without a sacrifice.*

Mother believed in the prophecy. Elena believes it. The Sisterhood believes it.

How will I stop it?

I retreat to the safety of my room, Mother's letter crumpled in my hand. I open the curtains and sit on her old velvet settee and inhale the very faint scent of rose water that still permeates it. I watch the sun rise, salmon and pink, over the hill. I listen to the bright twitter-songs of birds and the sounds of the house waking up around me. I think of what to do.

The Sisters will do what's best for the Daughters of Persephone, not what's best for the Cahill girls. Mother's letter made that painfully clear. But how can I keep us out of their clutches?

I don't want girls throughout New England to grow up frightened and powerless. But my first priority is my promise to Mother. First and foremost, I must keep my own sisters safe.

When I go downstairs for breakfast, I find Elena lurking in the hall. She gives me a serrated smile. "I was waiting for you."

"Why?" I demand gracelessly.

"It's time to tell me the truth. Can you do mind-magic, Cate?"

I fight the urge to back away. Instead, I draw myself up to my full height, looming over her. "I told you, I don't know."

Elena's brown eyes bore into mine. "I don't believe you."

I glare down at her. "Are you calling me a liar?"

She sidesteps the question, fiddling with one jade teardrop earring. Her dress is pink with mint-green piping today. "I think you're frightened. I couldn't break your glamour in the garden. Neither could your sisters. A witch that powerful would be welcomed—celebrated—by the Sisters. You're too powerful to fritter away your talents like this."

"What happened in the garden was a fluke." I avoid her eyes, looking into the gilt-edged mirror above the hall table. My face is paler than usual, with enormous purple shadows beneath my eyes.

"Was it?" Elena lays a hand on my arm, her smooth brown skin a contrast against the icy blue of my dress. "I know one of you can do mind-magic, Cate."

I pull away under the pretext of fussing with my hair. "I don't see how that could possibly be true."

"Your father's got some very interesting holes in his memory," she says.

I freeze. How could she know that? "My mother could do mind-magic."

"But these gaps are from *after* her death. He doesn't seem to have any memory of Mrs. Corbett suggesting that you go to the

Sisters' convent school," Elena says. "Funny, that. Who would have used such dark magic to keep you all together?"

Mrs. Corbett, that wretched old bat. I don't know why I'm surprised. I ought to be thankful she hasn't turned us in to the Brothers.

"Tess would have been only, what, nine at the time? Ten? That's too young for her magic to have manifested. That leaves you or Maura, and if Maura knew she could do mind-magic, she would have told me. So we're back to you." Elena's reflection gazes at me from the mirror. "I have an obligation to the Sisters. I don't think Maura is the one they want, but if you won't co-operate with me, I daresay she will. She's eager to go off to New London. She'd leave today if I suggested it—especially if she found out how many secrets you've been keeping.

"I'm quite fond of Maura," she continues slowly. Her chocolate eyes never leave mine. "I wouldn't want to see her come to any harm. Unfortunately, those who run the Sisterhood—they subscribe to some rather Machiavellian notions. They wouldn't harm her irreparably, but they aren't above using her as bait."

I whirl around, my heart pounding like a drum. Enough. "Leave Maura alone. It's me. I'm the one you want."

Elena peers up at me. "I'll need you to prove it. I can't trust you, Cate. I believe that you'd lie to me, even now."

I ball my hands into fists. "You pretend to be her friend, but you don't care about her. The only thing you care about is the damned Sisterhood."

Elena's hand twitches up, as though she's tempted to slap me. "*I'm* not the one putting her in danger—you are. If you'd just cooperate—"

My nails cut crescent moons in the center of my palms. "What do you want me to do?"

Elena's smile is serpentine and triumphant. "You can start by meeting me this afternoon for a lesson in mind-magic. Half past two, in the rose garden."

"Half past two," I agree, cursing her. "And if I prove that I can do it, you'll leave Maura and Tess out of this?"

"Insofar as it's in my control, yes," she agrees, cagey as always. "If you prove that you're the prophesied sister, and if you agree to join the Sisterhood and play your role in the prophecy, we'll keep them safe for you."

It's not much of a promise, but it's better than nothing.

"Fine," I snap. What choice do I have?

I tell Mrs. O'Hare I won't be having breakfast. I can't stand to see the smug look on Elena's face—not without hurling the china at her. I grab an apple from the kitchen on my way out the back door. All around me, the autumn air is as crisp as the apple. Fallen leaves drift across the path, crunching beneath my boots.

I stop beside a bed of blowsy white roses. Their plot needs a weeding. I listen for the sound of hammering up at the gazebo, but I suppose it's too early for Finn yet. My shoulders slump. Perhaps it's just as well.

Giving him up would be a heavy sacrifice—is that what Brenna foresaw? It's far more than anything Mother asked of me. I know a life with him would require sacrifices, too—learning to cook, to sew, to make do with twice-turned dresses. But if I could be with him, living in the Belastras' cramped flat would be like heaven. I could still see my sisters, still practice magic with Sachi and Rory, still visit my garden when I needed to get away from town and all its gossiping tongues.

New London is so very far away.

But if it would keep my sisters safe—what I want can no longer matter.

I drop to my knees, wrap my hand around the stem of a stubborn weed, and yank. Five minutes later, there's a pile on the path next to me. The plot looks much better, and I feel a good deal calmer. I glance at the next plot over—wine-dark roses in front of the Cupid fountain, just beginning to bud again. They could use some attention, too. I scoot over, humming to myself and smoothing the rumpled soil.

A shadow falls over me. "Stealing my job out from under me?"

My heart beats faster at the sound of his voice. "You can help if you'd like."

Finn kneels next to me, keeping a careful distance. We're in full view of the kitchen window. "You wouldn't mind the company?"

I smile at him, besotted. At his cherry lips and freckles and warm brown eyes. "Not yours."

"You love this, don't you?" he asks, gesturing at the flowers. "Not just the pretty result, but the work."

"I do." Mrs. O'Hare is always fussing at me about it. I never remember my gloves, and she's always going on about ruining my hands and getting dirt under my nails. Personally, I do not see how a little dirt hurts anyone. "I find it satisfying, leaving things better off than when I started. And I don't like being cooped up inside."

"I see that." He rubs the pad of his thumb across my cheek.

"You're beautiful, you know. I've been remiss in not telling you that more often. Like a modern-day Pomona. Or Venus—she was the goddess of gardening and fertility before she became the goddess of love."

He holds my eyes for a moment—long enough to turn me flushed and prickly—then begins to untangle the bindweed that's twisted its way through the roses. I rock back on my heels, watching his fingers move, gently separating the leaves.

He's so tempting. When I'm with him, I want to forget all about prophecies and obligations and sisters. I want to be a normal girl in love.

I move to sit on the lip of the fountain, trailing my hands behind me in the cool water. "What do you love?" I ask.

"Pardon?" He cocks his head at me like a parakeet.

"I garden. Tess bakes. Maura—" Maura dreams of escape. I shake my head, refusing to go down that path. "If you didn't have to work here, if you didn't have to work at the bookshop even, how would you spend your time?"

He takes a minute to think. "Cooped up inside, probably. Before my father died, I'd planned to go to university. There isn't much of a market for independent scholars these days, but I'd like to do my own translations of the myths. Orpheus and Eurydice is one of my favorites. Baucis and Philemon. All of Apollo's exploits."

I know those stories; they're the ones Tess has been studying with Father. "Well—you can still do your translations, can't you?" I ask, plucking a stray leaf from the fountain.

"I try. It's hard to find time."

"I'm sorry," I say, remembering that I'm not the only one

who's suffered a loss. "About your father. That must have been awful."

"It was very sudden. I don't know if that made it better or worse. Mother's been a rock, but I know it's been hardest on her. I try to help where I can."

"I'm sure you're immensely helpful."

Finn runs a hand over his already-rumpled hair. Does he even bother to comb it in the morning? "Perhaps. I wish there were more I could do."

I feel a great surge of protectiveness. I have enough worries of my own, I know, but somehow I want to take his on, too. "I want to know what worries you. I want to know *you*. Everything. Your favorite flower. Your favorite foods. Your favorite book."

Finn smiles. "There's plenty of time for that."

But there isn't! I haven't got any time left at all. Once Elena confirms that I can do mind-magic, will she even wait for my intention ceremony? Will I get to see him again before I'm shipped off to New London?

My mood darkens. I lean forward, yanking at more hapless weeds. A branch of the rosebush breaks under my careless hands. I snap it off and hurl it across the garden.

"Cate? Did I say something wrong?" Finn stands, hovering over me uncertainly.

"No. It's not you." A muscle tics in my eyelid. I press the back of a hand to it.

Perhaps the Sisterhood won't be so bad. They'll protect us from the Brothers; they won't send us to prison or the asylum. They want to help girls like us. Can I really blame them for their ruthlessness? I'd do anything to protect Maura and Tess, even if it hurt other people. The Sisters feel the same way, only their scope is much bigger.

I might be able to forgive their methods if they weren't aimed squarely at my family.

If they weren't willing to hurt Maura to force me into a future I don't want.

The future I want is standing in front of me, his forehead furrowed, his eyes full of worry. "What is it then? Tell me," he says.

"I can't." I push back onto my feet.

"If something's making you unhappy, tell me. Please."

I look at him—really look, beyond the freckles and the messy hair and the magnificent kissing. Finn is a clever, capable man, raised by a clever, capable mother. He likes me as I am—not just the laughing girl who caught minnows in her hands and climbed trees, but the stubborn, snappish girl I can be at my worst. I think he would still like me—love me—even if he knew about my magic.

But what if he knew I'd done magic to him? I stare at the cobblestone path beneath my boots. It's unforgivable.

I don't deserve him.

I brush dirt from the knees of my pale-blue dress. "I should go in. I'm not good company today."

He watches me go, plainly puzzled, and I can't say I blame him. I'm halfway down the path when he calls after me. "Lilies, I suppose. And a good apple pie, and the *Metamorphoses*."

I can't stop my answering smile. "Red roses, strawberries, and *Tales of the Pirate LeFevre!*"

Mrs. O'Hare scowls at me as I enter the kitchen. "Miss Cate!

Wash those hands before you touch anything. And take off your boots before you track dirt across my floors. You've been playing in the mud again, I see."

"I've been gardening," I correct, unbuckling my boots and stepping out of them. "The roses needed me."

"I thought we hired young Finn Belastra to take care of the roses."

"He's been busy." I bend over the sink to hide my blush, lathering my hands with soap. "With the gazebo."

She harrumphs and rubs a spot on my cheek. "You look like a street urchin. You might have fine airs now, but you're still the little girl who liked to splash about in mud puddles, aren't you?"

"I suppose I am." I give her a quick, fond squeeze. She smells like buttered toast—it's been her standard midmorning snack for as long as I've known her.

"Oof," she huffs, but she smiles. "And what was that for?"

"For being you. For always being here for us," I say, and she flushes with pleasure.

She must be getting on in years; she's always had gray hair and wrinkles. Sometimes, when it rains, her bad left knee protests, and she draws her chair up to the kitchen fire and calls it a sewing day. She doesn't show any other signs of slowing down, though, and it's a good thing, because I don't know what we'd do without her. Tess will need her more than ever now, if I'm gone.

Maura pops her head into the kitchen. She's wearing a simple, cream-colored day dress with a red sash, and her hair is in one long red braid down her back. She looks very young.

"Excellent," she pronounces, but her grin has a touch of nervousness to it. "I wanted to talk with you, Cate. It's important. Can you come upstairs?"

I follow her to her room, dread creeping over me like a shadow. Maura pushes the door shut behind us and ushers me over to the window seat.

"I know you won't like it, so I'll just have out with it. I'm going to write Father this afternoon. I've made a decision. I'm going to join the Sisters."

She can't. Not without knowing about the prophecy and what it portends. I bite my lip, torn between what my sister needs to know and what my mother asked me to do. "Maura, you don't have to declare yourself for an entire year!"

Maura turns, gesturing for me to retie the bow at her waist. "Why wait?"

"Why are you in such a rush? Are you that eager to leave your family?"

"I'll have a new family. Dozens of sisters." Maura beams.

My heart bangs, wounded, inside my chest. I give a hard yank on the knot. "You already have sisters."

"I know. I didn't mean—" Maura admires herself in the mirror, then turns to face me. "I know we've been arguing more than usual, but I'll miss you, Cate."

"But you'd still leave us without a second thought, just like that?" I snap my fingers.

"No." Maura sits next to me, pushing the yellow curtains aside. She looks out over the potholed drive and the red maples. "I've had second thoughts, and third and fourth ones, too.

Mother didn't teach us half of what she ought, and we haven't practiced enough. I'll be behind for my age. But magic is part of our heritage. I want to learn more about it."

"You can't go!" I insist. "Father won't allow it."

Maura rolls her eyes. She can get around him and we both know it. "Father might be surprised at my sudden religious fervor, but he won't fight me. He'll appreciate how scholarly and charitable they are."

"I'll tell him," I threaten, standing. "I'll tell him what they really are."

"You wouldn't risk it. Father's rebellious about his books, I grant you that. But if he found out his daughters are all witches, he'd have the vapors. His health might not withstand the shock."

I imagine myself knocking on the door of Father's study. Sitting in one of his leather chairs. Leaning forward, opening my mouth, and telling him that Mother was a witch. That Tess and Maura and I are witches, too. Then—what? What would he say? Mother loved him, but she obviously didn't believe he could handle it.

"You can't stop me. You might as well accept my decision. I'll write you. I won't be able to say much in case the post is intercepted. But you can visit if you like. I hope you will. Perhaps once you see how happy I am there . . ." Maura trails off, standing and taking both my hands in hers. "I *will* miss you."

She's right. I can't stop her; she won't hear anything I have to say. I can only go around her, and that means making a deal with Elena. "I'll miss you, too. Desperately," I say truthfully.

Maura wraps me in a tight hug. "Thank you. I didn't think—

I'm so glad you've decided to support me. You're the *best* sister, Cate. Really you are."

"You're welcome," I murmur, feeling like a traitor.

It's a full hour later when I storm into Belastras' bookshop. Marianne is perched on her stool behind the counter, her reading glasses low on her little snub nose. She pushes them up with her index finger. The gesture is heartbreakingly reminiscent of Finn.

"Have you got any customers?" I ask.

She shakes her head, putting her book aside. "No, but—"

"I found this," I interrupt, pulling the crumpled letter from my pocket. "Mother left it for me. The rest of the prophecy—it says that only two of the sisters will live to see the twentieth century—because one of them's going to kill another. Mother wants me to find a way to stop it. She thinks there's a war coming, and because of my *gift,* I'll be at the center of it. I don't see how I can avoid it. The Sisters are already threatening Maura to get to me. They're ruthless. Did you know that?" I stomp up to the counter and throw the letter down. "Because I must say I think it's an oversight on her part for not telling me before she went and died and left me in charge of everything!"

I'm full-out roaring, so I'm not surprised when Marianne's brown eyes go wide. Only—she's not looking at me. She's looking—past me.

I gulp. I have the uncomfortable feeling there's someone behind me, in the labyrinthine rows of bookshelves. And if it's not a customer—

I turn around slowly.

It's Finn, his face pale as a sheet. "You—Cate. What are you saying?"

My stomach claws its way into my throat.

He was not supposed to be here. Not supposed to find out like this.

The moment stretches out between us, interminable.

I can't lie to him anymore. "I'm a witch."

chapter

# 18

He looks—how? disappointed? His eyes are inscrutable behind his spectacles. The only clue is the rumpling of his forehead, that crease between his eyebrows.

"You didn't tell me," he says.

"No."

"Why?"

How can I explain it? He thinks I'm brave and strong, and I'm not. Not half as much as I'd like. Sometimes I'm scared and uncertain. Right now, I'm a whole host of emotions—desperate and angry and so, so resentful of being the one who's got to fix all this. If I admitted that—how would he feel about me then?

I don't want to give him up. But telling him how

I feel, how much he's come to matter to me in just a few short weeks—

I'm not sure if I'm brave enough.

"I thought perhaps you'd guessed," I say weakly. "When I came to see the register."

He shakes his head. "I thought one of your sisters, perhaps—"

"All three of us. And we're not just any garden-variety witches. We're the subject of a prophecy. You—I assume you heard that."

He shrugs. "You were shouting."

I look at Marianne, glancing between the two of us with curiosity written plainly on her face. I wonder how much she's deduced.

"I don't know what to do anymore." My voice comes out small and defeated. "They're going to force me to go to New London. The prophecy says one of us will be the key to either a second Terror or the witches coming back to power. They think it's me, and the Sisterhood—they're all witches really and—I'll have to leave Chatham forever and—"

My voice breaks. I gulp back tears, burying my face in my hands. I breathe evenly—in, out, in, out—struggling for control.

There's a hand on my shoulder, turning me. I peek between my fingers, and Finn is staring down at me, eyes full of compassion. Compassion and—something else, something that makes me feel as though it would be all right with him if I did cry, or wail and throw things even. That he might not think any less of me. He pulls me into his arms, right there in front of his mother.

He's braver than I am.

I sniff into the rough gray cotton of his shirt. "I don't want to lose you, but I don't want to lose my sisters, either."

"I know." He rubs my back. I curl into his chest and close my eyes, feeling fortified against the world.

His mother coughs. "Finn? May I speak to Cate for a moment?"

Finn's hands slip down over my back. I wonder if he's as reluctant to let go as I am.

"Of course." He pulls away, barely glancing at Marianne. "I'll just be upstairs."

We both wait until he's closed the door to their living quarters. Marianne eyes me over her glasses, and I feel like a recalcitrant schoolgirl who hasn't done her work. It must be obvious there's something between Finn and me now. She's been so kind, and now she'll hate me.

"I'm sorry," I say. I feel raw, all sharp edges.

Marianne puts her spectacles down on the counter and peers up at me. "For what?"

"You can't want your son caught up in all of this."

"Well, it does complicate things a bit, but we don't choose who we love."

"Oh—he—that is—he hasn't—" I stumble.

"He may not have said the words, but I know my son. I saw the way he looked at you."

"How?" I hate myself for wanting to quiz her on it.

"Like he'd do murder for you."

I think of the pistol strapped to Finn's calf. How he spoke of doing whatever was necessary to keep Clara and his mother safe. It intrigued me then, because it wasn't the talk of a timid bookseller's son. Now it terrifies me. Men are not punished as severely as women, but for rising up against the Brotherhood, or for serious offenses like murder, there are the prison ships.

"I can take care of myself. Of all three of us. I've made mistakes, I know, but my sisters are more important to me than anything in the world. I'd do *anything* for them."

"You're an impressive woman, Cate." Marianne smiles at me. "You're strong and capable and—"

"Capable?" I laugh, but there's no mirth in it. "Hardly. I've gone about things all wrong. I'm so angry with Mother—I know it's terrible because she's dead and she can't very well defend herself, but she kept too damn many secrets!" I slam my fist onto the counter. Pain splinters up my forearm. "She asked me to take care of them, and then she hobbled me!"

Marianne catches my fist before I can punch the counter again. "Anna was my friend, but she asked a great deal of you, Cate. Too much. Keeping it all a secret from your father—from your sisters—from everyone—it's a wonder it hasn't broken you."

"No. I can do this. I have to." I stalk away, staring out the front windows. At our neighbors passing on the street, going about their errands, oblivious to my heartache.

"But you don't have to do it alone," Marianne says, her voice mild. "Part of being strong is knowing when to ask for help. When to share things instead of keeping them in."

I take a deep breath. Ink and parchment and dust. I let it out.

She's right. I don't know what to do. I don't want to be the Sisters' pawn. That's why I came.

"Will you help me?" I ask quietly. "Please?"

Marianne smiles again. "Do you love my son, Cate? Do you want to marry him?"

I nod.

"Then let's see if we can find a way."

She pats the other stool, and I clamber onto it. "Maura wants to join the Sisterhood. Elena says they'd hurt her to get to me. If it's my freedom for hers—what else can I do? They'll keep her and Tess safe if I fall in line."

Marianne frowns. "How do you know they would keep a bargain like that? They could renege on it the very next time you refuse something they ask of you. The Sisterhood doesn't handle insubordination any better than the Brothers do, Cate. Why do you think they let the Brothers arrest Zara?"

I gasp. "They could have saved her?"

Pain flashes over Marianne's face. "Yes. But she was a rather outspoken critic within the Sisterhood. She didn't agree with some of their methods, and she made it very clear. That's why she left the convent to be a governess. It gave her a bit of freedom and allowed her to live nearer to Anna. I don't think the Sisters appreciated that two of their most powerful witches refused to further the cause."

"I appreciate what they're trying to do. But I don't want to hand over my power to them." I shake my head, cradling my aching hand against my chest. "I don't want to hand over my sisters, either."

"And marrying Finn *is* what you want? Not just a last resort against the Sisters?"

I meet her eyes without hesitation. "I've never been more certain of anything."

Marianne nods and pinches the bridge of her nose as though warding off a headache. "Will you ask him to come downstairs, then? I have an idea, but I think it might take both of us to convince him."

I climb the stairs to their flat and let myself in. Their sitting room is cramped but cozy, with a little fire burning in the grate. There are chrysanthemums in a glass jar on the end table, a basket of socks for darning beside the chair, and books piled helter-skelter. The juicy smell of roast beef drifts in from the kitchen and makes my stomach rumble.

Finn's lounging on the sofa, staring at the floor instead of the book in his hands. He jumps to his feet when I enter.

"May I see your book?" I ask. He hands it to me. A collection of essays.

The magic tugs at me, invigorated by my nerves. *"Commuto,"* I say, and the book disappears, replaced by a bouquet of fuzzy-headed gold chrysanthemums.

"I'm a witch," I say. I'm tired of feeling ashamed for the way I was born—a witch, and a woman. I've done the best I could with it, blessing or curse.

I raise my eyes to his. Despite Marianne's reassurance, I still expect fear. Anger. Instead, he takes the chrysanthemums from me, studying them from every angle, then lets out a low whistle. "That's amazing. *You* are amazing. I've never seen—for all the talk the Brothers do of magic, I've never seen it."

"I—I can do more," I say, hesitant. I focus on the cup of tea on the side table. *"Agito!"*

The teacup floats across the room and into my hands.

"Good Lord," Finn whispers. "What else?"

"Mind-magic. But I've only used it to keep my sisters safe." I look at his smiling freckled face. I'll tell him everything except what I did to him. And if we can find a way to make this work, I'll spend my life making it up to him. "Are you—does it scare you?"

"No. I trust you, Cate." He takes me into his arms, fierce and gentle at the same time.

"I wanted to tell you before. Weeks ago, when you showed me the register and talked about how you'd protect your mother and Clara, I wanted to tell you everything. I'm—I'm glad you know."

Finn grins. "So am I. I love you—all of you. Your stubbornness and your prickliness and your witchery and your bravery."

I laugh through the grateful tears blooming in my eyes. "You love my stubbornness?"

"And your laugh. And your pointy little chin. And your gorgeous hair," he says, tucking a wayward strand behind my ear.

"My hair's not gorgeous. Maura's—" I stop. I need to learn to take compliments without comparing myself with my sisters. "I love you, too. I want to marry you."

Finn pulls back. "I want that, too. More than anything. But I don't see how—I'd do everything I can to protect you, but you'd be under more scrutiny from the Brothers. And people will talk. You're marrying beneath you."

"Don't say that! I'd be proud to be part of your family. You have no idea—your mother has been so kind to me. Kinder than I deserve."

Finn seizes my mouth in a long, drugging kiss, and my arms twine around his neck. "I take it she's not worried about my virtue, if she sent you up here alone."

"No. Actually—" I take a second to catch my breath and settle my hands back at his waist. "Your mother wants to see us downstairs. She said she has an idea."

In the bookshop, Marianne sits behind the counter, her eyes rimmed in red. She waves off Finn's concern. "It's the end of one dream and the beginning of another," she says, twisting the ruby ring on her finger. Finn and I stand in the center of the shop, a row of bookshelves concealing us from the passersby who might look in the windows. Finn holds my hand.

Finn squints at her. "It's not the time to talk in riddles, Mother."

She smiles. "This is the last day Belastras' bookshop is open for business. We've had a good run of it, but I believe it's time to close our doors."

"What? No." Finn drops my hand and strides forward. "You can't make that decision without talking it through with me."

"Technically, my dear, I can. I'm the proprietor." Marianne keeps her voice light.

"Why now? What does this have to—" Realization slowly dawns over Finn's face. "You can't be serious."

"Serious as a cemetery," Marianne promises, standing up and patting his shoulder. "You may do whatever you like, but you can no longer be employed as a bookseller."

"I'm not following," I admit, feeling dim.

Finn swipes his hands through his messy hair. "She wants me to join the Brothers." He turns back to me, leaning against the counter. "Brother Ishida came by last night to offer me membership. He sweetened the deal with a job in the secondary school, teaching Latin. Your father's old position. They made the offer contingent on joining the council in Brother Elliott's place."

"No." I shake my head. "It's— You love the shop, both of you. You can't give that up for me."

"The shop's already out of the equation," Marianne reminds us. "Besides, Clara and I would be a good deal safer if Finn were a member of the Brotherhood. I'm far too old to be carted off to prison, and the Brothers don't seem as though they'll let up anytime soon. If Finn was stern enough to put his own mother out of business—why, that's just the sort of man they're after. And they would never suspect his wife for a witch."

"She *is* right," Finn says. "I could afford a wife on a teacher's salary. It wouldn't be grand, but—"

"I don't care about that," I interrupt. "I just—I won't have you hating yourself for it. It's too much. You'd have to arrest girls like me. Take them away from their families and lock them up in Harwood. They're hardly ever real witches, Finn. Even if they are—it's not right. You know that."

Finn takes my hand in his. "I wouldn't relish it, Cate. In fact, I'd hate it. But if this would keep you safe—" His voice catches. "You'd sacrifice yourself to protect your sisters. Let me do this for you. For us."

I bite my lip. It feels like too much. I should refuse him.

I should but I won't.

"What's to stop them from hauling me off to New London tomorrow? Once Elena confirms I can do mind-magic, I don't think she'll let me stay in town for another two months," I point out.

"The Brothers take the ceremony of intention very seriously," Marianne says. "It's a commitment before the Lord, almost as important as the marriage vows. It's rare, but occasionally, girls get a bee in their bonnet and ask for special permission to move up their intention ceremonies. The Brothers are so used to girls dragging their feet about it, they're happy enough to oblige." She gives me a grim, determined smile. "You could announce your betrothal to Finn early. Say—tomorrow?"

"And if I'm as important as the Sisters say, they won't want to risk calling attention to me with a broken intention." I turn to Finn, my eyes searching his. "Are you very sure?"

Finn leans in, resting his forehead against mine. My entire field of vision is swallowed up by him. "Yes."

I close my eyes for a minute, taking solace in his strength. Then I turn to his mother. "Marianne?"

"All any parent wants is for their child to be happy. In fact—" She pulls the ruby ring from her finger. "Perhaps this ought to belong to you, now. It was my engagement ring from Richard."

"I couldn't—" I protest.

But Finn takes it from her and weighs it in his palm. He holds my gaze, and the look in his eyes is a love letter in itself. When he speaks, his voice is rough. "Will you marry me, Cate?"

I go still, the question hanging in the air. I have never felt more accepted—for the girl I am, not the girl I want to be— never more loved and *respected* than I am in this moment. It's a choice, and it's mine to make.

"Yes," I breathe.

Finn slides the simple gold band onto my ring finger. I tilt it, and the ruby sparkles, catching the sunlight. He leans down and

brushes his lips against mine, sealing the promise. "I can't wait
to make you my wife."

"Cate Belastra." I try it out, and despite the solemnity of the
moment, despite knowing what this will cost him, I can't help
smiling. "Catherine Anna Belas—"

I'm interrupted by a scream. It goes on and on, howling, until
the hairs on the back of my arm rise.

Finn rushes to the window and peers out at the street. When
he turns back, his eyes look pained. "The guards are making
another arrest," he says.

The woman shrieks again. This time it's cut off abruptly with
a sharp crack.

Marianne goes pale. "Who is it?" she asks.

Finn's face furrows. Soon, he'll be complicit in this. "Brenna
Elliott."

My heart sinks. "I have to see."

Marianne throws open the front door and goes out. She
stops on the front stoop, clutching the cast-iron railing with
white-knuckled hands.

Across the street, Brenna's cowering on the cobblestones.
Beneath her cloak, her sunny yellow hem is splattered with mud.
A white handprint is stark on her red, tear-stained cheek. As I
watch, two of the Brothers' hulking guards advance toward her.
She scrambles backward on her hands and knees and lands in
the gutter.

There's a crowd gathering. "Witch! Witch!" Cries go up—
some high and excited with the sport of it, some low and hateful. A boy throws a rock at her. His aim is true—it hits her on
the forehead. Blood trickles down her face.

One of the guards snatches her roughly by the arm. Brenna screams. Her mop of tangled brown hair falls into her bloody face. The guard slaps her again and she goes silent.

The guards hold her up, one on each side. She's shaking like a new tree in a thunderstorm.

Brother Ishida steps forward. "This girl is mad. She will be taken back to Harwood Asylum straightaway."

Brenna rocks, keening to herself like a wounded animal.

"No!" Rory runs down the street, resplendent in a red dress. She didn't even take time to throw on her cloak. "Brenna!"

Sachi darts forward and yanks Rory back into the crowd.

Brother Ishida turns to the group gathered on the street. "Miss Elliott believes that she can see into the future. What is that but presumption, for a weak woman to think she can do the work of the Lord? At her grandfather's behest, we allowed her to come back to her family. We hoped she had been cured, but our leniency has not been rewarded. It is for the good of our community that we send the wretched soul back."

I turn on my heel and go back into the shop. I can't stand to see any more.

Finn follows me and closes the door behind us. He pulls me behind the first row of bookshelves and then wraps his arms around me. I'm dry eyed but shaking with the horror of what's just happened.

"You're safe," he says, over and over, stroking my back. "You're safe. I'll never let them do that to you."

I'm not certain which of us he means to comfort.

• • •

It's already well past two when I leave the bookshop. I'm going to be late for my appointment with Elena. I apologize to John for keeping him and the carriage waiting, and on the way home I go over the plan Marianne and I have worked out. I'll explain about Brenna's apprehension, how awful it was. It won't be hard to show my distress. I'll plead that I'm too upset to have a magic lesson today. No matter how loyal Elena is to the Sisterhood, she can't want a frightened, unfocused witch wreaking havoc with her memory. I'll promise her that tomorrow, after church, I'll cooperate.

By then I'll have announced my engagement to Finn—the newest candidate for the Brothers—and it will be too late for her to force me into joining the Sisters.

After I appease Elena, I'll go to Maura and Tess. I'll tell them about the prophecy, show them Mother's diary and her letter. They'll be furious with me for not telling them sooner, but faced with Mother's warnings, they'll understand. They have to. Maura might not believe me, but she'll listen to Mother. She'll see that the Sisters don't have our best interests at heart—that we have to stay together, here in Chatham, and look out for one another.

I'll tell them about Finn last. I hope they'll be happy for me.

I feel a great swell of gladness as the carriage comes up the drive. The house is still there—white, gabled, surrounded by maples shedding their summer skins. Home. I want to grab up handfuls of dirt and kiss it. I won't have to leave after all. Not far, anyway.

I hurry into the rose garden, ready to make my excuses to Elena.

Only she's not there.

Drat. I hurry inside. The sitting room is empty. Tess is reading in Father's study. Upstairs, Elena's room is empty. The one time I actually want the nuisance and she's nowhere to be found.

Annoyed, I throw open Maura's door without knocking. "Maura, have you—?"

I stop, stunned. Maura and Elena are sitting close together on the wooden window seat. Their skirts spill against each other, Elena's peony-pink and Maura's cream, a froth of lace and silk.

Maura has her hand on the curve of Elena's cheek. Her lips on Elena's lips.

chapter

# 19

"Maura, i need to talk to you," I choke, stumbling back into the hall. I retreat to my room, trying to make sense of what I've just seen: my sister, kissing the governess. Kissing her with her eyes closed, tilting toward her like a starved sunflower.

I never dreamed—but Elena is everything Maura wants to be: cultured and clever, pretty and powerful. She's paid Maura attention, encouraged her, listened to her and made much of her when no one else would.

When I put it that way, I don't know how I didn't see it before.

I drop onto my settee, head in my hands. Oh, this is going to complicate things. And Maura—is her interest in kissing girls specific to Elena? Is this just a schoolgirl crush, or something more? I think back over all her protestations against marriage, and I feel very guilty. She's right; she's been trying to tell me something, and I haven't been listening.

Maura comes to my room. Her cheeks are flushed, but her berry mouth is tilting up at the corners. She looks happy. Slightly mortified, but happy. She closes the door and stands on the flowered rug I took from Mother's rooms.

"How long has this been going on?" I ask. I have to know how compromised she is.

Maura's hands flutter like nervous birds. "Just now—that was the first time—but I've wanted to—I'm mad about her, Cate."

"Oh, Maura. Why didn't you tell me?" I lean back against the settee, remembering the girls from the register, the ones who were caught kissing in the blueberry fields.

"I've tried! I told you how wonderful and clever she is, but you wouldn't hear it. You don't listen to me, Cate. Elena *listens*."

I hate saying it, I hate hurting her like this, but she has to know. "Because she wants something from you."

Maura's mouth falls open. "Do you truly think so little of me," she gasps, "that I couldn't tell whether her feelings are genuine? Do you think I'm so awful no one could love me?"

"Of course not! Someone *will* love you someday, and it will be grand, and he'll be lucky. Or she," I correct myself. "But it's not Elena."

"How do you know what her feelings are? I know it's—unconventional, but we've been spending so much time together.

We've never been like pupil and student; we've been friends right from the start, and now—"

"She was sent here to *spy* on us. That's not paranoia; it's truth. I was supposed to meet her this afternoon in the garden for a magic lesson, and I was late. The Sisterhood wants me to join them and they'll use you to get to me. Elena told me that, Maura, straight-out. They would hurt you if they thought it would make me fall in line."

"Liar!" Maura's eyes narrow into sapphire slits. "She'd never hurt me."

"She would," I sigh. "She doesn't want to, but her first loyalty is to the Sisterhood."

"I don't believe you," Maura snaps. "Besides, why would they want *you*?"

I shrink back from the scorn in her voice. "I found Mother's diary. She wrote about a prophecy—it was made before the Great Temple fell. It says that before the twentieth century arrives, there will be three sisters, and one of them will be the most powerful witch in centuries. The Sisterhood thinks *we* might be those sisters. They want to get their hands on us before the Brothers find us. *That's* why Elena's here."

Maura paces across my room while I talk, back and forth, back and forth, between bed and window. "What makes you think it's you? It could just as easily be me. Or Tess."

I shake my head. "The prophecy said the most powerful can do mind-magic. And I—well, I can. Since I was little."

Maura pauses, one hand flying to her mouth. "Have you ever used it on me?"

"No! Of course not." I glare at her. "I've only used it once. To keep Father from sending me away to school. Elena—she wants to make me join the Sisters so they can use it against the Brotherhood." I reach into my pocket, touch the ruby ring hidden there. "Their cause is important, Maura. I believe that. But it's not as important to me as you and Tess. It's not right that they'd use you to force my hand."

Maura shakes her head, her red braid whipping back and forth. A little smile plays at her lips. "You're wrong. She's not using me to get to you."

"I'm not making it up. Do you truly think I'd go to these lengths just to keep you from seeing a governess?" I throw my hands up, exasperated. "You can see Mother's diary if you want."

I start for my bureau, where I've magicked away the diary, but Maura stops me. "I don't need to see it. Even if this prophecy is true, I know what I feel, and that's true, too. I don't care what the Sisters would do to me. I want to go back to New London with Elena. I'm in love with her, Cate, and she loves me back. She hasn't said it yet, but—"

Anger simmers through me. "She's manipulating you, Maura. She has been from the very first! I'm going to dismiss her right now."

"You can't!" Maura steps between me and the door.

I lean against the wooden bedpost, suddenly exhausted. I don't have the energy for another row with Maura. I hate fighting with her; I hate the distance that's sprung up between us since Elena arrived—before that, if I'm honest with myself. It's easy to blame Elena, but we've been at each other's throats for months.

Sympathy washes over me. Maura's so lonely. So mind-numbingly bored. She doesn't want to marry. She deserves to go somewhere she can use her talents—somewhere she belongs. If that's with the Sisters, so be it. I should let her go without putting up a fuss.

I push the curtains aside and stare out the window. I can see the rose garden from here, the goldenrod and evergreens forming a neat, protective square around the bright pink and red and cream-colored roses. Around the bench where I first learned to do magic, at the feet of my mother and Athena.

I put a hand to my temple, blinking. There was something—what was I thinking?

"Are you all right?" Maura asks. Her concerned eyes are trained on my face.

"My head—" It's such a peculiar sensation. Like there's something tugging on it. Not at my hair—inside. It's terribly strange.

Maura slides her arm around my shoulder and guides me to the bed, smoothing the rumpled blue quilt. "You look tired. Why don't you take a nap before supper?"

My mind feels fuzzy. Wasn't I angry with her a moment ago? I don't remember why; she's being so sweet. There was something wrong, something I meant to do, but I can't remember—

I push at the tugging in my head, and it dissipates.

Just like a glamour made by a witch who's not quite as powerful as me.

Maura kissed Elena. I was going to dismiss her and then—

No. Maura wouldn't.

I look up at my sister, her sapphire eyes still focused on me.

I can feel it plainly now, her pull on my memory.

"How. Dare. You?" I explode, pushing her away. She falls back against my dressing table and knocks over a little bottle of lavender water. It rolls off the table and smashes, dousing the room in scent.

"Stop it. I know what you're up to," I snap.

Maura's face falls. She backs away, toward the door. "I was only—"

"Don't you dare make excuses! I've never used magic against you. Never!"

I take a deep breath, trying to calm my racing heart. It's all right. I can still remember. It didn't work; she's not strong enough.

But what if it *had* worked? I turn to Maura, sick and furious. I will never do this to someone I love. Never again.

"Does Elena know you can do that?" Has Elena been playing us against each other all along, waiting to see which of us was the most powerful?

Maura nods. "She taught me herself. She was proud of me, how fast I caught on. But—" Doubt flickers over her face. "It doesn't matter. That's not why she likes me, Cate."

I head for the door. Every moment Elena's in this house is one moment too long.

"Where are you going?" Maura runs behind me, pulling at my elbow.

I rip my arm away. "Don't touch me."

Maura is crying now, tears pooling in her eyes. "Cate, it's not her fault! I'm the one who did it."

"Do you think that makes it any better?"

Maura leaps in front of me, barring the way. I shove her, hard, and she falls back against the wall.

I throw open the door to Elena's room without knocking. She's sitting in her green armchair by the fire, needle flashing through some sewing in her hands.

"I want you out of my house. Now." My voice is so cold, I don't recognize it.

"You can't do that!" Maura's tears are falling freely now.

I close the door—no point in the servants overhearing this quarrel. "I'm the mistress of the house; I can do whatever I like. That includes dismissing servants who displease me. Miss Robichaud, we are no longer in need of your services."

Elena looks at me, quietly calculating the strength of my order. I stare her down. Will she try to compel me, too? Is she capable of it?

Maura pushes past me to stand next to Elena. "Father won't like this, Cate."

"He's not the one who has to live here."

Maura puts one hand on the back of Elena's chair, protective. She juts her chin at me. "I'll write and tell him and he'll have to cut his trip short."

"Good," I say coolly, planting my hands on my hips. "Perhaps he can talk some sense into you. Or do you plan to try and bewitch him, too?"

"You act like I've gone beyond the pale. You just said you've done it yourself!" Maura shouts.

My jaw drops. I stare at her, disbelieving, furious.

Elena slides her needle neatly into her sewing and puts it aside. "Maura, you tried to compel Cate? But it was unsuccessful?"

"Yes," Maura says uncertainly. The doubt in her eyes is growing. "Does that matter?"

"Insofar as it means that Cate's the stronger witch. It's quite extraordinary, that both of you are capable of mind-magic. I've never heard of a precedent," Elena breathes. She walks toward me but stops a few feet away, at the edge of her canopy bed, her eyes wary. "I'm sorry that I went behind your back and taught your sister, Cate. I know you haven't trusted that our intentions are honorable, but—"

"Honorable? You kissed my sister!" I explode. The magic sways up, dizzying. I'd love to make that needle prick her. To smash all the pretty little bottles of scented water on her dressing table. To show her just how powerful I can be. I close my eyes for a moment, summoning up every ounce of self-control I possess.

"What's going on?" Tess squeezes in the door, closing it behind her. "Why is everyone shouting?"

I point a finger at Maura, hovering over Elena's empty chair. "Tell her! You tell her what you did. And you." I whirl on Elena. "I want you out of this house. Now."

"You can't just throw her out on the street," Maura says, hurrying to her side.

I ignore her, my eyes clashing with Elena's. "I'll give you until dusk to pack your things. John will drive you to the train station. We have some money for household emergencies; it ought to be enough to pay your way back to New London."

"If you make her leave, I'll go with her," Maura threatens.

I draw myself up, taller than everyone else in this room. Stronger. "Maura's not the one you want. I'm more powerful than her; I've proved it twice over. I swear I'll fight you every step of the way unless you tell her the truth. Your superiors in the Sisterhood might not mind your tactics, but I do. Letting her think you care for her won't win you any favors if I'm ever in a position of power."

Elena looks at me for a long moment. She's an ambitious woman; I hope I've chosen the right threat, the one that will mean something to her.

Finally, she turns to Maura. Puts a hand on her ruffled cream sleeve. "Maura," she says, "I think you've misunderstood my feelings."

Maura's blue eyes fill with tears. "Don't say that," she begs, taking Elena's other hand. "Don't listen to Cate. Please. I—I love you!"

Beside me, Tess lets out a little hiss of surprise.

"I'm flattered by your regard," Elena says, pulling away, "but I don't return it."

Maura reaches out a hand, then lets it fall. The same hand that cradled Elena's face so gently. "But you kissed me!"

Elena shakes her head. Despite all the fuss, she still looks perfect as a china doll, not a single curl out of place. "You took me by surprise. It was a mistake."

Maura looks past Elena to me. "You were right," she snaps, running from the room. "Are you happy now?"

The three of us stand in silence. Across the hall, Maura's door slams so hard, the floor rattles. "Possibly we could have handled that better," Elena says. She opens her armoire and pulls out her valise. "You can make me go, but they'll only send someone else. I'll tell them what I've learned. You can't pretend this isn't happening, Cate. You will find it easier to come willingly."

"And if I don't?" I want Tess to hear her say it.

"The Sisters would rather not force your hand. But if they have to, they will do everything in their power to convince you. And their power is considerable. They will not hesitate to use Maura and Tess." Elena gathers her things from the dressing table. "I'm sorry to say that, Tess. It's not how I would have things go."

"But you won't stop them, will you? Which means I can't have you in this house. Pack your things and get out," I snap. "Tess, come with me."

Tess has been standing back, leaning against the tulip-flowered wallpaper, taking everything in with her observant little storm-cloud eyes. She follows me down the hall to my room. I can hear Maura sobbing behind her door, and my stomach twists.

Tess perches on my bed, swinging her slippers over the edge. "You've been keeping things from us. Tell me everything," she says. And I do.

There's a knock on my door before supper. Tess is still here, lying across the settee on her stomach, reading Mother's diary with a frown of intense concentration.

"Miss Cate!" It's Mrs. O'Hare. Why has she climbed the stairs instead of sending Lily? "You've a caller. Brother Ishida is here to see you."

Tess sits up, alarm written all over her face.

"It's nothing," I say. "We haven't done anything."

Unless Sachi's told her father. Unless Brenna's tattled. Unless—

No. More likely, it's the second phase of the Belastras' plan in action.

"Try to tell Maura he's here, if she'll open her door," I tell Tess. "We don't need another scene."

I fix my hair in the looking glass and head downstairs to the sitting room.

A heavy wind's sprung up, sending leaves raining to the ground. Trees tap against the windowpanes with newly bare fingers. The curtains swirl into the sitting room like malevolent blue ghosts. I cross the room and shut the window. Brother Ishida is standing before the fire, his back to me.

He turns and smiles. "Good evening, Miss Cahill."

"Good evening, sir."

It's not until he gives an impatient gesture toward the floor that I realize what he's waiting for. I go to my knees before him, padding them with my skirts. It's hateful, pretending obeisance to a man I neither like nor respect. I think of how he fathered Rory out of wedlock, how he's allowed himself to be blackmailed by her mother, how he drove Mrs. Clay out of town when she became a liability. It's all I can do not to cringe when he lays a hand on my brow. His fingers feel too soft for a man.

"Lord bless you and keep you this and all the days of your life."

"Thanks be," I mumble.

I rise to my feet as he sits on one end of the cream sofa. He gestures for me to sit next to him. I do, keeping a careful distance between us.

"Miss Cahill, as you know, your intention ceremony is not scheduled until mid-December. However."

Nervousness swims through me. "Yes, sir?"

"Finn Belastra came to see me earlier this evening. As your father is away on business for some time yet, he asked me for your hand in marriage. He assured me that you had already agreed, and that the two of you are eager to announce your betrothal." Brother Ishida looks at me, his thin mouth like the slash of a knife. "I hope you have not compromised yourself in any way that necessitates this, Miss Cahill."

My head jerks up. Good Lord, is he suggesting—? I let outrage play over my face. "No, sir. Certainly not!"

"I'm glad to hear it. Particularly given your friendship with my daughter. Sachiko has a good heart, but I won't have her associating with girls who are not her equal in virtue or obedience. Believe it or not, I do recall what it is like to be young." Brother Ishida rakes his eyes over me, lingering on my bosom, and I fight the urge to cross my arms over my chest. "We must all be wary of the devil's lustful whispers."

"Yes, sir. I will pray to the Lord to strengthen my sinful heart." I inch away, folding my hands primly in my lap.

"I'm willing to move your intention ceremony up, as young Mr. Belastra requested," Brother Ishida continues. "I know your father thinks very well of him. He recommended Finn months ago for the position in our school. I can't imagine he would object."

"No, sir. I would never dream of making a match Father wouldn't approve of."

Brother Ishida's smile is slippery as a snake. "I trust you know that Finn has accepted our invitation to join the Brotherhood. He's already made a very wise decision in closing down his family's shop. I hope you are sensible of what a great honor it is, to marry a member of the Brotherhood."

"Yes, sir." I smile. "I shall do my best to deserve it."

"See that you do, Miss Cahill. See that you do."

There's a noise out in the hall. The repeated thump of John dragging Elena's trunk down the steps.

"Was Cate right? Did you ever care about me at all?"

Maura's voice is furious—and loud. If she doesn't know Brother Ishida is here, Lord only knows what else she might say.

"What's that clatter?" Brother Ishida asks.

I smile nervously, hoping his hearing isn't what it used to be. "Pardon me. It seems my sisters are having some sort of quarrel."

The front door closes and Maura wails. Her voice is closer now—in the front hall.

Something smashes to the floor.

"What the devil?" Brother Ishida is on his feet.

I run, terrified, into the hall. I'm too late. Mrs. O'Hare and Lily stand in the doorway to the dining room. Lily is cowering, one arm thrown up to protect her face. Mrs. O'Hare is sidling along the wall toward Maura, one hand outstretched.

Maura's lost control of her powers.

Maura, whose heart is breaking, is breaking everything in her path.

The cut-crystal vase is smashed, shards gleaming on the

wooden floor. Roses are scattered helter-skelter, bent and bruised. As I watch, the hall mirror flies off its hook and shatters. The portrait of Father's parents that hangs on the wall follows suit. A piece of glass sticks in Mrs. O'Hare's hand.

"Maura, dearie," she says, still inching forward.

I wonder how long she's known.

Another shard, several inches long, flies past my head. I freeze.

"Get back, Mrs. O'Hare. She doesn't know what she's doing."

Maura stands by the door, head thrown back, arms wide. Her blue eyes are helpless, unfocused. The rich mahogany hall table rises and dashes itself against the wall, again and again. The legs splinter.

The front door slams open as if pushed by an invisible hand. Outside, thunder rumbles. The sky is full of angry clouds.

"Good Lord," Brother Ishida says from behind me.

Maura looks at him. At me. "You—you made her leave."

The curtains from the hall window break away and float toward me. I step on the fabric to keep them down, but it twists around my legs like snakes. And then there are snakes—glossy and sinuous, hissing, tasting the air with their forked tongues. I will myself to see past the illusion. Curtains. It's only curtains. I push against the glamour, and it breaks. The curtains drop to the floor, harmless.

"Stop it! Maura. You have to stop."

Maura's hands are clenched in fists at her sides. "I can't."

The curtains rise up again. Now they're not curtains anymore but spiderwebs, sticky and horrible, with fat black spiders. I scream and brush at my face.

"They're not real, Cate," Tess says calmly from the top of the stairs. "You know that."

But Lily is screaming her fool head off, and behind me Brother Ishida is mumbling prayers, and I can't concentrate. Maura knows I hate spiders and she's using it against me and I can't make her stop and—

"*Intransito*," Tess says.

The spiderwebs disappear. Maura's frozen in place, her mouth stuck in an O of dismay. Her blue eyes are scared, pleading, and she focuses them on me. Even now, after everything she's done, I feel a pang of sympathy.

How did Tess know that spell? It seems my sisters are full of surprises.

The house goes silent for a long moment.

Then Brother Ishida steps forward. His cold marble eyes are shining. He points to Maura and then to Tess.

"Witches!"

It's the stuff of nightmares.

"Miss Maura Cahill! Miss Teresa Cahill! You are both under arrest for foul and flagrant crimes of witchery," Brother Ishida declares. He moves to block the open door, his long black cloak trailing through water, his boots crunching on broken glass. "Miss Belfiore, ask my driver to come inside."

If she tells the driver—that's one more witness—

"Lily, no. Don't. Haven't we always been good to you? Please!" I cry, desperate.

But Lily picks up her blue skirts and runs outside. Tess stares down at me from the top of the stairs, gray eyes frantic, looking for instruction. She doesn't know what to do. I don't know what to do.

"Should I—Maura?" she squeaks.

I nod, and Tess casts—silently this time, reversing

her *intransito* spell. Maura falls into a heap on the floor. Mrs. O'Hare, nearest her, wraps an arm around her waist and pulls her to her feet.

"Can you control yourself now?" I ask.

Maura nods. She has a cut on her cheek and another on the palm of her right hand. There's a jagged rip in one sleeve, a spot seeping scarlet just above her elbow. She sways, pale, as she stares at the damage she's wrought. At the family heirlooms in pieces on the floor. At Mrs. O'Hare's hand, wrapped in her blood-soaked apron. "I'm sorry. I'm so sorry," she cries, flinging herself at Mrs. O'Hare.

"It's all right, dearie," Mrs. O'Hare whispers, stroking her hair.

She is more forgiving than I am.

The coachman strides into the doorway, tall and broad-shouldered, with a sharp hooked nose and a wicked scar across his chin. I recognize him—he's one of the men who arrested Gabrielle Dolamore. He was in the street with Brenna this afternoon.

"Cyrus!" Brother Ishida barks. "Go to town and round up the council. Bring them back here immediately. I have identified two witches in this household."

Cyrus's eyes rake over us with a look of disgust. "Yes, sir," he says, and he turns on his heel and disappears into the dusk.

Brother Ishida paces back and forth in a tight circle. "I hardly need testimony. I have seen proof with my own eyes. Nonetheless, best to be thorough. Miss Cahill. Were you aware of your sisters' treachery? Have you seen them commit acts of witchery previous to this night?"

I am silent, staring at my own clasped hands.

"Answer me, girl! Were you aware your sisters are witches?"

I am silent.

He crosses the room and slaps me across the face. Hard enough to snap my head back and send me stumbling against the wall. "Cate!" Tess cries. I put one hand to my stinging cheek. Maura and I have shoved each other, pulled each other's hair— but no one has ever struck me before. The pain brings tears to my eyes, but I will them back. I won't give him the satisfaction of crying.

"You will not ignore me," Brother Ishida says, his dark eyes flashing in his lined face. "I am your elder and your better. You will answer. *Now*. Were you aware of your sisters' witchery?"

"No." I lower my eyes to the floor, biting my lip. I will not help matters by telling him what I think of him.

It's raining now, drumming on the porch roof. A cold wind blows through the hall, bringing with it the scent of wet leaves and dying grass.

Mrs. O'Hare moves toward the kitchen. Brother Ishida puts out a hand to stop her. "Where are you going?"

"To fetch some bandages and ointment for Miss Maura," she says.

"No. No one is to leave this room until the guards arrive." Brother Ishida turns to Lily, trembling just inside the door, her brown cow's eyes big and guileless. "Miss Belfiore, have you witnessed any other strange happenings here?"

Lily hesitates, and he frowns. "Miss Belfiore, your first duty is to the Lord. We must stamp out witchery wherever we find it,

314

lest it take root and spread through our country like poison. Speak up."

"I've seen things," Lily whispers. She fixes her eyes on his boots. A hank of brown hair swings forward into her face. "Things what don't seem natural. Flowers what bloom out of season. Food what's burnt black but tastes like heaven. Things are there one minute and gone the next."

Oh no. I've always tried to be careful not to let the servants see anything they couldn't explain away. Still, I never truly believed they would inform on us. Mrs. O'Hare loves us, and Lily—well, she's a good churchgoing girl, but she's always been so timid. She's been with us for years, since right after Mother died.

"Thank you, Miss Belfiore." Brother Ishida smiles. "You've been very helpful."

"You've been an ungrateful little sneak," Maura hisses.

"Silence, witch!" Brother Ishida thunders. "Miss Teresa, come here."

Tess walks slowly down the stairs. She holds her head high, but she's trembling—like Arabella walking the plank. She stands next to Maura.

Brother Ishida gives them a cruel smile. "When my guards arrive, they will place you in restraints. The other members of the Brothers' council will help me search this house for evidence against you, though we hardly need more. You will be taken to separate cells and held for your trial tomorrow. There can be no doubt as to your witchery. You will be sentenced to the prison ship or to the madhouse. It is, I think, better than you deserve.

When my grandmother was arrested for witchery, she was hanged in the town square. 'Twere up to me, I'd resurrect the burnings." The vicious calm of his voice is terrifying, as though he's discussing the weather instead of my sisters' murder.

They are both quiet. "Do you hear me? Do you understand what you deserve?"

"Yes," Maura whispers, glowering at the floor.

Tess raises her head. She looks first at Brother Ishida and then at Lily—long, searching looks, as if imprinting their faces on her memory.

*"Dedisco,"* she says.

I hold my breath. A momentary silence swells, filling the room. The rain pounds down outside.

Then Lily shakes her head. Her eyes grow round with surprise as she looks at the mess in the hall. "What's happened?" she gasps.

Lily doesn't remember. Tess's spell worked.

Dread blooms through me.

I thought being the subject of the prophecy was the worst possible thing. But the notion that it might not be me, that it could be Tess—

It frightens me even more.

"There's been a terrible storm," Tess says carefully. "The wind blew the door open and swept through. It was awful. Like a tornado."

Brother Ishida grabs the curved wooden newel at the bottom of the staircase. He leans against it for support, breathing heavily. "Are you all right, sir?" I ask, wiping my face of any trace of hostility. We must play this right.

"I'm feeling unwell." His voice is as gray as his face.

"It's understandable, sir. It was frightening. Glass everywhere. You were fortunate not to be injured."

"Thank the Lord," he murmurs.

"Indeed." I keep my eyes focused on his face. "May I walk you out? Thank you for coming tonight, sir."

He follows me out onto the porch. "You're welcome, Miss Cahill. I came to—to—"

He doesn't remember. He doesn't remember anything! Tess's magic worked.

The trees thrash overhead. Lightning illuminates the drive. "You gave me your blessing to announce my intention early. Tomorrow morning at services."

"Of course, of course. We'll have the usual ceremony. I don't believe anyone else is scheduled for tomorrow. And your father approves?" he asks.

"Oh yes, Father's very pleased."

"Excellent." He peers at the rain-dark drive. "Where's my carriage gone?"

"Perhaps your driver took it into the barn to wait out the storm," I suggest.

"Oh, here it comes now," he says, pointing at the carriage rattling up the drive. My stomach sinks, expecting another to turn the corner at any moment. Now what will we do? The three of us won't be strong enough to modify the memories of all the council members plus additional guards. We'll still be ruined.

But this brougham doesn't have the Brothers' golden seal on the side. "That's not mine," he says, just as it stops before the porch.

Elena Robichaud hops down almost before the wheels have stopped turning, splattering her black cape with mud. She makes a face and then turns back to the carriage, extending an arm, as Mrs. Corbett gingerly joins her. They wade up to the porch and stand there, huddled against the rain.

"Brother Ishida," Mrs. Corbett says, her fat face folding into a smile. "We just passed your coachman walking down the road."

"Walking?" Brother Ishida demands. "What the devil for? He's gone off and left me stranded here. Where's my carriage?"

"Just outside town. One wheel broken," Mrs. Corbett says. There's an odd glint of satisfaction in her brown eyes.

"It must have been the storm. The winds were fierce here," I put in. "Such a roaring. It might have been a tornado. Mrs. Corbett, do you suppose your carriage could take Brother Ishida back to town? He's not feeling well. Or we could get our man John—"

"You're welcome to borrow my carriage, sir." Mrs. Corbett interrupts my nervous chatter. "I'll stay here and see to it that the girls are all right."

"Thank you. Good day, Miss Cahill." Dispensing with the usual blessings, Brother Ishida hurries through the pelting rain.

Elena shivers in her cape. "We stopped the driver," she says, teeth chattering. "Gillian broke the wheel and I compelled him to forget his errand. What happened, Cate? What did you do?"

*We?*

I stare into Mrs. Corbett's toady face. The penny finally drops. I've been so stupid not to see it before. She's the one who recommended Elena. She's the one who told the Sisters we were witches. All her meddling since Mother died—how long has she been spying on us?

My mouth goes dry, and I have to swallow several times before I can speak. "You're a witch, too."

"And a member of the Sisterhood, before my marriage. After my husband died, I offered my services again. Both my own girls are useless. I was sent to Chatham especially to look after you three, make sure you didn't make spectacles of yourselves. You could have made it easier," she says. "A merry mess you've made of things. And I hear you've given our dear Elena some difficulty?"

"What happened to your face?" Elena asks.

I finger the welt rising from Brother Ishida's ring—the silver ring all the Brothers wear on their right hand, signifying their devotion to the Lord. "Impertinence."

Elena raises her eyebrows, a smile tugging at her lips. "I can't say you don't deserve it. Let's go in. It's freezing out here."

Inside, Maura's sitting on the bottom step in only her chemise and corset, with Mrs. O'Hare beside her, daubing ointment on her cheek. Her right arm and palm are wrapped in thick strips of white linen where she fell on the broken glass. Behind her, Tess is rebraiding her hair.

"Good heavens," Mrs. Corbett says. "What happened here?"

Maura scrambles up, clutching her ruined dress to her chest, two bright spots of color on her cheeks.

"The storm," Tess says.

"Maura," I say. Tess looks shocked, Maura ashamed. "Where's Lily?"

"We sent her home. She wanted to stay and help clean up

the mess, but I thought it better—" Mrs. O'Hare trails off, her wobbly chin set, her blue eyes fierce as she looks at the two newcomers. "I wouldn't let anything happen to my girls, not ever. I've known the truth of it since you were making things go topsy-turvy yourself, Cate. Maura, come up to your room. We'll start the fire and I'll see to your hand. You may need stitches; it's bleeding clean through that bandage."

"Wait," Mrs. Corbett says. "Lily Belfiore was witness to this, along with Brother Ishida?"

"Yes." Tess is holding Maura's hand in hers. Maura's watching Elena balefully. "But she doesn't remember any of it."

"Nor does he," I add. "It was a very thorough job."

"And which of you performed the magic on them?" Mrs. Corbett's beady eyes are hungry, roving over all three of us in turn.

This time I don't hesitate. They already suspect me. They can't know about Tess. "It was me."

Mrs. Corbett and Elena exchange a look. "Let's go into the parlor. We have several matters to discuss with you, Miss Cate."

"I'll come, too," Tess offers, bounding down the stairs.

"I believe it's a discussion best had in private," Mrs. Corbett says.

"Of course," I say smoothly. I don't want Tess to see how frightened I am. I run a hand over her soft blond hair. "You go help Mrs. O'Hare with Maura."

Tess gives me a dubious look. "All right."

In the sitting room, the fire is blazing. Mrs. Corbett takes off her cloak and settles on the sofa, Elena next to her. I take the tall blue armchair across from them.

"I believe you owe Elena your gratitude, and perhaps an apology," Mrs. Corbett says.

I grit my teeth. "Thank you for stopping the coachman. I'm very grateful that my sisters aren't being hauled off to Harwood in the morning."

Mrs. Corbett glares. "I did not hear an apology."

I cross my legs at the ankle and lean back in my chair. "I won't be giving one. This mess never would have happened if Elena hadn't made Maura think she had feelings for her—feelings of a romantic nature."

"No," Mrs. Corbett says, her voice sharp. "This mess, as you call it, would not have happened if you had simply cooperated with us. There would have been no need for Elena to employ any unsavory tactics. You have been obstinate at every step of the way. She has been much more patient with you than I would in her place."

I'm silent. "Cate, I'm truly sorry," Elena says. "I didn't realize Maura's feelings were so vehement. I realized she was losing control as I was leaving. That's why I went to fetch Sister Gillian."

"It's clear from what happened today that Maura is unstable," Mrs. Corbett says. "She is a danger to herself and, given what she knows, to the Sisterhood. She needs to be looked after, and by someone powerful enough to head off any more accidents."

I shift in my chair, leaning forward, desperate. "She's got me. I can look after her. I'll teach her to control herself."

"I'm afraid that's not a good idea. Elena says there is already a great deal of tension between the two of you. Given the nature of the prophecy, we are anxious to keep you on good terms. We don't wish to lose one of you just yet."

I smooth my skirts with a shaking hand. "You can't think—we argue sometimes, like sisters do. But Maura would never hurt me."

*Not on purpose,* a niggling voice suggests.

"We cannot take that risk. Not if you are the three sisters. And it seems increasingly likely you are. It's not an easy thing, modifying more than one memory at a time. That's the work of a very powerful witch, Cate. If the Brothers were to find out about you—the three of you—they would relish making an example of you. It might serve as an excuse for them to return to old ways. Uglier ways."

My eyes fall to the hearth. To the orange flames dancing. The wood crackle-snapping in the fireplace. The glowing red ashes beneath.

*'Twere up to me, I'd resurrect the burnings.*

"What would you have me do?" I ask. I glance up at the family portrait above the hearth, at Mother, cradling Tess in her arms.

"Maura and Teresa need to be taught to control their magic. They need to learn what they're capable of without your interference. Elena has offered to stay on and teach them."

"What? No!" I jump to my feet, but Mrs. Corbett throws up a hand, and I'm flung backward into my chair, the wind knocked out of my lungs.

"Sit and listen," she snaps. "Elena will not compromise your sister in any way, if that's what worries you."

I take a deep, shaky breath, guilty at what I'm about to suggest. "The Sisters—Maura wants to join the Sisters. Let her go. I'll stay here with Tess."

"What Maura wants is irrelevant. We think it best if the two of you are separated at present—for your own protection. If you are with the Sisters in New London, she cannot be there. And there's simply no other option for a witch like you."

I choose my words carefully. "I've had an offer of marriage. I want to accept."

"I'm afraid that's not possible." Mrs. Corbett's voice is smooth as a looking glass. "Your gifts cannot be squandered in marriage. A witch of your caliber belongs to the Sisterhood."

Anger rises in me, fierce and fortifying. I belong to *myself*.

I grip the wooden arms of my chair, fingertips going white. "What if I don't agree to it? Will you compel me?"

Mrs. Corbett leans forward. "You don't say who offered to marry you."

I don't hesitate. They can't know about Finn. "Paul. Paul McLeod. You asked me about him at tea, didn't you?"

"And you hardly reacted like a girl in love," Mrs. Corbett scoffs.

Elena stands. Walks to the fire and holds out her hands to warm them. "I saw you with the gardener," she says, her back to me. "Finn Belastra, isn't it? The two of you looked quite fond of each other, what with him holding your hand. And I suspect, given the way you lost control of the magic yourself, that you've done a bit more than hold hands."

"We won't modify your mind, or your sisters'. You're too valuable for that," Mrs. Corbett says. "We would certainly prefer that you come to us willingly. But if you don't—we will do everything we can to convince you. How would Finn feel if his mother were arrested by the Brothers? Or that little sister of his?"

"But they aren't witches." I want to stand up. To fight them with everything in me. But I know they'd only throw me back down. They're intent on proving their dominance. Still, it takes everything in me to sit there and listen. "They haven't done anything!"

"That won't matter to the Brothers," Mrs. Corbett cackles.

"And there's always *his* memory. It would be sad if he forgot you." Elena turns to face me, a dark silhouette against the fire.

Mrs. Corbett stands. "It's your choice, Cate. What will it be?"

# chapter
# 21

I sit sandwiched between Tess and Elena on the hard wooden pew. Brother Ishida drones on behind the pulpit. Any moment now, he'll call my name. I feel flushed and pale all at once, and ill with the anticipation of it.

Next to me, Tess fidgets with her necklace, a little gold locket Mother gave her on her eighth birthday. Last year when the clasp broke, she lost it in the garden and was inconsolable for hours. I helped her scour the grass until we found it. I think she wears it when she needs a bit of extra comfort.

One seat down, Maura sits still as a statue. She hasn't met my eyes all morning, though I can't tell if it's for shame or anger. She didn't bother to dress her hair to hide the cut on her cheek, and she's wearing one of her old unfashionable dresses instead of a bright new frock. She wanted to skip church entirely, but Elena wouldn't allow it.

I kept my mouth shut when Elena gave her orders, though it galled me. Just as I did last night, when she told me to keep away from my sisters until I announced my decision. She said it was for their good, to keep them from doing anything foolish. I cried myself to sleep, drowning my tears in my pillow. Then I woke before the sun, dry eyed and resolute.

"Miss Catherine Cahill," Brother Ishida booms. "Come forward to declare your intention before the Lord."

Surprised whispers spread throughout the room as my neighbors speculate. Faces swivel in my direction. In the pew in front of us, Sachi twists to stare at me. Rory's absent from church today.

"Already? Is it McLeod after all?" Sachi whispers.

Tess catches at my sleeve. "What are you doing, Cate?"

I don't answer her. I stand, smoothing my burgundy skirt, and make my way down the aisle to the front of the church. I stand with my back to the whispers, facing Brother Ishida. He seems fully recovered today, his face unlined and untroubled. It is strange to look into his eyes again, burning with their usual fervor but none of the bitter hate he evidenced last night, and know he remembers none of it.

Thank the Lord he remembers none of it. Thank *Tess*.

"Miss Cahill, do you recognize the seriousness of this ceremony? It commits you to the path you have chosen in the eyes of the Lord and of this community. It is not a matter to enter into lightly. Once you have declared your intention, the Brotherhood and all your neighbors will swear to support you in it."

"Yes, sir."

He moves aside and I step up, looking out into the sea of faces. It's the only time women are permitted up on the dais. From here, the congregation is enormous, hundreds of our neighbors packed together in their finery. All waiting with interest to hear what I've got to say. It's a heady feeling.

"Catherine Cahill, what is your intention?"

I do not hesitate. My voice is loud and clear and perfectly confident.

"In the hearing of the Lord and all those who witness my words, I offer myself to the Sisterhood."

The whispers explode. No one from Chatham has joined the Sisterhood in years, and I do not suppose I seemed a very likely candidate. Brother Ishida fumbles for a moment, and then he's speaking about the noble, honorable calling of the Sisterhood.

But his words seem faint and far off, as though they're coming at me from down a long dim hallway. It's done.

The next part is hardest. I raise my eyes to the back of the church. Paul sits next to his mother, handsome even in his heartbreak. I can see the clench of his square jaw, the way he works to control his emotions. My choice must seem incomprehensible to him. But I'm not the unfettered, carefree girl who waded in the pond and walked that pigpen fence. I'll never be that Cate again. It's better he know it now.

Sachi is whispering with Rose Collier behind her pink fan, the blue feather in her hair wagging furiously.

Behind her, Maura's listlessness has disappeared. She grips the pew with both hands, her knuckles white, her blue eyes swallowing her face. As I watch, Tess scoots closer to her. Somehow, in the last day, their roles have reversed; Maura has become fragile and Tess her protector.

Last—horribly—Finn. Brother Belastra, now. Sitting for the first time in the front pew with the others, dressed head-to-toe in black. He's already committed himself to this path. The shop is shuttered—I saw the sign on the door when our carriage drove past. He swipes a hand through his unkempt hair, his rich chocolate eyes stunned. This is not what he expected me to say.

Unconsciously, I finger the welt on my cheek. Finn's face darkens, and he reaches reflexively toward his boot. I give a tiny, almost imperceptible shake of my head. What could he do? Nothing.

There's nothing anyone can do. I chose this.

"Catherine Cahill, the blessings of the Brotherhood are upon you. You may go in peace to serve the Lord," Brother Ishida says.

I bow my head. "Thanks be."

The rest of the congregation echoes me.

Our neighbors rise and stretch. Some of them head in my direction—Finn included—but Elena beats him to it. She tugs me down the side aisle, separating me from the curious onlookers in their Sunday finery.

"Time to go, Cate. The carriage is waiting." She smiles, her perfect white teeth flashing, as though she's sending me off on a delightful picnic and not a prison sentence of her making.

Finn is at my elbow. "Could I have five minutes? To say goodbye?" I ask. I hate myself for the longing evident in my voice.

"I don't think that's wise, do you? Why prolong the inevitable?"

I won't beg. I won't give her the satisfaction. "May I go home to gather some of my things, at least?"

"Your sisters and I can take care of that for you. We'll send them soon. Come, Cate. No stalling," she says, leading the way down the aisle.

Finn puts his hand on my arm, his warm fingers encircling my wrist. He'd pull me through the crowd and away from all of this if I'd let him.

But I can't let him. I can't even look at him or I'll cry. I stare at the cinnamon freckles dotting the back of his hand. "Goodbye," I say to the wooden floor. I reach into my pocket and pull out Marianne's ruby ring. My engagement ring. I can't keep it; it wouldn't be fair; he should be free to give it to someone else, though the thought of it makes me want to die. I press it into his hand and close his fist around it.

"Cate," he says, and the desperation in his voice nearly undoes me. "Why?"

"Come along," Elena says.

Maura runs up, pushing her way through the crowd. "Let me go instead. Please, Cate, don't leave me here with her."

There's so much I want to say—to Finn, to my sisters. But not like this. Not with Elena and Mrs. Corbett listening, weighing my words, looking for raw places to strike.

"You'll have Tess. Look after each other," I manage. I find Tess's gray eyes, and a bit of understanding passes between us. She gives me a nod solemn as a promise.

I go. I walk down the aisle and out the wide door and down the cobblestone path lined with dying white chrysanthemums.

I feel as though I'm being dragged to my own funeral with my mourners behind me. My smile warps, but I keep my chin up.

I climb into a closed black brougham adorned with the Sisters' gold seal. Mrs. Corbett squeezes in beside me. She's to chaperone my journey to New London. To see to it I don't change my mind and run off, more like. She raps on the door and the coachman jolts us forward. We're on our way.

"You did the right thing, Cate," she says. "You'll come to see that eventually."

But I see it already. To protect the people I love, I'd do it all over again.

I only hope I can live with the consequences.

# acknowledgments

This book is a dream come true, but it wouldn't have happened without the help of lots of amazing people. Thank you to everyone who has followed my path to publication and cheered me on, whether online or in person. Your support means the world to me.

Thank you to Jim McCarthy, my awesome and patient agent, for taking a chance on me. I like to think of you as Yente, matchmaking authors and editors, and you made the best match I could have hoped for.

Thank you to Ari Lewin, my amazing editor, for loving my story. For pushing me and challenging me and never letting me settle for anything less than my best, and for being hilarious and generous. To Paula Sadler for genius ideas and for keeping me supplied with all those tasty ARCs. To Elizabeth Wood for the gorgeous cover. And to the rest of the team at Putnam and Penguin Young Readers: I'm more grateful than I can say for all your hard work and excitement about the Cahill witches.

Thank you to all of the authors who have inspired me and welcomed me into this fantastic YA community. To the Apocalypsies for being such a fabulous support group and sharing this strange, marvelous journey. I'm honored to be in your company, and I can't wait to read all your books! To Jaclyn Dolamore for loving an early draft and answering all my newbie author questions. To my agent-sisters, Robin Talley and Caroline Richmond, who have shared all the excitement and all the crazy and been extraordinarily supportive every step of the way. And to Kathleen Foucart Walker, the best critique partner ever, for reading every blessed draft of this book, exchanging flailmails, asking clever questions, and always telling me I could do it. I can't wait until it's your turn.

Thank you to the Washington College Drama Department, where I learned to love creative collaboration. You taught me how to ask questions and give constructive feedback, and even though I'm not doing theater anymore, it's been invaluable.

Thank you to the staff of the CUA Press for watching me grow up and for being excited for me and very understanding when I left to follow my dream.

Thanks to all my fabulous friends for being so interested and invested in this book. To Anne Chan for her fantastic author photos. To Liz Auclair and Laura Furr for prodding me out of the writing cave and for always asking how it's going, even though you've both had fantastically exciting, life-changing things of your own going on. To Jill Coste for distracting me with cute dresses and cupcake recipes when I need distractions and for being a kindred spirit. And to Jenn Reeder for being my best friend, alpha reader, and #1 cheerleader: I would be lost without you and our Tuesday night dates.

Thank you to my family for always, always being supportive of my writing. Special thanks to my sisters, Shannon Moore and Amber Emanuel, who make me laugh and make me crazy. Without you, I don't think I could have written Cate's relationships with Tess and Maura so convincingly. And to my parents, Connie and Chris Moore and John Emanuel—thank you for everything, especially for letting me sit inside and read all day instead of mowing grass. It seems to have paid off. I think you always knew this was what I was meant to be doing, even when I didn't.

Last but absolutely not least, thank you to Steve Spotswood, my brilliant playwright husband. For reading everything, for bringing me tea, for brainstorming on the porch, for feeding me the best sandwiches ever, for making me laugh when I'm anxious, and most of all for believing in me when I don't believe in myself. I love you.

Turn the page for a preview
of the spellbinding sequel!

THE CAHILL WITCH CHRONICLES: BOOK 2

# STAR
# CURSED

## chapter

# 1

I feel such a fraud.

I stand with Alice and Mei in a dim, narrow tenement hallway that stinks of boiled beef and cabbage. We are all dressed alike: black woolen cloaks covering stiff black bombazine dresses, heeled black boots peeping out beneath floor-length skirts, hair pulled back simply and neatly. This is the uniform of the Sisterhood, and while none of us are yet full members, we are on a Sisterly mission of charity. We carry baskets of bread baked in the convent kitchen and vegetables from the convent cellar. We keep our eyes lowered, our voices quiet.

No one must ever suspect us for what we really are.

Alice knocks. Fine onyx ear bobs swing from her small seashell ears. Even on a mission to feed the poor, she finds a way to flaunt her family's status. Someday, her pride will be her undoing.

I half relish the thought.

Mrs. Anderson opens the door. She's a widow of twenty-three with blonde hair a shade lighter than my own and a perpetually harried expression. She ushers us inside, her hands fluttering like pale moths in the November gloom. "Sisters, thank you so much for coming."

"There's no need to thank us. Helping the less fortunate is part of our mission," Alice says, grimacing at the cramped two-room flat.

"I'm grateful." Mrs. Anderson presses my hand between her icy palms. She still wears her gold wedding band, though her husband has been dead three months now. "My Frank was a good provider. We always made ends meet. I don't like to depend on charity."

"Of course not." I give her an uneven smile as I pull away. In the face of our deception, her gratitude makes me squirm.

"You've had hard luck. You'll be back on your feet soon," Mei assures her. The fever that tore through the city in August claimed Mr. Anderson and their elder boy, leaving Mrs. Anderson to fend for the two surviving children.

"It's not an easy thing, to be a woman alone in the world. I'd take on more hours at the shop if I could." Mrs. Anderson slides the jug of milk into the icebox. "But it gets dark so early now, and I don't like to walk home alone."

"It isn't safe for a woman to be out at night," Mei agrees.

"So many foreigners in this part of the city. Most of them can't even speak proper English." Alice's hood falls back, revealing golden hair that waves prettily away from her pale forehead. You'd never know to look at her what a harpy she is. "Who knows what kind of people they are?"

Mei flushes. Her parents immigrated from Indo-China before

2

she was born, but they still speak Chinese at home. She's the only Chinese girl at the convent, and she's very conscious of it. I daresay Alice knows that; she has a talent for poking at people's bruises.

The old Cate Cahill would have taken Alice to task, but now, as Sister Catherine, I help Mei unpack sweet potatoes and butternut squash onto the scratched wooden table. Sisters do not have the luxury of losing our tempers—at least not outside the convent walls. In public, we must be models of ladylike decorum.

I loathe these visits.

It's not that I lack compassion for the poor. I have plenty of compassion. I just can't help wondering how they would feel about us if they knew the truth.

The Sisters pose as an order of women devoting our lives in charitable service to the Lord. We deliver food to the poor and nurse the sick. That is the truth—but it's also true that we are witches, all of us, hiding right here in plain sight. If people learned what we really are, their gratitude would turn to fear. They would think us sinful, wanton, and dangerous, and they would have us locked up in the madhouse—or worse.

It's not their fault. That's what the Brothers preach at church every Sunday. Few would risk going against them, and these poor people already have less than most.

No matter how kind Mrs. Anderson may seem, she'd give us up. She'd have to, in order to protect her children. They all would.

"Sister Cath'rine! You're back!" A small boy runs out of the bedroom, his hands full of jacks, his mouth smeared with the blackberry jam we brought last week from Sister Sophia's cellar. Alice shies away from his sticky fingers.

"Good day, Henry." This is my third visit to the Andersons' flat, and Henry and I have become fast friends. He's lonely, I think.

3

Now that his mother goes out to work, he and his baby sister are left with an elderly neighbor all day. It can't be much fun for him.

"Henry, leave Sister Catherine alone," his mother scolds.

"It's all right. He's not bothering me." I take the final item—a jar of juicy red tomatoes, seeds floating in the pulp—from my basket. As I kneel, my eyes fall past Henry to the pallets stuffed with straw ticking. The first time we came, they had a nice mahogany sleigh bed, a matching trundle for Henry, and an armoire, but Lavinia's had to sell them. Now her pretty blue wedding quilt is tucked neatly over her pallet and their clothes are stacked in cardboard boxes.

Henry sits, scattering jacks across the floor and giving me a gap-toothed grin. I'm out of practice, but I was a champion at jacks in my day. A memory flashes through me: Paul McLeod squatting across from me on the cobblestone walk in my garden, the hot summer sun beating down, the smell of freshly cut grass all around us.

Once upon a time, memories of my childhood friend would have made me smile—but not anymore. I treated Paul poorly, and I'll never be able to apologize.

He's not even the one I hurt most. The thought hammers at me, relentless.

"I been practicing," Henry announces, tugging at the grimy white shirtsleeves that end halfway up his skinny forearms. "Got up to ninesies yesterday. Bet I can beat you now."

"We'll see about that." I settle across from him while Alice and Mei and Mrs. Anderson cram together on the stained, lumpy brown sofa, joining hands and bowing their heads in prayer. I ought to join them, but my relationship with the Lord is fragile these days. I am in good health and safe from the Brothers' meddling eyes, but it is hard to feel thankful when everyone I love is at home in Chatham and I am here in New London alone.

I miss my sisters. I miss Finn. Loneliness carves a hollow in my stomach.

Henry and I are up to sevensies when there's a furious pounding on the door. I freeze at the sound, the red rubber ball bouncing right past my outstretched hands.

The baby stirs in her wooden cradle. Mrs. Anderson leans over her for a moment on her way to the door. "Shhh, Eleni," she says, and the tenderness in her voice makes me miss my own mother, gone four years now.

Mrs. Anderson opens the door to a nightmare of black cloaks and stern faces. Two Brothers push past her into the flat.

My heart stops. What did we do? How did we give ourselves away?

Alice and Mei are already on their feet. I scramble across the room to join them, and Henry rushes to his mother's side.

A short, bald Brother with a long face and piercing blue eyes steps forward. "Lavinia Anderson? I am Brother O'Shea of the New London Council. This is Brother Helmsley," he says, indicating an enormous red-bearded man. "We have received a report of impropriety."

It's not us, then.

Relief courses through me, followed closely by guilt. Lavinia Anderson is a good woman, a good mother, kind and hardworking. She doesn't deserve trouble from the Brothers.

Lavinia presses a fist to her mouth, her wedding ring glinting in the fading afternoon light. "I've done nothing improper, sir."

"That will be for us to decide, won't it?" O'Shea turns to us with a smug, self-important smile. He stands like a bantam rooster with his chest thrown forward, shoulders back, legs spread wide, in the way of a small man trying to seem bigger. I take an immediate dislike to him. "Good day, Sisters. Here to deliver weekly rations?"

"Yes, sir." Alice bows her head, but not before I see the flash of mutiny in her blue eyes.

"It's a pity your charity's been wasted on the undeserving. Poverty is no excuse for wantonness," Helmsley snarls, running one great paw over the squash. "Just lost one husband and already setting her cap for another! It's scandalous, is what it is."

Mrs. Anderson clutches Henry's thin shoulder, her face suddenly white.

"Do you deny that you allowed a man to escort you home last night? A man who was no relation to you?" Brother O'Shea asks.

"I do not deny it," Lavinia says carefully, her voice quavering. "Mr. Alvarez is a customer at the bakery. He was leaving the same time as me and offered to see me home."

"As a widow, Mrs. Anderson, your behavior must be beyond reproach. You cannot consort with strange men on city streets. Surely you know that."

I bite my lip, face cast down. What other choice did she have—to walk home alone and risk being robbed or accosted? To hire a carriage with money she cannot spare? To beg her employers for an escort? This problem would never present itself to girls like Alice or me. Before we joined the Sisters, our movements were shadowed by ladies' maids and governesses. A proper lady rides hidden away in a closed carriage, not down in the dust and dirt for anyone to stare at and take liberties with.

But Mrs. Anderson cannot afford a carriage or a maid. She has neither parents nor a husband to look after her. What, precisely, would the Brothers have her do? Stay home and starve?

"I wasn't consorting. I mourn my husband every day!" Lavinia insists. Her shoulders are thrown back, her chin up, and she meets O'Shea's eyes straight on.

"You're a liar." O'Shea nods at Helmsley, who slaps her across the face.

I flinch, remembering the way Brother Ishida struck me. My hand flies to my cheek. The cut from his ring of office is healed now, but I will always remember the indignity of it, and the vicious pleasure on his face.

Lavinia stumbles back against the cradle. The baby lets out a wail.

Henry launches himself at Helmsley's knees. "Don't hit my mama!"

He shouldn't have to watch this. No child should. "Should we take the children into the other room, sir?" I ask O'Shea, who is clearly the brains behind this visit.

"No. Let him see his mother for the slut she is." O'Shea leans down and grabs Henry's small shoulders. "Stop that. Stop it right this instant, you hear? Your mother is a liar. She betrayed your papa's memory."

Henry stops fighting, his brown eyes wide and frightened. "Papa?"

"I haven't!" Lavinia protests, tears coursing down her face. "I would never!"

"Your neighbor reported seeing you arm in arm with Mr. Alvarez," Helmsley continues, looming over her. He must be six feet tall.

Lavinia cowers away from him, pressing back against the peeling blue-flowered wallpaper. "I stumbled over a loose brick, and he caught me before I fell. That's all there was to it, I swear! It won't happen again. I'll be home before dark from now on." But that means giving up several hours of work—and pay—that her little family can scarcely afford.

"A woman's proper place is in the home, Mrs. Anderson," O'Shea says. He turns to Helmsley, sneering. "You see, this is what comes from permitting women to take on outside work. Gives them false notions of propriety. Turns their heads from the Lord."

"Makes them think they can do for themselves just as well as men," Helmsley agrees.

"Do you think I want to go out to work?" Lavinia shrills, and I want to clap a hand over her mouth. Arguing will only make this go worse for her. "I only took this job after my husband died, to put food on the table for my children. We can't depend entirely on the Sisters' charity. We'd all starve!"

"Hush!" Brother O'Shea roars, strutting right up to her. "Your insubordination does you no favors, madam. You should be thankful for what you get."

Mrs. Anderson takes a deep breath and offers up a watery smile. "I'm sorry," she says softly, looking at Mei and me pleadingly. "I am very grateful. I'll do whatever you want. I'd swear on the Scriptures, I've done nothing wrong!"

O'Shea shakes his head as though she has committed another grave sin. "Then you would forswear yourself."

A grin settles on Helmsley's ugly bearded face, and I sense a trap closing around her. "Your neighbor said Alvarez kissed your hand when you parted. Do you deny that?"

"I—no, but—" Lavinia sags against the wall. "Please, let me explain!"

"You've told us enough falsehoods for one day, Mrs. Anderson. I think it's clear what's been going on here. We are arresting you for crimes of immorality."

The baby begins shrieking. Henry is crying, too, clinging to Lavinia's skirts.

8

"We could stop this." Alice's lips barely move. Her voice is so low I can hardly hear her over the commotion, but I catch her meaning immediately.

What she's suggesting is dangerous. Doing magic outside the convent puts every one of us at risk. And mind-magic is the rarest, wickedest kind of magic there is. Erasing one memory can take other, associated memories with it; performing mind-magic repeatedly on the same subject can leave devastating mental scars. Long ago, when the witches ruled New England, they used mind-magic to control and destroy their opponents. The Brothers tell those old stories to keep people frightened of us, though Alice and I are the only two students at the convent even capable of it.

"No," Mei begs, her dark eyes frantic. "Stay out of it. It's not our business."

"Four of them. We could do it, together." Alice's soft hand clasps mine. "Count of three."

What the Brothers are doing is hateful and wrong; it wouldn't trouble me overmuch to use magic on them. But Alice is more confident in her skill than I am. I've never performed mind-magic on more than one subject before, and certainly never on a child. What if we fail, or it goes wrong, and we damage Henry's mind permanently?

I snatch my hand away. "No. It's too risky."

Then the moment is gone. Helmsley is binding Lavinia's wrists together with coarse rope.

"Our work is never done, Sisters. I'm sorry to subject you to such a scene," O'Shea says, though it's obvious he's rather enjoyed having an audience. He gestures to the fresh bread and the vegetables piled on the kitchen table. "You'll want to take that to someone else in need. No point in letting it go to waste."

9

"Yes, sir." Alice snatches up her basket from the floor and begins to gather up the food.

Mei steps toward O'Shea. "Sir? What about the children?"

O'Shea shrugs, and I cringe at his indifference. "We'll take them to the orphanage, if there's no one else to look after them."

"There's a neighbor," I suggest. It's the least I can do.

I hope the neighbor will agree to take them. Two more mouths to feed isn't an easy burden. If Lavinia is sentenced to hard labor on a prison ship, she might be home again in a few years—if she survives the backbreaking work and rampant disease. If she's sent to Harwood, though, that's a lifetime. She'll never see her children again.

"Mrs. Papadopoulos, two doors down," Lavinia says quickly. "Henry, go with Sister Catherine. Don't worry. I'll be back soon." She gives Henry a smile, but her voice cracks on the lie. "I love you."

"Stop delaying." Henry yanks Lavinia away from her son and out the door. I hear her stumble on the steps, and my breath catches. Could I have stopped this? Have I become as cruel and cowardly as the Brothers?

"Come here, Henry," Mei says, reaching for him, but he darts past her.

"Mama! Come back!" He surges after Lavinia like a small, sobbing lion. Mei scampers after him, and I follow, cursing the steep stairs and my heeled boots.

Outside, Henry runs to his mother and buries his face in her skirt. There's a ragtag crowd gathered: the Spanish and Chinese boys who'd been playing stickball in the empty lot across the street. Above us, curtains twitch, and I wonder which of those nosy neighbors informed on Lavinia.

"Don't take my mama!" Henry begs.

"Don't you see he's scared? Let me say a proper good-bye,"

10

Lavinia pleads, reaching for him ineffectually with her bound hands.

O'Shea's thin face is hard. "He's better off without a mother like you."

Helmsley shoves her toward the carriage, and Lavinia trips, falling to the sidewalk in a heap of black skirts and blonde hair.

"Take the boy inside," O'Shea orders us, his pale eyes cold.

"Mama!" Henry screams, fighting, kicking Mei as she tries to grab him.

I see the crowd of boys stirring restlessly, grumbling among themselves. I cringe, remembering the last arrest I saw—Brenna Elliott—and the way onlookers called her a witch and threw stones at her.

One tall boy draws his arm back, and I almost shout a warning as he lets it fly.

The rock smacks O'Shea right between the shoulders. O'Shea turns and glares at the group of boys, and I glance at Mei, suppressing a smile.

I've never seen anyone fight back against the Brothers. It's rather marvelous. Foolish, too—but then they are boys, not girls, and they've got less to lose.

More rocks fly through the air, pelting O'Shea and Helmsley in the back and shoulders, accompanied by angry shouts in foreign languages. O'Shea spins around, bellowing something about respect, but then he gives up and sprints for the carriage like the coward he is. Helmsley yanks Lavinia to her feet, dragging her down the sidewalk.

As Mei bends to grab Henry, a rock slams into the side of her head. She screams something at the boys in Chinese. I dart forward and grab Henry by the collar. The boy buries his tearstained face against my hip as the Brothers' carriage rattles away with his mother sealed inside. The hailstorm of rocks stops as suddenly as it started. The crowd drifts away; the curtains flutter shut. It's over—except for Lavinia Anderson, whose nightmare has just begun.